# Remnants

Thank You So much, Suzanne.
You don't know how much it means
to me for MY boss to genuinely
support me. Thanks!

# Remnants

## Trials and Tribulations

AUSTIN AYLWIN

Library of Congress Control Number:     2015919487
ISBN:           Hardcover               978-1-5144-2844-3
                Softcover               978-1-5144-2843-6
                eBook                   978-1-5144-2842-9

Print information available on the last page.

Rev. date: 03/31/2016

Back cover photo by Baptiste Esteban

**To order additional copies of this book, contact:**
Xlibris
1-888-795-4274
www.Xlibris.com
Orders@Xlibris.com
729872

# Author's Note

*Well hello there! Before you proceed, I would like to draw your attention to one tiny detail: Grammar. I'm only eighteen years old and I'm far from perfect. While I have read and re-read this book more times than I can count, it's inevitable for me to miss the occasional hiccup. I'm sure as more readers find my book, my inbox will become increasingly full with 'generous' and 'not-soul-crushing' comments to inform me of my mistakes. But listen here: If the day ever comes that I become famous, you, my dear reader, now own physical evidence of my failures! This in turn will only make it more valuable. So, you're welcome.*

# 1. "...there's a difference between bad and evil."

**Year 0017: On the outskirts of Kyoto, Japan – 1 of 17 Nuclear Zones**

Jade slivers of grass stroked my bloodstained cheeks. My mind was vacant and my body was numb. The air was heavy with smoke and fire, filling my lungs with wasted breath. I'm lost…where was I? The taste in my mouth…was it blood? Was it *my* blood? My questions were only met with uncertainty. There was only one truth that accompanied me in that field as everything else burned: After seventeen years, my past had finally caught up with my present.

The paralysis faded sluggishly, providing me with a strained exercise of simply flipping onto my back. Crinkling the muscles in my neck, I looked down at my lower half and exhaled in realizing pain. A bone in my right leg was askew, struggling to penetrate through flesh on the opposite side. The base of my foot was angled to nearly touch the sky. Walking was futile, but I couldn't stay. They were coming.

I tugged at the shaggy earth and pathetically began to crawl away. My barn was embraced with flames, tickling the dull blue sky with slender fingers. My vision distorted with a harsh crack and a flashback rolled in like a crashing wave. The sky was now black and I was once again in a field but not of Japanese origin. There was another barn on fire, but this one had burning teenagers bursting out of it. They screamed unrelentingly as I simply watched. I blinked, and the barn became mine again. The sky was of the day and now only burning horses and cattle raced by. Christ…I thought I lost that memory. I thought that was one of them that were taken from me. But as my home was scorched away, I remembered everything. I didn't want to.

I hoped that I would asphyxiate on the smoke and gulp it down like bleach before the memories rolled in. I didn't want to remember them. I didn't want to remember *her*.

Two men laid before me without an ownership to life. One dangled nearly a foot off of the ground with an anchored pitchfork punctured through his abdomen. The tines tasted his insides and met the air with lustful delight. The other *may* have been a man, but his caved-in skull made certainty impossible. Next to him was a shovel originally used for manure that was coated in his juices. I…think I did this? Before my vision faded entirely, I saw a heavy silhouette looming over me. It was a gorilla. This was not abnormal. He was my only friend in this sea of death and I could only watch helplessly as armed guards pumped him full of tranquilizer. I called out his name but my voice wasn't audible. His tree trunk arms swung brutally and he managed to break the majority of one guard's ribs before collapsing next to me. Their three-eyed masks looked at me and began to approach but I blacked out before they arrived. The last thing I remember was pinching the sides of my watch. It was a habit that would never fade. Then I was gone.

When I woke up, recycled air caressed my teeth. I was underground. That much was certain. I reached for my watch but braces latched around my wrists prevented me from doing so. The room that held me was blank and cold. A lone bulb of light dangled from the ceiling, swinging back and forth to tamper with the shadows. My sight fell to my leg where a cast had just been applied and then to my right forearm where a red-blotched bandage was tightly wound. It took less than a second to understand that they had taken my blood. That was the only thing that I feared: clear, irrevocable evidence of my identity. Looking down at my hands, the familiar scars casted over the ends of my fingers relinquished an unsettling tingle. Unfortunately, slicing off one's fingerprints was not an act that an innocent person partook in. Oddly, it wasn't my guilt I was trying to hide. Rather, it was the very existence of the crimes themselves; and these were struggling to remain dormant. They had my blood but that would only prove my existence. My momentary fear quelled. Eventually, I'd find my way out. Always did. They may have thought that the dark ambience would instil fear but I was not a victim. It was *my* presence that horrified them.

A door opened and the frighteningly clean light that it allowed in had shown the entirety of the room that held me. It was an interrogation room—one-way mirror and all—and a chair across from me stared me down. Then, a ginger-haired man with a trimmed beard and a receding hairline entered and by the look of his face, he had already tested my blood. He was convinced that I was a fraud. I mean, how could I not have been? I hated the Empire with every fibre of my being but even I couldn't deny the genius of their identity database.

He sat down, took a breath, and cautiously looked up. Luckily for him, the light refused to show the damaged side of my face.

"Do you know where you are?" the man asked with a voice soaked in nicotine. He looked like a Tom…that's what I called him from then on.

I focused on a water stain on the ceiling. It shifted and mutated like a transitioning Rorschach test. The ceiling vibrated and rattled, causing a pulsating hum to erupt. No, this wasn't actually happening. The hallucinations…they sifted through my mind and plucked at whatever deemed interesting. There was no real or fake; everything merged and refused to separate.

"You will answer me, rebel," Tom attempted to demand. "Do you know where you are? Why you are here?"

My eyes blinked, dampening the parched lumps of fat that forgot they stared. I licked my upper lip and touched wiry hair that scratched at my muted taste buds. The thought of him actually believing he would force me to speak was amusing. I exhaled a chuckle that rattled the mangy hair on my face. I looked at him with a single eye that broke through the shadows but still didn't speak.

"…The database has a 100% success rate," he stated. "Every drop of blood contains a face, contains a story, they're never wrong…except with you. So, would you like to tell me where you got this sample?"

Even though my hands were bound, I held authority with a vice grip.

He continued. "You…you killed two men. Brutally. Horribly. But you are not in charge here. If you're not willing to speak…then we have no use for you."

His voice was like an annoying recording that was put on a loop: It wouldn't stop unless I interrupted it. So, shaking the dust off of my barren vocal chords, I *chose* to speak.

"I know…you. I know what you're trying to be…I know what you're trying to hide…"

"And what would that be, exactly?" he asked, teetering on the border of caution.

"You're not…one of them. You're not. You try to be…put me in this room…cast shadows…trying to get inside my head? But if you were really one of them…none of this would be necessary. Their presence… that is enough. But you? You're just simply…there."

His skin flushed with aggravation. He leaned in with a vial of crimson fluid pinched between his forefinger and thumb.

"I'm gonna ask you one more time. Where did you get this?"

I directed my gaze down to my bandaged forearm where a red dot hovered over my vein.

"*You* got it from *there*. All I did was make it."

Now he was laughing. But it wasn't the kind of laughter that ended with a smile. It faded and became a look worse than how it began.

"We've had imposters over the years. They try to make noise but we don't listen. Their words lost their meaning in a time that no longer exists. But you've gone the farthest. You've somehow brought a sample that belongs to a myth; it belongs to a dead man. You're not him, even if you want to believe that."

My eye twitched and I craved a massacre. I stopped listening after the third word.

"Not imposters…*recruits*. That's what they are. Ya know it's…it's cute seeing you commit to the charade…but there's no point. I knew the moment you walked in. You people…" I inhaled the air through my flaring nostrils. "You got a scent. And you brought me here for one thing…to recruit me. It's smart…wearing the same outfits as them? Hiding in plain sight. But I know that you're them…I know that you're the resistance…the problem, however, is that we don't share the same reason for being here. I'm not here for you…I'm here to get my friend back. You fucked with my farm. Burned it down. And that's…that was a mistake. So you've got one of two options."

He waited an extended period of time for me to continue but I made him ask for it.

"…What are they?"

"One, you voluntarily let me go and set us both free, and we don't turn back. Two, you keep talking…you keep flexing your muscles, and

I'll *show* you what's going on in my head. I'll paint the walls with your blood…I'll shove your femur down your throat until you shit it out…I'll skin you alive and wear it like a coat, then go to your house…and fuck your wife…but that's your decision to make."

Getting in people's heads, that's what I had to resort to for fun. He was breaking but his fear turned into anger. A thick vein popped out of his forehead and he chewed harsh grit.

"You…you are not him…"

I smiled. "…You haven't even said his name. Are you scared? I know you know it…I can see it…hanging on the tip of your tongue. But you don't want to believe that your god…your saviour…is this," I finished, pointing to my skull.

Before he either had a panic attack or lunged at me from over the table, a voice of sheer prominence interrupted him over the echoing intercom.

"It's him," the female voice spoke.

Just the person I was looking for. The resistance made the mess but she's the only one who could make it right. She was the only one who deserved my attention.

"You…ya heard that too, right?" I asked him playfully. "I got, uh, voices in my head…but that's not one of them. Well, I don't think…"

I watched thoughtfully as the colour drained from his face. Without a word he backed out from the room and left me alone. With him gone, I pulled off that mask of controlled instability and became my true self. There were two people in the room with me, built and formed by my unapologetic excuse of an imagination and I conversed with them. They were my family. They were the only ones who I didn't want to murder.

Arguing arose through the one-way mirror. Muffled words made no sense but I already knew exactly what they were talking about. It went like this: He didn't trust me, she was trying to convince him that I was who I said I was, he needed proof, yadda yadda yadda. He was going to get it. So when he returned, I gave it to him before he could take a breath.

"Which case study would you like to hear about?"

"…W-what?"

I grinned. "Everyone starts with the genocides. That's the easy one to read. Well, *easier.* Then there's the child experiments, the fire, the…

execution, my death, etc. etc. But you…you have one in mind. You want to know about what happened with Atlas."

That was the turning point. I knew that name was all it took.

"My god," he breathed. "It's you. You're…Levi."

"Took you long enough."

He didn't speak. Being in the presence of such a nefarious monster would take a toll on anyone. That was a title forced on me, not one I accepted nor did I create.

"So…are you going to ask?"

"A-ask…?"

"If I did it? That's the million-dollar question. Clearly you must carry some doubt if you're a part of this…Levi…fan club."

"…No…no! We don't need you…Even if you share the same blood and name as him, what you have become…you are not my saviour. I *refuse* to work with you."

I filled my cheeks with bubbles of air and puffed out with a shrug.

"Well, I'm sorry to hear that, but I don't think I could physically care any less. Your involvement is that of a cockroach. I'm here for the one the voice belongs to…sitting across from me…looking in my eyes. And no, not from that one-way mirror."

He fiddled with his wedding ring nervously. I wondered if it still had a purpose. I wondered if there actually was someone who carried its counterpart.

"Y-you don't just simply ask to meet her."

"Well I just did."

To hurry things along, she made the decision herself and entered the room.

"Hello, Levi."

If the rebellion was a show, she was the puppet master. There was no one she answered to. Well, not yet.

Her eyes were aged but still retained youth. Her slender wrists were sprinkled with liver spots and she wore a draped, knitted cardigan. Her black hair was cut in a bob and a single streak of white brushed down. It was both familiar and utterly foreign.

"…Are you Godmother? That's what they call you right? You're the head of the rebellion."

She nodded her wrinkled head.

"Good…good. I'm going to ask you a question…I believe you have the answer. What the fuck did you do with my ape?"

Tom had no idea what I was talking about. Surely he thought me as a grade-A wackjob. But she didn't.

"Your ape…" she repeated, as if speaking to a friend. "Your ape is safe. No harm will come to her."

That pissed me off. It was the little things that made me…volatile.

"It's a *he* you wrinkled, cancerous shit. Don't you dare speak to me like I'm your hostage. There is no bargaining. No trade-offs. Every single moment here proceeds under my authority, got it? I'm not here to gossip and I'm certainly not here to be interrogated. You've taken my friend because he tried to save me—"

"—After you brutally murdered two officers," she reminded. "We took both of you before they could."

I scoffed. "That's besides the point. The only reason for me being here is to get him back. Your rebellion means nothing to me."

"I don't believe that," Godmother stated with balls far superior to Tom's. "Your friend is here in the safe house and I know that you are more than capable of apprehending him. You could've killed us all but you didn't. Why?"

I was about to deliver a harsh retort but I couldn't bring myself to do so. She was right. No…dammit, people don't do that. They don't make *me* ask questions. But she was capable of the impossible. Why had I remained there? Was I not over it? Did I still want to fight? I looked down at my hands and realized they had yet to be cleaned. I stared attentively at the blood they carried, both figuratively and literally. Her words were like a lingering scent; they clung to me. She saw me for who I was. Not Levi, no, but the monster that borrowed that name. I was a wild animal locked in with a group of tamed beasts. I was of the same species, but I could never be one of them.

"…You ever heard of Clear?"

"I'm sorry?" Godmother asked.

"Clear. It was part of all the scientology bullshit, but even Hubbard and the psychos had a silver lining. Cult nonsense, sure…but a valid ideal doesn't cease. To be Clear is to atone for your sins. Clear your conscience. That's…that's what I came to do. I owe that to her."

"Her?" she repeated like an unforgiving reporter.

"Them," I replied coldly. "I said I owe it to *them*."

Tom spoke up, presumably feeling left out. "Jesus Christ…seriously? Godmother, we don't need him. We don't—"

"Tom, your mouth is open," she acknowledged. "I suggest you shut it."

I glared up at him and like an opposing magnet he immediately averted any connection.

"I could leave right now, you know that, right? You people are murderers. But even then there's a difference between bad and *evil*. It's been one thousand and seven days since the last reported sighting of a halfie, and yet…nothing has changed. We won the war, but is it really considered winning when you've lost everything in the process? War… it can never be won because no one wants it to end. Why is that?" I paused, waiting for an answer that I didn't receive. "…It's because of me. I'm the figure of controversy at the heart of it all. See, most of them believe that I plagued them all and *he* was the saviour. But…there's still truth…you people have that…and you waste it. Hundreds of people die every week because they're either killed in order to eradicate my existence or groups like you kill them in my name. My name is *not* to be a death sentence. Well, not unless I'm the one handing it out. But I never wanted it to be used as if I was a god. We all know there's only one man who thinks of himself as such. I *chose* to be here. The reason I came out of hiding wasn't because I wanted to start a revolution. I came out of hiding so I could end it. End it all. Take him down and be at rest. I am his last loose end and something tells me that I'll be tied up very soon. I can't stay hidden much longer. I need to make sure his story is told as well as mine before I'm killed…so that someone can end it for all of us. I don't give two shits about you…but you are committed, I'll give you that. Once it's done…my hands are clean. I'll be able to die peacefully and become…Clear. You get it?"

Her sad, aging eyes twinkled with hidden heartbreak. "You've got a whole life ahead of you. Why would you want to die?"

"If you put expired milk in a brand new container, does that make it any better?"

"No," she answered.

"Exactly. So…okay…all right, I'll help, but it's on my terms. You give him back and when we're done here, you let me die in peace."

Godmother nodded. "I'll make sure *he* is brought back to your farm without the Empire knowing, you have my word."

"…Okay…what do you need?"

Godmother looked at me with a heavy glance. "I'm sorry but we need to know everything."

I bit the inside of my cheek. I immediately regretted my commitment. "Everything? Look…it's not that easy. That's seventeen years of… nightmares…"

She fiddled with a locket around her neck solemnly. "We have just over a week before the freedom parade swallows the city. If tradition holds true then he'll be there. Our plan is to expose him for the tyrant he truly is. All the people under his control are more than capable of overthrowing him but they're just too scared to act on it. If we can find any leverage or a way to take him down before then, we'll win. If we don't have anything before then, we'll have to wait another decade and that is something we will surely not survive. You need to tell us everything, Levi. I'm sorry but you can't spare any details."

"…Fine. But if you want to know what I did and the repercussions, we're going to have to start from the very top: the outbreak. You'll understand why later on."

She nodded, failing to hide her excitement. Tom fiddled with his ring once again, this time for an entirely different reason.

"Thank you for doing this, Levi. It won't be easy but it's for the salvation of every single victim under his power. Start whenever you're ready."

I leaned back in my seat until the darkness swallowed me. I crossed my arms, a breath exhaled, and it all began.

## 2. "—At least three limbs and a pulse."

**17 Years Ago.**

**90 minutes until Day Zero.**

It all started with a nightmare. No, let me rephrase that: a *recurring* nightmare. To be fair, most mornings began this way, shuffling through my extensive library of horrors until a juicy nightmare was dug up. I'll share the most-played one; the title song off the Greatest Hits of Levi's subconscious. This one in particular was like a record that skipped and repeated at a constant rhythm, playing only on a certain occasion: a death in the family. Now, family is used loosely in this sense as hardly known great-uncles and friends of friends had taken center stage with me as the sole audience member.

In this...ordeal, I would find myself in an abandoned warehouse where burning sunlight pierced through foggy windows, illuminating my surroundings with a passionate red hue. Smoke enveloped my feet and stretched out to the man/woman/animal that motionlessly stood opposite of me. Dead eyes locked on me with final-moment gazes that would leave me with a sense of ridicule and despair. They looked at me as if I had killed them; punished them to a fate worse than death. Then, without any kind of warning, we fast-forward a few moments and this was usually when my outside body would start to shiver and sweat. I would be forced to watch as the body of the newly deceased individual was thrown into various pieces of heavy machinery. Gears and ropes ripped the flesh from their bones and blood spurted in the air like an overpowered hose, all whilst their mindless eyes stared up at me. Looks not of agony, but of disappointment. This unnerving stare would last until the grinding pieces of metal forced them downwards and their eyeballs exploded from their sockets. Keep in mind that these dreams first appeared when I was four years old.

The worst part of these night terrors was this eerie sound of silence. All that could be heard was my elevated heartbeat and everything else was muted, from the sounds of breaking bones to the machines roaring. The victims wouldn't even make a noise. All that they gave me was that god-forsaken look of disgust. Picture this: A seven-year-old kid waking up with piss in his pajama bottoms because he just watched, in vivid detail, his dead dog being ripped apart limb by limb. It doesn't take a rocket scientist to understand that I was a messed up kid.

The moment I had woken up that morning, I was already drained. My muscles ached from nightlong tension, my arrhythmic heart pulsed in a chaotic manner, and a heavy layer of sweat covered my skin that was seasoned and sunken from years of cutthroat anxiety. My body remained paralyzed for a few moments as my brain climbed its way out of the limbo that separated the subconscious from reality. Like a recently switched off light bulb, it was a dream that still momentarily lingered after I had awoken before disappearing entirely. The question that would inevitably arrive plastered itself on the crumbling walls of my paranoia-driven mind: Was it only a dream?

I looked over to my bedside clock and blinked at the glowing green numbers. 7:14 AM. With a drawn-out sigh of defeat, I lifted my body up from the warm enticement of my quilt and climbed to my feet like a puppet held up by strings. The unseen puppet master directed me to the other end of my room to inhale a granola bar from my breakfast stash, to the bathroom where I brushed my teeth and urinated simultaneously, to the shower where I was able to wash away the remaining gleam of sweat, and finally to the foggy mirror where I got the first glimpse of myself that morning.

The teenager that looked back at me had a thick head of dark brown hair that swiped to the side and dark, solemn eyebrows to match. There were two hazel eyes that produced an image about three dials out of focus, with contacts that helped clarify the blurry end product. Dull, pink lips peeled apart in the middle, creating a gap that exposed my post-braces teeth to the outside world. I looked at the reflection, understood that it was me, and yet continued to believe that what I was looking at was simply a broken man trapped in a teenager's body.

At the ripe age of seventeen, I had already suffered more hardships and tribulations than what would be deemed socially conventional. Standouts would include a broken family, years of being subjected to psychoanalysis, proposed shock therapy sessions, and most recently, a broken heart. Yes, the classic situation of high school romance, but with a twist of mental instability. My romantic life was the love child of a John Hughes movie and a Freudian essay. Is it worth explaining? Yes. Right now? Nope. I wouldn't say that this was the catalyst for my teetering sanity, but it surely didn't help. All that you need to know is that I successfully accepted love with open arms and in return I received a broken hand and thirty hours of court-mandated therapy.

*Seventy-two minutes.*

After using up every excuse to remain upstairs, I finally came down and inspected each room while a forgotten radio played static news. First the kitchen, where only used dishes in the sink and takeout boxes stacked up against the beige walls could be found. *Zzt—as of today, there are officially eight billion people—Zzt* Then the bathroom, which was only occupied by stale vomit spiraling in the toilet. Next was the dining room. *Zzt—Environmentalists are becoming increasingly concerned about overpopulation and exhausting global res—Zzt* No one. Finally, I crept into the living room where the familiar stench of bourbon and tobacco wished me a good morning. Sprawled out on the couch was the unconscious body of a snoring, gray-haired, pathetic excuse of a human being.

"Morning, Dad," I said to his sleeping corpse.

To say that my relationship with my father was complicated would be a hilarious understatement. When I was three years old, something happened. This was the event that fractured my well-being and ruined everything that was right about my family. It was no one's fault. No one could've anticipated it. It happened, we moved from Kansas to Alberta, Canada and we never spoke of it again. Unfortunately, ignoring the reality was like putting a Band-Aid over a bullet wound.

Mom was the first to go, leaving my dad and I behind after I found her in the bathtub one night with her wrists slit. We rushed her to the hospital, me too young and too oblivious to understand the implications of what she had done, and when we got home, Dad told me that Mom was moving away. The last time I saw my mother, she was being rushed blood-soaked on gurney down a sterile white hallway.

My dad left too, but in a different way. The charismatic, wisecracking, rock and roll loving guy who had accompanied me during my early childhood slowly faded away over the years with each bottle he drank. His hair grayed, eyes sunk, and his lips formed a permanent look of grimace that was incapable of curling up into a smile. More often than not our nights consisted of greasy takeout and juvenile insults to one another, followed by a collapsed father and a boy struggling to carry him to bed.

Ignoring him most mornings, that day I decided to reminisce on the times I still had my dad, imagining myself in a one-person theatre watching vintage, grainy home videos. The numbers counted down and the image blew up on the screen. Those sweaty, summer days spent in Baskin-Robbins, stuffing my face with an ice cream cone that never ceased to leak. Dad would let out that booming, lively laugh of his and showed me how to clip off the tip of the waffle cone and drink from it like a straw. Cut to the springtime, which was puddle stomping in my rubber boots and those frustrating days of learning the physics of a two-wheeler. Now my superhero-themed third birthday party in the fall where an inflatable superhero jumpy castle anchored on our front lawn and my cape billowed in the autumn wind. I was dressed as Batman; my father was honoured to be my Robin. Then the film reel changed and flashes of the summer fourteen years prior flickered on the screen. I remember how desperately I tried to vacate the thought, only for it to come back stronger and more potent. Through my fingers that attempted to cover my face, I caught quick glimpses of the screen, each blink a new image.

Circus...Clowns...Ring toss...a stranger...Lost in crowd... Blindfolded... Mirrors...Mirrors...Music...Mirrors...Pools of blood...

I forced myself to return to reality. The alcoholic remnants of a loved one were still on the patchy sofa in front of me. I clutched my forehead, embracing a pounding headache that was rolling in like storm clouds.

Scurrying off to the kitchen, I popped the lid off of a transparent, neon orange pill canister and with a swig of orange juice I swallowed a single red pill. Temporarily satisfying the unruly beast that rested within, I released a heavy sigh, tucked the container in my backpack, and slipped out through the backdoor with only the sounds of drunken sleep mumbles and clinking beer bottles to send me off.

Let me be very clear. I would never say that I hated my father. The reason being that my father had been gone for a very long time. I loved my dad. I absolutely despised the man who had occupied the same house as me.

*One hour.*

The walk to the bus stop was uneventful and forgettable. I'd say my memory is average but I couldn't even tell you what I was wearing the day of. Odds are you could imagine a pair of slim, black jeans, matching Converse sneakers, and whatever pattern of plaid that you find appealing. Beneath it would probably have been a dark gray t-shirt since I seemed to have a personal distaste for graphic designs of naked women or cats in space. My point is, not every moment of my life is worth recalling, but there are certain things that I'll never forget. The only thing that I remember on that walk was one of those rare metaphors that would've been a photographer's wet dream. A dewy aroma momentarily attracted my attention and my nose guided me to an expansive bed of flowers sprouting in my neighbour's yard. The first half of the plot was filled with a diverse selection of vibrant and delicate flowers blossoming from the soil. The other half, however, had contained only the dead carcasses of once beautiful flowers, with shrivelled-up heads and wilted petals that fell to the base of their yellowish stems. It was almost as though life and death were handed out equally in a random fashion. Luck of the draw I guess.

Another thing that I remember is a prime example of an average teenage boy conversation that took place on the steps of our school. Because whichever way you look at it, teenage boys are pigs. There is no getting around it. They cover uncertainty with shaky bravado; a veneer of cockiness counteracts inexperience. Sexual themes make up the better part of every conversation if only to try and suss out from others if they are as manly as they don't actually feel. Let me set the scene.

The brick-covered school casted a gloomy and soul-draining shadow that engulfed each and every student as they reluctantly entered the premises. Girls of all shapes and sizes strolled up the cobblestone steps and male commentary/ratings followed them closely like an inglorious shadow. Resting on the bike racks were two boys that were judging each passerby more favourably than usual. One was a scrawny, Asian boy named Nick, who had a greasy ponytail and wore a *Legend of Zelda* T-shirt two sizes too small. The other boy, Logan, had thick, charcoal glasses and to put it bluntly, a Jew-fro. To a variety of conservative teachers and simple onlookers, we may have been considered burnouts. That doesn't imply that I was a pothead. I had never even tried the stuff. What I'm trying to say is that if our student body had a directory, we would be found under *other*.

A girl with a sultry, hourglass feature walked by and Nick obnoxiously licked his fingers.

"I'd like to get a piece of that," he stated.

Logan shook his head with his curly hair wiggling with a slight delay.

"Kacey? Keep dreaming. She has like a 3.9 GPA and was offered a full-ride scholarship to NYU. Not to mention that she's absolutely breathtaking. And you? Well you're just…you."

Nick jumped off of the bike racks. "What are you tryn'a say? I've flirted with girls twice as hot as her."

"You consider it flirting, they consider it as a creepy Asian dude staring at them from across the hall," informed Logan. "Half of them probably think you're some ugly-ass lesbian with that ponytail of yours."

Before the argument grew, I broke into their conversation.

"Hey guys."

In every group of friends since the dawn of man, there is always that one person who is unintentionally the wet blanket. I was that guy. At any type of social gathering, there was this stench of sympathy that clung onto me, making it difficult to have a conversation where eggshells didn't litter the floor. Everyone was hesitant to talk to me because they were worried one slip of the tongue would cause me to snap. In my three years of high school, I hadn't forged the most popular reputation and every time I messed up, the events preceding high school were always raised. My past was a popular topic of discussion throughout the school and though no one had guessed correctly, everyone possessed their own theory of why I was a social pariah.

"Levi," Nick already began, "be honest with me. On a scale from one to ten, how hot do you think I…"

"Three outta ten," I quickly responded.

It also didn't help that I could sometimes be a dick.

"Ahh screw you guys!" Nick flipped us off. "I could get any girl I want. Hell, I'd need a canoe just to swim through all the pus—"

"In the duration of one week, I've seen you get rejected by four separate girls," I interrupted him. "One of them was a blind girl from learning strats."

Logan snickered. Nick wanted to snap back. I could see his skin flush with embarrassment. Yet, he refused to poke the bear.

"She was wearing sunglasses, okay?!" explained Nick. "She seemed fine until she walked into the trophy case."

"Right. Well that doesn't exactly go against your prerequisites, does it?"

"—At least three limbs and a pulse," piped up Logan.

They both chuckled while I was able to form something passable for a smile. Unfortunately, my limited access to happiness was a gift from my dad that I wasn't able to return.

As we started to make our way up the steps, a bubbly, blonde-haired bombshell strolled towards me with her books held across her chest. The joints in my legs locked into place and my mouth formed a hesitant O as she came closer and closer.

"Hey Levi!" she smiled. "D'ya mind if we talk for a second?"

Both Logan and Nick were just as dumbfounded as I was.

"Uh-hey Britney," I stumbled. "Yes! I mean, no. Yes we can talk. No to that I don't mind…continue?"

She felt obliged to giggle and lessen the awkwardness. I felt obliged to jam a brick into my mouth. I guess you could say I was pretty smooth.

"Well, I was planning on going stag with the girls to grad but then Kara just had to go find a date! So our plans kinda got screwed up and, well, I was wondering if you wanted to go with me?"

I turned around to see if she was speaking to someone behind me.

"Me…?" I asked. "Uhm…why? Do you need a ride there or something?"

Britney rolled her eyes flirtatiously. "No, idiot. As my date."

With my heart pulverized into an undistinguishable mess, the idea of another girl being attracted to me was inconceivable. It was unclear if she was being sincere or a bitch. Instinctively, I assumed the latter.

"…I'm still waiting for the punch line."

Though I gave her multiple opportunities to retract her offer, she continued to persist.

"Levi, you're an attractive guy," complimented Britney. "You shouldn't be so shocked that someone would ask you to grad."

I shook my head. "I don't doubt my looks, Britney. I also don't doubt the fact that my charm is equivalent to that of a lamp. I'm not even sure why these guys have stuck around."

"I'm just as shocked, buddy," muttered Nick. Logan smacked him in the stomach.

"Besides," I continued, "I'm thinking of skipping grad."

Britney worryingly grabbed my bicep like we were in a B-list soap opera.

"What? Why?"

The touch of a girl was both electrifying and unnerving. Instinctively, I pulled my arm away.

"What's the point?" I asked rhetorically. "Grad is just an excuse to spend one last time with people that we pretend to be friends with and celebrate a milestone that couldn't be more meaningless. Not my kinda scene."

The threshold of her tolerance was reached as she finally came to her senses.

"Jesus. Aren't you a buzz kill," she snarled.

With a spin of her heels and a twirl of her golden curls, she stormed away towards her glaring friends who had somehow already shared a universal hatred for me.

Nick and Logan approached on either side of me as I slammed my palm onto my forehead.

"Nailed it," I murmured.

"Are you that surprised?" asked Nick as he unceremoniously picked something from his teeth. "I don't know the kind of girls you're into but most of them on *this* planet don't exactly get turned on by comparisons with home decor."

Logan slung his arm over my shoulder. "Don't worry 'bout it. You'll find a honey soon enough. If ya want, just go on one of those sites like Mormonmingle.com. You can always rely on the Mormons to marry, fuck and repeat. Bastards breed like rabbits."

"I feel so much better already."

As the warning bell blared through the outside intercom, Nick and Logan gave me a farewell nod and stumbled for the doors, leaving me to my natural state: Alone.

I looked up to the cloudless, pale blue sky and suspiciously peered into it like it was some sort of one-way mirror. I'm not sure if it was hearing the word 'Mormon' or something else entirely, but my thought led to the contemplation of a higher power. Was there this big man in the sky watching over us? Tinkering with our lives like a spoiled child with too much time on his hands? Religion was never brought into my household. Dad was unable to believe that what happened to us could've possibly been a part of God's plan. I didn't know where I stood on the religious spectrum, but I did know one thing: If God was real and directed our lives to his choosing, I had no interest in meeting him. When I looked into the sky, I didn't see some sort of supernatural meddling. All that was there was the hazy sun in my peripherals like a child's depiction of a yellow slice looming in the corner. Flickers of shadows passed over me. Hundreds of migrating bird flying overhead, their flight patterns were erratic and violent, as if each bird was suddenly responding on instinct to avoid a terrific threat.

I exhaled, not thinking anything of it, and dragged my feet up the cobblestone steps to the school. I pulled the door open to reveal the various players in the high school drama. Each of us was a cog in the machine that was this school, and there was me, a gear that just didn't fit.

"This is going to be a long day," I sighed.

# 3. "Shit got fucked."

*Seven Minutes.*

Class was nearly half over when a fit, shaggy-haired boy decided to show up at school. His rule was that if he missed the first five minutes of class, it was already a lost cause. The burning hatred that he carried for school was both humorous and downright ridiculous. One time he intentionally broke two of his fingers to avoid writing a trigonometry exam. This was Atlas Jordan. He was a protagonist in the classic tale following the delinquent-with-a-heart-of-gold, but at the time this story wasn't one I was familiar with. To be honest, I thought he was nothing more than a stoner douchebag.

To summarize Atlas would be like trying to slam a revolving door: it couldn't be done. Everything about him was merely a contradiction. Atlas was a juxtaposition of himself. His wide, innocent, sapphire eyes clashed with his rebellious, weed-smoking persona. He teetered with failure in nearly every single one of his classes, yet he was able to recite every lyric in Eminem's *Rap God* after only a few listens. He could be one of the most arrogant, stubborn, and narcissistic assholes I've ever met and I would've never believed how important he would eventually become to me.

Girls adored him, guys envied him and teachers despised him. He pulled more pranks and caused more shit than any other student in the sixty-four years that my school had existed. A picture of Atlas hung up in the teachers lounge over a dartboard with a massive crater of punctures collected between his eyes, proving the collective hatred the teachers shared for him.

Mr. Sperling, one of the many advocates for Atlas's expulsion as well as an adamant dart player caught Atlas ditching class.

"Mr. Jordan," Sperling announced, "what a pleasant surprise. Taking a morning stroll, I presume?"

"Not this time, Teach'," he replied. "I recently learned that Chipotle and Red Bull for breakfast is not a combination to be reckoned with. Now I'm venturing off to the little boys room to make myself well-acquainted with the porcelain."

Sperling's lip snarled up in revulsion. "You disgust me, Jordan. Get to class."

"I'm being serious! My colon is a-rumblin'."

"You couldn't have gone in all of the time it took you to get here?" Sperling questioned.

"Well, I mean, I was physically capable of shitting," he remarked. "I was also capable of shitting last night. But the thing is, I didn't need to shit then. I need to shit now. So either you let me go or I'm going to let go. Right now. In my pants."

Sperling waved his hand to Atlas and marched off bitterly. Atlas grinned to himself and made his way to the bathroom where he proceeded to pull out a Gameboy.

*Four minutes.*

Back in the classroom, my intelligence was in the process of receding into a coma. With every word uttered by the monotone, pot-bellied teacher, a powerful stench of stupidity and abused prescription drugs slapped my face. Thirty-eight classmates encompassed me, each with a varying expression of boredom and dissociation. We were the patients and he was the anaesthetic that slowly coated our cells with a dreary covering.

"So, Class," the teacher had begun with incredible energy, "last week we were discussing *Catch-22* by Joseph Heller. That's J…O…S…"

I slammed my head on my desk and contemplated whether or not breaking my legs via jumping out of the window would be worth leaving the classroom. My eyes rolled into the back of my head and my eyelids fell down like the velvet curtains of the final act. Parallel lines of sunlight poured through the window and onto my face, trapping me with jail-like bars. Seeing as though being educated was a lost cause,

I looked outside and began to daydream. The next thing that went through my head was something that I would soon regret.

*Three minutes.*

In the bathroom stall, Atlas swiped his precisely unruly light brown hair out of his piercing, blue eyes that the Gameboy screen bounced off of. His tongue casually stuck out of his mouth while he performed his daunting task. As his Italian plumber lost his last life and a series of swears ensued, a pathetic looking freshman entered the bathroom. Atlas peered through the thin sliver between the stall doors and saw the innocent keener, causing him to shake his head and laugh. Not that he was making fun of the kid, but rather noticed how he had seen himself and so many others in the kid before the harsh reality gave them an abrupt wake-up call. Atlas recognized all of the flaws in society and didn't give in to any of the bullshit that was delivered from the 'paid professionals'. It was often the times that his pants were at his ankles when he became surprisingly philosophical.

*Two minutes.*

I truly believed that some of the most psychotic and demented thoughts that an individual may conjure up would occur with a lethargic mindset. The middle of English class + a droning teacher + a panel of the outside world to my left = a perfect mentality to daydream about a massacre.

The stage was set. Mr. Pot-belly traced the fading marker all across the whiteboard, exposing his perspiring armpit to the audience. Robotic sounds escaped his wheezy breath, a catalyst for a hypnotic slumber to infect the classroom. A redheaded girl stared down at her phone flickering from her crotch. A sniffle. A grunt. Nick doodled a squid-like monster terrorizing a beach. Chairs screeched across the tiled floor. Then, a man wearing a vintage hockey mask kicked down the door, dropping an immediate silence on top of us. From head to toe, he was clad in different shades of black and with a flick of the wrist he pulled out a machine gun that matched. The red marker didn't even reach the floor before a frenzy of bullets eradicated Mr. Pot-belly's brain into purple and gray mush.

Pandemonium. Kids that begged for mercy were blown apart with an unforgiving wave of gunfire while the remaining students ducked beneath their blood-splattered desks. Teenage screams filled the room like a humid atmosphere and beneath the mask of the murderer, a glint of smiling teeth flashed into my eyes. Using the carcasses of my fellow classmates as cover, I army-crawled to the front of the class with a pair of scissors clenched between my trembling teeth. While he was busy with lighting up a huddle of girls burrowed in the corner, I climbed to my feet and stealthily tiptoed until his leather-coated back was nearly pressed against me. The scissors left my mouth and the open blade wrapped around to his jugular. I sliced it open and watched gloriously as a heavy red mist sprayed onto his victims. He dropped to his knees. I smiled calmly and knelt down to the dying gunman. Pulling away the hockey mask, my smile dropped fast as what I looked down at was my own reflection.

"Pay attention, Mr. Finch!" the teacher called out.

I shook my head back into reality and sat up in my chair.

"Sorry, Mr. Nesbitt."

The teacher scoffed and continued to scribble his chicken scratch on the white board. I looked around at my living classmates and swallowed the disgust I felt. My forehead mindlessly slumped to the flat surface of my desk again and with that, the final lap was coming to a close.

*Forty-five seconds.*

Looking back on it now, I've come to realize that what happened next shouldn't have been much of a surprise. After millions and millions of years of evolution, humans were the final end product. How depressing is that? We once had the colossal, seemingly mythic dinosaurs walking the planet and somehow ended up with the selfish, disgraceful humans that we all were. We had been created and educated to utilize the finite resources on the planet for our own personal benefit, knowing very well that there would be inevitable consequences that would leave no man unharmed. Unfortunately, I was a part of the generation that suffered the fallout.

*Twenty seconds.*

In the seventeen years that followed the incident, I've lost track of how many times I've been asked the same question: "What do you think caused it?" My response: "Does it matter?" I personally discovered the cause in the winter of that year and I can honestly say that I have gained nothing from it. Sure, it made sense and was something fairly expected, but my outlook on life hadn't shifted in any sense. The only thing that I can and should say about the event is that the world was a living organism and we were the viruses that were taking over. It was time for a vaccination. A rebirth.

*Five seconds.*

A young boy rode a train with his backpack resting on his lap. When he approached a tunnel, his eyes shut fearfully.

*Four.*

A mother filled her tank at a rural gas station as her daughters gossiped in the back seat.

*Three.*

Deep within the confinements of an insane asylum, an elderly, bearded man awakened.

*Two.*

Atlas continued to play his game as the boy entered the stall next to him.

*One.*

I lifted my head up from my desk and examined the class. Something felt very wrong.

*Zero.*

A ghostly, spine-chilling drone filled the air for a few moments before disappearing entirely. Just as the teacher turned to continue on with his lecture, it all began. In the classroom, half of the occupants started to make choking noises and clutched their throats. Almost instantaneously, their pupils constricted and foam arose from the corners of their mouths. Various students were puking violently and grabbed at their hearts as they fell to the floor. Red gore secreted out from their eyes and dribbled from their ears as the remaining half of the class—myself included—sat in utter confusion and panic. A loud popping sound erupted from Mr. Nesbitt's chest as a growing pool of red soaked through his crinkled shirt. His heart had exploded. Within seconds, the bodies of half the class lifelessly collapsed to the ground in puddles of blood and fluid.

"What the FUCK!" classmates screamed.

"What happened?!"

My legs buckled and my breath faded as I pulled myself away from the drooling and convulsing body of my English teacher, leaking beneath my front row desk. Everywhere I looked, death followed. Though my mind was paralyzed with dreadful fear, I couldn't help but feel a sense of guilt due to my colourful daydream. Was this somehow my fault? Was this a new species of terrorist attacks? Would I soon suffer the same fate as the fresh corpses around me? The only thing courteous enough to answer me was the thin veil of death that swarmed half of everything. The questions continued to rush in when I lifted myself up to the window, only to see that this mysterious illness had reached the outside world. Dozens of cars swerved and collided with one another. Pale, dead bodies scattered the streets as others desperately struggled to hold onto life. Brothers, sisters, mothers, fathers, friends, all let their final breaths out into the tainted air and blood bubbled through their teeth as their unaffected companions were forced to watch helplessly.

Back in the men's bathroom, Atlas continued sitting on the toilet completely unaffected and unaware of the disease that had randomly taken so many lives. While he was mid-wipe, he received an urgent text message from one of his friends in Home EC, getting a quick glimpse of an abundance of exclamation marks and full caps on his phone that rested on the toilet paper dispenser. The two buzzes vibrated on the metal and shook until it teetered off. His fragile phone descended to the ground and made a loud popping sound, shattering the screen to the point of becoming opaque.

"Awe balls," he said angrily.

Before he could retrieve his broken phone and see what his buddy had sent him, the boy in the stall next to Atlas began to moan and splutter as blood dripped onto the floor.

"Uhm, the girl's bathroom is next door..." joked Atlas. The lack of a response caused him to feel bad for his badly timed joke.

"...That was rude," apologized Atlas. "Do you need any help, bud?"

The boy whimpered like a suffering dog, followed by screams of excruciating pain that sounded as though his insides were being eaten away. Atlas pulled up his pants and reached for his phone when thick, arteriole blood pooled at his feet and engulfed the overpriced piece of technology. His hand jerked away and Atlas immediately scurried out of the stall with his face scrunched up in disgust.

"What the hell kind of nosebleed you got, bruh? You bled all over my goddamn phone!" he shouted at the metal door that separated the two. Silence. "...Also, are you dying in there? I probably should've started out with that."

Atlas could see most of the boy's dormant body from where he was standing when out of nowhere, his limbs and torso contorted sickeningly on top of the fractured porcelain. The boy convulsed vigorously on the tiled floor as if another being had possessed him. After Atlas fearfully backed away to the sink counter, the poor boy's body became still. Atlas slowly crept towards the dented door and knocked lightly.

"Ok, what the hell is going on in there? From where I'm standing, things are looking slightly more *Scarface* than I would like."

Through the crack, Atlas saw the boy's twitching body slump to the gory mess below. He could hear the thunk as his head hit the ground and land in the goo, followed by a wheezing sound that resembled a collapsed fireplace bellow. Atlas bent down to his knees and peeked underneath the stall to see the aftermath of what he'd just semi-witnessed. He looked down to see lifeless eyes staring back at him with a demented, blood-curdling smile that brutally stretched across his pale face.

"Jesus fucking Christ!!" Atlas yelled as he scrambled to his feet. Within seconds, he was gone out the door, leaving the poor boy to marinate in his tainted blood.

"Holy shit! Holy mother shit!!" Atlas screamed.

He exploded out into the halls and realized that this anomaly had spread from the washroom as countless bodies were piled on top of each other.

"What the hell did I miss?"

As each second passed, the school became more disoriented and powerless as its list of occupants was cut in half. This blacklist included Logan and Nick. After severing my trance on the outside world, I noticed their still bodies resting on top of each other near the front of the class. Both were sprawled on their bellies like that of a drowned person, except instead of water filling their lungs, it was blood. I slumped down to my knees and flipped them over, praying for a shimmer of life that would never come.

"N-Nick? Logan?" I stammered. "Guys…wake up! Wake up!"

While I stayed back with my fallen friends, the remainder of the living felt it necessary to evacuate the premises in a chaotic fashion.

The sound of teenage screams and scuffling shoes filled my ears, but I was still able to here a small, almost overlooked splutter. I tilted my head down to realize that Nick had still been able to hang on.

"Nick! Nick, stay with me!"

My first thought was to issue CPR. I supported his head with one hand and pressed firmly onto his vibrating and pulsating chest as if it were a geyser on the brink of expulsion. Just as I lowered my face to his, he demonstrated one final sign of life as a projectile cough of blood sprayed me with a warm, cranberry red mist. The tiny bubbles fizzled away from his gaping mouth and just like that, his chest permanently deflated.

With a trembling hand, I wiped the droplets from my cheeks and forehead that blended with a solution of perspiration and tears. A part of me was surprise to see tears, indicating true sadness, but they were only the product of exposure to such rancid smells. True tears would never come.

Fellow classmates traumatized by the gruesome genocide pushed their way to the exit, worried that the mysterious illness would take their lives as well. I kept my solemn gaze onto Logan and Nick with the exhaled blood dripping down my chin, wondering how all of this could've happened. I decided that my best course of action would be to leave the classroom and find a way out, so I lifted myself off of the infected floor and delicately stepped in between the teenage corpses. Just as I reached the door, a girl with her mascara smeared down her cheeks beat me to it and selfishly slammed the door in my face. Clearly panicked, she thought that she should keep the dead bodies in quarantine, so as I reached for the handle, I heard the outside lock snap into place.

"Hey! Let me out!!" I yelled.

My fists pounded on the door and the sudden realization of being locked in a room with dead people began to sink in. Yelling proved to be of little help as the screams of hundreds of students drowned me out. I was utterly helpless in a classroom straight from Hell.

Through the barbaric halls filled with cold bodies and blood painted on the walls like a canvas, Atlas sprinted to the exit. With each step he glanced at a new fallen body and a new concoction of swears popped in his mind. In all the chaos erupting through the school, Atlas almost missed the sound of my screams for help. He *almost* missed it.

Atlas stopped and faced the L-shaped hallway, standing against the strong current of students. His eyes were locked on my face pressed against the window of the classroom door. I looked at him and he at me, and right then and there, he had a decision to make. He had to decide whether he would go and rescue me or save himself to leave me in the makeshift graveyard. I can guarantee that he didn't care about my well-being. He just didn't want the guilt on his conscience.

"Son of a bitch," he exhaled.

Atlas reluctantly embarked on his rescue mission for a complete stranger and as he pushed through the terrified students, he caught snippets of various dialogue.

"-goddamn terrorists!"

"-he just collapsed on me!"

"-did we survive?"

Atlas reached the tail end of the hallway and faced the glass pane, reflecting my worried expression. There was an awkward pause.

"Are you locked in or is this just something you're into?" he asked. "Please tell me you're not one of those necropheliacs."

"I got locked in! Open the door!"

Atlas flipped the lock open and yanked the door to reveal me standing above a sea of corpses.

"Uh...thanks," I said hesitantly.

"Don't worry about it," he replied sternly, trying to disregard his act of selflessness.

With a nod of acknowledgment, Atlas turned to walk away. I felt as though our conversation wasn't finished.

"So that's it then? Isn't there, like, an obligation to talk about what happened?"

"Shit got fucked," he answered without stopping.

"Clearly," I said with a short-tempered tone.

Atlas turned and gave me a look of annoyance.

"What else do you want me to say? I was taking a shit and this kid went all *Exorcist*in the stall next to me. I was thinking it was some kind of seizure until I saw everyone else. It's messed beyond belief but pointless dialogue isn't going to bring them back, dude. You can come with me to get the hell out of here or you can sit here and wallow with them. Your choice."

"…I appreciate you opening the door but I don't need your help."

He scoffed, shaking his head at my bluntness.

"You do you, bud. Nice talking to you."

As he continued on with his exit, an abnormal sound could be heard, as if the wind was being split apart by a bullet. The sound grew closer and closer until it made our ears ring.

"What the hell is th—"

As the words escaped his lips, the unthinkable happened. Clouds shattered into wispy strands as an uncontrollable hunk of metal hurdled towards the school. An unmanned plane twirled through the air and produced a roaring sound of shifting metal that echoed into the heavens. The reflection of the school rooftop became bigger and bigger in the plane's shiny, metal nose before it ultimately impacted.

The deafening boom of shattering bones and steel tearing apart played like a soundtrack for a disaster movie. A colossal explosion swallowed the rooftop as the new flames licked the crushed carcasses in between the crumbling rubble. The metal shell of the plane buckled in like a collapsing slinky as it pierced through the defenseless school and burrowed inside. Each and every living passenger aboard the plane was ferociously killed as his or her bodies became scorched and unrecognizable. The ceiling of the school caved in on the student body, engulfing us in concrete and pipes. Approximately two-thirds of the school was now completely obliterated and the charred smoke filled the lungs of both the living and the dead. Though we managed to avoid the worst of the crash, Atlas and I were still thrown into the air and submerged in dust and rubble that made it nearly impossible to breathe. A metal rod lodged in the split concrete pierced into the side of my leg, creating a steady stream of blood to dribble out of my body. We were trapped. Not only in the decimated high school, but also in a world that we would soon discover had been cluttered with billions of deceased individuals. This indeed was just the beginning of the end.

# 4. "Can't you understand me?!"

Somewhere in Alberta.

The air reeked of madness. All it took was one catastrophic event for the civilians to downgrade to barbaric, devolved beasts that instantly turned on each other. Riots broke out in the streets, countless cars attempted to escape only to collide with one another; a local gas station erupted with gasoline fires, slowly roasting the trapped people inside. As the downtown metropolis abruptly disintegrated into an uncontrollable state of chaos, a careless man looting an electronics shop noticed an immense cloud of smoke billowing miles away.

Broken concrete crumbled to the ground as thick, ash-embedded smoke surrounded the classroom. After ten or so minutes locked in a comatose state, I awoke with nothing but pain and agony gushing through my body. My heavy eyelids peeked open and squinted through the dense air to see the outline of a boy trapped across from me. Gravelly dust coated my throat, making it impossible to inhale without facing the chances of coughing up a lung.

"What…was that…" I wheezed, rubbing my ashy forehead.

I lifted my head up to examine the piece of metal penetrating nearly two inches into my right leg. Unable to reach the iron rod, I laid there pathetically paralyzed.

My vocal chords felt like barbed wire. "Hey…you good?"

There was a moment filled with heavy grunts and exhales until a silhouette was cast over me.

"What the hell…did you do…" a familiar voice crackled.

I opened my irritated eyes and focused on the teenager in front of me. Atlas had a weak frown that shook. There had been a large, hook-shaped gash traced down his left cheek that dripped red frequently.

I released a sigh drenched with annoyance. "Can you please just get whatever's in my leg out?"

It was clear that he wanted nothing more than to leave me behind and flee out the door, which unfortunately for him was nowhere to be seen as slabs of ceiling formed a barrier around us. If he wanted to get out, he needed my help. Atlas knelt down and brushed the onyx powder off of my trapped leg. Before he chose to rescue me however, his gaze was drawn to a pool of thick black gore and an unrecognizable object a few steps away. As he slid to it, he realized the object was Nick's head, decapitated by sharp sheets of stone from the fallen walls. His long, black ponytail snaked through the blood, absorbing it like a sponge.

"Oh man…"

He crawled swiftly to the gaping hole in the wall and puked up the remaining contents in his stomach over the broken ledge.

"What is it…?" I asked.

"S' nothing!" lied Atlas, turning back to me. "Just…stay there and shut up!"

Thanks to his abrupt turn, his arm smacked into what was left of Nick and knocked him over the edge. It tumbled into a blazing fire created by a ripped apart jet engine that crash-landed on our school's front lawn. Nick's head spun with drops of blood spraying in every direction like a perspiring football. The permanent look of suffering befuddlement on Nick's face was the last thing Atlas saw before it disintegrated in the fire.

"Can you just help me?" I shouted, lacking any patience.

Atlas extracted the metal without warning and I shrieked in struggling pain. A build-up of blood spurted out at the removal of the rod and the increased pressure started to dwindle.

"There," Atlas replied with a sharpness in his voice. "Happy?"

I looked over at a deceased classmate next to me and though it felt morally wrong, I tore a long strip of fabric off of his shirt and wrapped it tightly around my wound. Now that that was taken care of, I took my first real glance at my surroundings that seemed to produce more questions than it provided answers.

"D-did we just get hit by a plane?" I muttered in shock. "That's not…that's not something that just happens…"

Muggy, late-morning sun twinkled on my tilted face, as the ceiling failed to exist. A constant rumble was felt beneath me. The classroom-turned-prison cell had only three walls as the fourth had been exchanged with the outside world. The three-story trees that were once planted on the wide lawn were reduced to stumps cleared by a Boeing 737 carcass. It had one wing, zero engines, and was forever parked in the middle of the passing road, certainly taking dozens of untainted lives with it. As if the population of the nearby area being sliced in half hadn't been enough, God decided to take a shit in the form of a plane crash on our heads. Super.

"Still think it's a good idea to stay here?" Atlas wondered, already clearing rubble from the doorway. "If you're ready to relinquish your bitch-in-distress title, get off your ass and help me."

Using a split desk for assistance, I was brought back on my wobbling feet and limped to his side. It was instinct to isolate myself from others; disregard their care and emotion. Still, he did help me, and I felt it best to at least attempt to show the ability to connect.

"…My name is Levi," I told, apparently to no one.

"Great, good to know…" he brushed off.

I persisted. "What's yours?"

"That is literally the least important thing right now," he spat, cringing at the sound of my voice. "Just dig!"

He demonstrated signs of claustrophobia. Being surrounded by death and broken concrete, a surge of desperation arose. I was not going to do anything until his heart rate lowered to a somewhat human level.

"My name is Levi," I repeated, extending a limp hand. "What's yours?"

He dropped his head and sighed a breath filled with frustration. "…Atlas," he finally replied back, meeting his hand with mine. Before I could pull away, the palm of my right hand was doused with a dampening sensation. I looked down at our handshake and I jerked away with an audible cry.

"What's your problem?!" Atlas blared out.

"Look at your hand!" I replied swiftly.

Atlas raised his right hand up to his squinty gaze and realized that half of his ring finger had been sliced off as well as the entirety of his pinkie. In the middle of the stumps were white circles of bone that could only be seen for a moment before being completely swallowed by oozing blood. His eyes widened and his mouth gaped as blood steadily poured down his butchered hand.

"M...my hand..." said Atlas in a curious fashion.

"Y-you're in shock, Atlas. Don't freak out..." I muttered, not knowing what to say.

I ripped off another piece of cloth from the shirt and applied it to Atlas's hand, which at a single touch he screamed with such brutality that it gave my eardrums a bruise.

"SHIT!! Motherfucking horse cock!!"

"Shh!" I hushed. "You need to be quiet!"

Atlas gripped onto my stained flannel collar and looked into my eyes maniacally.

"Q-quiet? I got my freaking fingers chopped off!! Do not tell me to be quiet!! No one can hear me 'cause they're all dead!"

"Cool it!" I yelled. "This...this isn't something that they prepare you for! I'm lost and so are you...but I'll work with you. We'll get out of here, just like you said. But you need to breathe...that's all I can tell you."

Atlas groaned in pain and frantically paced as he clutched his missing digits.

"Ya know...I don't get you."

"Not many people do."

He cradled his mutilation and dropped his eyelids. "Let's just get the hell out of here."

I brushed the remainder of the debris away and found the doorway. Stumbling through, we made our way out from the school in silence. All that could be heard among the shifting metal and plaster was the pattering of our blood hitting the scorched floor. Secreted from Atlas's mutilation and my sliced calf, the red liquid converged with one another into a singular pool. We may not have been friends, but at that moment we were blood brothers.

The first time we saw the outside world post-infection was like seeing a hazy photo of a war-stricken country. Witnessing countless flames breaching through the hoods of cars and local shops, a cavalcade of panicked citizens sprinting down the frenzied road as if it were a city-wide marathon, the anguish and suffering tattooed on the faces of mothers clutching the bodies of their lifeless children and vice versa, it was surreal. I felt as though I was obligated to do something. But what? Literally thousands of bodies were scattered every which way, each with a look of unforgivable uncertainty on their faces. With only their bloodshot eyes they asked me what they did to deserve such a fate, and it took everything to keep my knees from buckling. Obviously, I never would've shown it.

"I don't understand…" I directed to Atlas but spoke to the sea of bodies washing at my bloody sneakers. "How could this be a terrorist attack? Why would terrorists want to attack Alberta??"

Atlas shook his head and rubbed his strained neck with his good hand. His mouth formed a flattened O and his eyes flickered with reflections of fire found in every direction.

"I don't know, oil?" he assumed. "Whatever it is, my passive commitment to atheism is all I need to know that this wasn't any 'divine intervention' crap."

We weren't able to stand in the same spot for more than two or three seconds. Either we were constantly pacing out of paranoia or equally traumatized schoolmates and pedestrians pushed past us. Being in the presence of both the dead and the living was nauseating and their fear was dangerously infectious. So with that in mind, we knew our best bet of falling out of that pathetic spell of wallowing and helplessness was to find a way out of such a populated area as soon as possible. The teacher parking lot was to the left of us—across the football field that was redder than it was green—and we sprinted for it. Not until we stepped on the crackled pavement of the lot did we realize what had been occupying half a dozen spots: One of the plane's engines.

"Christ…" we breathed unanimously.

Resting on top of two pancaked station wagons was the torn engine that billowed charcoal black smoke into the sky. The attached wing was like a broken arm fractured in three places. The turbine spun drunkenly and pointlessly, as if it still fought to lift off of the ground. Grease fires circled the perimeter of the wreckage like some kind of ritual and as our fight or flight instincts had pre-set on the latter, violent coughing arose through the flames.

"You hear that?" I asked.

Atlas slowly dropped to the concrete and pressed his cheek to ground, peering through a sliver vacant of any fire or rubble.

"Great. Looks like someone's trapped under a piece of the wing."

The person imprisoned beneath the slab of metal must've just awoken as cries of help suddenly played at full volume. However, the cries belonged to a familiar voice; a voice that was bubbly and outgoing and asked me to grad an hour prior.

"Britney!" I realized.

Her charred face snapped up at the sound of her name. Scraggily lines of skin were made visible down her otherwise blackened cheeks by a heavy downpour of tears.

"Levi!! Help me!"

I moved side to side like a dodging football player, frantically trying to find an opening. Atlas and I were able to body check a teetering chunk of uplifted pavement and create a path to the wing that slowly compressed her.

"Hold on, Britney! We'll get you outta there," I said in a shaky, unsure wheeze.

I knelt down and felt the tender flesh on my leg beginning to tear. Through clenched teeth and an abundance of obscenities, I was able to rest my knee on the ground and slid my palms under the hot belly of the wing. With an overdose of adrenaline I attempted to lift it, but to no avail.

"A little help here!" I snapped at Atlas.

He examined the jagged, frayed wing, looked down at his injured hand, and shook his head.

"Look at my hand," told Atlas. "Do you want me to get fucking tetanus?!"

"Just lift the damn thing!"

Reluctantly, he joined me and together we were able to hoist it up just far enough for her to pull herself out. Once her medium rare body escaped the smoky entrapment, the sweet, horrid smell of cooked human flesh wafted into my nostrils. It was then that the engine had run out of stability and began to go haywire. The turbine spun at head-slicing speeds and interior machinery of the engine started to choke, warning us that destruction was imminent.

"I think that's our cue to RUN!" Atlas bellowed.

We each wrapped an arm over our shoulders and painfully heaved her body up with us. As fast as we could, we leapt over the overturned concrete and made a run for it down the parking lot. The ferocity of the engine had become too deranged and released a breathtaking explosion. The force of the outburst sent our bodies airborne as a grand fireball spewed out and licked the air, looking for anything to feed its endless hunger. Our bodies crumpled onto the lawn and the bright orange fire singed the hairs on the nape of our necks. There was a brief moment of stillness where neither Atlas nor I were entirely sure if we were living. Then a series of oxygen-deprived wheezes cleared any confusion and we flipped over on our perspiring backs, taking in overwhelming breaths of fresh air that washed away the dust coating our lungs.

"What...the...wha..." Atlas exhaled.

I squinted up at the dull sun overhead and achingly lifted myself upright.

"You okay?" I asked in a breathless voice.

Atlas mumbled and waved his hands away out of complete exhaustion.

"...Just peachy."

I army-crawled over to Britney, who had remained abnormally still.

"Britney? You good? Anything broken?"

Her glassy eyes peered over to me at a delayed speed and suddenly she broke out into a wretched sob.

"Muh-my friends! Oh god...they just kept on choking! They w-wouldn't stop! Blood came from their eyes...ears...everywhere! What the hell is going on?!"

Before I could console her in some way, she wrapped her arms around my neck and cried into my chest. Though I was uncomfortable, no way in hell was I going to stop her from mourning.

Now on his feet, Atlas tapped my shoulder. "Uh...you need to see this."

With Britney glued to me, I awkwardly stood up and turned to face the street that I would have never believed could've existed.

Less than three feet of solid ground could be visible among the hundreds and hundreds of scattered bodies. Nearly half a dozen fights broke out in the middle of the street. Water from demolished fire hydrants soared into the air. Dogs raced down the block, barking and howling for their owners that would never answer back. A symphony of sirens echoed into our ears, orchestrated by the dozens of cop cars, ambulances and fire trucks that didn't know where to start. A woman carried a bundle of bloodstained blankets in her hands, sobbing and sniffling down the middle of the road. Only caring about his own well-being, a man frantically drove over fresh human carcasses and completely disregarded the mourning mother that walked with her head hung low. She could barely let out a scream before her body slammed against the windshield and tumbled down the entirety of his truck. The vehicle continued on without any regret as the broken woman remained on the pavement with a vertebrae protruding out from her spine. Her eyes rolled into the back of her head and the contents of what was in the blanket would never be revealed.

I clamped my hand over my mouth at the brutal reality that unfolded before me. People that had been good, hard-working individuals less than an hour ago had been transformed into volatile animals while their kin and companions laid dead in the dirt.

"If you want to see this fucked-up fuckness then by all means go ahead, but I'm gonna find myself a one-way ticket out of here," Atlas continued to speak as I replied with silence.

Seeing as though most of my initiative had parted from me like the spine of the deceased mother on the road, Atlas walked away from me disorientated and embarked on his first venture: boarding the school bus.

When the day began, this vehicle's sole purpose was to take biology students on a trip to Elk Island. Now, it had become a life raft that illuminated a fading world as students and pedestrians alike clung to it like a terrified child dodging the lava floor. The bus's schedule had been revamped and its new destination was the Edgar Warren Military base outside of the city. The logic behind the desire for military protection against still, dead bodies may have been rather flawed, yet that didn't prevent Atlas and soon Britney and I from finding salvation on the helpless bandwagon. The mustard yellow body of the school bus was bursting at the seams as the maximum persons limit tripled. As fate would have it, Atlas and I seemed to have really pissed off the big man upstairs. Just as we reached the brimming entrance of the bus, the accordion door slapped close and the engine roared awake.

"Wait! Let us in!!" Atlas protested, banging the bases of his fists on the door until they became red and tender.

Squished faces mushed against the glass, each giving us looks of varying empathy. Though no matter how much a person felt sorry for us, it was ludicrous to think they would give up their spot. One person on the very edge of the inside door stood out. His name was Josh Valentine.

"Of course," Atlas said, bubbling with anger.

Josh was your run-of-the-mill basketball star that cared more about the number of times he's hooked up than his grades. His hair was an electrifying yellow with a front spike as tall as his ego. He had baby blue eyes, unnaturally black eyebrows, and a painful sense of ignorance as he was unable to comprehend how disliked he truly was by the general public. Oh, and he was Atlas's archenemy before they could even wipe their own asses.

"They can't just leave us here!" Britney screamed with a dry voice. "There's enough room for us!"

There wasn't enough room for us. Take away two dozen people and there still wouldn't have been enough room.

The cringing sound of tires screeching rang through our ears and the bus viciously pulled away from Atlas's grasp. Josh gave him a shrug and his eyes averted, frightened at the glare that lingered on them.

"You son of a bitch!!!! Burn in Hell!!" he screamed at the racing vehicle that shrunk into the distance.

"We'll find another way, okay? Just calm down," I said to Atlas and put my hand on his shoulder, which he quickly slapped away.

"Not now, dude. Just…not now."

With nowhere left to go, he stormed off to a group of people crowded around a display of televisions in a raided pawnshop.

Before I could speak to Britney, she had already run off in search of another vehicle to hijack. She had adapted a sense of desperation to cope with the recent events while Atlas took more of an apoplectic approach. Me? Disorientation would be the word to use.

Eric Crowley. Thirty-eight years of age. A struggling barber that lived paycheque to paycheque, Eric was one of the countless that lost Mother Nature's coin toss for their lives. To be blunt, he was a completely insignificant human being until twenty-four minutes after the commencement of Day Zero. You see, Mother Nature had been planning this randomized omnicide for centuries, and the destruction of half the global population was everything that she hoped for. That was it. What happened next wasn't something that she had ever anticipated, but as it has been proven time and time again, there'll always be a fault in a seemingly faultless system. All it took was one mutation in one DNA strand in *seemingly* one human to devastate the world far worse than it had already been.

While I had accompanied Atlas to the horde of despaired humans, Britney had frantically searched left and right for any sign of escape. With each car parked along the sidewalk that was keyless or drenched with corpses, the lunacy dripping in her bloodstream continued to pour. After eight or nine fails, Britney had caught a break when she came across a navy Camry that had a trail of blood exiting through its gaping passenger door. Assuming that the red path vacating the vehicle belonged to a victim of the outbreak, Britney followed it in hopes of finding a set of keys. She would find some, along with their owner: Eric Crowley.

Britney had been following the bloody trail of breadcrumbs and we were moments away from finding out the impossible truth. The bodies of the anxious and the volatile clumped together like a cornfield, forcing us to push our way toward the source of the distress. I told myself time and time again that I wished I could've heard the news on a different day so that I'd be more prepared. But the thing is, no amount of time could prepare someone for this.

The fuzzy screens projected cities all over the world, rapidly disintegrating into dreamlike states of sheer terror. Towns and villages decimated, resembling a massive graveyard with traumatized men, women and children cradling their decomposing loved ones. Cameras panned over bodies of water with ships being swallowed in the endless blue sea. Red hues of blood formed wispy strands in the water that caressed the lifeless individuals bobbing up and down.

**London.**

People were clawing out their throats, screaming to the unmerciful heavens. Their pleas were left unanswered. The Big Ben crumbled to the ground, as it had been hit by one of the hundred of aircrafts that plummeted to the ground. People ran aimlessly past the fallen clock tower as a new time period had begun.

**New Delhi.**

The overcrowded streets were flooded with millions of dead bodies. Knee-high pools of blood swallowed the city and survivors piled on top of each other like an anthill. Survival was all that mattered now.

**Vatican City.**

In the streets of the religious capital, confusion and questioning of faith had filled the public. Crowds questioned the supposed Judgment Day, holding family members who had shared the same beliefs. Why did they deserve this? The pope unsuccessfully attempted to calm the mass of Catholics, as he hopelessly stood high up on his balcony. His palms were clammy and a bead of sweat dripped down his creased forehead. This was out of his control.

**Tokyo.**

Cherry blossom trees were splattered with red and black by the mouths of the infected. The bright lights of the metropolis flickered in the dying city where hundreds of thousands had believed a third atomic bomb had struck their beloved country.

**New York.**

Dozens of helicopters with cameras zoomed over the Big Apple. Central Park, Times Square, Grand Central Station, all of it with dead bodies scattered like ashes. Citizens run amok, giving off the impression that the second 9/11 had taken place. But this was different. For the victims weren't only trapped in two towers, but trapped in the entirety of this fallen world. Death loomed above each individual's cowering head and the light at the end of the tunnel had burnt out.

There was nothing to be said. Nothing could be said. I opened my mouth and aching silence was all that followed. My stomach felt overturned and inverted, as if I had hit turbulence on a plane. I tried to reassure myself that all of this was simply a setback and that in a few months time, this day would be only a stained memory in the back of our minds. But I couldn't convince myself with something that I knew wasn't true. Whatever happened, it was more than just a revamped 9/11. Order had evaporated in less than an hour and all of us now wandered this planet like chickens with their heads cut off. People who begged for assurance surrounded me front, back and sideways, but as I previously mentioned, there was nothing to be said. Whenever it came to situations where a proper bedside manner was desired, I was nowhere to be found. A kid next to me—couldn't have been older than six—was staring at the television with innocent eyes as his parents collapsed to the pavement in sorrow. His doll-like eyes fixed onto mine and I began to reach out to pat him on the shoulder, but ultimately pulled back and looked away. The touch of a stranger wouldn't bring the two halves of the world back together.

I turned around and saw Atlas facing a shattered window of a sporting goods shop next door. Carefully, Atlas reached inside and pulled out a chrome baseball bat. He formed fists around the white-taped handle and nodded to himself.

"What's that for?" I asked.

"Batting practice," he said sarcastically. "C'mon, have some common sense. People are starting to lose it. Every moment that passes, the public is going to become more and more volatile until the military roll in. This is for our safety."

I frowned sceptically. "Military? What're they gonna do? Shoot up the dead bodies? Everyone's freaked out but there is no immediate threat."

I don't think I have ever been more wrong.

Atlas stretched his neck and looked through the heavy stream of panicked bystanders for Britney. Eventually he was able to spot her as she was bending down to rummage through the pockets of Eric's body.

"What is she doing?..." he muttered to himself as he started to cross the street.

I followed behind with clench teeth as a new bout of pain sprouted from my spliced leg. My ears perked up at an encore of the symphony of sirens. The ascending and descending alarm of what sounded like a convoy of police cars drew closer and closer. Just as Britney felt the jagged edges of the keys in his jacket pocket, Eric's fingers began to twitch.

"Oh Jesus!" she exclaimed as she scampered up to her feet.

Eric's feet trembled erratically and his bloodstained eyelids flickered open, revealing a set of crimson red eyes mixed with a deathly gray. His chest pulsated upwards, the result of death paddling his chest with an infected defibrillator. Constricted, pale skin stretched over his face like a tightly wound drum. From cheeks to forehead, an intricate map of protruding, varicose veins formed. While Eric endured this terrifying experience, Britney was sent into a petrified state. He hadn't come back from the dead, but rather awoken from a dormant state as his DNA became unwound and unchained. Something had taken control of his body and the sight of human flesh made Eric increasingly agitated when suddenly, he released an abnormal, inhuman shriek.

Atlas and I stopped in our tracks.

"What was that?" yelled Atlas.

The infected man reached his contorted arms into air and grasped his hands around Britney's neck. Whatever infected him had created an unruly hunger for any protein available. He tore away a piece of her trachea and was lathered with a bright red mist as he chewed her flesh savagely. Blood gushingly poured down her collarbone and flooded her throat, causing her to splutter and choke. She slumped to her knees and began to slam her head on the grass, as if she was trying to crush something crawling within her skull.

While I stood there with absolute incertitude, Atlas showed a surprising act of selfless valour as within seconds he was between Eric and Britney. He threw a sucker punch at Eric, causing his jaw to break.

"What the hell is wrong with you?!?" Atlas screamed.

He was completely unresponsive and continued to snap his unhinged jaw at Atlas. Without hesitation, Eric leaped up and attacked once again with just as much devotion.

"Can't you understand me?!" Atlas asked in desperation as he held him away by the neck.

Eric's teeth drew increasingly closer to Atlas's neck and forced to think fast, Atlas swung his newly received bat at his head. The steel bat smashed into his infected cranium with enough momentum to splatter blood across Atlas's face. He fell to the ground and groggily attempted to climb back to his feet. With one final swing, Atlas's weapon struck down onto Eric's face, putting him down for good. Breathing heavily, Atlas wiped his face and looked to Britney, who was writhing on the ground. Something was seriously wrong. Britney wasn't dying. She was transforming.

All while this had transpired, I was busy finding someone to help. Given that every surrounding citizen had kicked into survival mode, I was ignored and overlooked. So when the convoy of police cars drove down the road at great speed, I saw a careless opportunity and knowing that they had a prioritized schedule, I decided to interrupt it.

With my teeth tightened and a held breath locked in my chest, I raced into the streets and jumped in front of the oncoming boys in blue.

"Stop!" I yelled.

They hastily hit the breaks and the cars screeched to an abrupt stop. The front bumper of the lead car collided with my shins, sending a fresh burning sensation into my open wound.

"Help me please!!" I spoke again.

The policemen exited their respective vehicles with their guns at the ready, incredibly pissed off.

"Are you stupid, boy?" yelled an officer. "We could've killed you!!"

"I'm sorry! But there's something wrong with my friend! She's still alive!!!"

The fact that she was still living had intrigued the officers and they became more interested in the situation.

"…Where is your friend?"

I spun on my heels and ran towards Britney and Atlas. Five policemen chased after me while the rest tried to contain what little peace remained. When we arrived to the chaotic scene, Atlas had backed away from her and held his bat at the ready. I got my first good look at her and it was at that moment when true fear finally struck me. She was convulsing and her eyes were flooded with blood. Britney climbed to her feet and looked as though she was fighting something internally.

"Nuh…gygh…" she gurgled.

The policemen raised their guns and nervously pointed them at her. A sixth police officer started to converge toward us.

"What are you doing?" I asked with a violent tone. "You need to help her!!"

She clawed at the festering bite mark and pulled out clumps of hair from her head. Her blurred vision directed toward me and she emitted a loud bellow that sounded almost primal. I was terrified. Every inch of my body was noticeably trembling. But what stood opposite of me wasn't just horrific, but intensely fascinating. The body that Britney once occupied was completely foreign, but her innocence still remained imprinted in her ivory eyes. So, high off of the adrenaline that coursed through me and hanging on a shred of hope that human connection was the solution, I raised my arms in a comforting manner and crept towards her.

"Stand down!!" ordered one of the police officers.

"Uh…" Atlas warned.

The voices were unidentifiable mumbles that passed through me as I sustained eye contact and she curiously looked back.

"She's sick," I said, without breaking eye contact. "But I can do this. I can calm her down."

As I carefully walked toward her twitching body, my foot snapped a dry branch and the crack seemingly awoke a frenzy that was constantly teetering. She snarled her foaming teeth and lunged at me ravenously.

"Get back!" a female cop yelled as she jumped between us.

Britney managed to lock her teeth onto the skin of the officer's forearm, tear a chunk off, bite the next closest officer on their shoulder, and begin to hobble toward her third target before a booming sound echoed through the air. I felt the warm spatter spray my chest, and then visually developed the image of Britney's skull shattering as a single bullet pierced her forehead.

"Christ! What did you just do??" screamed Atlas.

With the fearful, innocent emotion tattooed across her face, Britney collapsed to the floor with blood trickling down her eyes and was left with only an everlasting reminder of the deteriorating world. I was dazed and confused, still coated with the remnants of the blood that poisoned her. I frantically wiped my shirtsleeve over my pulsating chest and felt the vice grip of police officers forcing me to the ground. While the sixth officer approached the group with smoking pistol in hand, Atlas struggled with two burly officers, desperately fighting their grasp.

"Get off me, you bastards! She was sick! She needed help, not a bullet!"

"On the ground! NOW!!" one of Atlas's officers commanded.

Both now forced to the grassy floor, we knelt next to the two infected officers who were clutching their respective wounds. Their downfall is imminent.

The group of officers was broken apart to let in another. The sixth officer was clearly in charge and immediately pointed her weapon to Atlas's forehead. He slowly looked up at his potential executor and became face to face with a much more dangerous figure than he previously anticipated.

"Mom?"

# 5. "Well fuck me sideways."

Two officers convulsing on the grass were transforming into mutated, devolved savages, both the city and the humanity around us was in shambles, and yet, Atlas was transfixed on the woman who steadily aimed the barrel of her pistol perfectly between his eyes. Of all the people that could've came in contact with him—a cult of psychopaths, a league of cannibals, even a handful of necropheliacs—anyone would've been more preferable than the woman that gave him life.

Atlas nervously stood up and repeated himself. "Mom? Jesus, what're you..."

She took a step forward, still retaining that icy glare.

"Are you bit?" she forced through her tightened teeth.

"Bit? Mom, you shot Britney! She was…she was…"

"Answer me!" she ordered. "Are you bit?"

Atlas looked over at the vibrating bodies at both of his sides, foam erupting from their inhaled lips.

"N-no! What is wrong with them?"

His mother snapped her glare to me, back at him, and then finally lowered her weapon.

"Get them to the car, Rogers," she directed toward the flashing red and blue lights. "Now! We need to get out of the city."

A muscular, dark-skinned officer with vinyl-framed glasses heaved both Atlas and I onto our feet and physically forced us into an assisted sprint. We gave each other a quick, blink-and-you-miss-it glance that insinuated our time together wasn't over yet. The corpse of a third-grade girl got caught under my foot, giving me a moment to regain balance and look behind. There I saw what was once two infected become five, cops and citizens too slow to act before getting a chunk of meat ripped away from their respective limbs. My ears popped at the ripping sound of reckless gunfire that was diluted with blood-curdling screams of the living. Then with a thrust, I felt my back kiss the leather seats and the world outside became barred as the police car door slammed shut. Rogers spun around on his heels and wiped away the beads of sweat emerging from his scalp when the chaotic surroundings reached his pupils. His 6 foot 5 inches of height and muscles bulging through his uniform as if he were a stripper was simply a façade, hiding the scared little kid that burrowed inside all of us. Instead of rescuing his comrades, He hopped into the front passenger seat, fumbled his fingers over the lock on the door, and proceeded to call his pregnant wife at home. She would've just finished her yoga class. It went to voicemail.

"We were supposed to go to San Diego next week!" Rogers spoke aloud. "Sasha and I...we never been. Wanted to see the zoo, ya know? The tigers! First with the bodies 'dat dropped dead, now we got infected running 'round!" He burst into tears. "...Just wanted to see the tigers, man."

While Rogers let a steady stream of tears roll down his cheeks, I turned to face Atlas, who raised his sliced hand to his drained face.

"So...that's your mom?" I asked, biting the inside of my cheek. "She's lovely."

His eyes growled at me. "Why does it seem like you're always looking for a fight?"

"As much as I appreciate her ordering me into a police car, I can't neglect the fact that she murdered our friend in cold blood."

"She wasn't my friend," he replied, emotionless. "Neither are you."

I folded my arms and let out a breath strained with attitude. "Now I can see where you get your charm."

"Screw off, Levi. Seriously. Why are you still here? Go! Go to your family!"

My mouth tasted something bitter. "...I have no family. Well, no one that I *consider* family. I just need to lay low and wait until it all blows over."

"Look out the window! Whatever happened to Britney isn't stopping. They're passing whatever they have to us like a game of tag. They're turning in seconds!"

"Turning?" I repeated with incredulity. "What're you saying? That these are zombies?"

A ballistic man with foam of multiple hues dripping down his mouth slammed against the passenger window, causing Rogers to nearly wet himself.

"Got any other ideas?" Atlas asked forcefully.

"It's rabies! A side effect to whatever killed everyone. I guarantee they're not zombies."

"How?"

"Because they're still alive! They couldn't die and come back in five or six seconds! Calling them a zombie would imply that they're dead, and I can assure you that they're not. Britney... she was volatile, but I looked into her eyes and saw this shred of humanity that remained. She was still in there."

"These could be hybrids or something!" suggested Atlas.

"Do you hear yourself? You sound delusional. They're sick and... and in a few weeks time the CDC will have a cure."

Even I could hear the uncertainty that lined my voice.

The driver door ripped open and in came Atlas's mother alongside an overweight officer by the name of Tibbs, side-tackling me to make room for his fat ass in the backseat. His ill-fitting uniform had large, circular sweat stains emerging from his armpits and he constantly swiped the loose strands of hair across his balding scalp with a trembling hand. He was obviously not going to last very long.

"Get us outta here, Jordan!" he blared.

She twisted the idling keys forward and with a movie-like screech of the tires, we drove away from the dispersing sickness. As expected, the majority of the dialogue being thrown up was as pointless as it was uncertain. The initial death toll, the infectious panic seeping through the streets, Britney and the sick people, (I eventually coined the term halfies) and blah, blah, blah. While the three partook in this filler conversation, I was occupied with a not-so-subtle examination of Atlas's mom. Her black hair was pulled back into a ponytail so tightly drawn that the hairs on her scalp were anxiously trying to remain rooted. Her nose was crooked and misshapen from years on the job and there were dark circles hovering beneath her eyes, only furthering her grizzled demeanour. Wisps of gray dabbled above the peaks of her ears, just enough to estimate an age of late-thirties to early-forties. Everything about her was either intimidating, livid, or a mixture of the two, except for one key ingredient: Her eyes were full of innocence and youth. The colour of sapphire with a gentle hue, this was the single resemblance between her and her son.

My focus was pulled to the rear window, where the fallen bodies trampled beneath the cop car were forming a red carpet for the virus to trail behind. Regardless of our whiplash-inducing speeds, more and more of the halfies came to life as the recycled process followed us like a deformed shadow. Pedestrians stranded on the side of the road begged for a ride and while Officer Jordan carelessly drove past them, I caught a glimpse at the sheer terror smeared on their faces. I had to turn around because the infected would catch up with them shortly after.

We were given a taste of the aftermath in different parts of the city. When we approached a hilltop a few blocks from the school and entered the parameters of the downtown skyline, it was at that moment that all of our hearts had skipped a beat. The city was on fire, both figuratively and literally. Apartment buildings and churches had been set ablaze. Perhaps word had gotten out and the people attempted to prevent the fallen from reanimating, or an accidental mishap in the terrible chaos, or a man-made creation to release their stress and frustration, or possibly all of the above. Dozens of buildings stood tall and proud as the city beneath them had been reduced to ashes and littered with bones. The monotonously stern overcast shrouded the city with gray, viscous clouds that contained the rumbling of thunder within. Instantaneous flashes of lightning came and went in the sky, but never touched down. It was as if our world below was unworthy of the striking light from the heavens and was to live its finite life in darkness. Hundreds of civilians flooded the streets with personal belongings in one hand and something stolen in the other. Tiny specs were seen resting on top of these skyscrapers, and then falling. It was only when they were halfway down to the concrete floor did I realize those tiny specs were people.

"-and you?" she spoke to me.

I blinked and looked at her stinging gaze in the rear-view mirror.

"I'm sorry?"

"My son told me you're injured. What happened?" she replied in an irritable tone.

I looked down at my left foot and saw that I was wearing a pale red sock that was white when I put it on.

"Oh, uhm, a metal rod cut my leg when the plane hit. It's nothing serious, though." I added, not wanting to sound weak.

"Hold on, plane crash?" she said, now taking her eyes off the barely visible road.

"Yeah. You know, the plane that hit our school? We were still inside when it crashed, but we survived…somehow."

Her eyes scrutinized me and she shook her head determinedly.

"Impossible. I saw what was left off your school. There's no way you two could've sur…"

Then in a split second, a female pedestrian thrown from a horde collided with the windshield, cutting off Officer Jordan. The rioting and pillaging of the streets had made her unaware of the high-speeding police vehicle driving by. The glass shattered to the point of becoming opaque, creating thousands of miniature fragments barely held together. The pedestrian—a burka-wearing elderly woman—ricocheted off of the glass and tumbled to the pavement as the car skidded to an abrupt stop. She hit the ground with such force that the sound of her bones crushing was heard with precise detail. As blood started to pool, her body ceased to move.

"Oh my god…" Ms. Jordan whispered.

"Jesus Christ, Julie!" Rogers screamed. "You killed an old lady!"

"She jumped in front of me!! Dumb bitch killed herself!" she yelled back, trying to reassure herself.

Atlas looked through his window and noticed a crowd of disgruntled civilians approaching.

"…We might have a problem."

It didn't take long before a cluster of people had surrounded the crime scene and almost instantaneously pointed their fingers to the cops and their passengers.

"You murderers!!" a man screamed.

"You're supposed to help the people! Not kill them!!" another joined in.

Tibbs gulped. "Well fuck me sideways."

In the heat of the moment, the crowd of people started to push the car, which led to them rocking it back and forth. We could only see angry faces through the windows and the closed off environment became increasingly claustrophobic. They heaved left and right continuously, gaining more and more momentum to the point that our vehicle had been lifted off of the ground. With each time we landed, more harm came to the exterior of the vehicle and the wheel axles had begun to give away. A man broke through the crowd with a metal pipe in hand and smashed the end into the driver seat window, spraying a burst of glass into Ms. Jordan's face.

"Auyyrghhh!" she screamed as microscopic fragments burrowed into her skin. "You bastard!!"

She released her pistol from its holster and shot into the air through the broken window. The crowd yelped in terror and dispersed from the vehicle, letting it land hard onto the pavement.

"Drive!" Rogers begged.

The car darted out onto the road, driving over the mangled corpse of the female. I could feel the thud beneath me and wistfully closed my eyes. This was painfully familiar.

"What the hell are you doing?" Atlas complained as the car swerved side to side.

"I can't see shit!" his mother yelled back.

She stuck her head out of the window and guided herself through the hectic streets. Seeing no point in looking forward, I glanced at the side view mirror and saw the beginning of a massacre behind me. Biters had toppled into the streets and converged onto the shouting pedestrians to feed their empty stomachs. The pale bodies surrounded the group of people and herded them like cattle, where they then began their feast. Screams rang through the air and with a metaphorical snap of the fingers, their screams turned into infected moans.

"Oh god! Oh my god! Oh my god!"

"Help us! Please!"

Officer Jordan glanced down to the gun in her hand, realizing what she'd done.

"Looks like their ears still work! Gunshot must've caught their attention." She had this smug, fake look of concern that made me believe she had found slight enjoyment in her actions.

We continued driving until we reached the sketchy, rough parts of the city. On the corner of 26th Avenue laid a beat up garage where dozens of junk cars parked in the lot were in the midst of getting fixed. The wide garage was dingy and faded, with a flickering neon sign propped up on top of the roof that read *Rhodes Auto Repair.* The building was the colour of burnt coffee and had crimson stripes along the top, with the stereotypical pennant streamers strung up high between two poles.

There were muscle cars left and right, all giving off a similar odour that matched an owner who had put more money in their car rather than paying for their children's daycare. Ironically, as we approached the garage, the front axle of the squad car had been unable to maintain the bearing weight and collapsed out from under us. The front end of the vehicle slammed down on the pavement as two tires shot out to the sides. We skidded to a stop with sparks flying as the metal belly of the car scraped alongside the gravelly road, stopping directly in front of the auto garage.

"Damn," released Ms. Jordan.

"Maybe your tires are low," Atlas joked, too disillusioned to care.

"Shut your mouth, boy. You're lucky I didn't leave you behind."

The temperature of Atlas's anger heightened. "Leave me beh— you're my mom!!"

Sounds of gurgling and gnawing meat projected behind me like surround sound speakers. The barred back window showed that both the living and the undecided were narrowing on us.

"What! How are they here already? That's not even possible!" I cried out.

Everyone examined the approaching mass and in the time that we flooded out from the broken squad car, the number of infected had seemingly doubled.

"God, it's like they're breeding!" exclaimed Rogers.

Atlas peered over to his receding mother and recognized something foreign on her face: the look of fear. A characteristic that was not only unnatural but also deemed impossible in the eyes of Atlas. Yet as Ms. Jordan stood motionless, her pupils dilated, her breathing rate skyrocketed, all symptoms of terror. She didn't feel this way as a result of the amount of biters but rather what was on some of their faces. They had stretched, sadistic smiles pulled so far apart that their cheeks were tearing. Black gore oozed from the corners of their mouths as they drew closer to the fresh meat, increasing their speed to a full-on sprint. Atlas caught a glimpse of their faces, sending shivers down his spine as the thought of the poor boy in the bathroom popped into his mind.

"W-what are we gonna do?!" Tibbs stammered, frustrated that no one else was taking action.

Ms. Jordan had a reputation of attacking a potential threat head-on, not worried to break a few bones or getting blood on her hands. This reputation had now been diminished as she spun around and bolted for Rhodes garage, leaving behind her fellow officer and us two teenagers.

"Son of a bitch," I exhaled, following after her with a still-noticeable limp.

Atlas and I galloped away with Rogers following shortly, leaving Tibbs in <u>dead</u> last.

"Don't leave me behind! Please!" he begged, but as selfish as it sounds, I didn't even consider stopping.

Ms. Jordan, in the lead, spotted a metal grate for arriving vehicles and noticed that it elevated slightly above the ground. The five other garage doors had been shut, leaving the small opening our only chance of survival.

Tibbs panted heavily as wheezes were exhaled out like a broken squeaker toy. He ran as fast as his short, stubby legs would allow him, but it wasn't enough. It was relatively simple for two approaching pale ones to catch up with him, and with a single pounce, they brought the fat man down to his demise.

"No! Fuck God please no!!!" he bawled as they submerged him.

While Ms. Jordan and Rogers slid underneath the metal grate, I stopped and looked back at the suffering cop. Quiver-inducing screams shot from the mess, followed by the sounds of flesh tearing from bone and the slurping of bloody meat. Tibbs's legs kicked vigorously as death had refused to take over in a timely fashion, allowing him to feel everything that was being done to his body. I saw lumps of white fat spewing from the feeding pit, causing me to gag.

It was Atlas's turn to pull me away. "He's dead! Forget about him!!"

As I backed away, I couldn't help but be both fascinated and horrified at the severity of this disease. It had been thirty-six minutes since Eric Crowley—who I believed to be the sole anomaly at the time—had released his tainted DNA to the world and it had already trickled into the downtown area. The exceedingly turbulent nature of this "Zombie" virus made the black death look like the common cold.

I was finally removed from the viewing gallery and rolled underneath the grate less than a second before Atlas shut the outside world out for good.

The interior of the garage wasn't much of an improvement from what we'd seen outside. A lone light bulb hung from the ceiling, swinging from the faintest gust of wind. The cold cement floor had tools and containers of oil scattered across it. Two cars on opposite sides of the garage had been raised in the air by a lift, both spending the rest of their existence without an owner or the feeling of the road beneath their tires. We spent a few moments on our knees catching our breath, readjusting to this uncontrollable world, too exhausted to mind the puddles of engine grease on the dank floor. The eerie silence hadn't lasted more than twenty seconds before banging and scratching were heard on the metal grates. That was when we discovered that we weren't alone in the garage.

A teetering toolbox came crashing down to the floor as a man brushed past it with a crowbar raised.

"Can I help you?" he asked calmly.

Ms. Jordan had her gun raised at the man before she completely turned around. I jumped to my feet and looked at the man, who gave each of us a two-second preview with his eyes. He had a burly, Tom Selleck-esque moustache and a Vancouver Canucks baseball cap on his head with little wings of hair flaring out the back. He wore a grimy white tee with the torso of his navy blue overalls tied around his hips. His lanky figure was completely misleading, as a lone glance was all it took to see that he could take me down with a single blow.

"Drop the weapon, sir! Drop it now!" Ms. Jordan commanded.

He released the crowbar from his grasp without further debate and raised his hands in the air.

"I ain't no threat, missy."

"Who are you?" she asked coldly.

"My name's Jim Rhodes. The owner? So it's not a stretch that you'd find me in my own shop." He took a step forward. "Can I help you? Judging from what's happening out there, I think it's safe to assume that we're closed."

Atlas jumped in. "We had to find shelter. It's not just a bunch of dead bodies out there. There seems to be some sort of infection too."

"Hmm, Interesting." Rhodes nodded his head slowly and scratched at his forearm, which was dressed with bandages. The sight of this put Ms. Jordan on high alert.

"What happened to your arm?" she asked knowingly.

He looked down at his wound and scoffed. "Ahh, just a scratch while I was working this morning."

Ms. Jordan didn't budge. "A scratch? That looks more serious than just a scratch. Blood is seeping through your bandages. Speaking of which, they look pretty new."

"It happened a few hours ago," he explained. "I was about to head out to the hospital when everything happened. Seeing as though the hospitals have got more concerning matters, I wrapped myself up."

She shook her head and cocked her pistol.

"Mom? What're you doing?" Atlas asked nervously.

"He's infected."

Rhodes frowned in confusion. "Infected? Lady, what the hell are you talkin' about? I told you I got scratched. Working on that car behind you. My blood is still on the goddamn bumper!"

"Stop lying!" she persisted. "Have you seen what happens when you get bitten? You become an animal; an animal that needs to be put down."

It was clear that she was being serious and Rhodes started to become more desperate. "Listen, I'm not infected! I've got a family, okay? Just like you. My kids—the same age as those two—they'll be waiting for me. Don't do something you're gonna regret."

"Jordan…I think he's telling the truth," warned Rogers.

"Shut up! You don't know shit!"

The fear had taken total control. The woman pointing the gun was simply a host for the terror that latched onto her brain.

"He's infected. Just like those psychos that killed my officers! Don't you understand?! We need to stop this virus before it becomes unstoppable."

"Ms. Jordan?" I finally spoke up. "You're frightened. I get it. You should be. But you can't let it take over your sense of reason. He said he wasn't bit, so shouldn't we believe him? Even if he were lying he'd have a fate worse than death. Think about his family. You would be ruining their lives."

She hesitated. I saw it. A moment or two of silence filled the room before she eventually looked over to me.

"…I'm not ruining their lives. I'm saving them."

She turned her head to Rhodes—completely unarmed—and shot him in the heart.

"NO!" Atlas yelled until his throat dried up and became nothing.

His lifeless body slumped to the grease-stained floor. The Canucks hat blew off from his head and soaked up the blood from his spliced organ like a sponge. I simply closed my eyes and shook my head. It was at that moment that I knew the world was beyond saving.

# 6. "...I'm not peeing in your mouth!"

**65 Days Later**

There was a hum; the sound that accompanies a blazing sun producing dry and uncensored heat. The buzzing of crickets having passionless sex and the rustling of parting grass, it was a looped soundtrack that was as constant as it was numbing. There were worse sounds, I guess. Sounds like rumbling hunger blaring from my seemingly inverted stomach, or the music of groans and infected mouths, or even worse, the sound of silence. As long as something kept my ears company, my sanity remained generally intact. But the heat...I was sweating like a whore on thanksgiving. That's the saying...right? Regardless, trudging through rural Alberta was made devastatingly worse as the climax of summer was upon us. Food and water were desirable, yes, but winter was what I craved. The best part of winter is that you can put on as many layers as you want and no one questions it, but with the sun, there's only so much I could shed away before my skin was next to go. Perhaps my desire for winter stemmed from childhood delight of the mythical coldness that plagued the maple leaf country annually. Living in Canada, it was coded in our genes to embrace the winter as if it was written in piss and snow. When you're caught in a snowstorm, forced to push through frostbitten temperatures, your mind stops. Survival instincts kick in and all you think about is getting home. I wanted that...I wanted to go home instead of spending every minute in the wilderness starving and suffocating.

We've been out here two months. We stuck to the wilderness mostly since trees gave us shade and protection from any threats both living and…the alternative. I've lost track of both the time and day, for I only lived vicariously through the hopes of making it to the next one. I hated the infected, but mosquitoes had created a new tier of detestation. My skin was littered with itchy, red bumps that gave me an everlasting state of aggravation. The only water that I had to drink was lukewarm at best and always contained various twigs and pebbles to add a nice crunch. I was peeing a bright orange and the last thing I had to eat was a raw onion. Every hour that went by, I could feel my stomach feeding on the layer of fat that hugged it, all whilst the sun sucked the water from my skin like a girl who was a little too eager to give head. So… things weren't exactly looking up for us. In fact, things weren't looking anywhere. Everything was blind.

A snap of a twig sent my head to the right. With my blurry, un-pellucid gaze, I was able to make out the furry shape of a deer.

"Gotcha, Bambi," I whispered to myself.

I had been tracking the deer for nearly three hours. The very sight of the animal caused my stomach to gurgle and moan, loud enough for Bambi to flick her head up cautiously. I bit my lip, drew in my breath, and only released it in small spurts as the deer began to continue on. The handle of the bow that I stole/borrowed indefinitely was clenched with waning strength. My stomach was being a goddamn traitor.

"Don't turn on me now," I spoke to my belly. "I'm tryn'a please your ass."

The buck found a bush of berries—the same berries that I spotted earlier but was too afraid to risk trying some—providing it with a worthy distraction so I could take the kill. I loaded the slightly warped arrow and drew back the fraying string toward my cheek. I had the ideal shot—just below the jaw and into the trachea—but then something happened. The son of a bitch looked at me. Not just a glance in the general direction. The bastard saw me. She saw me and didn't move. Even though I couldn't see it clearly—since daily contacts came at a minimum in an apocalypse—I felt the gaze. It was a situation where I was aiming at an unarmed beast and in the strangest way, the animal was pleading for survival. She wasn't ready to die; and I wasn't strong enough to defy that wish. So I took a step forward on a dry tree branch and Bambi fled. As I watched her dash away with a sleek prance, I realized naming it was a bad idea. If she was Bambi then that made me the hunter. That movie was too traumatizing for me to ever accept that comparison. God…If I was comparing life to Disney movies, I must've been more gone than I thought.

After a long trek back and my stomach giving me the opposite of a silent treatment, I finally made it to our living quarters. If I had to describe it in one word it would be dank. Definition: uncomfortably moist. Our humble abode was a graffiti-covered power station deep in the bush in the heart of…nowhere. Inside the palace, our decorations included: six used condoms, the carcass of a dead garter snake, dozens of cigarette butts, and a syringe. We had been living there for three days. That was a record for us.

I unlatched the door and swung it open to be greeted by two teenage boys resting in their claimed corners. Dehydration was a bitch that all of us had fallen for.

"Do you think…a bite…would be a hard way to go?" Josh wheezed. "I think I've lost any shits to give…but hey, two months of living? That ain't bad. That ain't bad at all."

In case you were wondering, yes, it was *that* Josh. Choosing partners in an apocalypse was not like choosing kids for your flag football team. You got who you got because they were lucky enough to share the same fate as you. Josh…he would not have been my first pick. Hell, he wouldn't have been my eighth. Our paths intertwined because of dumb luck and our series of unfortunate events that I'm sure will be brought up in later storytelling. We were in the wrong place with the wrong people at the wrong time. It had been nearly two months on the road with him and still I couldn't entirely believe him to be innocent that night. To be fair, none of us were. It was a stain that we each took turns to wash away, but to no avail.

Atlas fed on his fingernails impatiently. "I'm surprised you lasted *that* long, Sonic."

He coined the nickname 'Sonic' because of Josh's spiky hair and the disturbing resemblance it had with a hedgehog. It may have sound playful but their relationship was anything but. It took Atlas a long time to forgive Josh even though I personally thought he did nothing wrong. Having a spot on that bus was like a golden ticket and no one would've given it up out of the good of their heart. I believe that Atlas's anger did not arise from Josh's helplessness but rather the events that proceeded to unfold because of it. What would have happened if we, or at least he had gotten on that bus? Atlas finally accepted the fact that our shared company was for survival and not something voluntary. He accepted it, yes, but his anger never faded. It was in his nature to constantly carry a tremendous burden. Hell, look at his name for Christ's sake! I could never blame him for feeling angry but I just wish he didn't unload it on us, namely me.

"No food?" he asked, rising up from a tattered blanket he called a bed.

I shook my head.

Atlas laughed the way he always did when he was pissed off.

"Why is that whenever we go out for food, it's always you that comes back with nothing but your dick in your hands. C'mon, even Josh found that case of yogurt! …Granted it was six inches deep in mould, but it's something! You didn't come across anything even remotely edible?"

I thought about lying, but for how long I was gone, even I wouldn't believe me. "I was tracking a buck for a while."

"And?" Josh asked, still hopeful.

"I shot and missed."

Josh threw his head back and sighed in frustration. Atlas kept a sceptical eye on me. Eventually I called him out on it.

"Can I help you with something?"

"We weren't friends, but remember how we went to Vimy Ridge Academy for junior high? We were in Sports Rec together."

"Yeah. Your point?"

"Every week we'd do a different sport…one of those included archery."

I was starting to see his point but I still played dumb.

Atlas continued. "I remember there weren't enough bows for everyone so we had to go in groups of two. We were partners; and every time you took a shot, you'd hit that red circle like it was nothing. So, getting to my point, how in the holy hell could you hit those dink-sized targets but miss a fucking deer?"

"You saw those arrows we found!" I argued. "The wood had the durability of a straw and they had one feather on the end…if you were lucky."

"Ya know what I think? I think you pussied out. You could've shot the deer but you didn't. What? Did your balls drop dead along with the other 50% of the goddamn world?"

Josh attempted to breach himself between our clenched fists.

"Guys! We need to keep quiet! They'll hear…"

He was cut short as what his eyes saw instructed him to do so. Peering through a grated window, what was a luscious scenery set seconds ago had been altered and tampered with. As if it only took a blink, Josh saw a pale one appear and stand motionlessly, observing the power station. It watched delightfully and angrily, breathing heavy, tainted breaths. It tilted its head and looked side to side. Then more approached, all with the same intention and devotion.

"Oh Jesus Christ…" he murmured.

What started as a meaningful walk turned into a terrifying sprint. They arrived with seemingly fictitious speed and swarmed the station. A grimy, pale arm thrust through the window panel and contorted erratically as the glass shards dug into its skin. We instinctively rushed to the back room where a large, rectangular generator was anchored in the center.

"Shit…how many are there?"

"Can't be any less than six," I guessed.

"We can take them!" stated Atlas. "That Indian restaurant a week ago had nearly double!"

"Atlas, This isn't a movie. All it takes is one bite. Hell, maybe even one scratch and we lose. We have kitchen tools and sporting equipment. We're all drained. This is not a battle worth fighting."

"I-I agree with Levi," inputted Josh.

"Of course you do, you coward. I haven't forgotten the farm," spat Atlas.

There was a moment where we all said nothing and only the snarls and screams from outside filled our ears.

"…What else can we do?"

I slid my backpack off and unzipped the first pocket. "Just because I didn't find any food doesn't mean I came back empty-handed." I pulled out a half-empty air horn. "Josh, you have the duct tape in your pack, right? Hand it over."

He grabbed the thin roll and gave it to me. I squatted down and hobbled over to the broken window where three other arms had joined in the attempt to break in. The adhesive taste clung to my tongue as I ripped a strip of tape away with my teeth. With that I proceeded to wrap it around the plastic button on the air horn. The screeching was deafening and reminiscent of a hockey game. I tossed it out of the gaping window as if it were a grenade and the ribbon of sound that followed it faded into the outside world. Soon, the pounding on the door ceased and we found our precious opportunity to escape.

"Alright…looks like we're moving. Again," declared Atlas. "Say goodbye to this home, not-so-sweet home."

While the infected were intrigued by the blaring horn, we snuck out of the door and slipped away into the bushes. As we ran, I began to think if this was how I had to live my life from then on. Was it worth the struggle? In the end, I convinced myself it was. Because at that time we all had an actual goal that we could strive toward: Safehaven.

Seven hours went and dragged the burning ball of gas into a fading sunset. We were walking and as lost as can be.

"What the hell am I even doing?" Josh asked.

"You're supposed to try and find out where we are," replied Atlas. "Uh, look for rivers and landmarks, something like that!"

"This map is from the seventies, dude! If I'm reading this right, the road that you said we're on should be in the middle of a lake…so that poses as a slight issue. There may be a *tiny* chance we're not where we think we are."

It had been nearly two weeks since we had been even slightly certain of our whereabouts. We knew our endpoint, Vancouver, but we needed to know where to start and, well, we didn't.

The three of us stumbled down this long and winding road like we were a trio of lost tourists. Except instead of fearing the possibility of missing the world's biggest taco or some shit like that, we were slowly dying. The malnutrition and dehydration had taken its toll on us, each in varying ways. For me, the physical symptoms were noticeable yet bearable, but the thoughts that conjured in my head were so sickening that I wouldn't dare repeat them. Atlas had become even more of a self-righteous prick and found his only cure in ordering us around. Josh, well, it only seemed to affect his already questionable intelligence.

"I once watched this movie about this guy who had his arm trapped under a boulder and had to cut it off with a Swiss army knife," Josh recalled. "No idea what it was called…that guy from *Freaks* and *Geeks* was in it I think. Anyway, he had to drink his own piss like twice so he wouldn't die and yeah, that would suck doing it to yourself but maybe if we each…"

"Fuck man, I'm not peeing in your mouth!" yelled Atlas.

"Hey! It's not like I get off to that kind of thing! I just don't want to die!"

I shook my head. "How you made it to grade twelve is beyond me."

Before the conversation delved deeper into kinked-up territory, we came across a translucent gas canister resting on the side of the road. I hobbled toward it cautiously, somewhat expecting it to be booby-trapped or explode.

"Is that gas?" Josh asked stupidly.

I knelt down and examined the beer-like solution. "Well, it's either that or urine, and no, Josh, we are not going to drink it."

I lowered my nose to the nozzle of the twenty-litre container and took a whiff.

"It's gasoline…thankfully."

"Won't be much use to us without a car," Atlas pointed out.

"I'm sure the people with a car are saying the same thing about this. We're halfway there."

"Yeah, but why'd someone leave a full container of gas? Stuff's more valuable than gold these days," said Atlas.

"I don't think it was left by choice…" I responded, directing attention to the ditch next to us.

Lying in the ditch was a half-eaten corpse wearing a *Rebel Without a Cause* red windbreaker.

"Score!" said Josh as he reached for the jacket.

"Dude," halted Atlas, "you're going to raid a dead body? I'd say that's quite the faux pas on morals."

Josh flashed his award-winning smile. "Think of it like this: This new world we find ourselves in is like one big garage sale. There's a whole lotta shit in it but occasionally you'll find something worth while."

"Hmm, you actually didn't sound brain dead there," smirked Atlas.

Josh flapped the jacket in the air and zipped it up. "We found gasoline *and* I get to look like James Dean? This day can't get any better!"

But it did. A few minutes later we spotted a gas station peek behind a strip of forest down the road.

"That isn't some kind of mirage, right?" Atlas asked us. "That's only in deserts…please let that only be in deserts."

"Nah, I see it too. Probably where this came from," I said, shaking the filled container.

It felt like a lifetime had come and gone since the last time we had seen a structure that wasn't either overrun, burnt to the ground, or both. Wasn't anything special, just a dingy looking gas station. Yet, I felt my heart pulsating rapidly and a reservoir of fresh saliva secreted into my sandpapered mouth.

"D'ya think anyone is in there?" Josh wondered aloud.

Not a second passed before a loud, neck-cringing scream erupted from the structure and diluted into the hazy air.

"That answer your question?" Atlas replied.

As our instincts kicked in, Josh and I did a little kind of dance: I took a step back as he took a step forward, demonstrating that he was willing to save anyone in need of it, which was nothing but a pile of horseshit. Josh was the kind of person who told everyone to do something and then proceed to sit back while shit was actually getting done. By the sound of it, the scream belonged to a girl, probably around our age, and clearly in danger. Josh wanted us to believe that he cared, but deep down I knew that all he cared about was himself; like me.

"We…we need to do something!" Josh implored.

Atlas and I glanced over to each other, a look of disengagement filling our pupils.

"We live in a world occupied by cannibalistic D-bags who'll take a chomp outta you faster than you can tell them to bust off…and you think we should go *toward* a scream?" inputed Atlas. "That's a big no-no in my books."

I nodded. "I'm with Atlas on this one. People don't scream like that because they saw a spider. Whoever they are, they're as good as dead."

Josh just wouldn't give up. He almost made me believe that he cared. Almost.

"We can't just leave them to die! Besides, we're running on fumes here. Whether or not you care about saving someone else's life, don't you want to save your own? No way in hell that place is any less than half-stocked."

He had a point.

"How can you be so sure it's not another dead end?"

"I'm not," he replied, "but if we don't at least try, I *can* be sure that we won't make it another day."

Atlas sighed and unsheathed his bat that dangled from his belt loop. "Fine. But I'm expecting a goddamn spectacular welcome basket. Crackers, jerky, lavender soap, the whole nine yards."

With what little energy that remained in our muscles, we hustled over to the gas station with weapons at the ready. Josh and I took the front while Atlas swooped around to flank from behind. Parked near the pumps was a gas tanker that had its tube permanently lodged in the underground gas reservoir and a charred carcass of what appeared to be a Winnebago. Why it had been burnt was not our concern and we passed it without a thought. We reached the tinted doors of the gas station and to our surprise we were greeted by nothing. Not a groan, not a scream, not a slurp, nothing.

I frowned. "…I don't get it. Was this some sort of gag?"

Atlas appeared behind me with the same look of confusion that I produced.

"Are we too late?" asked Josh.

Atlas gestured his bat to the door. "Check inside. Maybe they're playing hide and seek."

I pulled the handle, which was unlocked. The inside was completely black, preventing the dull light that lingered outside to creep in. I got that feeling you get when you race up the stairs from the basement or leap onto your bed once the lights go out. But I wasn't going to show it. Sure, I might have been selfish, but I wasn't a bitch.

Nothing presented itself. "Guys? I think it's all clear."

I took a step further inside to let the others follow behind. Once we were all in, however, the door slammed shut and a bright blue flash of electricity briefly illuminated the room. One blink later, my neck tingled with agony as a bolt of blue lightning bounced through my skin.

"Gyuhhh!" I yelped between clattering teeth, dropping to the floor.

"What was that? Levi?" Atlas asked, panicked.

Suddenly, the light powered on and in front of us was a teenage girl with a rifle aimed at us.

She giggled. "This just keeps on getting easier and easier."

# 7. "These bitches are *Gone Girl* insane."

"Drop the bat," a second girl with a Taser said to Atlas. "Now."

While Atlas frustratingly lowered to the ground and let it go, I remained on the ground, occasionally convulsing. I was still conscious, however, but they didn't need to know that just yet. I kept my eyes closed and listened in.

"Check to see if he's breathing," Rifle girl ordered.

I heard the sound of footsteps and noticed my closed vision had darkened as the other one approached me and lowered her ear to my mouth. I felt the urge to lunge upward and rip away her ear with my teeth. No, I thought. Deep breaths.

I kept still and she finally got up. "He's alive. Just knocked out cold."

"I think, and this may just be me spit balling here, but I think that none of you might actually in danger," muttered Atlas.

"Quite the opposite actually," Rifle girl said, laughing.

She had hair the colour of liquid gold that permanently held a sprinkle of seductive perfume. Her pink, pouty lips smirked at them with her top teeth only just peeking through to say hello. She wore a tight, white tank top that barely contained a set of large, seemingly fake breasts supported by a clearly visible pink bra. Her figure was elusive and made the sands in an hourglass halt. This girl was clearly in charge of the two and though he couldn't place it, Atlas knew that he recognized her.

The other girl emerged from her hiding spot behind the door and joined her companion, Taser still in hand. "We'll cut to the chase. We are going to take your stuff. Then, we'll let you go. But if you try anything stupid…" she squeezed the trigger and a fresh strand of electricity licked the air, "you're going to wish you hadn't."

This girl was different from the other. Instead of a bubbly, outgoing persona that her colleague had adopted, she was brooding and dangerous. Her hair was liquorice black that formed harsh bangs just below her eyebrows; a jagged line of hair like it was an active lie detector. Her eyes matched Atlas's, reflecting that light shade of sapphire back at him. Contrasting her partner in crime, she wore a black T-shirt and dark blue jeans with a plaid-shirt tied around her waist. The face on this girl was both delicate as well as frighteningly piercing. Already she had an arrogant aroma that tickled my clenched nostrils. A single look at her, Atlas knew that this girl didn't let anybody screw with her. He was immediately attracted.

"Listen, honey, if you're trying to seduce me…you can bet it's working."

Taser girl grunted in disgust and slapped Atlas across the face.

"You're a pig."

"Oh…straight to the role-playing? Alright, I can dig it."

Rifle girl scoffed and gestured at the two boys with her weapon. "Get them on their knees, V."

"Yes, ma'am," Atlas said flirtatiously.

Taser girl forced both Atlas and Josh down to the floor. While Atlas made the best of the situation, Josh did not.

"Atlas! This isn't a joke. Don't you see they have a gun?"

Atlas chuckled. "All I see is two girls who don't have the kahunas to find their own supplies so they trick the good guys into delivering it to them on a platter." He surveyed the interior of the gas station and saw that they were well stocked. "Greedy too, by the looks of it. Ya know, we were going to help you."

"That's cute," said Rifle girl. "Really! Problem is, this is how things work now. You do what you need to do to survive and those morals you once had are nowhere to be found. Besides, you can never have too much food, too much water, and most importantly…too many weapons."

Atlas shrugged his shoulders. "Sorry to burst your bubble, tutz, but we've run dry on all of the above. That was the main reason we came here."

"Doesn't seem to be the case from what I can see," she replied. "Your sleepy friend's got that nice looking bow. You've got that bat of yours. I can also see a mighty fine crowbar sticking out of your backpack. Still, judging by how nasty you three look, I'd assume you've been out there since it all started. No way in hell could you survive with just that."

"You're flattering me," smiled Atlas. "Like I said, we ain't got shit."

The bubbly attitude faded and her voice suddenly became strained. "Is that…gasoline?"

A collective "FUCK" went through our minds, now realizing that we indeed had something to lose.

"It's piss!" Josh lied.

"Why would you be carrying it around with you then?"

She had us there.

"V, check it out."

The Taser girl, the one addressed as "V", came toward me for a second time and when she reached for the container beside me, I found an appropriate time for my grand reintroduction. Just as she knelt down, I jabbed my elbow into her jaw, sending her flying back. The Taser escaped her grasp and I caught it before either could even hit the ground.

"I thought you said he was unconscious!" yelled Rifle Girl.

I flipped it on and took its previous owner as a hostage. The Taser was drawn mere inches away from her neck.

"Atlas, would you kindly?" I asked.

He nodded with a grin on his face, demonstrating the first time that he was actually impressed with me. Atlas extended his hand out to the rifle girl, whom was now trembling.

"Hand it over, tutz."

She lowered the gun and passed it over in defeat.

"Much appreciated."

I released my hostage and slowly climbed up to my feet, legs still feeling like noodles.

"It's one thing to knock me out from behind, but electrocute me? Seriously?" I yelled at the girl on the floor who was glaring back at me. "It's been what? Two months? Isn't this a little too early in the game to be pulling this ambush shit?"

"We have a system!" the blonde girl exclaimed. "We do this for our safety, not because we enjoy it!"

"Hollering out at the top of your lungs so that every infected for miles can hear you? That's what you call safe?" wondered Atlas.

"It's worked so far," the black-haired girl intervened.

I rubbed my throbbing neck and turned to face the door where she was wiping blood from her nose, eyes still locked on me loathingly as if *she* was the victim.

"Yeah? How about now? What happens when your plan doesn't work?"

The sound of a cocked rifle arose from a storage closet in the back of the room, causing the hairs on my neck to prick. I turned back around and laid my eyes on an innocent, doe-eyed girl wearing a summer dress with a bow around her waist. Hazel irises and a precise cluster of freckles around the nose were a few of her angelic qualities. The demonic, however, were not concealed. The chestnut-haired girl aimed her gun at the center of my heart without even the slightest tremble.

"I'll kill you," she spoke at a solemn whisper.

I looked at her for a moment, completely hypnotized by this unexpected ruthlessness. I was struck with fear. Confusion flooded my mind, not understanding why she was threatening me. Then I examined my surroundings and realized that my innocence was hard to find. I did in fact hit a girl.

"Just…just lower the gun. This isn't what it looks like," I pleaded.

The blonde was your run-of-the-mill bombshell. "V" was more unconventional yet her clique would still be found in the schoolyard. But this girl…she was an aberration. Her initial appearance belonged to the innocent but her face was the product of a lobotomy. Her blank, emotionless gaze didn't quiver. Neither did the gun. This girl truly terrified me.

"Now just wait a goddamn minute, Sarah Connor!" Atlas spoke up, his stolen rifle aimed at her. "Lemme get this straight. We come here to help you, we get jumped, Levi gets a neck full of Taser, we fight back, and you make it seem like the *men* are to blame? Man, that's some grade-A feminazi shit right there."

I knew things weren't looking good for us, so I decided to take a chance.

"Atlas, lower your gun," I said.

"Excuse me, what? Sorry, I thought I heard you say *lower* the gun. Levi, ya see that bitch in front of you? She is about to kill you."

"No she's not," I replied.

"How do you know?"

These girls were smart, but they lacked the little details. I dropped the Taser and kicked it aside. "Because her gun is empty."

I took a shot that actually hit a nerve. For the first time, the brown-haired, freckled girl showed a slight shift in facial expression. Though barely recognizable, it was enough for me to keep going.

"You're wondering how I know? Ya know, guns…they're intimidating. It's encoded in our genes to be frightened whenever we catch a glimpse of one. They're unnatural and they don't make us think straight…which is why it's very easy to overlook something as small as a missing ammo magazine."

She winced but didn't say anything. Just stared. The girl with the bangs spoke on her behalf.

"We always keep one in the chamber," she lied.

Her words were lost on me for I was in a muted world were only the gun-wielding marvel that stood before me existed. There was definitely a chance that a bullet was agitatedly waiting so I took a leap of faith and stepped toward her until the barrel of the rifle was kissing my chest.

"Levi! Back off!!" Atlas yelled at me.

"No," I muttered back without taking my gaze off of hers. "If you think I'm wrong, pull the trigger."

I felt the ring of the barrel increase and decrease with pressure onto my chest as she was having an inner debate with herself. Finally, she slowly lowered the gun and looked away, allowing me to breathe again.

"Okay," I exhaled, "Now that we got that taken care of, can we…"

Then I felt the butt end of the rifle jam into my face, knocking me to the floor for a second time. Blood dribbled from my split lip as my cheek swelled up almost instantaneously. Bitch.

"What…the hell…"

"Levi, we're leaving," urged Atlas. "These bitches are *Gone Girl* insane."

"Wait a second!" the blonde girl stopped. "You can't just leave!"

"What're you gonna do? Shoot us?" spat Atlas as he helped me up and grabbed his bat.

I gave one last look at the freckled girl and shook my head. "This is what I get for *trying* to care."

We were halfway out the door when Josh finally opened his mouth.

"Why did you want the gas so bad?"

"Josh, let's go," Atlas said, short-tempered.

But he didn't move. He stood his ground and addressed the blonde leader. "I saw the look in your eyes. Why is it so important to you?"

She hesitated, unsure if it was some kind of trick. After a moment of scepticism, she replied.

"We have a car."

Josh's eyes widened. "You do? Where are you planning on going?"

"Why do you want to know?"

"Where are you planning on going?" he repeated.

The black-haired girl was clearly urging her friend to keep her mouth shut. The brown-haired girl kept her eyes glued to the floor.

"…Jasper. Our dad has a cabin there. We're supposed to meet him."

"Quinn!" snapped the black-haired girl. "We don't know these guys!"

Josh hadn't been prying because he was nosy. He had a plan and it was finally brought to the surface.

"Quinn, right? My name is Josh. We're on a mission. What do you think about working together?"

"How about not!!" blared Atlas.

"We're heading to Vancouver," Josh persisted. "To the coast! We've been told that there's a place called Safehaven that's completely free of infected."

Atlas yanked him back by his shirt collar, causing him to splutter.

"Are you out of your mind? These girls tried to kill us!" he reminded.

"And you want us to work with them?" I added.

"Stop putting your egos on the line!" argued Josh. "We have no food, but they do. They have the car and we have the gas! It's perfect!"

"*One* container of gas," I corrected. "What happens when we run out?"

At that moment I was trying to convince myself that it was a bad idea, yet I knew what the real answer was.

"Then we find some more or we walk or I don't know! But I do know that the more people we have, the better are chances of surviving."

"Hold on, why are you making it seem like we want to go with you?" Black hair said in a snarky tone. "We have our own agenda thank you very much."

"I agree with Bangs over there!" said Atlas. "We are *not* all on the same page."

"Jasper is on the way to Vancouver! We work together, help each other out, then we can go our separate ways."

"What do you have that helps us?" asked Quinn. "Besides the gas, obviously."

"That guy holding your rifle? His name is Atlas," Josh introduced, "and the guy next to him is Levi. Besides a...detour, we've been out in the wild since the very beginning. Surviving. We may not get along too well, but these guys know what they're doing and so do I." He paused, allowing for their inevitable judgments to unfold. "How long have you been held up in here?"

"That...that's not important," stammered Quinn.

"We can help you and you can help us," promised Josh. "So, what do you say?"

"I'll tell you what I think!" Atlas butted in. "This is a dick of an idea. Ten minutes with these strangers and we're already at each other's throats."

Finally, I caved.

"I hate to admit it, but Josh is right. We can't get our differences in the way and forget about the real threat that is out there."

Atlas turned to me, clearly pissed. "Need I remind you what happened the last time we were with other people? It didn't really work out now, did it?"

"That's different," I said angrily. "What happened there was a mistake."

"And this could turn out to be just as well!" he argued. Man, was he ever stubborn. Did he forget that he was just as guilty as Josh in regards to the farm?

Josh ignored him. "Quinn? What do you say?"

She looked at her compatriots, weary about the recent events. But like I said, sometimes you just need to take a leap of faith.

"...That quiet girl is Annabelle. This Goth-looking one is Veronica, my sister."

"Hmph," sighed Veronica.

"It's going to be dark soon. You three can take the space behind the cash register for the night. We'll head out in the morning."

Atlas was angry with me. After what happened at the farm, trust was not something to be handed out lightly. He was still with Josh and I because we all experienced it and turning on one another would only produce a no-win situation. He had lied down and thought about his family, or…lack thereof. Josh was a difficult person to read because I never knew where his loyalty lied. He found an expansive cupboard beneath the wall of cigarettes and condoms and slept in there. Annabelle had disappeared, fading into the mythical world that I was almost convinced I had conjured up. The sisters slept next to one another, though Veronica's focus was solely and professionally stuck on the three strangers inhabiting her home. And me? I thought about many things, but my mind was trained to return back to the event that made me. It was times like these that I wished I had never been born at all.

# 8. "I'm so hard right now."

The morning came with a subtle breeze that kissed our faces and tussled our hair. After a painstakingly awkward night of little sleep and distrust on both genders, we rushed at the opportunity to keep ourselves busy and awoke at seven in the morning to start packing. While Josh, Veronica and Annabelle found cardboard boxes and loaded up the maximum amount of junk food and energy drinks, Quinn escorted me to the vehicle.

It was a grand reveal that received increased anticipation as the metal awning of the nearby garage slowly crinkled up to tease the car. When the full model was shown, however, it was nothing less of an anti-climactic buzz kill. The car in question was a 1982 Ford Bronco pickup truck that looked like it spent a couple years too long in the sun and stunk of cheap, expired leather.

"I don't mean to be rude, but this car looks like someone swallowed a chunk of rust and shat it out," I sighed.

Quinn shrugged her shoulders. "It was the only one left. We came here in an RV…but that obviously didn't work out in our favour."

As I began to fuel the rust bucket, Annabelle walked outside and loaded up a ratty cardboard box into a trailer that would attach to the truck. She looked over at me and I found myself staring back with constricted tunnel vision. It wasn't a look of affection, but rather a look a tamed beast gave to a wild animal. What had yet to be determined was figuring out who was who.

I was the one to break eye contact, immediately feeling defeated; treating it like some sort of competition. Before she returned inside, however, I cheated a quick, momentary glance back to her. I witnessed her brush a strand of caramel hair behind her ear, exposing a large, jagged scar that hooked all the way around the back of her neck. Then, she was gone.

"What's her story?" I investigated, shaking out the final drops of gasoline.

"Who, Annabelle?"

I nodded.

"If I'm going to be completely honest, we don't really know," admitted Quinn.

"What do you mean? I thought she was a friend of yours?"

Why was I asking these questions? I didn't care about her. I didn't...I couldn't.

"No, not at all. It was just V and I for a while, surviving day to day in that gas station with no one to talk to but each other for nearly a month. Then, a couple weeks ago, during a brutal storm, we heard tapping on the glass. It was almost two in the morning and whether it was rain or those sick people, we sure as hell weren't going to check it out. But it kept on tapping. After ten minutes or so, we finally investigated what was making that sound and there she was...standing outside of the doors...covered in blood."

"I'm sorry, blood? What happened to her?"

"She didn't say," said Quinn. "She never said anything. Like, at all."

I let out a dry chuckle. "Well that didn't seem to be the case when she pointed that rifle at my heart. She made it very clear I was not welcome...vocally."

"We were just as shocked as you were!" she explained. "That was the first time she ever opened her mouth." Quinn looked over to Annabelle who reappeared with another box. "Poor girl. She was trembling like a dog for the better half of two days. Had to throw away her clothes—too stained, ya know? Those are actually my clothes that she's wearing."

She saw that I had clearly looked perturbed, as if I was in the midst of processing bad news. I honestly didn't realize it until she pointed it out.

"Don't worry, you did nothing wrong," Quinn assured. "We were all at fault in that whole situation last night. I'm sure Annabelle will be fine. She just obviously went through a very traumatic experience."

As Quinn strolled off to help with packing, I stood motionless, lost in thought. For I had believed that Quinn's assumption was wrong. I understood what trauma meant, arguably more than anyone. But the look on Annabelle's face wasn't a traumatic one. No, it was the look of someone who had died.

While this had happened, Atlas was sprawled out like a starfish, sleeping like he had just discovered what it was. He was the kind of person that could fall asleep anywhere at anytime, be that in a hot tub or in the midst of taking a shit. Veronica, who had spent already an hour of loading up the remainder of the supplies, did not take kindly to this ability of his. Or maybe she just didn't like his face. Either way, she approached the space behind the cashier counter and kicked Atlas in the stomach.

"Wake up, you lazy shit. We're leaving."

Atlas awoke with a tremendous groan and began tapping her shoe.

"What're you doing?" she asked.

"Trying to find the snooze button," Atlas mumbled.

Instead of coming up with a suitable comeback, Veronica reached into the last box and pulled out a lukewarm Mountain Dew that she proceeded to pour all over Atlas's face.

He spluttered and shot upright. "Wh-what the hell was that for?"

She grinned sarcastically. "Your wake-up call. Now let's get a move on. We need to attach the trailer to the truck."

Atlas sighed. "You didn't have to go and waste a perfectly good bottle of Dew on me. If you wanted to see me in a wet shirt, all you had to do was ask."

After wiping his face on his moth-ridden Loverboy baseball tee, he stumbled outside dazed and confused after a wild night of hard sleeping. While walking behind her, he spotted something rather peculiar in the grassy area between the garage and the gas station. There had been a risen mound of dirt with a cross made of sticks that protruded out from the front, acting as a makeshift headstone. What was concerning though was the fact that next to the grave was the charred remains of a burnt corpse.

"Friends of yours?" Atlas asked to a leading Veronica, causing her to stop mid-stride.

"What did you say?" she replied hesitantly.

He pointed to the grave and she instantly drew in close to him until they were less than an arm's length apart.

"Let me make something very clear," she began. "We are not friends. I don't know you and you don't know me. Whatever happened to you before now, it doesn't concern me and frankly, I don't give a shit. That's your business. So I'm telling you, not asking, to not give a shit about my life. Those people over there? They don't concern you and they never will. You got me?"

Atlas raised his hands defensively. "Easy there, Bangs. I was just asking a question."

"We may be working together but that does not mean that we have to enjoy it. Besides, it's better for us to not care about each other because it'll make our deaths much easier to handle."

"Our deaths?" asked Atlas.

"Do you really think we have a full life to live? The average lifespan in this world is a couple weeks, a month if you're lucky. We're all going to die, it's just a matter of when."

Atlas sighed. "Lovin' the optimism. Anything else you'd like to share with me?"

Veronica pointed at Annabelle, who was kicking a lone rock across the gravel floor, and glared at him.

"That girl there? She's been through more than I could even imagine. She is incredibly vulnerable and incredibly unstable. All you guys do is think with your dicks and prod anything with a pulse. But if any one of you three so much as lay a finger on her, so help me God, I'll rip your guys' manhood off and shove them so far up your asses that you'll taste them. Understood?"

She spun around on her heels and produced a whirlwind of hair to follow. Atlas watched her walk away and smacked his dry lips

"What a freak…" he muttered beneath his breath. "…I'm so hard right now."

All the supplies from the gas station were loaded up, the trailer was hooked up to the tailgate of the truck, and we were ready to head out. The six of us huddled up to discuss any last-minute details.

"There'll be one bathroom break every two hours."

"Don't stop for any survivors."

"What's the music situation?"

When everything seemed to be taken care of, we saw no reason to stick around for another minute.

"Well, let's get going!" said Quinn.

"Shotgun!" declared Atlas.

Everyone filed into the dust-ridden truck and claimed their respective seats: The three girls in the back seat, Atlas in the passenger seat, Josh forced to ride in the trunk, and me. That was when I realized there was one small detail we overlooked.

"Uhm, guys? Does anyone know how to drive?"

Everyone was silent.

"Really? We made sure what music we were listening to but we didn't discuss whose going to drive?"

The passengers inside of the vehicle listed off their own excuse.

"Never got around to it," said Veronica.

"Same here," added Quinn.

"Failed twice!" Josh called out from the trunk.

Annabelle said nothing.

"I got an instant fail for trying to flirt with the driving instructor," stated Atlas, as if he was proud. "Almost got her number too."

Again, I was all that was left.

"What about you, Levi?" asked Quinn.

"Well," I began, avoiding eye contact, "Technically, yes. But that's only because five minutes in, my driving instructor went into labour and I had to drive her to the hospital. She passed me while they gave her an epidural."

Atlas laughed. "Well, that's better than any of us! Get in the hot seat."

I shook my head and with hilarious disinclination, I sat down in the driver's seat. The keys fell out from the sun visor and onto my lap. While I adjusted my rear-view mirror, I caught the glimpse of the four backseat passengers and realized that their lives were in my control. This was a feeling that I did not desire.

The engine awoke in a fit of coughs and with a kick we were off. That is, until I came to a stop no more than twenty seconds later.

"Uhm, where are we exactly?"

"Vermillion," answered Veronica.

"What??" exclaimed Atlas. "Vermillion? No, no you must be mistaken. That's from *Pokémon*."

I closed my eyes. "This is going to be fun."

# 9. "Do you suck or blow?"

I lied to you. It was not fun. The entirety of the one hour, fifty-six minutes and forty-three second car ride was spent in an awkward limbo that felt like a drawn-out first date with vacant attraction to one another. The music didn't help ease the molasses-like tension, seeing as we had a choice between Tina Turner's Greatest Hits or an audio book for *The Catcher in the Rye* in Spanish.

I often found my eyes drifting to my left, gazing out at the intriguing devastation painted in blurs outside of my window. There were burnt barns singed into the fields, rotting corpses of half-eaten cows and horses spread out and hidden like Easter eggs, infected humans varying from clumps in the dozens to a lone walker, an overturned school bus that dripped red at a constant, innocent rhythm, and a totaled Pontiac Sunfire lying in the ditch that caused me to clench the steering wheel and immediately avert my eyes.

The trip was cut short and though I should've been overjoyed, it was not by choice. Once one hour, fifty-six minutes and forty-three seconds came and went at a deadbeat pace, the gasoline had entirely dissipated, leaving us nearly fifteen miles out from the big city. We came to a lurching halt and I released a defeated exhalation through my nostrils.

"Why're we stopping?" asked Veronica. "Do you see something?"

"We're out," I explained.

Veronica leaned forward. "Are you serious? What're we supposed to do?"

My mouth scrunched to the side in uncertainty. "I guess we walk."

"With the trailer full of supplies?" wondered Quinn.

Why were they asking me questions as if I was in charge? That wasn't the kind of person I was! That isn't the kind of person I *am*! I'm the supporting role; I'm the right-hand man. I'm never the leader.

I looked over to Atlas, hoping he would take over the highly undesirable command seat.

"…There doesn't seem to be any cars around. Plus, we ain't got any tubes lying around to siphon gas and frankly, I don't even know how you do that. Do you suck or blow?" He paused, not receiving an answer. "Forget it. Do you see that building there?"

Atlas pointed to a sleek, shimmering hotel in the distance due east of us.

"We can hold up there for a night or two until we find more gas."

Veronica squinted through the sun glare bouncing off her window and frowned.

"What, we're supposed to walk there? Are we going to just abandon the supplies?"

Atlas thought about this for a moment, peered out his side-view mirror and nodded to himself.

"I've got a plan," he announced.

Before I could ask what it was, he opened his door and walked toward the bumper of the trailer. I looked back into my mirror and noticed that a lone biter with a missing jaw was hobbling towards him.

"Atlas…whatcha doing, bud?" Josh asked in both a casual and nervous manner.

Without answering back, Atlas proceeded to reach his arm around the pale one and grasped onto a greasy tuff of hair. He dragged it to the bumper and without warning, he forced the head down onto it, driving his fist into its putrid, rotting cranium.

Josh gagged. "A little warning would've been nice."

Now with a lifeless corpse at his disposal, he hoisted the bloody heap up on the covering on the trailer. He gave the head a couple more squeezes to allow the gooey juices to coat the lid. What he had done wasn't a random act of murder but rather provide an effective repellent to humans and infected alike.

I exited the vehicle. "Smart thinking. No one's gonna even think about going near that."

"Well, except us," Veronica pointed out. "Ya know, when we have to get to our stuff back?"

"One step at a time, Bangs," grinned Atlas.

Josh hopped out of the trunk, slung his backpack over his shoulder and puffed out his chest like the hero he wasn't.

"I made sure to put enough food and water into everyone's backpacks for a few days," he pointed out, expecting gratitude that wasn't delivered. "Let's head over to that hotel and see what's happening!"

We each grabbed our backpacks and started moving east, but like some sort of animalistic impulse, I turned over my shoulder and scavenged for anything that could even remotely pass as a weapon. The only thing that I came across was a rusty tire rim off of a charred carcass that was once a Toyota.

We made it seven minutes without any problems. On the eighth minute, the pale ones grew to a number that made them unavoidable. I feel as though I don't give the infected the proper calibre of seriousness that they deserve—given that they have been prominent for nearly half of my life—and I often make them sound like they were nothing but a nuisance. They weren't. At that time, the shit was scared out of us on a daily basis. With the level of adrenaline that pumped through my veins, I felt like a junkie that never understood what normalcy felt like. I forgot what being safe was like and life started to resemble one in a war-torn battlefield, except there, all that you had to fear was death.

A swarm of cold ones emerged from deserted cars and ditches, all immediately obsessed with the very sight of us. The hotel was five hundred metres away, but it had a forest of infected encompassing it. This was when Atlas and I discovered who these girls really were.

"Everybody stay close," ordered Atlas. "Anyone that breaks ranks…"

He pulled a pale, white-collared man by his red and gray tie and stabbed a scavenged kitchen knife into his eye socket.

"…is as good as dead."

One lunged at me—a particularly fucked-in-the-face individual—and I whipped my hands around its body and proceeded to snap its neck. I didn't even need to turn around to feel the petrified gazes of the three girls, like a depiction of the three wise monkeys. Veronica was the least frightened but even her butch persona couldn't hide it. The mixture of gasps and held breath coming from the females told me that they were cowards in every sense of the word.

"Atlas, to your left," I called out monotonously.

He swung without looking, jamming the blade into its gelatinous-like temple. It was indeed a confirmed kill, but the flimsy nature of the knife meant for vegetables and cheese had reached its expiry date and snapped into its skull.

"Great…" exhaled Atlas. He pulled out his bat from his backpack and gave it a few flourishing swings with his wrist.

"Josh, clear a path!" I yelled.

There were a trio of teenage girls of the infected variety that pushed toward him like a blockade. The look on his face was like he had been impaled. Clearly he wasn't going to be much help.

"Josh!" I repeated.

They reached out with slimy hands and Josh felt their cold, raw flesh on his James Dean jacket before a living hand pulled him away; a hand that belonged to Veronica.

"Move!" she ordered.

With a flurry of her hand, she produced a bent pipe, something that I still don't know where she got it from, and proceeded to knock all three onto their cute, decomposing asses.

"There's a clearing!" Veronica pointed out. "Now's our chance!"

She yanked Annabelle away by the hand, whom had stood completely frozen and dead, hidden among the infected. She didn't even seem to be phased.

We all followed behind at a complete sprint, swerving and diving by bodies like a dodgeball deathmatch.

Just keep running, I told myself. There was a space between contorted bodies that I would've just been able to fit through and at that point, all that mattered was saving myself. Why would I risk my life for people that I just met? Yes I'd known Atlas and Josh for a couple of months, but after what happened at the farm…I didn't think I could trust them again. And Annabelle? She meant nothing to me. So when she tripped on a mutilated leg, twisted her ankle, and was left as nothing but a fresh meal, why should I have cared? If I didn't care about her, why did I spin on my heels mid-stride before she even hit the grass to save her? Why did I fall to my knees, lifted her up into a piggy-back, and carved a path through a clump of no less than fifteen walkers with just the metal rim and crowbar? Why did I risk my life for a girl that meant no more to me than someone passing me on a street?

Answer: Because I'm a boy, and boys are idiots.

## 10. "Make me care."


The grinding, clinking sound of the metal gate tore through the air, playing a cringing solo on my eardrums. Our collective bodies slumped on the square patch of grass in front of the plaza. Dozens of roamers gripped their greedy appendages through the diamond holes, rattling the caged area like an overly exaggerated wrestling match. I took a few moments to catch my runaway breath, only to realize I was still holding onto Annabelle.

She pushed away and glared at me disarmingly, as if I had attempted to take advantage of her. I was expecting a fury of insults and complaints, but then I remembered she was a practicing mute.

"Sorry for saving your life?" I said confusingly.

She backed away to Veronica, averting her blank, beautiful eyes.

Josh rubbed his bruised skull. "I gotta say…zombie apocalypses kinda suck the major wang." He stumbled up to his feet and retreated from the fence, the look of a pathetic child plastered on his face.

Atlas's signature scowl arose as he approached him. "So I guess we know everyone's true colours after that shit storm. Yours is a nice hue of pussy pink with a dash of shit-my-pants brown."

Veronica stepped in. "Back off. This isn't something we're used to, okay? We're not murderers!"

"Neither are we!" Atlas snapped back. "We're survivors! We do what we do because we have to. If we show any weakness, even for a second, we're biting the freaking dust."

"Enough!" yelled Quinn. "These fences won't hold for long. Let's get inside!"

For being the first building we came across, we struck a goldmine. The words *Cobalt Hotel and Resort* cursively danced onto the skyline and just like its name, the modern structure glimmered with an ocean blue. The fact that there had been construction-like fences surrounding the perimeter implied that it had yet to be open to the public, making the interior both bodiless and desirable. The hotel was a sleek, semi-circle style tower with the curved edge facing us. Warped, spiralled steel beams that spun like DNA strands elevated the entire building. The edges extended out with artistic glass that resembled paper-thin ice. The building was truly a sight but what could only be seen as an architect's wet dream were the windows. Weird, I know. What made them noteworthy was that every single window was one-sided, turning it into a mirrored masterpiece.

Atlas crinkled the back of his neck to extend his sight to the peak of the hotel.

"I feel like I'm looking into my soul," he muttered.

We pulled the metal rod handle toward us and were embraced with the cold remnants of what had been a pristine, marble coated lobby that would've scoffed at the sight of me and the weight of my wallet. To either of our sides were thick, Greek-style pillars leading to a grand staircase that split into three directions. At the base was the receptionist desk where a secretary sat face down in a puddle of her own blood and drool. We all stopped for a moment to listen, only to be answered with the unfamiliar sound of silence.

"I don't mean to sound ungrateful, but where are all the bodies?" Quinn asked.

"There was a sign on the fence outside that said the hotel would be opening in the fall of this year," explained Josh. "We might've came across the only building in miles that isn't a cemetery."

"I wouldn't be so sure," Veronica disregarded, as her pipe remained raised. "This skank seemed to have worked here. Surely she's not the only person in the building."

"Only one way to find out," I muttered, stepping forward to the desk.

My index finger tapped the ringer on a pearl white bell and waited for a few moments to see if anyone would answer my call. Surprisingly, all that could be heard were our simultaneously held breaths.

"I don't buy it," Atlas said, unconvinced.

"Neither do I," agreed Veronica. "Let's get out of here."

"Whoa now, that's not what I said. I said I don't buy it, as in, let's go investigate. I don't give a flying hoot if that cabin of yours is diamond encrusted overlooking a lake of liquid gold. This shit right here is real shit that is too good of shit to pass on."

While Veronica was dumbfounded by his genius vocabulary, Josh spoke up.

"There's no way that there is any power left in the building. Even if there was, we'd need to find the generator and that's not something that I would fancy doing in the dark."

"We have flashlights, dumbass," retorted Atlas. "How about this: we split up in two groups. One of us investigates the upper levels while the other goes into the basement to find the generators. That'll save us a butt load of time."

"Split up?" I asked. "Have you seen any horror movie that has ever been made? That is the shittiest of ideas."

"Got any other ideas?"

I didn't.

"Good. So, Veronica, Quinn and I will check out the basement. Since you boys have misplaced your testicles, you two can sweep the upstairs. Bring the Helen Keller wannabe with you too. Check, the, uh, sixth floor? Yeah, sixth floor. That's a good number. Try and find a couple rooms for us to hold up for the night. If all things go according to plan, we'll meet you up there via the elevator."

This assigned grouping wasn't something that sat well with Veronica. "How about us girls go find the power and you three search the rooms?"

Atlas shook his head, swooping his dangling strands of hair sideways. "Nah, I think I should go down there with you. Ya never know what could be down there."

Veronica was offended. "What? You don't think we could handle ourselves?"

He ignored this and put his hand in the middle of us. "Fifteen minutes, okay?" He then threw it up into the air. "Go team!"

With a dying flashlight, Atlas embarked toward the basement stairwell door that was slightly ajar. With a sigh of reluctance and a few missteps of hesitancy, Veronica and Quinn trailed after him. Josh, Annabelle and I were left in a cloud of awkwardness. It was clear that Annabelle was at the pinnacle of her discomfort with me, but I didn't care. It's not like she was going to protest.

I was vomiting. Violently. This is something I should probably expand on, huh? Let me explain.

We had made it to the sixth floor without any complications. The fact that we hadn't seen a single infected/deceased other than the lady at the desk had worried me. This worry of mine was quenched once we reached the sixth floor. There had been five rooms on each side of the hallway, all locked. Since construction hadn't been finalized, none of the key card slots were installed. Simply for safety reasons, a standard lock was attached to the handle of each door.

"How are we going to get the rooms open? They need a key," Josh inquired.

Let me tell you some things about Josh: He was a tremendous basketball player, cared about his hair more than the air he breathed, and above all, stupid. Grades were fine, yes, but I'm referring to the street smarts or to be blunt, common sense. So when I jokingly suggested he break down one of the doors, what do you think his response was? Yeah, you guessed right.

Less than a second later he was writhing on the floor clenching his shoulder, while the door had walked away from the fight without even the slightest dent.

"…" said Annabelle silently as she shook her head disdainfully. While I helped the fool off of the ground, we noticed that Annabelle had knelt down to the door with a bobby pin pinched in her fingers and another between her teeth.

"Oh, yeah right," Josh scoffed. "As if that'll work. That's only done in the movies. There's like seven notches you need to press with such precision that an average girl like you…"

There was a click and she swung the door open.

"Alright, well…" he said, biting his lip.

We filed into the room and found…nothing. It was simply a free living space that we would soon occupy. The room to its left, 643, was next and once again Annabelle knelt down to pick the lock.

"Listen, once was luck, but twice? No w…"

She opened it again.

"…Sorry."

Before going inside, she gave me this glare that felt as though she wanted to take my soul, rip it out and shove it down my throat until I shat it out so she could do it again. Yeah. All that from one look. I had absolutely no idea what I had done but hey, that's just me being a boy.

Oh right, you want to know about the vomiting. Well, behind door number two was certainly not nothing. We peeked inside and curled up on the floor was this grayish, pus-covered beast that resembled Golem more than a human. It was extremely skeletal, its bloodshot eyes bulged out further than its skull, and the odour was enough to induce a coma. There was a bite mark on its ankle, assuring me that it wasn't a spontaneous zombie production. On its forehead was a tumour-like bulge the size of a baseball that seemed to cause its head to droop a certain way. It wasn't until the frail beast began to snap its teeth at me did I realize that it was still *alive*.

"Jesus…what happened to it?" breathed Josh.

Since there had been no immediate threat, I had the time to examine it. Most of its teeth were either broken off or missing completely and its stomach had sunk in so much that it looked like a wrecking ball had hit it.

"It's starving," I realized.

It's funny, you never think of the stereotypical zombie to actually starve. They just seem to 'live' and feast on humans not because they have to but because it's a convenience to them. This…thing, however, was not a stereotypical anything. It looked like an anorexic cancer patient multiplied by ten. Seeing it produced a theory in my mind, though I kept it to myself for the time being as I had to put it out of its misery. My crowbar was up to bat but due to its pathetic size, I had to kneel down and endow an uncomfortably close vicinity with the creature. So, with my teeth bitten deep into my tongue, I jammed the forked end into its fragile face. It was an instant kill, but I hit the tumour and caused a spurt of blackish pus to shoot out. It lathered my face and the smell was enough for me to taste it vividly. I can assume you know what happened next.

While the interior of my stomach took a nice stroll on the hotel room carpet, Atlas and the sisters descended into the basement in search of power. It was an unfinished T-shaped hallway that was ceilingless and had walls without plaster. Each door had led to a room with a specific duty. One was the *Surveillance Room*, another had been the *Water Filtration* and at the end of the hall was the *Generator Room*.

As they slowly inched their way with only flashlights to illuminate the path, it was in this moment that Atlas truly wished that he was gay.

"It appals me that even in the end of the world, a guy can't trust us women to do something other than sucking their dick or making them a sandwich or both. You just had to come along with us to flex your muscles, huh?"

Atlas looked at her confusingly. "…What? No, that's not…"

"Roni, shut it. We might not be alone here," whispered Quinn.

"All you guys are the same. You think we're nothing but walking, talking sex toys in short skirts and high stilettoes and…"

Atlas's ears perked up and suddenly, he clasped his palm over her babbling mouth. Veronica squirmed and flailed her arms like an aggravated toddler, but Atlas had a vice grip on her. He held her in place and pointed to the generator room door, which had been slightly trembling, almost shivering.

"We get it, Ms. Hepburn! Men are beasts. Women are freaking angelic. So could you please keep the ranting in your head and shut up!" he snapped. "Quinn is most certainly right. We are not alone."

She pulled away from him. "Asshole."

They crept up to the door as if it was their prey. He pressed his ear against the cool, stainless steel and listened to the rhythm of what sounded like limp scratching. It sounded as if a dying animal was begging for the lethal injection.

"I'm going to open the door on three," told Atlas. "I'm trusting that you can handle yourself."

"As you should," she replied steely. "Open it."

"Okay. One…two…THREE!"

Atlas swung the door open and like a bullet, a vile stench ripped through their nostrils and licked at their watering eyes. Quinn nearly fainted, Veronica seized into a fit of coughs, and Atlas plugged both his nose and mouth with his lifted shirt. With a few inhales of fresh air, he peeled away from behind the door and flashed his torch at the interior of the room. Inside had been no less than seven rotting bodies, all wearing hotel uniforms, each with a bullet hole in their respective foreheads save for one. Varying from cheeks to entire legs, large amounts of flesh had been eaten away from nearly every occupant in the room and the culprit was found sprawled at the opening of the door. With six bullets and seven bodies, one had to draw the short straw and endure the transformation. At Atlas's feet was a grossly enlarged, bloated biter that pathetically clawed at him. It bathed in a puddle of its own excrement and intestines that were forced out through its ruptured stomach. With enough mass to make up two fully grown adults compacted into its body, this infected had to be the fattest thing that Atlas had ever seen. Bones of its victims pierced through its stomach, sending bile and fluid out from a calcium pipe.

"Christ," breathed Atlas. "This is seven kinds of fucked up."

"No arguments there," agreed Veronica, in between coughs.

Atlas directed his flashlight at a panel on the far left wall that was barricaded by a fallen beam. "You see that? I'm not small enough to reach that. One of you will need to flip it on."

Veronica looked to Quinn who looked back at her. "After you," beckoned Veronica.

"…Fine," exhaled Quinn.

While she carefully tiptoed through the expansive casket, Atlas looked down at the obese mess. "If you think I'm a worthless, women-oppressing piece of inferior trash, would you be willing to take care of our little friend here?"

Veronica glanced down at the beast, which attempted to glance back up at her. This was impossible, however, as both of its eyeballs had been squeezed out of their sockets.

"I'll let you take this one," she muttered.

Atlas chuckled. "Women. You all think you're some kind of self-righteous, independent young female until the jar of pickles comes out."

"What??"

"It's a metaphor. Bust off."

Just as he drove the bat down, the power booted up just in time to show the eradication of its inflamed skull. Its contents formed an intricate Rorschach design that actually moved due to the expelled maggots. I can assume you know what happened next.

We managed to clear enough rooms on the sixth floor for each of us to get our very own suite. Unfortunately, the short straw was in my hand and I was put into the room with the gray, headless body. I was able to open the window and create a makeshift garbage disposal for the body but its brain seeped into the carpet, infecting it beyond recovery. I assumed that the others were either sharing a meal or partaking in the immortal sport of gossip. I, on the other hand, preferred the highly desirable isolation that I loathed with a fiery passion. It was a love-hate relationship with myself that was put on the back burner for the majority of the past two months, but now I was free to let my mind crumble. In this hazy, scathingly raw hotel suite, I was, for the first time since it all began, truly alone. This was my nature and no matter how comfortable I was with the four walls and a roof preventing me from human interaction, I despised it. Being socially inept is not a sought-after trait but rather an illness that had poisoned my teenage body for close to fifteen years. I hated everything about the social normalities of people, yet my envy for them was unmatched.

The porcelain lamp on the bedside table flickered at a periodically erratic rate. With each change in light, I was taken in and out of this world as my mindless focus stabbed into the brain stain on the carpet. The mess was a putrid eminence swirled with paint strokes of a steel gray and an intoxicating red. I was disgusted and hypnotized. As my eyes grew weary and blurry, the decorated splatter morphed and evolved into a pool of freshly discharged blood. The carpeted floor became a cold, harsh ground made of hardened cement that laid a base for a painfully expanded hall. Ropes were tied around and around my body, squeezing the adolescent life out of me. A broken mirror was on the floor. A body was in front of me, behind me, and all else that reflected her. She was dead.

The rattling of knuckles on the door shook me awake from my trance, sending me straight to my numb feet. I had returned to the hotel and that horrible nightmare was buried once more.

"Hunh...?" I grunted through my sand-coated throat.

The door creaked open and in the frame stood Annabelle.

"Oh...hi?" I greeted cautiously. We stood in a heavy silence that even made me, a man of little words, desperate to lift it.

"Is there...what do you want?"

She glanced at me for a moment, silently judging my perspiring body with her alluringly robotic eyes. Then she spoke.

"You shouldn't have saved me."

I was taken aback. This was only the second time I had ever heard her speak, the first being with a gun aimed at me.

"She speaks!" I stated. "I was beginning to think you could only speak when you're threatening to kill someone. Namely me."

"You shouldn't have saved me," she repeated.

"What are you talking about?"

"Outside. When I tripped. That was my time to go. I know it was. But you took that away from me."

Her voice disarmed me. Now finally hearing more than a threat, I could listen to it like a linguistic vinyl. It was slightly heavy and raspy, like she was the dame in a classic 40's noir. She had been able to break my barrier, so now it was my turn to make her feel the same way. To do that, she needed to know how wrong she was.

"Let me tell you a story about how my grandpa Frank died," I began. "This man smoked so goddamn much that he made Humphrey Bogart look like a teenage boy that snuck a pack from his dad. My only memories of him were literally clouds of smoke or the frequently seen whiskey on the rocks; I was usually his personal bartender at the age of four. Anyway, he eventually got a severe heart attack. It was his time to go, right? Nope. Nuh-uh. He made it to the hospital and after regaining consciousness he realized that the nurses had given him a catheter. Ol' Frankie wasn't too happy that they tampered with his wee-wee and in protest, he yanked the catheter out. Shortly after, he haemorrhaged and dropped dead right then and there in his hospital room."

Annabelle gave me a look of tremendous disgust that sent a flush through my chest. Seeing this girl show any kind of emotion was like witnessing a unicorn barf rainbows.

"What was the point of telling me that?" she asked coldly.

I grinned slightly. "To explain to you that death happens according to a plan. I am not a religious man, but I do believe that someone or something up there has our fate determined. They or it has our names scribbled in some kind of death notebook and with it is our cause. It is not random and it is impossible to tamper with. Why did my grandpa survive a heart attack only to die a much more painful death? Because that was how he was supposed to go. That and he was a total dick."

"Yeah but what does…"

"…that have to do with you?" I interrupted. "Because you weren't supposed to die as pathetically as that. I know that because I wouldn't have been able to save you. My hands would've been tied and you would've been swarmed…but guess what? We're both still here."

Her lip trembled and forehead creased. I made her feel and yes, I was proud.

"So what, exactly? Are you looking for some sort of thank you?"

"I don't care about what I did. I'm not looking for someone to pat my back and pinch my cheeks every time I do something half-decent. That's bullshit. What I'm looking for is the real reason why you came into my room."

"Excuse me?"

I was now in arms reach of her. "You didn't come in here because you wanted to start a fight. I don't know much about you, hell I don't know anything about you, but I'm pretty damn certain you're not like those other girls. You came in here for a reason. What that is, I'm not entirely sure."

Her eyes darted side to side, looking for a lifeline that wasn't there. Then, she looked at me. Not just at me, but into me.

"...The other guys, they put up a front. They act as if whatever this is...is normal. Clearly something happened to you three that are above and beyond the hardships of an average person. But they are pretending that it was nothing but a hiccup and it makes me want to snap their weak little necks. But you? You at least offer a realistic outlook to this world."

She took one step closer, a cloud of painstaking intimidation following closely.

"I don't trust you. I don't trust anyone. When you saved me, I was pissed because we actually need to care about each other if we want to survive. So, I'm asking you to give me a reason to trust you."

I tilted my head and frowned. "And how do I do that?"

"Tell me what happened to you before this. Make me care."

I exhaled and looked down at my feet. How I lived was by constantly developing a new layer of skin to cover up the scars and wounds on the previous one. Right then, she was making me go against my nature by making me...open up? No, I didn't need to do anything that she asked of me. The weird part, however, was that I wanted to. So, I sat down on the bed and started to peel away my skin.

# 11. "I can fix it! I can fix everything!!!"

**66 Days Ago**

It was eleven o'clock at night and the tedious scratching on the grate continued with equal haste. Not a word had been spoken after the bullet ripped through the life of the owner. We all had separated from the crime scene and found corners or back rooms to shut everything out, attempting to avoid the guilt that loomed over like a stubborn storm cloud. Everyone that is, except me. Staring mindlessly at the gaping hole that split his heart into two, it was then that I understood how we as a species were too far gone. This seismic event was simply a wake-up call and not until I witnessed the death of an innocent man did I truly comprehend how justifiable this apocalypse was.

What made my muscles tense with rage, what made my jaw tighten until my teeth ached, what put my entire body into a seizure of frustration were the sounds that night. No, not the fingernails of ravenous humans clawing on the grates, not the rhythmic echoes of suffering moans of shortcoming deaths in the distance, no, it was the sounds *inside* the garage; the sounds of snoring. How despicable must we have been to either stand by or take part in a meaningless murder and have the malice in our hearts to be capable of sleeping? The answer wasn't needed because the snores and heavy breathing of my fellow survivors was an answer in itself. We deserved this punishment and anything that was to follow.

I was not a good man. Never in my life had I even attempted to sugar coat the reality. What I had been was a selfish, passive, inconsiderate robot, yet a robot that nonetheless had the ability to feel pain. I could feel it, yes, but never would I show it. I was physically unable to cry after the…incident, and genuinely caring about someone was utterly inconceivable. I didn't care about this lifeless man. I didn't care about Atlas. I didn't care about anyone but myself. However, I will give myself the credit of at least attempting to care. I thought about this man that laid in front of me and his life and how I would never know whom this man was. The cliffhanger of this tragedy was more excruciating than the tragedy itself. All that could be done was to forge imaginary concepts; possible lifestyles that may coincide with this man's life. He could have had three sons who all despised him. Perhaps he had a beautiful and loyal wife that he shared a cramped one-bedroom apartment with alongside their three-legged husky. Maybe he had no one in his life and the bullet that was tucked near the centre of his spine was his saving grace. Whatever life he lived, it simply didn't matter anymore. He was dead and despite contrary belief that was scratching at our door, there's no way to come back from that.

I laid next to his body with my head at his feet and vice versa and stared at the metal rafters where pink fluff burst from the seams. Then the hallucinations crept in. For hours on end I watched shapes become animals and animals become liquid until a new world of fractured mentality was locked into the garage. Lights flickered and danced and screamed as I stored away my constant trauma for once and thought about the one who made love a broken concept.

The foggy, surreal atmosphere engulfed everything below my torso as I walked through an empty hallway. It was of my high school, yet it looked nothing of the same. Broken windows were boarded up with rotting planks of wood. The taste of aerosol filled the air, wafting from spray-painted lockers. The floor was blanketed with glass shards and rubble. The few windows that remained intact had the dusk rolling through them, creating elongated shadows of the windowpanes on the jagged floor. At the end of the corridor was a brown-haired girl of my age, standing motionlessly, allowing the moonlight to absorb into her skin and create a sterling outline along her figure. She wore a tight, cherry red dress and a silver chained necklace with a small heart pendant that sparkled mystically. Her face, however, was concealed by the shadows, making her unrecognizable. I felt pressure in my throat, like I had yelled something to get her attention, but all that I could hear were muffled sounds as if I were underwater. The girl slowly emerged from the shadows and revealed herself, sending me into a sudden paralysis. It was my ex-girlfriend, the girl who, if I still had a heart, it would have ached for.

"E-Electra?" I asked in awe.

My pulse quickened and breath became obnoxiously erratic. I began to move toward her, going at a frighteningly slow, almost immobile run, but just as I was in arms reach of the girl I once adored, thick ropes spontaneously appeared from the rafters and pulled me away. They jerked my body back and wrapped around my wrists, sending sharp pains through my strained shoulders that were one tug away from popping out of their sockets. With no other choice, I dangled there helplessly as she closed the remaining distance apart. With each step, the light illuminating from the windows flickered, progressively altering her appearance. When she finally reached me, she had not been the mesmerizingly beautiful girl I had remembered, but that of a newly reanimated corpse. Her flesh ripped away from her cheekbones, she had a mouth of putrid teeth that carried a yellowish tint, and protruding veins had encompassed a fresh bite mark. She looked at my wide eyes disappointingly.

"How could you let this happen?" she softly spoke.

The interior of her mouth was clearly visible through the strands of tainted muscle exposed across her torn cheeks. Ropes tightened. The light shined brightly on her whilst leaving me in complete darkness.

"No…this can't be happening…" I stubbornly whispered.

"You didn't come for me. I waited and waited, but you never saved me."

"You don't understand what I've been through. I was going to look for you! I promise! I just got side-tracked…"

"It's too late, Levi. This is what I've become. There is no coming back from this."

My squirming body was further bound as ropes now grabbed onto my legs.

"No! Don't say that!! I can fix it! I can fix everything!!!"

Her decomposing hands clasped around my neck as she looked deep into my eyes.

"This is what you deserve," she whispered as she proceeded to pierce her teeth in my neck. Blood oozed from her festering mouth as I could feel the life draining away one drop at a time. This was what I deserved.

"Levi! Get up!" a sudden voice yelled.

I shot up from the cement floor gasping for air and looked up to see Atlas hovering over me. His iron bat was dangling between his exhausted fingertips, drooling gooey blood onto the floor next to me. Before I could even ask what was happening, the shrieking moans of the breached infected answered thoroughly.

"Get outside!" he urged, pulling my body up onto my yet-to-be-awoken legs.

Forgetting to take out my dailies, a crusty, gelatinous layer formed over top my eyes, making my vision dry and dreary. This made the situation increasingly maddening since I could hardly even see the erratic creatures encompassing me. Through heavy squinting, I counted nine pale bodies in the tight vicinities of the garage and spotted the collapsed gate where more would surely arise. Atlas had partaken in batting practice with two former construction workers, Rogers and Ms. Jordan had vacated the area and forced themselves a path to the nearest available vehicle guns blazing, and I had crawled myself into a corner where three and a half infected converged on me as if I was a blonde bombshell at the local gym.

Besides Britney, I had yet to see a pale one up close. In case you're wondering, let me explain something about them. The misconception is that these stereotypical George A. Romero-type zombies had overrun the world and what they were was in fact the complete opposite. Instead of slow, lethargic movements, these beasts were personified viruses that had claimed the human body and constant signs of rejection were clearly evident. From frenetic twitches to bone-snapping movements of the neck and limbs, it was clear that an inner battle was taking place. This instability was all the more reason to fear them. Fear them, as well as sympathize for them in the smallest, almost miniscule way. It was their eyes. Instead of being cloudy, dead balls of useless fat, any sign of life that remained in their bodies would be found in their eyes. They actually looked at you with an expression that was a hybrid of prolonged suffering and barbaric hunger. Three sets were on me—as well as a fourth that lost its duplicate—and this point marked the moment I lost my infected-killing virginity.

Reaching behind me for anything useful, my hands felt the shaft of a crowbar resting next to its previous owner. Indeed, this crowbar was the same weapon Jim Rhodes dropped without any hesitancy. With that guilt nicking at my insides, I lunged all my weight forward, thrusting myself onto my knees and jammed the snake-tongue edge into the closest one's forehead.

**Note**: You know all the movies and comic books that make killing someone look as easy as slicing a cake? What a bunch a crap.

The end got about two-three inches deep before getting caught on some type of gray matter. It continued to snap its jaw like everything was fine. The other two full bodies were reaching around the leader with greedy hands, snagging on my shoes and pants. I didn't have much time.

"Get…off!" I squeezed through my fastened jaw as I forced the body away with my foot. Luckily, I was able to push it away and slide my crowbar out from its skull, but what I didn't anticipate was the domino effect that would follow. The first collapsed into the second, the second into the half body, the half body into the third, who just so happened to be up against the elevated car held up by a rickety lift. With no power and the sketchy mechanisms that struggled to hold it up, the weight of the three bodies caused the car to tilt downwards and ultimately come crashing down. At a four-foot drop, the front of the car flattened the heads instantly and sent a splurge of blood in every which way. That, ladies and gentlemen, is what you call a first kill.

Before I knew it, the morning dew caressed my flushed cheeks as I was outside of the garage, sprinting for the getaway car. Atlas was in second place behind me, ducking and dodging the lunging bodies as if it were a sick, sadistic obstacle race. At the end of the lot, with the streamers guiding us like runway lights, a Pontiac Sunfire was being revved up, leaving momentarily whether or not we were in it.

"We're gonna make it, we're gonna make it!" yelled Atlas.

With Rogers in the driver seat and Ms. Jordan in the front passenger seat, the backseat was all that was left. Quickly approaching, Ms. Jordan opened her door to open the backseat door just seconds before we dove in.

"We made it? We actually made it!" Atlas said surprisingly.

Just as we made the familiar sounds of tires screeching, one stubborn biter was able to latch on and stick its head into Ms. Jordan's open door.

"Get off!" she yelled.

Instinctively, she slammed the door on its head, creating a cracking noise. Then again, then again, then again, until one last slam forced its head to explode. The blood and juices decorated the interior of the moving vehicle, as well as Ms. Jordan's eyes and open mouth. She spluttered and coughed nastily, absorbing poisonous blood into her taste buds and tear ducts.

"Fuck!!" she shrieked, rubbing her eyes numb. Blindly, she closed the door permanently and Rogers glanced over.

"Jordan, you hurt? What happened?"

She lifted her agonized face from her clutching hands and glared at him with reddening, swollen eyes.

"Just. Keep. Driving," she ordered.

Terrified, Rogers nodded his head and glued his eyes onto the road ahead of him. We managed to escape the city and besides Ms. Jordan, we were all profoundly lucky. The first day had come and gone and, for the first time, everything seemed all right. Well, for eight minutes.

Eight minutes later.

*WHAM*

I was kicked out from my daze—spent thinking of Electra and how surreal the out-of-place daydream had been—and sent back into the claustrophobic containments of the car with a vibrant pain striking through my shins. I groaned in pain and looked past the leather upholstery of the passenger seat to witness Ms. Jordan shivering painfully, whom had just thrown her body back like she had been electrocuted.

"Jesus, what was that for...?" I muttered, rubbing my bruised legs.

I was able to catch Ms. Jordan's reflection in the side view mirror, which had looked no less than a product of a distorted carnival mirror. Thick beads of sweat drenched her forehead, trailing through long lines of creases. Her nails dug into the armrests as if her life depended on it, though I was starting to think that was already a lost cause.

"Jordan, you alright?? Rogers asked. "You ain't looking so hot."

Atlas's mother had been huddled up in a collapsed ball pressed against her door, her eyes shielded from view. They watched drearily as the vast fields and clumps of countryside forestry passed by. Besides an occasional barn or convenience store, civilization was scarce. Good, she thought, glad that there would only be a minimal body count. This was the last sane thought that Ms. Jordan had.

"J-Jordan?" Rogers repeated. He reached over and pulled her shoulder towards him, revealing her morphed state.

"Holy Christ…" he gasped, the sight of her too unbearable to comprehend.

Blood seeped from her purple eyes, swallowed by a complex maze of varicose veins and bubbling blisters. She reeked of burnt flesh, the product of her blood boiling beneath her face. The pain became unbelievably excruciating that she couldn't contain it for another second, releasing an animalistic yelp as she clawed at her corrosive face.

Atlas awoke from his eight minute nap at the ear-ringing sound of what seemed to be a suffering dog. He laid his eyes on what had become of his mother.

"M-Mom?"

With no shred of humanity left, she whipped her head side to side, cracking her passenger window. She shook in her seat vehemently, being restrained by only the frayed seatbelt that was coming undone. White foam spewed from her snapping mouth and she shouted unrecognizable sounds.

Rogers fixed his dark-framed glasses and frightfully looked next to him. "What is wrong with you?" he asked fearfully. "Are you hurt?! Oh my god, are you…"

…I knew what was about to happen. Death was squished between us in the back seat and soon we would all be making a pit stop. I suppose there were worse ways to die. If I were to look on the bright side, I had outlived half, hell, more than half of the world's population. While any Asian would be disowned at the thought, anything above a 50% was considered a pass for me, thus a reasonable death.

You may be wondering why I seemed so comfortable with the idea of losing my life. Let me make something clear: I have never been an advocate for suicide since I believe it to be weak. I guess that's the kind of mindset one has when they find their mother's bleeding body in a bathtub at the age of five. However, I can understand the appeal of death. At this moment of time, driving down the road at a hundred and twenty miles per hour, I realized that I had virtually nothing to live for. A father that meant nothing more to me than a cold sore, a mother whose whereabouts are unknown, an ex-girlfriend who almost needed to file a restraining order on me, no friends, and a sis…the point is, I was starting to understand the desire of death. But, if I were to die, I was going to do so safely. I buckled my seatbelt and turned to Atlas, who had demonstrated the highest calibre of uncensored terror.

"Atlas? Put your seatbelt on," I ordered.

He looked to me in confusion and disbelief, trying to hold onto any piece of doubt that was left in his brain.

"But, I..." he stuttered.

"Do it now!!"

Atlas jammed the metal into the slot and let it click, his eyes remaining fixated on his infected mother.

"Mom? Mom!!"

Rogers was in complete shock as was his body, restricting his foot from lifting off of the gas pedal. He could only watch in horror as his superior officer transformed and became a monster that had an endless craving for any available flesh.

"God have mercy," he whispered.

He reached for his pistol to end Ms. Jordan's life, but it was too late. The fully infected officer attacked her fellow comrade by ripping away the tendons of his trapezius with her bare teeth, causing the nerves in Rogers's arm to spasm. His flow of nerve impulses was shattered and the abruption forced him to jerk the steering wheel sideways.

"Arrygghh!!!!" screeched Rogers as blood ejected from his open meat.

As both the life and blood drained out of him, he lost control of the Sunfire and the vehicle began to swerve recklessly across the desolate highway.

Atlas's head smacked on the side of the window and the blunt head trauma knocked him out, leaving only me to fully experience what had happened next.

The uncontrollable car swerved too deep and the buckling pressure forced the front tires to pop. I felt the rapid burst from underneath my feet and as the vehicle gained enough momentum, it was unable to remain on all fours and flipped over. It tumbled down the road with shards of glass and car parts flying in the air. Rogers's body launched out of his broken window and slid through the jagged opening, tearing off the skin of his face and torso. His body splattered on the road with the majority of his skin inside out and rolled up like a sleeve. The innocent officer's head smashed onto the pavement and right there he was pronounced dead.

Unfortunately, the accident was far from over. The flimsy, metal deathtrap flipped over and over like a blockbuster car crash and my flailing body repeatedly slammed against the inside. I smashed into the roof of the car, making such an impact that I could actually hear the sound of my bones cracking. All while I had been tumbling, Atlas was able to remain in his seat, but the initial collision that his skull made with the window had split open his eyebrow, creating a long, vertical gash down the length of his eye socket. The car door on his side dented inwards and with his arm completely vulnerable, it snapped like a twig.

His mother's head was sent straight into the windshield and pierced through. Her head had broken through the glass, yes, but her body still remained inside the spinning car. Her scalp scraped against the rough cement with each flip until it was unrecognizable mush.

The tumbling car finally came to a devastating halt after smashing into a pack of pine trees on the side of the road. The vehicle landed upside down and my fractured body dangled upside down like a strung-up animal carcass.

"A...Atl..." I tried to speak, but only coughed up blood from my overturned mouth. I was already fluttering in and out of consciousness and when I took in a breath of air, a shooting discomfort rippled through my chest. Most of my ribs were broken.

"H...He.….H..Hel.."

As the swelling of my torso constricted my breathing, more and more blood spilt from my mouth. The last sensation I had before blacking out was feeling a warm wetness above my stomach but below my skin. I faded with the realization that I had been hemorrhaging internally.

# 12. "You're welcome."

With his eyelids like two collapsed tents, Atlas fought with fierce weakness to keep them up. His mouth was riddled with imaginary sand and all the saliva he could gather from his dry, brittle reservoir wasn't even close to adequate. Everything felt like glass. He could only see through one eye. His physical ailments weren't of precedence, however, as he found himself tucked in a single bed in a candlelit bedroom.

"…W-wha..?"

Atlas couldn't keep his eyes open for more than a few seconds at a time before shutting down in exhaustion. So, he had to make each waning glance count. What he saw: A white door with a gold brass handle…a painting to his left of a sinking ship…a large metal machine with plastic tubes running from a pump…my comatose body in the adjacent bed…

"You survived," an aged voice called from the doorway.

Atlas creaked his head to the left and through fading vision saw a woman in her late seventies smirking at him. She had hair the colour of steel that was tied into a braid slung over her shoulder. Her face was full of wrinkles yet a fresh youthfulness was embedded beneath. Through his good eye, all it took was one glance to know that this was a woman that meant well, yet wasn't above knocking some heads whenever needed. Atlas had so many questions, but first, the basics.

"Wh…where am I?"

"My farm," she replied. "My son and a few others were out looking for survivors in the area when they came across some terrible wreckage. They saved ya and brought ya to me just in time. Your friend? That's a different story."

"He's…not…my friend," Atlas mumbled.

"Well whatever he is, boy's in serious condition. He's broken nearly a dozen ribs and sliced open an artery as well as his liver. I was able to stop the bleeding for the most part, but there ain't nothing much more that I can do. His breath is shallow and don't seem to breathe properly by himself which suggests one of his lungs may be punctured."

"For an old bag...you seem to...know your shit."

"This old bag is the reason your radius isn't sticking out of your skin so watch your tone, boy. I sewed you up, I can take that back."

To his amazement, Atlas looked down and saw his arm in a sling pressed tightly against his chest. The pain was moot, however, as he was too busy thinking about something else.

"...In the wreckage," Atlas began, "did...did they find anyone else?"

The old lady's head lowered, candlelight casting a morbid shadow over her tilted features.

"Two bodies, yeah. They were...too disfigured to determine what they looked like. All that my son told me was that they was wearing police uniforms. You close with them?"

Atlas rested his head back onto his doubled pillow and exhaled.

"...No."

She may have been old but she was far from oblivious. His pain was hidden in plain view and made it clear that he needed some sort of sympathy.

"Well, you're welcome to stay as long as you see fit," she offered. "We've taken in more than twenty others, most of your age actually. When we brought you in, a lot of kids seem to have known you."

She waited for a response that never came.

"I'm Blanche, by the way," she greeted with a veiny hand extended to him.

He looked at her and gently stroked his blind eye, which had been covered in a thick layer of gauze.

"Well, Blanche, do you mind...telling me why I can't see...out of my right eye?"

"You received a rather large gash down your eye. You have a scratched cornea but fortunately no permanent damage other than a rather gnarly scar."

Atlas let out a wheeze of a chuckle. "Too bad...eye patches look badass..."

Blanche smirked with a lop-sided grin. "Get some rest. In a couple of hours, we'll show you 'round the place, get you meeting the rest of the folk. Sound good?"

Atlas hated nothing more than being talked down to. It made him feel inferior, like an idiotic child. But she did save his life and no matter what he thought, that did count for something. What made it so difficult for Atlas is that he had to put his fate in the hands of someone else, something that he had seldom done. You see, what separated the two of us was that I didn't rely on others because I couldn't. He didn't rely on others because he was too proud to.

"…Fine."

She gave him a polite nod and walked out of the room but paused again in the doorframe.

"Atlas?"

He squinted over at her.

"You're welcome."

She left, leaving Atlas befuddled. Not only by everything that has unfolded, but also the fact that she knew his name without asking. The mistrust took hold before another bout with sleep commenced.


Seven hours later, Atlas took his first steps up from the bed and ventured out of his homemade hospital room. The sun was a dull burn on his skin, shining a 5 o'clock haze through the four-pane windows. Outside of his room was a stout hallway with five portraits on either side, staring Atlas down with judging eyes and posed smiles. The end of the hall had branched out to the kitchen, a cramped square with a glossy, mosaic floor and cupboards in a thrust-style staging. The living room sat next to it, a simple arrangement of two angled couches and a rocking chair aimed at the clunky television. A door that led to their vast, seventy-acre farmland was all that bridged the two sections. At a slow, almost dreamlike pace, Atlas emerged into the amber-lit area and was met by the swaying hips of a lively, red-haired woman whistling along to the tunes of the fifties.

Slightly disoriented by the eerie normality, Atlas cleared his throat to address his entrance.

"Ehh hmm," he announced.

The red-haired lady spun around with the skirt of her floral dress following with a twirl.

"Oh my, you're awake!" she spoke joyously. "How wonderful!"

She scuttled over to the active record player and lowered the volume. Now revealing the front of her body, Atlas realized that she was incredibly pregnant.

"Blanche didn't warn me you'd be up and moving so soon or I would've saved you some beet soup! Boy, you must think I'm the worst host, don't you?" she assumed, the hue of her cheeks matching her hair. "Not to worry, I'll whip up a new batch! God knows you kids won't let it go to waste."

As she returned to the kitchen, Atlas stood stiffly, too baffled to speak. Her mother-like charm and compassion was a foreign sight that he didn't simply welcome with open arms. In the mere seconds of meeting, she had shown more love to him than the entirety of his deceased mother's lifetime. Frankly, it was off-putting, seeming completely unnatural. The barbaric nature of society that unfolded just days prior didn't assist the situation either. This lady seemed like Atlas was nothing more than a houseguest spending the night rather than a fellow survivor in an apocalyptic world.

She obviously noticed this and gave him a sympathetic smile.

"I'm sure this seems a tad odd, huh? I've been told that I can come off a little strong. My name is Cecilia. And you? You must have a bundle of questions."

He gently grabbed his slung arm.

"…Atlas," he responded, his voice cautious and low.

"I'm sorry?" she asked.

"My name is Atlas."

"Ahh, yes! Atlas…what a lovely name. Well, Atlas, what would you like to know?"

He thought for a moment, sifting through the thick bushel of confusion that littered his mind.

"Where am I?" he asked for the second time.

"Why, you're on Blanche's farm! It's been in her family for--"

"I know that," he said, irritated. "But where am I?"

Cecilia frowned. "I'm confused. What do y—"

"The city!" Atlas raised his voice. "Am I in the city? The country? How long have I been out? Are the dead still walking?"

Cecilia began to cower, tilting her head down like a child that had done wrong. Atlas looked at this woman, this poor, innocent woman, and retreated.

"…I'm sorry. After seeing what happened out there, coming back to this…normality? It just seems like one sick joke, you know? I, uh, I shouldn't have yelled at you."

Immediately, her frown receded and her jolly, bountiful smile stretched cheek to cheek.

"Awe, honey, don't you worry," she assured. "The rest of the kids are just like you. Even though it's early on, all that death'll certainly have an effect on you. This place just takes some getting used to."

Atlas glanced out the kitchen window above the sink and absorbed the rustling leaves and summer breeze.

"It's…pretty nice. Especially for you and the—"

He pointed at her bloated stomach.

"—The baby?" she replied.

Atlas smirked. "Well, you can never be sure until the woman says it herself. I learned that one the hard way."

Cecilia giggled. "I can assure you that I am very pregnant and very overdue. I was already a week late before the craziness started to happen. Felix and I were on our way to the hospital when all those poor people dropped dead. Figured the hospitals had more than enough to worry about."

"Felix?" Atlas wondered.

"My husband," she clarified. "Blanche's son. He was actually the one that found you and your friend in the wreckage! Him and one of the boys out there, I think. He's out patching up the barn if you'd like to go say hi!"

"I might just go do that," Atlas thought aloud. "But wait a second… you've been mentioning these kids a lot. Who're you talking about?"

Cecilia frowned again, but this time it was out of astonishment. "Wait, you don't know?"

"Know what?"

She smiled to herself and gestured to the back door. "Why don't you go take a look for yourself?"

Atlas nodded and slid on his pair of torn-up sneakers resting by the porch. He pushed the screen door aside and before he took a step out, he hesitated.

"...Can you keep an eye on him? On Levi?"

Cecilia nodded. "Of course. Is he a friend of yours? Your brother?"

"Just please keep an eye on him."

"I'll let you know if anything changes," she said with another one of her sympathetic smiles.

Atlas nodded with gratitude and headed outside. The first thing that his eyes fixated on weren't the roaming livestock or the towering trees or the alarmingly red barn, it was the yellow school bus parked in the field. The very same bus that left him, Britney and I stranded at the school.

"Son of a bitch," he breathed.

Nearly thirty teenagers of all shapes and sizes filled the farmland, taking part in various activities. Anthony, Jake, and Matt from track were throwing a football to one another. Brienne from chemistry was reading *Game of Thrones,* slowly swaying side to side on a tire swing attached to the branch of an oak tree. Teresa and Avery, the picture-perfect couple at our now extinct high school were playing fetch with a scruffy-looking dog, their faces gleaming. The picturesque lifestyle contrasted nicely with Atlas's broken, battered and bruised reality. Then, as if it were one simultaneous snap of the neck, the twenty-plus teenagers had their eyes on Atlas. A wave of sympathy nearly crushed his body all over again.

"Oh my god you're alive!" exclaimed Trevor from math class.

"Atlas you poor boy!" Stacey sympathized, a caked-up blondie.

"What happened to you?"

"Most of the others were bit!"

"We didn't see you make it out of the school!"

"How did you find us?"

It became too overbearing. Atlas had many friends, yet he had already come to terms with the fact that they were either dead or that he would never see them again. Seeing them again was like a reintroduction into their lives and that wasn't something that Atlas found desirable. With great reluctance, he told them about how he survived the spontaneous plane crash, Britney's death as well as her transformation, and how he came to receive his injuries. Unsurprisingly, he opted to leave out the part about his mother.

"—and then I woke up here. The in-between part is a little hazy though and Levi is in a coma. Does anyone know who brought us here? I think they deserve…"

Then, an individual emerged from the barn that made Atlas's skin crawl. His pupils constricted and his brows furrowed. Steam flushed through his ears and his only operable fist clenched into a cement-like ball at the sight of the one person he felt had deserved a slow and agonizing death along with the other half of the world: Josh.

"…H-hey Atlas…" he stood starstruck.

All he had to do was let them on the bus. That was what had been swirling around in Atlas's head as he stood silently. The single move was a catalyst that not only caused the deaths of Britney, Rogers and his mother… but potentially me: Someone that he barely knew and might not ever know because of one selfish act. This was enough for Atlas to start moving toward Josh.

"Listen…" Josh began. "Everything was so hectic, ya know? That bus was way too full and there were dead bodies everywhere. Don't think that what I did was to—"

*SMACK*

With the crack of the cartilage in Josh's nose, Atlas let out a heavy sigh.

"You…you broke my nose!" Josh yelled.

"It's an improvement," Atlas remarked.

He towered over Josh with unrelenting fortitude, a look in his eyes that was ready to kill. Punch after punch, the ground became increasingly red and a crowd grew of fans and protestors, both without the motivation to try and stop it.

"You worthless *PUNCH* piece of *PUNCH* shit!" screamed Atlas as he unleashed his one-handed fury on Josh's splitting face. Finally Atlas was able to release his emotions in the only way he knew how. He had been in more fights than either of us could count—before and after the outbreak—but this was substantially different. Every punch he threw was soaked in agony that had been building up for years, never taking a moment to stop. From the lack of respect that was thrust upon him to the delinquent label branded across his chest to a life filled with exasperating conflicts with his mother, this fight was the release of it all, and Josh didn't stand a chance.

"That's ENOUGH!" a harsh voice ordered from behind.

Atlas's bloodied fist wavered as he locked eyes with a storming Blanche.

"What on earth is going on here??!"

Atlas rose to his feet and looked at her, but his vision had started to become wet and murky. He touched his bandaged eye with his fingertips to feel a steady stream of blood pour out of his ripped stitches.

"You don't *huff* realize the kind of person *huff* you brought into your house," informed Atlas as he compressed his open gash. "He's nothing but a selfish, inconsiderate, damn near murderous piece of horseshit."

The silence that encapsulated the crowd was like a ring that was being smelted by Blanche's furious eyes. "You're calling him the murderer? You've beaten the boy half to death!"

Atlas looked down at Josh's spluttering body and then to the frightened crowd and then back to Blanche.

"You don't understand," he insisted. "If it wasn't for him—"

"—You'd be dead! That boy and my son were the ones that helped pull you out of the wreckage!"

It was the moment where he knew that he was in the wrong, but was just too stubborn to try and find any sense of redemption.

"That's…that's not the point!" Atlas hesitated. "He doesn't deserve…"

"Enough of this. I'm taking you back to your room and you will stay there for the rest of the night until you've come to your senses. Cecilia will re-apply your stitches while I clean up *your* mess."

Atlas was infuriated. He couldn't understand why no one had sided with him.

"Look, lady, you don't have any right telling me what to do."

"Well I just did," she snapped back. "Now go."

Wearing the hefty cloak of an antagonist, Atlas left with a final spit to the ground and weakly stumbled back to the house.

The sun was setting and Atlas was cursing.

"Shit ow! Ow! OW!" he yelped as Cecilia crossed in another stitch.

"My god, you're worse than my three-year-old niece. At least with her all it takes is a Kit-Kat to shut her up. Would that work on you?"

"I'd be just dandy if you didn't shove pins in my eye! Besides, how do you know what you're doing?"

"Farming mostly," said Cecilia. "Spending time with Blanche, you pick up a thing or two when it comes to first-aid. To be honest, you're the first human I've ever worked on!"

"Oh that's great to hear," sighed Atlas.

"Alright, last one...aaaanndd... done! Good as new!"

She handed him an oval mirror and he took a look at himself. There was now a blue, frayed lining inside his large vertical gash that seared with sensitivity after each blink.

"Thanks..." he muttered.

Cecilia set down the small pair of scissors and crossed her legs. She took a moment to ponder, allowing the rumbling of my breathing machine to fill the void.

"So," she finally began, "you going to tell me what happened?"

"What happened is that I hurt someone that deserved so much worse."

She sighed and gave him that downward glance the way mothers do. "Atlas, violence is never the answer. Especially now! We live in a time where we need each other more than ever before."

Atlas chuckled almost maniacally at her obliviousness. "You know... your arrogance would be cute if it wasn't so sad. If God, Mother Nature, fucking Cthulhu, whoever was behind this had wanted us to work as a team, it would've been because of some kind of multi-national terrorist attack. That way we could've held hands in a circle and sang kumbaya. But instead they eradicated half of the world's population because they understood how undeniably screwed up we are. There's no fixing who we are, just preventing it from getting much, much worse. How can we work together when we are the problem?"

Cecilia averted her gaze, implying that she had lost. Atlas stood up from his chair and began to exit.

"I appreciate your concern," he said on his way out.

As he shut the door, Cecilia looked over to my comatose body and began to tear up. She grabbed my hand and shivered.

"You poor boys," she whispered. "What happened to you?"

## 13. "Unless it's in real life, I sincerely hope to never see you again."

I was comfortably numb. A euphoric sensation trickled through my veins like a buzzing intoxication. My eyelids were dormant and though my sense of touch was temporarily vacant, a tingling breeze stroked my face, indicating that I had been outside. Wherever I was, however, was not something that I cared to know. For the first time that I could remember, my mind was weightless. There wasn't a scolding burden that both compressed my skull and constantly fought to claw its way out. There was only the simplicity of nothingness. Whatever happened before and whatever will happen were two sides of a spectrum that had ceased to exist. All that had happened and all that will ever happen was simply then. Deep, I know.

"Levi? It's time to wake up."

A voice that was velvety smooth had oozed into my ears, causing me to salivate. I opened my eyes and was immediately blinded by a scorching ball of light levitating above. The lone shadow produced was a silhouette of a girl whose head had blocked the slightest fraction of light, making her identity unknown. The only thing to grab hold of was her hypnotic voice that was eerily familiar. Like an old tape gathering dust at the back of a jukebox, its foot-tapping groove was unveiled once more.

"Who…Mom?"

The silhouette laughed. No sound escaped her lips; only the slight vibrating of her shoulders had been visible.

"No, silly," she replied. "It's me."

A small, angel-like hand produced out from the shadows and into the light. It reached out for me and I took hold, lifting me up onto my jelly-filled legs.

"I've missed you," spoke Electra.

The sun bounced off of her skin like a mirror, making it nearly impossible to look at her; my eyes were not worthy. Her chestnut-roasted hair had a single braid tied along her temple that reached to the base of her skull. Her eyes were a burning brown, almost cinnamon colour that complimented her fiery lips. She wore a white lace dress and was barefoot, allowing her toes to curl into the grass. Being in her presence was surreal in every sense of the word.

"How…Where am I?" I asked in a drunken slur.

She leaned in closely and stroked both of her forefingers on my biceps.

"You're home," she whispered before pulling my face into hers. Her lips pressed firmly onto mine in a fierce, yet passionate fashion. Her tongue gently licked the backside of my teeth, causing me to grin stupidly.

The happiness was short-lived, however, and the reality kicked in.

"Wait a second…I was in a car," I pulled away and began to remember, "and there was an accident…and I remember tumbling… rolling and rolling and rolling until…"

I stopped myself out of confusion and gently placed my flattened palms onto my stomach, feeling no abnormalities. I lifted my shirt and saw no bruises or bulging bones.

"That can't be right…unless…crap, am I dead?"

"No, Levi. This is a dream."

Sceptical, I pinched my arm and felt the tiny pain in full effect.

"This certainly doesn't feel like a dream," I remarked.

Electra smiled. "It's a dream that you don't have to wake up from. It's a place where we can be together. Finally."

She embraced me warmly and pressed her cheek against my beating heart. My nostrils were filled with the smell of her natural perfume, a smell that made me want to fall in love all over again. Unfortunately, I was still sceptical.

"Electra…" I hesitated, "believe me when I say that I want nothing more than to be with you. You make me feel…well, simply that! You give me the chance to actually care about someone other than myself.

But still, this just doesn't seem right. The real you, wherever you may be, wouldn't even attempt to acknowledge me after the incident."

She took a step away and dipped her head down to deliver a sultry, one-eyebrow-raised kind of look.

"This is the real me, ya loser," she said confidently.

Then she stepped inwards, closer than before. Her firm breasts pressed against my body and she leaned in until her bottom lip grazed my ear lobe.

"—and the real me wants to fuck you. Right now."

Before I could react, she pushed me to the grassy ground and leaped on top of me.

Then, well, you get the idea.


I sat up after three back-to-back rounds of lovemaking and looked down at my exhausted crotch.

"Boy, if this does turn out to be a dream, we're going to have one serious mess to deal with back home."

Electra rose from the grass and placed her chin on my naked shoulder. "You were always so awkward after we did anything," she reminisced. "I remember the first time I took of my shirt and you thanked me."

I exhaled laughter, which soon faded, and that irreparable uncertainty pulsated back to life. I stood up and listened to a nearby bird chirping.

"What is it?" she asked.

"This…this isn't the world that we live in. Well, that we *attempt* to live in. I like it here but I have moral obligations! Duties!"

"Duties?" she repeated sceptically.

"Yes," I replied shakily.

"Listen, Levi, you are truly wonderful, but you're not the stick-your-neck-out kinda guy. What did you do that made your life above the billions that died?"

"Well, uhm, I saved Britney!"

"—only for her to be brutally killed minutes later," reminded Electra.

"Yeah, well, Atlas needs me! We don't really know each other, b-but he needs my help just as much as I need his! Hell, he could be injured or dead or in the same place as me—wherever that is—but there's this obligation to myself that I need to be certain. I don't know why but I just do."

Slightly annoyed, Electra stood up to face me, our naked bodies inches away from each other, and looked down at her feet. Then, with a sound of crackling thunder and the unlawful rawness of godlike eradication of the earth, the ground split between us and our surroundings receded into ash. The air became distastefully gloomy and morose. With each blink, the world around me contorted and crumbled further and further until I was no longer in the forest but in the middle of an overturned street in the downtown metropolis. Buildings that once were ceased to exist and in their place laid mounds of charred bones of men, women and children. What I first believed to be snow was actually ash; the remnants of the sacrificed bodies.

"This is the real world," whispered Electra. "Not what you would expect it to look like after only two months."

"Two months?" I replied in disbelief. "How is that even possible?"

"What will happen is a tragedy, yes, but it's one that you can avoid if you stay with me. This?" she said, gesturing to the scorched graveyard of a city. "This is the real world. What you have the chance to experience is the *ideal* world."

She stepped in and just like that, the earth sealed itself back into the perfect summer day as if nothing had happened. Everything had returned to normal, except for the goose bumps littered across my skin. Those had remained.

"If you still have doubts, I have one last thing to show you," said Electra.

Her sparkling body spun around with her hair following like a silky, bronze cape and she wandered into the trees. Then, with a single blink, she was gone.

"Electra?" I called out. "Where'd you go?"

I put on my eerily immaculate white T-shirt and jeans and chased after her.

The nature around me was precisely chaotic. Everything grew in such an erratic pattern—the mossy bed, a fallen log, and dead leaves sprinkled among the living—and there was this atmosphere to the place that felt a few breaths too heavy. Like a sauna, my chest felt compressed and drained as I chased after her. I didn't stop to check, but I'm fairly certain that I passed by a red hair bow dangling on a branch.

I reached the end of the tree line and suddenly the new world I had only just been acquainted with morphed into something utterly foreign. The tide from the ocean splashed up and down onto white, sandy beaches. Crashing waves plummeted to the tiny grains of sand and pebbles, creating bubbly foam that quickly sizzled away into the scorching sun. Two children in their bathing suits chased down the shoreline to obtain their respective affection. Siblings took turns flying a kite in the shape of a butterfly that contained each colour on the spectrum, the water never ceasing to lick at their ankles. Dozens of families and couples lounged on the sandy beach, each sharing a moment that would forever be glued into their scrapbook of life. It was as if I stepped into the 1920's, my eyes visualizing a sepia-toned world where only certain things had deviated. Like the light blue waves, the vibrantly black rocks near the basin of a cliff, and especially, the cherry red bikini that Electra was wearing. She wore lipstick to match and her lips peeled back to reveal blindingly white teeth.

"You cannot deny how beautiful this place is. And it will never change. This is where we can start again and have a new life. Together."

She was right. Everything about it was so unbelievably perfect. So why was I so unbelievably hesitant?

Electra recognized my all too familiar scepticism. "What is it? Why can't I convince you?"

The truth flickered on my tongue. I didn't want to speak out and shatter this place, but I simply couldn't contain it anymore.

"Because…because I don't trust you! You say all these things about us, but they're all just a ruse to keep me here. I know you, Electra. You would never say these things. They are just all the things that I've wanted you to say."

"You're wrong," she told me. "I've always felt this way about you."

"Yeah? Well what about when you…you know, the *incident*?" I recalled. "How could you have done that and truly believe the things you're saying?"

"That…it was all a mistake! I never meant to hurt you."

I nodded and let out a chuckle. "No, just put me through thirty hours of court-mandated therapy. Did you know they were considering shock treatment? They thought I was too unstable. Well, they weren't wrong."

Her forehead frowned into a look of empathetic sadness. "I didn't know…Levi, what can I do to make you believe me?"

I didn't answer. Instead, I looked at the obsidian rocks and the matching cliff above it. I then looked at her and when I looked down, I saw the crowd of people on the beach. I was now on top of the cliff and she had the exact same look on her face.

I sighed. "…I've seen both sides of you, Electra."

"What do you mean?"

"The first night of the outbreak, I had a dream. Well, not really a dream…I wasn't asleep. More like a vision, as cheesy as that sounds. Kind of like this one. Except, here, you're happy, caring, compassionate, loving…all of which are lies. In the other one, however, I got to see you for who you really are. And, well, you literally ripped my flesh away while I was strung up. If that's not the most symbolic shit you've ever heard than I don't know what is. You were…horrible to me. I am not deserving of true and absolute love, I know that, but I at least deserve the bare minimum; something you failed to reach."

I stepped out and approached the edge of the cliff, facing the vast ocean beneath me. "You said that I have no attachments to the real world. No friends, no family, nothing. Well, you're absolutely right. But I know deep down that I'm not finished with my time there. I still have things I need to do and I'll admit that I don't really know what those things are. But whatever they are, they're enough to convince me that this is not where I belong…just yet."

I turned my head around and saw that there were tears brimming in her eyes. She finally spoke up. "Levi, if you jump, you will die and you will never see me again. Is that what you want?"

I turned my head back. "Unless it's in real life, I sincerely hope to *never* see you again."

Then I jumped.

As I fell, the same sensation as when I first arrived here had returned. Loud pockets of air blared into my ears as I drew closer and closer to the jagged rocks penetrating from the earth. Before I could hit the ground, my blurred vision was pulled toward a group of unidentifiable individuals on the beach. To this day I still am not certain, but I believe that Atlas was among them, playing an acoustic guitar and, most surprisingly, with a smile. I couldn't make out the rest of the individuals except for a few distinct features. There was a boy with dark-framed glasses and hair the colour of champagne. Two girls were across from him. The first girl by Atlas's side had blindingly white albino hair that sparkled like a fresh snowfall. The other girl had light golden brown locks and for some unknown reason, this other girl was different, almost hypnotic. That was the last thing I saw before I imagined the sharp rocks plunge through my insides.


Atlas was lying on his bed adjacent to mine, arms folded beneath his head, when I began to convulse.

"...Wha?" he said, looking over to me.

He got up from the bed and went to mine. Getting a clear look at me, he realized that I had been foaming at the mouth.

"Blanche! Cecilia! Hell, anybody!"

Cecilia was the first to enter, followed shortly by her mother-in-law.

"Oh my god," breathed Cecilia.

"What's happening to him?!" Atlas asked frantically.

"He's going into shock," explained Blanche. "Either it's from internal bleeding or a brain injury that we didn't see. His heart is stopping."

"What do we do? What do we do??!" cried Atlas.

For the first time, Blanche was at a loss.

"I...there might not be anything—"

"You shut your wrinkled mouth right now!" Atlas halted. "You're a doctor, for God's sake! There must be something!"

"W-we have those old paddles out in the garage!" remembered Cecilia. "They might work."

"His ribs are too fragile to take the shock. It could cause further harm!" informed Blanche.

"Further harm than death?? Go get the goddamn paddles!"

With no other option, Blanche and Cecilia rushed out of the room. Atlas leaned in closer to me.

"Listen, I don't know you that well, alright? I shouldn't be having to deal with this kind of shit. But, here we are! Now, I stuck my neck out for you and saved you from that class and because of that, we got in the plane crash. Saving *you* nearly killed *me*! So don't you dare go out on me! Don't make that worth nothing! Wake up! WAKE UP!"

Honestly, I don't know how. Maybe God was doing me a solid or someone wanted me to keep going but as the demands escaped Atlas's lips, my eyes opened. I gasped for breath and choked on the tube lodged down my throat. Half-shocked, Atlas pulled the slimy, two-foot tube out and finally I could breathe.

"Holy shit," he said frightfully. "It actually worked."

Everything hurt. My bones were broken glass and my lungs felt like tissue. I was in searing, unbearable agony, but above it all, I was back. Through a painful effort, I slowly reached my hand into my pants and felt my crotch.

I rallied up enough strength to wheeze out a chuckle. "…Knew it…"

## 14. "Yeast flavoured cat piss. My favourite."

"Get off your ass and keep walking!"

I rather enjoyed the mud. It was a refreshing bath that allowed myself to momentarily forget about the stabbing pain rippling through my torso. Then my eyes opened and through my dirt-speckled eyelashes I could see Blanche lurking over me.

"You enjoying yourself?" she asked.

"We've been…walking…for hours…" I huffed.

She looked down at her watch. "It's been twelve minutes. And you ain't no more than twenty feet from the porch."

"…Spectacular…"

She stuck her hand out and pulled my rigid body upwards. "Boy, you've just had yourself a terrible ordeal. Somethin' a helluva lotta people would've been dead three times over. But don't you be thinkin' you some miracle 'cause you ain't. I've fixed up people with mangled legs and people that've taken a gunshot to the twat."

"Glad your…bedside manner…is up to par…" I said.

"Now, you ain't my kin but I was unfortunate enough to mend your sorry ass, meaning you are my responsibility. I can't be havin' sad little farts on my land while there's the demented runnin' amok. So until you can walk and shit and jack off by yourself, don't be giving me attitude, boy. Now get up."

That was the first day. Now, there's no point to disclose every single second of my four-night stay at the farm. My days consisted of shallow breaths and painful shits. Blanche continued on with her torturous ways. It wasn't until the fourth day that the storyline started to become enthralling.

It was around 1 PM when Atlas was taking a stroll around the lot. He had finished dinner in record time, as he couldn't handle another minute in the limelight. To the average, uninteresting majority of teenagers that occupied the farm, Atlas was a god among men. He was like a star soldier returning home to the swooning girls. The girls adored him. The guys wanted to be him. And, on any other circumstance, Atlas would've swallowed that love and affection whole. But after the car crash and the death of his mother, he wanted nothing more than the quiet serenity of the dying world. This was interrupted as Atlas was passing by a dingy-looking shed and an arrow grazed by his face before puncturing into the rotting wood.

"Jesus!" he yelped in shock.

Atlas spun around and caught Felix holding a raised bow in his right hand.

"Sorry, I didn't see you there!" he apologized.

"I'm sorry, I didn't think I had to watch out for fucking arrows flying about," sighed Atlas as he tucked fallen hair back into the mangled mess atop his head.

"I thought I was all alone out here," Felix explained. "Usually the kids will hold up in that farm until they're licking their plates clean. It's amazing how much a kid can eat."

Atlas nodded out of obligation. Clearly this conversation was going nowhere.

"Well, I'll let you get back to your Robin Hood…ing," he said, turning to walk in the other direction. Not three steps were taken before voiceless, unwavering sobs pulled Atlas back. He turned around to see Felix hunched over as if he were going to vomit.

"Uhm," he hesitated, "was it something I said?"

"No," he croaked. "I just—I just don't know how *sniff* how I'm supposed to raise a k-kid in a world *sniff* like this."

To Atlas there was only one thing worse than seeing a girl cry: seeing a grown man cry.

"Well, uhh, shit…" he muttered, trying to form words of sympathy. "I mean, you got yourself a pretty sweet farm! There's lots of land and plenty of food and you'll never have to worry about being snuck up on, ya know? And who knows, there might even be a cure being sent out right this very minute."

Felix scoffed. "Yeah? You mean, before those things kick down our fences? Sure, we're pretty far out from the majorly populated areas, but whatever's infecting them spreads like wildfire and we're just waiting to burn. Cecilia is overdue and ever since she showed me that little pink cross I've been pulling out my hair just thinking about being a dad. And now this? It's not fair!"

He started to cry again, this time more violently and now accompanied with sound. Atlas reluctantly stumbled over and patted his back with his good arm. "Don't be so down in the dumps about it. Parenting is easy! Do you know how many books they've got for this kinda' shit?"

"How to raise a baby in a zombie apocalypse?" Felix asked sarcastically.

"Hey, if Kim Kardashian can publish a selfie book, anything is possible."

Felix chuckled. "Heh, yeah I guess you're right."

"On to more pressing matters," Atlas said, changing the subject. "What's the deal with the bow and arrow? Planning on going up to those biters and telling them how they've failed this city?"

He flipped the bow over so it rested on his open palm and looked down at it. "My pops used to take me out hunting with this when I was a kid. We never really talked—ya know, classic conservative father butting heads with the liberal son—but hunting was the one thing we could actually do together. He'd always say that the bow and arrow was the best weapon for both stealth and precision. You won't scare off an animal and there's none of that kickback. I'd then go on to argue its efficiency with reloading, which he would go on to reply with, "then don't miss"."

Felix walked over to the painted target on the shed and pulled out the arrow that was dug into the near-gaping centre.

"You see, Blanche never liked guns on the farm. We would only be allowed to use a captive bolt gun for the cattle and that doesn't even require bullets. My only concern was if there were any foxes sneaking up on our livestock or, heaven forbid, an intruder. They're not going to be scared of a pointy stick and some string. We're in the middle of nowhere but eventually they'll come so the more practice the better."

"And you really think that'll be enough?" questioned Atlas.

"Absolutely not. We need more weapons. And more food because we're…" he stopped himself.

"Because what?"

Felix became beet red and avoided Atlas's curious, criticizing gaze. He had accidently revealed an issue that would prove to be just as devastating as the infected.

"I shouldn't have said that," he squeaked.

"Tell me," Atlas ordered.

"…We had a lot of food stored up. In case there was a snowstorm or a tornado, ya know, stuff like that. It was meant to last us months. Now that we're feeding a classroom of kids three square meals a day and then some, we've been reduced to scraps."

"How's that even possible?" Atlas asked with an increasingly resounding voice. "This is like the fifth day!"

"Like I said, it's amazing how much a kid can eat," Felix muttered.

Atlas paced erratically, trying to gather his thoughts. He wasn't mad that they were running out of food, he was mad that he had been categorized alongside those selfish, undeserving teenagers that weren't worthy to know the truth.

"Well, now what?" he asked impatiently. "Do we go on runs to try and scavenge Doritos and Twinkies from the local gas station?"

"That would be swell, if we actually had the weapons to do so. We'd be torn apart out there," Felix replied.

"You got any ideas, Mr. Optimism?"

"In fact, I do," informed Felix. "There's talk of a place that is free of infection. A place built for tens of thousands of refugees to live comfortably. I've heard that it's called…Safehaven, I think."

"What a lovely fairy tale," Atlas said caustically. "You'll have to make sure to tell your baby that story when he or she pops out."

"Just listen to me for a second," Felix urged. "Obviously this is the go-to thought in any story similar to ours. The only difference is that this place is real."

"And how do you know that, exactly?"

"Because I can prove it," he replied confidently.

Atlas sat down on an overturned garbage can and gestured to Felix. "I'm listening."

"I worked as a civil engineer for Davidson and Perks. Ever heard of them? Of course you have. They've basically had a stranglehold on the architecture market for nearly half a century. I'll admit, my job wasn't as exciting as the rest, but I had a high enough reputation to occasionally be informed on some of the hush-hush business that took place. One of the things that I'd heard is that in the sixties, both the Canadian and the American government hired Davidson and Perks to lead a project that was a direct result of the Cuban Missile Crisis. They wanted a place that was safe from any type of nuclear attack and to do so it needed to be somewhere that was completely off of the radar. Their best bet was to look to the water. Why? Because to this day, ninety-five percent of oceans remain unexplored. They found a substantially large island off the coast of Vancouver and in less than a decade it was a fully functional city. Now, I haven't heard much about it in a couple years, which suggests that it's done its job."

Atlas was dumbfounded. "That's…there's no way. This is way too *Bioshock* for my liking. There's no way! How could it go without being detected by a satellite or a plane or a flipping submarine?"

"It has a no fly zone encompassing it. There are certain laws that prohibit submarines and boats from entering the jurisdiction. There are even jammers that can mess with a ship's system and force it back. And the satellites, well, who do you think controls NORAD?"

Atlas shook his head. It was a perfect idea, thus making it completely and utterly flawed. Still, it was intriguing.

"…Even if there was this supposed Safehaven, wouldn't we have heard about it by now? Like, wouldn't they have made some sort of broadcast?"

"Even with the 50/50 outbreak, there's probably close to four billion left on this planet. Do you really think that they'd send an invitation to everyone? The island couldn't be bigger than Maui," Felix reasoned.

"So then who the hell is there?" Atlas asked.

"The rich and the geniuses. You'd either pay your way in or prove your intellectual capabilities."

"Great," Atlas said in a snarky tone. "We're 0 for 2 in those departments."

"Atlas, there's probably only a million people in the world that know about this place. The fact that *we* know gives us a huge advantage. Trust me, they wouldn't turn down kids."

Atlas rested his hands behind his head and whistled.

"That's one hell of a plan, Felix. I'll certainly give you that. Just one question: Why haven't you told anyone about it? We could be halfway there by now!"

Felix frowned. "I'm a civil engineer and my wife is a botanist who is nine months pregnant. We currently have twenty-six children to take care of—one of whom is barely able to walk—and we have nothing more than this bow and a couple of farming tools to defend ourselves. You do the math."

He slid the shed door open and placed his bow on a hook next to his quiver. "I'll tell everyone when it comes to that. There's no need to cause any panic until we're ready for it. Until then, just keep doing what you're doing and don't tell anyone."

Felix started to make his way back into the house to his wife when Atlas spoke up again.

"You said that there's barely any food left," he reminded. "Is there anything that we have a lot of?"

"Booze," he said without stopping. "Lots of booze."

While Atlas was busy contemplating about our potential salvation, I had taken it upon myself to sneak off from the gruelling rehab and found a large oak tree to sit against. I could've ventured off into the barn for lunch but the problem was that there were people there. People that I had never seen before looked at me with awe and uncertainty, as survival was unheard of in my condition. I wasn't much of a social butterfly before all this; more like a social pariah. So the life-altering injuries and cane didn't really help my cause.

No more than two minutes after settling in did a silhouette darken the light bouncing off my closed eyelids. I opened them—half-expecting Electra—only to see a grade eleven brunette who bit her lip nervously. You have no idea how sick I was of that innocent, lip bite act.

"H-hi," she managed to say.

I nodded in acknowledgement.

"Most of us were, uhm, planning a little party tonight? Ya know, keeping up our spirits? We found nearly half a dozen kegs of beer behind the barn and uh, well, would you like to join?"

I smirked weakly. "Yeast flavoured cat piss. My favourite."

She laughed uncomfortably. "Yeah well you don't have to drink. Some of us girls were thinking some mingling would make you feel better. Ya know, with your…uhm…"

"How sweet," I exhaled as I shifted in place, causing me to wince in pain.

"You must be in a lot of pain," she attempted to sympathize.

"It's not that bad," I said through clenched teeth. "So long as I don't stand, shit, smile, inhale, exhale, or pretty much anything else that includes physical movement."

"But that's like everything," she realized.

"Nothing gets by you."

"Well, if you want to have a good time, just stop by. I'm sure it'll be fun."

"House music pumping with drunk teenagers screwing and screaming at the top of their lungs? During an apocalypse? Sounds like a great time."

With my hockey stick-turned-cane I heaved myself up, leaving her behind in a cloud of sarcasm.

While I walked toward the house I crossed paths with Atlas who had a facial expression demonstrating that he had been deep in thought.

"I need to talk to you," he said gravely.

"What, you're inviting me to the party too?" I assumed. "No thanks."

Atlas scrunched both his face and neck back in confusion. "The hell you talking about?"

"Have your party," I told dismissively. "I don't care. Just don't expect me to come save your ass when you draw them right to you."

"What party? The hell you smoking?"

I rolled my eyes. "*Surprise* party. Got it."

Atlas's eyes deepened. "Listen, asshole, I don't know what in dick's name you're talkin' about but I'd appreciate it if you didn't speak to me like a total shit."

I could feel my cheeks flush with rage. "These people…they don't know what it's like out there. Instead of spendin' your days getting praised for living, maybe you should start help preventing them from dying."

"Me? I'm just trying to get by but it's *you* that's weighing me down. These past few days…you've only given me problems."

I smiled. "Well maybe you should've just left me in that classroom, asshole."

"That's something I've thought about. A lot."

I rubbed my neck and pushed past him to the house. "Have fun tonight."

I avoided Cecilia's pleasantries and Blanche's complaining and shut myself in my room to be alone. Alone as always.

The bass vibrations of the floor rattled me awake. With a medley of groans and aches I pulled myself up into a sitting position and peered out the window. The teens had transformed the barn into a full-blown rave that blared music and secreted immediate regret. There were many times that my introverted religion took hold and prevented me from experiencing what could be known as enjoyment. However, occasionally there were times when my common sense kicked in and I realized how idiotic an idea was. Here, I was sure it was the latter.

A gentle tap was heard against the door. Immediately I knew that it was Cecilia.

"Yeah?" I said.

Her lava-like hair spilled into the room and in her hand she carried a steaming cup of an unidentifiable liquid.

"Just checking in," she spoke sweetly. "I brought you some stuff that'll relax your muscles and help your stomach."

I waved it away. "Thanks, but I—"

"Drink it," she ordered. At least I didn't need to worry about a lack of strictness when it came to her raising that baby.

She forced the cup into my weak hands and as I drew it to my lips, I instantly spluttered.

"*Guh* Jesus, what's in this?" I choked.

"Neocitran, ginger, and more Tylenols than I would dare to count."

I gagged obnoxiously. "Did you get a cat to pee in this? Jesus, why does everything here taste like fucking cat pee?!"

"Just shut up and drink it! Boy, you're a bigger baby than Atlas."

"I'd rather drink the beer," I said bitterly under my breath. I then looked out at the outdoor rave and shook my head. "Am I the only one that thinks that their 'little' party is the stupidest possible thing they could be doing?"

She carefully sat down by my feet and released a day's worth of sighs. "I can understand the desire to have a little fun now and then, but this is just dangerous. We don't know what's out there."

Cecilia clutched at her stomach and made a face of mild discomfort.

"Baby not enjoying the music?" I asked.

"No, it's not that. I've been feeling weird all day. Must be the stress just getting to me."

"Worried that you're going to be a terrible mother?" I guessed bluntly.

"That's part of it," she admitted. "I don't know, lately Felix has been acting strange. Like he's not telling me something. And it might be thanks to the hormones but I can smell dishonesty a mile away." She thought for a moment. "Do you think he's cheating on me?"

I smirked. "What, with the wide selection of eligible women out there?"

She let out a reasoning laugh. "I guess you're right." Cecilia looked down at her feet and decided to pry into the vault of my personal life. "What is your mother like?"

My smirk fell straight from my face. It was as if I was always only able to dip my toes into the pool of joy before having to dry them off.

"*Was*," I corrected.

"I'm sorry?" she asked.

"What *was* my mother like?"

"Oh," suddenly realizing, "I'm so sorry. Is she…?"

"Dead? No, not dead. Just gone."

Cecilia nodded and smiled apologetically. This was a response that became routine whenever I was willing to open up. The 'awkward nod and uncomfortable smile' was almost synonymous with what little memories of my mother that remained.

"…It isn't my business to pry," she apologized. "Opening up old wounds isn't healthy in your state."

I looked outside, then to Cecilia, then down to the floor.

"I found her body in the bathtub after coming home from a soccer game. She had cut her wrists open and she was bathing in her own blood. I was five."

"Oh my god," gasped Cecilia.

"At the time, I didn't know what was going on. I just kept asking, "What's wrong? What's wrong?" In the bathroom, on the ambulance ride over, in the waiting room, over and over, that was all that I could say. After that night, my dad told me that Mom was going away to get some help. Whether that meant she was sent to the loony bin or to some kind of 'farm', I have no idea. All I know is that the last time I ever saw her was watching her pale body being rushed to the ICU on a gurney."

There were tears in Cecilia's eyes. She opened her mouth, then closed it, realizing that no words of consoling would be effective.

"I…I should probably let you have some alone time," she said, avoiding eye contact. "I'm sure Blanche and Felix could use my help in the front yard or in the barn or somewhere."

Cecilia turned on her heels and retreated for the door when suddenly, she froze and gripped the doorframe. It was as if she had been sculpted and was left to dry.

"Cecilia?" I called out confusingly.

She turned to face me and released an ear-popping shriek. I don't know what was worse: the look of legitimate, uncensored terror in her eyes or seeing a stream of diluted blood pour out from between her legs.

"It's coming," she whispered.

## 15. "You're worthless."

"Are you sure you have a condom?"

Josh lifted his head up from the girl's crotch and wiped his mouth.

"Of course, baby!" he assured. "Trust me, there's nothing quite like doing it in the forest. Really gets you in tune with the nature, ya know?"

The girl smiled and threw her head back in a moan as he continued to pleasure her. Her name was Rachel Draw, and in any other circumstance she would've seen Josh as the overly sexual, pubescent douchebag that he infamously was. Unfortunately, chugged beer and cheap vodka surged through her veins and made her susceptible to his persuasive confidence.

Josh awkwardly shimmied his jeans down to his ankles and proceeded to slide his banana-flavoured condom on—with a colour to match—and positioned himself into a missionary pose. Before he could stick it in, however, a snap of twigs caused Rachel to glance back.

"Did you *hic* hear tha?" she drunkenly asked.

Josh kissed her collarbone. "You worry too much," he told, almost annoyed. "We're way too far out for anyone to interrupt us. No one's going to find us, baby."

"Bu wha 'bout those things? Th' sick people?" she asked worryingly.

"Those whacks are too stupid to take three steps forward. We don't have to worry. But if they do," he leaned in and bit her ear lobe, "I'll protect you."

From his discarded jeans he pulled out a snubnosed revolver and waved it in the air. "See?" he displayed.

Rachel shot upright, further dizzying her already blurred vision. "You have a gun? Where'd you *hic* get that?"

"On the bus ride. When it shut down and the driver bolted, I peeked into his glove compartment and found this," Josh explained, returning it back to his pants.

She folded her legs into her chest and rested her chin on her knee. "That… guns scare me."

With a flourish of his fingers, he stuck two inside of her and caused her to fall back onto the grass.

"Then let's pray it won't be used," he whispered.

She nodded and reached her arms back, suggesting that she was ready. Josh was so eager that he accidently shoved it…elsewhere.

"Wrong one!" Rachel yelped.

"Oops, my bad," he apologized in an insincere voice.

He finally got it properly inside of her and immediately he began thrusting like a dog humping a leg. Josh's moans overpowered Rachel's mediocre enjoyment while she was now on top, making it impossible for either of them to hear an encroaching figure.

"Oh damn, I'm gonna cream!" he joyously called out three minutes later.

"Already?" she asked, bouncing on top of him.

"Yeah baby," he said proudly. "Get ready for me to drop the load!"

Just as he was about to finish, a grayish, red-eyed human with blackish teeth and scaly skin crept up from behind Rachel and took a ravenous bite out of her shoulder.

"Aieghh!!" she screamed.

He came.

"Shit!" Josh cried mid-ejaculation, thrusting her body off of his.

She fell backward with the biter underneath her and screamed for help. "Josh! Help me! Help!!"

Completely naked, Josh scrambled for the gun buried in the pile of clothes. He pulled it out, aimed it at the snapping jaw of the beast, but hesitated.

"Shoot!" she pleaded.

Clenching his eyes shut, he pulled the trigger and was only met with the sound of the hammer clicking against an empty round.

"No, no, no!" he said as he unhinged the cylinder. He saw that there had been two bullets in the bottom right holes and turned the dial until they lined up with the barrel. Once he clicked it back into place and returned his aim, he saw that the savage had already torn into Rachel in three separate locations. It was a lost cause—at least in his mind—and decided to leave her behind.

"No, you asshole!" she yelled in-between screams as her flesh was being peeled off of her back. She reached forward and grabbed his ankle.

"Get off of me, bitch!" he said, kicking his leg viciously.

His foot hit the mark and broke her jaw. With a howl of excruciating pain, Josh was able to jimmy his leg free from her grasp.

"I'm sorry…I'm sorry…" he muttered through tears as he sprinted away. He took a final look backward and above Rachel's mutilation, he saw the pale, bloodshot eyes of no less than twenty infected breaching through the forest.


The room was spinning. I saw blurry resemblances of Felix frantically lifting his withering, bloodstained wife to the bed, Blanche putting a pot of boiling water on the bedside table, all moving images that added a noticeable buffer to the reality. Then I heard her voice at full volume as it finally breached my audible threshold.

"Get it together, Levi!" Blanche ordered. "We need your help."

I looked at her wide-eyed and blinked rapidly. "Help…" I repeated, "Right. Yes. W-what should I do?"

"Alcohol for sterilization and my tool kit. Both should be in the shed. Felix, can you go with him?"

Felix looked back at her with Cecilia's limp hand clasped in his. "N-no…I'm not leaving her! S-she needs me!"

Blanche turned to me and placed both hands on my shoulder. "Looks like it's just you. I know you're barely healed, but ya need to forget about your injury for a while." She looked back at Cecilia. "…This isn't good, okay? I need ya to go as fast as ya can."

I nodded nervously and with a great, painful inhale I forced myself out to retrieve the supplies.

"Alcohol…Tools…Alcohol…Tools…" I reminded myself while I looked left and right with only the moonlight and background illumination to examine the interior of the shed. I spotted the red lid of a vodka bottle, snatched that, and noticed a black briefcase. This posed as a problem as it was on the top of a four-layer shelf eight feet off the ground. I stepped onto the first ledge and reached up on my tippy-toes, which only sent an electrifying burn through my stomach. I fell back onto my feet and gasped for air, feeling that one of my stitches had ripped out.

"Guh...SHIT..." I squealed through my locked jaw. There was no possible way that I would be able to reach her tools by myself. This led me to look over to the lit-up barn and shake my head.

"Atlas..." I realized.

So I was off. In what could only be described as a muscle-tearing, blood-spitting combination of a sprint and a disoriented stumble, I dribbled blood all the way to the party.

When I reached the patch of grassless dirt ahead of the barn doors, I could feel the bass of the idiotically loud music rattle my ribs. Before I was able to crash the party, however, the hand of a drunken female flopped onto my shoulder and whirled me around in a spin of aching bones.

"You came!" she said ecstatically.

It was the girl that had invited me to the party hours prior. Discarding the innocent schoolgirl look that I was introduced to, she had a tank-top two sizes too small—accentuating boobs two sizes too big—and her hair was the product of one too many drunken hook-ups.

"This is not the time," I said coldly. "H-have you seen Atlas anywhere?"

She ignored the question and 'accidentally' tripped into my arms, causing me to wince with a jolt of unexpected pain.

"Would you fuck me?" she asked innocently; like a sex-starved child. "I'd want nothing more than to fuck you."

She may have seen this as sexy and a turn-on. I saw it as nothing more than an obstruction that was putting a woman and her arriving child in jeopardy.

"Are you seri...how old are you?"

"Fourteennn," she slurred. "But I'm tuuurning fifffteen in, like, twooo months!"

I was done wasting my time.

"Out of my way," I ordered, placing my palm on her forehead and shoving her aside.

"No! Come back!" she called out from the dirt.

I heaved the barn door open with my shoulder and was immediately slapped across the face with the intoxicating smell of cheap booze and cow manure. Kids dangled from the rafters, tormented trembling livestock, screwed in piles of hay, painted the walls and stalls with their vomit, you name it. There was a woman struggling to hold onto her life less than one hundred metres away and everyone was too drunk and high to hear her birthing screams. I wanted to set the barn on fire and let them burn.

At the heart of the rave, I finally found Atlas slumped down in a horse stall. He had a red solo cup in his weary hand that he extended over to a horse to take a sip.

"Atlas!" I yelled, not wasting a single syllable. "She's going into labour. Something's not right. I need your help with something."

He swung his head to me like a pendulum and squinted. "…Stop spinning, you whore."

"For God's sake, you're drunker than the rest of them!"

"Spank me!" he spluttered. "You shit…you ain't know fuck all 'bout my dick!"

I knelt down and slapped him harder than I anticipated, though the satisfaction wasn't lessened.

"Can you just *not* be yourself for a second and listen! This is not a game. She might be dying!"

Atlas tossed his cup of beer aside and clumsily staggered up to his feet as if he had taken a serious beating.

"Lemme tell you something, bitch!!! You almost died and I saved you! I saved you! Me! You would' a been a puh-pancake if I didn't getchu out of th' classroom."

"What are you even talking about?? The plane still hit! This is not the time for this, Atlas! Not now!"

Atlas scoffed. "I'm so done. I'll wreck you."

He swung for a punch that I avoided, causing him to lose his balance and come crashing down. His head slammed against the wooden railing of the corral and he rolled in the hay, dazed and disoriented.

"You're worthless," I spat.

As he rolled and tried to recuperate, I stormed out of the barn and raced back to the shed for round two.

With a newfound surge of adrenaline, I returned back at neck-breaking speed. The medical supplies had remained in the same place, mocking me pitifully. The pain was inevitable but my body was filled with so much anger and disregard that it didn't matter. Before the burning sensation of agonizing tearing had the chance to reach my brain, I scaled up the shelf and latched onto the leather handle. Then, as if it was predetermined, the entirety of the shelf buckled and I tumbled down with gardening tools and paint cans joining the descent. I landed on my back and the twenty-something pound briefcase settled on my ribs with gut-blowing force.

"FFUCK!!" I bellowed.

The adrenaline had conveniently worn off, allowing the indescribable pain to sink in. I rolled so the briefcase slipped off of me and I was face-first on the dirt floor. My entrails were being teased with outside air. Every stitch had violently split open, as if my wound was an envelope that contained information that couldn't go unread.

"Cecilia...I'm coming..." I choked.

In what had to be one of the greatest physical struggles of my life, I pulled my shattered body up with assistance by the remaining beams of the shelf and collected the supplies. With vodka in one hand and the dragging briefcase in the other, I limped and wheezed back into the house, bringing a blood trail that had now made a full circle.

"I'm *cough* here! I...I have it!"

Felix rushed out of the delivery room—his face swollen from tears—and basically dragged me into the room. Blanche had removed Cecilia's pants and underwear and stuffed pillows beneath her, raising her pelvis. Her bloody crotch was the first thing that I saw when I entered the room and, well, let me put it this way: I would have rather scooped my eyeballs out with a rusty spoon than have to see that again.

"Levi! Where the hell have you been?! She's dying!!" exploded Blanche. I slumped next to the radiator and looked to the floor as blood dripped everywhere. "...What happened to you?"

I pointed to the vodka and decrepitly looked at Blanche through my overturned, mangled hair. "A...are...you done...with that?"

She uncapped the bottle and drenched her hands and her tools with it before confusingly passing it over to me.

"Thanks," I gurgled.

I peeled my wet T-shirt off of my torso as it clung with dear life and examined the wound. The split stitches stood up like prickly, blue hairs, encompassing the six inch wide slice. Blood poured at a steady but not life-threatening rate, demonstrating that I was not at risk. Yet.

"This...is gonna suck..."

After taking a good luck swig from the bottle and letting the nail polish taste coat my mouth, I drizzled it across my wound and, judging by the facial expressions of Blanche and Felix, I must have made quite the sound.

"…She's not…is she?" I asked, releasing my bottom lip from the grasp of my biting teeth.

"Just unconscious," Blanche clarified. "But we need to start the delivery *now*. Unfortunately we don't have any anaesthetics so she's going to feel everything."

Felix released a hoarse cry. "B-but…women give natural births all the time! It shouldn't be that painful, right?"

"Do you see the blood?" she pointed out. "There's nothing natural about this. If we want the baby to survive, I'm going to have to perform a C-section."

"What? She'll die! I can't let you do that!" protested Felix.

"She's may be *your* wife but that's *my* grandchild in there! If we don't take the chance, both of them will die. I can promise you that."

Felix looked to me for help but I was too busy trying not to barf up my esophagus.

"You…she'll…okay," he finally agreed. "Just…make it quick."

Blanche nodded and positioned herself over Cecilia with knife in hand. She drew a line on her inflated stomach and just as she was about to make the first incision, a collection of teenage screams echoed into the house.

"Now what??" Blanche yelled infuriatedly.

I squinted out through the window and once again saw the barn. This time however, teenagers that were originally passed out or having unprotected sex were now running for their lives or writhing on the ground. It didn't take me long to spot the red, animalistic glow of the infected eyes through the darkness.

"What is it?" Felix nervously asked, crouched next to the bedside table.

I rubbed my face with both hands and exhaled gruellingly. "…Where are your bow and arrows?"

"I-I put them in the shed…on a hook…why?"

I nodded and turned to Blanche. "When we were rescued, did anyone find any kind of weapons?"

She thought for a moment. "Yes. A baseball bat and a crowbar."

"In the shed too?"

"Yes," she replied. "Why?"

"They're here," I said.

Blanche scoffed. "And what are you going to do?"

I shook my head. What I wanted to do was go to sleep. Unfortunately and ironically, I was the only one on the farm that wasn't in the midst of losing their mind, thus giving me an unwanted level of leadership.

"I'm going to take care of them," I told her, exhaustively annoyed.

"By yourself?" they asked together.

Ignoring the question, I looked to Cecilia's stomach and saw moving lumps bulging in and out of it. "When I get back, I want to see a baby. Deal?"

Before either of them responded, I walked through the doorway and back outside.

# 16. "What...what have you done?"

It was a drunken massacre. The teenagers outside were too buzzed to realize that their flesh was being eaten away until it was too late. Pale ones clawed through the flimsy panels of the barn and their contorted, jolting bodies joined the oblivious kids on the dance floor. Tongues were ripped away, eyeballs gorged, ears gaped, tracheas plucked, and about any other horrific way to resurrect occurred all while the music continued to pump. There was a boy two years younger than Atlas and I, fallen to the grass with a tumorous infected straddling him. The boy was begging for help as the pale one was shuttering, as if something was crawling up its throat. Then, without warning, it vomited vulgar acid onto the boy's face. Like a fly prepares a meal, his face was corrosive and burned inwards as the infected snacked delightfully.

It seemed as though the night could not have gotten worse until it did. Amidst all the spilt alcohol that coated the straw and dirt floor, a teenager with a lighter in his hand and a blunt between his teeth was trying to escape when a tainted child bit his ankle. As he screamed, the lit blunt fell from his mouth and onto the flammable ground. One spark was all it took for the floor, as well as the teenager, to be set on fire. In the process of 'dying' and coming back, he continued to burn.

While this expected tragedy unfolded, a shirtless boy sprinted across the field with his yellow-coated penis flopping out from his unbuttoned pants. Josh zipped them up and passed by the barn to see Atlas lying inside of it.

"Atlas!" Josh called out. "Get outta there!"

Not responding, Josh made his first and only act of valour in his entire life. Taking a chest full of breath, he dove inside the barn and retrieved Atlas while the remaining teens boiled and bubbled. Josh and

Atlas's dead weight breached through the barn door and slumped down onto the gravel. Then, as fast as the ignition of the fire, Josh's heroism faded. He slammed the doors and slid a plank of wood through the handles, locking in kids that had still yet to turn. They banged their fists until they bled and pleaded but Josh simply backed away.

I had just picked up Felix's bow and my crowbar when I noticed the fire slithering through the cracks of the barn roof.

"How did…Jesus," I muttered in disbelief.

Boys and girls were transforming left and right in a matter of seconds. Kids that I knew, kids in my English class, or sitting at the lunch table next to mine, or riding on the same bus, the people that they once were was gone for good. Now I had to kill them.

"Hunh," I grunted. "Let's dance."

First was Bailey Quinlan: crowbar jammed into the eye. Next was Matt Spiegl: arrow through the nose. Then it was Tristan Murphy— who was substantially larger than the rest—making it a tad challenging. I lunged forward with the crowbar in my left hand and my bleeding stomach in my right, only for the forked end to get caught in the flab of his neck. He growled and pushed back at me, forcing it out of my grasp.

"Shit…" I mumbled, reaching behind my back painfully for an arrow.

Just as he came at me with his jaw wide open, I managed to pull the last one out from the quiver and forced it into his mouth. The arrowhead pierced into the base of his brain and after a sudden widening of the eyes, they rolled back into his head and he collapsed.

"Thank you," I said to him as I retrieved my crowbar.

Now that I had no arrows left, the bow was moot. I dropped it and placed both hands on my crowbar as if it was a bat, making me realize that it might've been a poor choice to leave Atlas's weapon behind.

Then, something caught me off-guard. "Oh man…"

It was the girl that invited me to the party and tried to seduce me. Regardless of her disgusting, drunken state, she was innocent. No more than a child. Her eyeball—which had a bite mark in it—dangled out of its socket and for one single moment, I froze. This let her take the advantage and before I could stop her, she had tackled me.

My ribs shifted as I landed and while I bellowed, the girl was smiling maniacally. She chomped down at my face closer and closer, her eyeball getting as close as grazing my cheek, and I realized that I couldn't get my arms out from beneath her.

"No…no…no!"

I could feel her teeth against the hairs on my neck and just as I had conceded defeat, two hands suddenly appeared on either sides of her head and twisted. Her neck snapped with a fantastic echo that sent a numbing shiver down my spine. The two hands forced her off of me and I looked up to see Atlas struggling to stand.

"Oh, you're alive," I acknowledged.

"Yeahh…screw you too…" he replied.

Josh pulled me up and I looked ahead to see that forty walkers— double the original amount—were approaching the only living things left. Even with the three of us, we couldn't take down half a dozen before they mowed us down.

"What do we do??" Josh asked. "WHAT DO WE DO??"

We collectively backed away and with the thrust-style audience closing in, there was only one thing we could do: Go back into the house.

"Head inside!" I yelled.

Our feet clambered across the grass as we ran at life-dependent speeds. Josh tripped on a detached leg and dropped his gun. We were able to make it to the house but just as I was in the midst of shutting the door, I realized that we had just rung the dinner bell.

Felix rushed to the door and to his surprise was met by the three of us.

"W-what are you…?" He couldn't finish his sentence. He looked to have lost five pounds on sweat alone and his eyes sunk into their respective sockets, forming two traumatized craters. The copious amount of blood splattered on his plaid implied that he was a newly entitled widow.

"…Dead?" I asked breathlessly.

He shook his head and fresh tears squeezed out from his drained ducts. Before he could speak, a furious wave of cold bodies crashed into the house. The rafters rattled from their gut-wrenching moans. Felix surveyed left and right and then looked at us with a sudden realization.

"What…what have you done?" he choked.

I opened my mouth to answer but his hand was clasped around my throat before any sound could escape.

"WHAT THE FUCK DID YOU JUST DO??" he roared.

Felix cocked back his tightened fist but Blanche interrupted his justified anger.

"Felix!" she called out. "Get in here. NOW!"

He dropped me like a sack of potatoes and re-entered the operating room before my body could hit the floor. We chased after him and as we entered, the screams of the presumed dead stabbed into our eardrums. There laid Cecilia—the insides of her stomach revealed for all to see— and she was screaming. Unfortunately, she was very much alive.

"Oh dear god," Felix gasped. He scampered over to her and knelt beside her convulsing body. "Shh, you're okay...you're okay!" he assured her, kissing her drenched forehead with trembling lips.

"It...hu...hurts..." she spoke almost inaudibly.

"I know baby, I know. Just hold on. Everything is going to be okay."

He looked over to Blanche who was still hard at work.

"For god sakes, get it out of her!" he pleaded.

She held the red blade in between her teeth and dug her fingers through Cecilia's muscles and organs. "The baby is upside down! I can't even see it through all this blood!"

Cecilia released another wave of shrieks, facing the highest magnitude of agony.

"Keep her still!" Blanche ordered.

"Guys! Help!" Felix screamed at us.

We awoke from our trance and awkwardly stumbled to Cecilia, each grabbing a different part of her body. Her screams were only tempting the outside threat, causing them to grow louder and more desperate. Felix held her mouth and begged her to keep quiet, but it didn't matter anymore. Their excited fingers clawed through the windows and shattered the glass. The front door pushed inside further and further until their arms could reach through. One especially ravenous infected found their way to the bedroom window and—as if it were paper— lunged their fist inside and grabbed a hold of Atlas's shirt.

"Get off you bastard!!" he yelled, yanking his body away.

"I've almost got it out!" informed Blanche. "You boys need to take care off those things!

We looked at each other with nervous gazes and understood that there was no way around it. So, we picked up our balls from the ground and filed into the living room.

"Josh, get the door!" I said, raising my gray-mattered tool.

He tackled the door with his back and had a pushing match between him and the outside force. I had a pretty good idea who was going to win.

Atlas grabbed a frying pan from a drawer underneath the stove and forced his way to the pair of front windows. His breath stumbled as did his feet and his vision zoomed in and out, putting his target in a dozen different locations. A teenage boy—Atlas's go-to weed dealer—pushed his mutated body through one of the two windows and snarled at him. Atlas grabbed a hold of the sliding windowpane and slammed it down on his head. He did so again and again until the boy's brains popped out like a zit.

Unable to hold the weight of more than ten starving beasts, the rusty hinges came loose and the door collapsed, trapping Josh underneath it. They filed in like a cafeteria line up—each trampling over Josh's quivering body—and all that stood between them and Cecilia was a drunk and a cripple.

We stormed ahead with wordless battle cries and swung frantically at the oncoming freaks. The first victims were two girls, a blonde and a brunette, and we each swung simultaneously at their craniums, slamming them together. I jabbed and thrust, stabbed and kicked, but no matter how passionately we fought, the threat did not cease. With broken bodies and operating on fumes, Atlas and I knew that we had to retreat with a single glance.

We limped away and into the room where Felix had ceased to move.

"Is there a basement??" I asked desperately.

He looked past me at a door at the end of the hall. Without consent or any care left worth giving, I forced him onto his feet and passed him over to Atlas, who knew exactly where to go.

"No! NO! I'm not leaving her behind!" he belted.

"I'll get them!" I said, not knowing that I had been lying. "Now go!"

Despite being blackout drunk, Atlas retained a tremendous amount of strength and was able to pull Felix's squirming body away. Atlas raced for the basement and I slammed the door in the face of a jawless infected.

"We can escape through the window before they reach us," I told to no one listening. "I'll help you with Cec…"

I stopped and looked at Blanche, her existence perfectly silent. In her hands was a bloody lump that released broken breaths. They didn't last for more than five seconds before stopping forever. With what little life remained, Cecilia reached out to Blanche, silently begging to hold her baby. Blanche looked at me with glassy eyes and that was when they broke into the room.

"Blanche! Move!"

But she didn't. She simply sat in her chair and stared down at her stillborn grandchild as they swarmed her. They bit into Blanche's throat and her pressurized blood splattered across my face. The droplets were each a punch that flung me to the wall.

"I'm s…sorry…" I spoke through a closed throat.

I leapt through the window and landed on a bed of white roses that became red at the touch. I was safe for the time being since the beasts were too busy with their delicious feast inside. The sounds of slurping and gurgled screams from Blanche and Cecilia haunted me, as I could do nothing but watch through the broken window.

"YOU SONS OF BITCHES!" I screamed despairingly. "I'LL KILL EVERY LAST ONE OF YOU!"

That was a white lie as I could barely stand. Hopped up on my endless epinephrine, I feared that my body would completely shut down when the rush was over. Unfortunately, there was still more to come.

I staggered to the front entrance and was met by Atlas and Felix, who had climbed out from a basement window. Josh, somehow alive, crawled out from the doorway and tumbled down the steps and onto the grass. He released a fractured exhale and coughed up blood.

"Where are they?" Felix asked.

I said nothing. All that I could do was wipe away Blanche's blood that was dripping into my eye.

"But…you said…" Felix stammered.

I looked into his eyes and nearly buckled from the guilt.

"…I tried. I'm…I'm sorry."

Felix saw red. He spotted Josh's gun lying on the grass, picked it up and pointed it at me.

"Stop! You don't wanna do this!" Atlas urged.

"SHUT UP!" spat Felix. He looked back at me through tearful rage. "You… I knew I should've left you to rot in that wreckage. You and those FUCKING TEENAGERS are what brought them here! It's your fault! IT'S YOUR FAULT THEY'RE DEAD! My mom…my wife…my BABY…"

I raised my hands as high as I could without splitting open my stomach. "I tried to help her. You know I did! I tried…"

"There's been too much killing for one day," Atlas pointed out. "Don't do this. Please."

Felix shook his head and collapsed to his knees. He then looked up to the sky so that only the whites of his eyes could be seen.

"I'm coming, baby."

He put the barrel beneath his chin and pulled the trigger. The blood of his eradicated face coated my own, joining the blood of his mother.

# 17. "It could be God's fault..."

Annabelle looked down at her feet, weary and unsure of the heavy burden that I had finally unloaded.

"…All that happened to you? There's no way."

I was envious of her idealistic thinking. Unfortunately, she couldn't have been more wrong. To prove it, I took a step away from her and awkwardly lifted up my shirt.

"The first couple of weeks were the worst," I explained, gently caressing my swollen stomach. "Without proper stitching, the cut got seriously infected and was screwing with the rest of my body. The only reason I made it was because we found some penicillin in a dead one's diabetes pouch."

She stared at the many repugnant colours splotched on my stomach as if it were a hypnotic painting. The bruises were a multitude of hues, each within a wide variety of abnormal shapes that spread across my upper torso. Ranging from a garish purple to a fading, putrid yellow, my stomach looked like the remnants of roadkill. Just above my belly button, poorly re-applied stitching was etched into my skin. This seemed to finally convince her.

"And you survived?" she asked in disbelief. "Huh, I guess you are tougher than you look."

"How sweet," I replied sarcastically.

She walked over to the bed and slowly lowered. I noticed that she moved as though she was constricted; as if she was afraid to be touched by the air that surrounded her. Her gaze gently met mine and then looked away, implying that my interrogation was over. Now it was her turn.

"What about you?"

Her head tilted in confusion.

"What's your story?" I asked. "I showed you my skeletons, now it's time for you to do the same. Like for starters, what's up with the silent treatment?"

"You don't say much either," she directed back at me.

I chuckled. "Yeah, well, something that happened to me as a kid really shut me up. But even then I didn't go full mute. What's your excuse?"

It became clear to me that she had never confided in someone before. The fact that I was even taking an interest in her was unheard of. I couldn't explain it, but being around her was both suffocating and intoxicating. I never knew what I wanted except that I wanted more.

"…What shut you up?" She ignored my question for the second time.

"I asked you first," I countered like an eight-year-old boy. "What happened? Does it involve the night where you met the girls? When you were covered in blood?"

She shot me a horrified look that caused me to cringe. Then, leaving me hilariously unsatisfied, the door opened.

"Uh, I don't mean to interrupt," interrupted Atlas. "Dinner's ready in the conference room if you'd like any. We…we're going to sit down and talk."

"About?" I asked.

"Stuff?" Atlas replied sceptically. "Things? I don't know, whatever people talk about at dinner."

"We'll be out in a minute," I answered for the both of us.

He gave me a nod and left. Since the farm, neither one of us could stand looking at each other for more than seconds at a time. Where the guilt lied was uncertain.

Annabelle closed in, her eyes watering. "How…who told you about that?"

"I'll take that as a yes," I replied smugly. "Listen, we're going to be around each other for a while. You said it yourself—we'll need to learn to communicate. To do that, you need to actually use words."

She bit her lip, holding back a prolonged build-up of tears. "We should go eat."

As she turned to go, I grabbed her wrist, which she pulled away almost immediately.

"I'm…sorry," I sighed. "I didn't mean to hurt your feelings. You're just the only person that I've had the chance to open up to and, well, it feels kinda nice."

She shrugged. "Well, I guess talking to you isn't horrible."

I smiled and scratched the back of my head nervously like a boy in a family channel sitcom.

"So…if you'd want to hang out again and talk some more, I wouldn't mind."

She backed away closer to the door. "Uhm…are you asking me out on a date?"

I was suddenly flushed with embarrassment. "No! Well, yes, but no… I'm confused."

"That makes two of us," she replied.

"So? What do you say?"

Her eyes trailed off in thought, each blink a judgment on my character. After what felt like half an eternity, she responded. "Maybe. I guess we'll have to see."

With that, she slid out of the door and left me unsure how to feel. I smiled, thought about it, and then frowned. Frenetic butterflies fluttered through my stomach, a feeling that I loathed. It made me feel weak. No, let me rephrase that: It made me feel *human*.

The conference room was as spacious as it was uncomfortable. Seeing a room lit with actual electricity still took some getting used to, but the problem that I had resided inside of the room. Turned out that the employees were setting up a party for the grand opening just as the outbreak hit, producing an eerily ironic picture. Three workers were sprawled out at their respective stations, equally dead. There was a just-out-of-college-looking brunette who had her head resting against the stage, streamers strangling her cold corpse. One ginger-haired man with a handlebar moustache rested on the peak of a standalone ladder, his head and limbs accompanying gravity to the floor. The last person's gender could not be determined as the decomposition had advanced impressively and only left a no-name body collecting dust. Our collective exhaustion heard through our constant groans and sighs declared that these would remain as their final resting places and that our noses would be forced to deal with it.

"So," Atlas began just as I decided to enter, "here's the situation. Veronica and I did a little snooping and managed to break into the kitchen. There, we found a couple dozen platters of sandwiches and meats—"

"Dope!" cheered Josh.

"—Forty-some days past their expiry," finished Atlas. "Looked like the meat was growing new meat."

Josh slammed his head down on the round table that everyone excluding me had been seated at. "Gahh! Why couldn't we have taken shelter in a goddamn Pizza Hut? I don't want to resort to cannibalism but Veronica's looking mighty fine right now!"

"Ew, creep!" Veronica jabbed as she pushed away from the table.

"What??" he asked defensively. "I just said I would eat you! Compliments don't get much better than that!"

"So what, then?" I interrupted and asked Atlas as I sat down.

"Good news is that they left their pantry unlocked and it's stocked full of non-perishables. The bad news, we've got a selection of dried fruit, spam, canned fruit and more spam."

"And to drink?" Quinn asked.

Atlas couldn't help but smile. "What they lack in food they make up for in soda and booze."

Quinn's mouth watered vehemently. "Booze? Jesus, I'd give my left tit for a couple of Mike's Hard."

"Can I get that in writing?" joked Atlas.

As everyone converged into the kitchen where the walls glimmered with white marble brick and stainless steel coating on every shelf and drawer, Josh caught a glimpse of the appreciable stash of alcohol and shook his head.

"That…that's not a good idea," he said regrettably. "I'll have to pass on that."

He gave a solemn look my way and picked up a bottle of water. Atlas saw this and stared at the variety of flavoured poison the way an army vet would stare at the dog tags of his deceased brothers. He wanted to prove that he was willing to seal the past and pretend it didn't affect him, but it did. I saw to that.

"Atlas…" I warned.

He shot me with an annoyed glare. "I know, buddy. Don't need your parenting, thank you very much." Atlas grabbed a root beer, an armful of various foods and made his way back to the table without giving me so much as an afterthought. He was pissed at me but he despised himself.

We all returned to our seats and set our mounds of food in front of us to gawk at. Each of us shared a belief that there had been enough food to not worry about rationing, something that we'd probably regret, but we were too tired to care. Then, as we had all settled in and stuffed our faces, the unrelenting cloud of awkward silence was cast over our heads. I was eating cherry-flavoured Jell-O with a side of tuna and almonds. Atlas ate the entire stash of beef jerky and washed it down with a tub of chocolate pudding. Josh scarfed down a full box of Cheerios and in between each chug he would slather a dollop of peanut butter on saltine crackers. Quinn chowed down on a bag on tortilla chips and salsa alongside a can of pears. Veronica ate a can of flaked chicken, a can of flaked turkey, a can of lentils and a can of spam, giving Atlas a middle finger of superior masculinity as she did it. And Annabelle, well, she *had* a granola bar and bowl of trail mix in front of her but she scarcely touched it. Perhaps she had been too busy processing my abounding recollection for her to consume anything. Since she was an impenetrable, emotionless stone, the thought of her thinking about me was an achievement in itself.

"Sooo…" Josh tapped on the ice in hopes of breaking it. "What's everyone's favourite movie?"

"Wha?" Veronica asked with an annoyed tone through a mouthful of chicken chunks.

"I'm tired of how awkward everyone is with each other!" exclaimed Josh. "Have you seen *The Breakfast Club*? They became besties in like an hour! It's been almost two whole days and we're still on a shitty first date with each other."

"Because we're incompatible!" explained Veronica. "All of us! Even you guys alone, you couldn't hold a conversation that doesn't involve food or who should search the next room. Sometimes even in the worst of times, people just can't click. Besides, the bonding scene wasn't until the end and even then they said that they wouldn't stay friends outside of detention."

Josh smirked winningly. "So you *have* seen it. Well then, what else have you seen? What hits your ranks?"

Veronica rolled her eyes and reluctantly decided to play along. *"Jurassic Park."*

"Pfft, as if!" jeered Quinn. "You hate those movies!"

"I do not!" Veronica said as if she took great offense. "How would you know what movies I like?"

"I'm your sister, remember? You're a *Clueless* girl at heart if I ever saw one."

Veronica scoffed. "Oh blow me. What's yours then, Mr. Ebert?"

*"The Princess Bride,"* Quinn said proudly.

Atlas released an obnoxious groan and rubbed the palms of his hands into his eyes.

"What? What's wrong with that?" asked Quinn.

"If you go up to a person that doesn't care about movies, nine times outta ten they'll say Princess *Bride* is their favourite," explained Atlas.

"What's yours?" she asked him, prepping for an insult.

"Are you basing it on films for their critical reception or personal enjoyment? Because the best movie ever made is *2001: A Space Odyssey,* but my favourite movie is *Pulp Fiction.* Each perfect in their own way."

Quinn bit her lip.

"Nice choices, Atlas!" said Josh. "Levi? Annabelle? What about you?"

*"Butch Cassidy and the Sundance Kid,"* I said almost instinctively, not looking up from my intriguing gelatine.

Everyone looked at Annabelle, causing her cheeks to flush ever so slightly. "…I don't really have one. I haven't seen that many."

"What? Really?" Josh asked, surprised.

"Yeah. I think I saw *The Good, The Bad, and The Ugly* when I was little but that's it."

Josh smiled. "Well, we have a lot of time on our hands! We'll make sure you see the essentials."

"This is good," Quinn said cheerfully. "Conversing? I miss it. What does everyone want to be when they grow up?"

"Isn't that like asking someone on the electric chair what they want for dinner the next day?" I wondered sarcastically.

"Hey, I'm trying to be optimistic here. Like me, I'd want to be a lawyer. I can be pretty persuasive when I want to be."

As if he were a sleeper agent, that phrase clicked in Atlas's brain and finally made him realize why she seemed so familiar.

"Holy tits," he whispered to himself.

He hadn't known her as Quinn but by a different name: Crystal Simmons: a camgirl and occasional girl-on-girl pornstar.

"Something wrong?" Quinn/Crystal asked.

"Nuh-no. Nope. I'm good Crys…Quinn."

She caught his slip-up and her eyes widened expansively. Her mouth opened and then closed, unable to respond. Quinn cleared her throat and diverted her gaze from anywhere near Atlas. "L-let's change the subject," she spoke frantically.

"Look, it's not that bad of a topic, I'm sorry," I said.

"No it's fine. Different topic," she nearly begged.

I lifted an eyebrow in confusion and frowned but thought nothing of it.

"Well I do have a topic," I admitted. "I don't know if it may, uh, bring up some religious futility but whatever. What do you think caused it?"

The question that was on everyone's mind but no one had any desire to answer. Everyone became quiet. This was really the first time that we were all relatively safe and not preoccupied with trying to survive, allowing us to ponder the countless possibilities of origin. The idea was truly frightening.

"Half of the entire world's population wiped away like bird shit on a window," said Atlas, almost as if he had to convince himself. "The thing that I'm more curious about is why we were left unharmed. What makes us so special?"

"It could've been a government hush-hush project gone awry," suggested Josh. "That or your run-of-the-mill terrorist attack."

"9/11 was one thing, but this?" Quinn wondered. "There's no way this could all be thanks to some bearded guys in a couple caves."

"It could be God's fault," Annabelle spoke softly.

Everyone turned to her with a curious head tilt.

"I didn't know you were religious," I said, somewhat surprised.

"I'm not. But I guess if you really think about it, it's plausible. Whatever happened, it's not something caused by man. So if you put it in the hands of someone that might've created the earth, it makes sense that he or she has the power to destroy it."

Josh let out a Doppler-style whistle and grinned. "Droppin' some hardcore religious bombs, huh?"

Annabelle attempted a laugh.

"Well whatever happened, happened," bluntly stated Atlas. "There ain't any second chances, do-overs, mulligans, nothing. Ya see, the past is set in stone. No tinkering with that. But the future? That's something that we got going for ourselves." He looked to the three girls. "I think it's time we start discussing it."

Veronica released a sarcastic, stabbing chuckle. "We? Now that's where you're mistaken. You boys have your future and we have ours. Oil and water, bud. There aren't any interconnections there, all right? We're here because we have to be. Once we reach Jasper, we fly solo."

Atlas dramatically widened his mouth in unbearable pain and placed his hand upon his heart. "Ouch. That stings, Bangs. Seriously though, what's so bad about us? I mean besides the fact that Josh has a brain the size of his schlong and Levi is a physical embodiment of a country song—"

"—And Atlas is a drunk," I added coldly.

"…Besides that," he continued, ignoring what I had said, "we ain't that bad. C'mon, tell us why you think you'd be better off without us."

The girls looked to each other, wondering who would speak. As expected, Veronica took the podium.

"We don't know you," she stated. "Sure, we know who you are right now, in front of us, but what about behind closed doors? We can never be certain what your true motives are. I mean, how can you expect us to trust a couple of stragglers we found on the side of the road?"

"Keep in mind that you were the ones pointing the guns and we gave you the benefit of the doubt," Atlas pointed out.

"Exactly! What person in their right mind would stay after that?"

I rubbed the corners of my eyes impatiently. "This is getting us nowhere. Though we hardly get along, us guys know from experience that it only takes one screw up for everything to come crashing down. And because of that reality, we are forced to work together whether we like it or not. We do it to save our individual lives. Now, I don't know what to think about you three and honestly I don't really care. I told this to Annabelle and I'll tell you now: We watch after each other and we survive. That's fact. I didn't think that at the beginning…Atlas can attest to that…but I've come to terms with it. I understand you have this nauseating pride to yourself but you can't push away the people that are trying to help. If you do, it's gonna get you killed."

Atlas let out a breath of disbelief. "We may be at odds but Mr. Roboto sure can make one hell of a speech."

Veronica blinked her ocean blue eyes, as if each blink processed a new word of mine. It was evident that she was having an internal struggle as her small army of common sense was clashing with the empire of her stubbornness. Funny, she reminded me so much of someone…

"Trust him," Annabelle encouraged her. "He told me about what happened to them. Everything he's saying is completely valid."

I had to look away from her in fear of my cheeks blushing.

"…Damn, all right," Veronica said, forcing a smile. "You win."

Josh threw his fist in the air. "Fuck yeah!" He let a moment of silence pass before he spoke again. "Am I the only one that feels like we should turn on some *High School Musical* and get freaking weird?"

"Yeah you can stop right there," ordered Veronica. "We're not listening to any of that crap. Luckily, I found an iPhone charger and I can show you what real music is. The sixties are where it all began."

She took out her phone and as she scrolled through her library, I looked around to be greeted by smiling faces. There was this newfound acceptance that even Atlas was able to deliver with a subtle yet meaningful nod. For the first time, I actually believed that things would be okay. But—as I have demonstrated on multiple occasions—happiness could never last.

Veronica settled on a song and when she hit play, it was as if my mind boiled.

PLAYING: I've Told Every Little Star by Linda Scott.

The all-too-familiar duh dums sent me into a wave of indescribable agony that forced my body to shake vigorously. I rubbed the sides of my head to try and flatten out the increasing pressure that I felt on my skull, to no avail. My throat tightened and my shirt dampened with perspiration. I felt the sudden urge to shatter someone's femur; to unhinge someone's jaw and rip it away from their face; I felt the urge to kill.

"Levi!" a voice brought me out of my trance. "I asked you a question."

Through weary eyes I saw Veronica with her brow furrowed. I rubbed the dripping sweat from my vibrating eyes and looked up. "I'm sorry… what?"

My focus was still completely and undoubtedly devoted to the music blasting through her phone speakers.

"Who do you like? Is or was there anyone special in your life?" Veronica asked once again.

Annabelle stirred in her seat, intrigued by my answer. Atlas looked over at me, sensing that something was terribly wrong.

I just wasn't able to concentrate. "Uhm, D'ya mind t-turning that off, please?"

Veronica was offended. "There's nothing wrong with my music!" she angrily insisted. "Just answer the question!"

I bit together and shook my head, trying to free whatever had been cluttering my thoughts and tampering with my focus. I was desperately trying to contain my building anger and frustration.

"Who I like?" I repeated. "Uh, I-I duh-don't know. Please t-turn off that song."

She increased the volume.

"V…" warned Quinn.

She waved her off. "I can see that you're trying to change the subject. Why? Is this a touchy topic for you?" she tauntingly asked.

I kept my gaze to the ground, my bottled-up anger starting to pour over the brim.

She thought that this was about a measly crush. Oh how she had been so wrong.

"Awe, did poor wittle Wevi get his heart bwoken??" she laughed.

That was it. She had crossed the line.

"SHUT THE FUCK UP!!" I erupted.

Silence. I found myself on my feet, fists clenched together so tightly my bones were on the verge of cracking. My eyes pierced like daggers, stabbing menacingly at the girl who had pushed me over the edge. She was speechless; she was absolutely terrified to see someone who had been so calm and collected overcome with such infuriation. Josh, on the other hand, was fascinated. Seeing the red burst through my skin made him question who I really was.

The sudden burst of hatred began to fade away, leaving me awkwardly standing above the scared group of teenagers. They looked up at me like I was a monster. I had to get out.

"I…" Veronica began, unsure what to say.

With my eyes glued to the floor and my face burning with mortification, I pushed my seat backward and delicately placed it back as if that would redeem everything.

"Uh, where are you going??" Atlas asked.

I continued walking to the door that seemed like a million miles away and only turned my head to speak. "My room. Goodnight."

Atlas stood up. "Buddy, ease up. You don't have to take things so hard all the time. We're just trying to have fun."

My feet stopped and my head drooped with a heavy exhale. I turned around with a shame-ridden face and immediately felt the intoxicating stare of Annabelle. Her head tilted like a lioness watching the curious onlookers through the large panes of glass of her container. She was judging me, I told myself. She looked at me as if I was a freak. I didn't care about what anyone thought about me and I never had until she came along. I constantly walked on eggshells around her in fear that I would embarrass myself like the way I had just done. I couldn't know exactly what she was thinking but it was too insufferable to endure it for another second. I picked up my feet and before they could blink, I was out of the door.

Once they heard the click of the door, the inevitable gossip ensued.

"What a dick…" Veronica snapped. "What's his problem?"

"You shouldn't have kept pushing him," defended Annabelle.

Offended, Veronica turned to her. "Excuse me? I was just joking around! He didn't have to flip shit! Jesus, are you on his side now? Saved your life and now you're fuck buddies?"

"Screw you," Annabelle spat as she stood up from the dinner table and made an abrupt exit.

Veronica looked at each of the teenagers left in hope of receiving assurance.

"Please don't tell me that I'm the bad guy here!"

Atlas looked silently at the bottom of his tub of pudding. "I don't know what to think."

He looked at the closed door and pondered the thought of our skewered relationship. Atlas thought about if things were different and if he would currently be alongside me instead of trapped on the wrong side of the door. He would be lying to himself if he said that he wasn't lonely. What made him hesitant was whether or not it was too late to change that.

He also left the conference room, leaving Josh and the sisters.

"Well, that was a mess," acknowledged Josh.

Veronica sat back in her seat and let her mind wander. "He's finally shown who he really is. Did you see the look on his face?" she asked to no one in particular. "He wanted to hurt me. Levi cannot be trusted. And if he snaps like that again," she reached for a steak knife, "I won't hesitate to gut the bastard."

Quinn solemnly looked at her sister with a prolonged, teary-eyed stare. "After what happened with James, I don't doubt you."

# 18. "So...are those real?"

I fucked up. I fucked up real bad. They were given—even if only for a split second—a glimpse at my true nature. A borderline psychotic rawness rested beneath my skin like a dormant volcano and it finally spewed. Making a dash for my room, I slammed the door and flipped the lock closed with a now-residing tremble in my fingertips. The light of my two-bedroom suite flickered with fluorescent life, making that tingling hum that would set anyone's teeth on edge. I locked myself in the marble utopia that was my bathroom and stared at the blood-spattered mirror with an inquisitive disgust. As I examined the sweat dribbling into my bold eyebrows and the glossy layer that slicked across my eyeballs, I found myself frightened at what reflected back. I was scared because I knew that the person they had seen was only the utmost minimalistic example possibly given. As of that moment in time I hadn't even seen my full potential and I wasn't going to wait around to find out.

While my eyes continued the staring contest with themselves, my hands found the X-shaped knobs of the faucet and twisted them. There was a nauseating gurgle that shook the entire sink before the nozzle finally spurted out milky water. I looked down at the murky liquid and doused my face with it in hopes that it would eat away at my skin, rendering me faceless. Unfortunately, all that was given was lukewarm water that reeked of pennies. Then, with my pale, bloodless hands, I pulled downward on my face to dry it forcefully. Clawing down at my cheeks like I was a cat scratching at its post, the whites of my eyes were exposed and precisely matched the colour of the fading droplets. When my eyelids shot back like elastic and blinked away the irritation, I looked into the mirror once more and found myself not alone. Behind me in the shadows lurked the figure of a little girl. She took a single step out of the darkness and revealed herself, bloody and skeletal. Her fragile hand rose to her face and she tucked a strand of once chocolate hair turned arterial red behind her ear. Drenched with redness from head to toe, the only thing that lacked the gore were her pearly white teeth that smiled maniacally at me.

"No!!" I screamed until my voice cracked. My fist was thrown into the mirror, shattering it along with the little girl into a million pieces.

I spun around and was faced with only darkness and the lingering presence that someone or something had recently brought. I was alone and only the buzzing of the light on the opposite side of the door accompanied me. Slumping to the floor, I clutched the toilet and trembled with tearless sobs.

"Please don't come back," I begged despairingly. "Please don't come back…Please don't come back…"

Peeking my head up like a scared infant, I managed to stand and immediately reached for the pill container next to the free conditioner and shower caps. I popped the lid open with my thumb and jammed my fingers into the cylinder, feeling only a single pill. Confused and in denial, I looked down into it as if it were a telescope and to my utter disbelief, I saw that only one had remained.

"Oh god…" I whispered in defeat.

My breath was sliced and my heart thumped at an improvised tempo. I looked down at the mess that littered the bathroom counter and saw my fractured reflection being held together with adjacent glass shards. It was then that I knew I had to vanish.


On the roof of the hotel, free of the walls and judgment that circulated within them, Atlas laid on a lounge chair next to a monolith-shaped pool. Beneath the ribboning water was an almost neon illumination of piercing blues and vibrant purples from an array of lights pointing up, down and sideways. An oak pergola that housed a hot tub and sauna had casted slants of darkness across the surface of the pool. Glass orbs were mounted at each corner of the rooftop, shining four deep, fiery lights into the night sky. It was as if the world had come to a standstill and for a brief moment, Atlas could sit and suffer in silence.

A beer rested in his hands, sealed and un-sipped. Atlas looked down at it with burdened eyes as his alcoholic thirst was causing his mouth to salivate. He popped it open on the side his chair, drew it to his lips, paused, and closed his eyes in frustration. Whether he liked it or not, I had gotten under his skin.

"Awe hell," he said to himself before throwing the bottle over his head and over the rooftop's edge. He counted to six before he could hear the minute sound of the bottle breaking on the earth below him. Just as he was about to jump in the pool and drown out the recent events that haunted him, the metal door creaked open and out came Quinn.

"Hey Atlas," she said simply, breaking the ice of awkwardness that he would surely attempt to carefully walk across. "Can we talk?"

He sat at the edge of his chair and rubbed the back of his strained neck. "About what?" Atlas tried and failed to act oblivious.

"Don't play stupid," she insisted. "About your little...realization at dinner. About me."

He clicked his teeth and avoided eye contact. "Ahh yes. Porn."

She carefully approached him and loomed over the neighbouring chair until he gave her a nod of approval to sit.

"Yeah...Honestly, I'm not mad at you for finding out. I'm more shocked than anything. How could you have even seen me before? I'd only get jobs on sketchy and perverted websites."

Atlas chuckled. "I once came across a video where a girl fucked three guys in pterodactyl suits. What you do is child's play."

Her lips grew even more pursed than normal and her cheeks flushed. "You...you don't think of me as a slut...do you?"

Atlas finally looked at her. "The one good thing about this apocalypse is that you get a fresh start. Whoever you were doesn't matter. If you sucked dick for money, well, you sucked dick for money. Having sex doesn't make you a bad person."

"I only really did webcam stuff—"

"My point still applies," he stated.

Quinn smiled fondly. "Yeah but...I'm not a good girl. Isn't that what guys want?"

Atlas shook his head. "Whenever us guys say that we want a good girl, we never actually mean it. What we want is a girl who looks innocent and is a good girl around everyone else but when alone they're into some kinky and borderline-illegal stuff. That's the dream."

"Weirdly enough, that makes me feel better," she said with slight confusion.

"Glad I could help," he muttered, placing both of his hands behind his head and leaning back on the chair. Atlas looked over to her and his eyes drooped down to her impressively large breasts. "So…are those real?"

Quinn let out a pump of shocked breath and lifted her forearms to shield her suddenly shy chest. "Atlas! You can't just go and ask that! We've only known each other for like two days! Would you be okay if I just asked how big your dick is?"

"Well I don't go flaunting my dick around," Atlas pointed out. "Unless you give me tequila. That shit sheds the pants like nobody's business."

Quinn laughed, though still embarrassed. "Yeah, but still…" She slowly lowered her arms from her the top of her ridiculously short dress and looked down at them. "What do you think?"

Atlas frowned. "Real or fake? Hmm…" He took a prolonged moment to stare at her triple D cup as if they were an intricate painting.

"Fake," he finally said. "There's no way boobs can be *that* round and *that* perky and still be natural!"

She let out a vocal laugh, her too-perfect boobs jiggling at a slight delay from her body. "They're real."

Atlas sat up, fully captivated. "Bull. Shit. I've seen enough boobs to make my twelve-year-old self pass out from unbalanced blood flow. There's no way!"

She tilted her head all cutesy and shrugged her shoulders. "What can I say? I got the body and the looks; Veronica got everything else."

Crossing his arms like a too-cool-for-school toddler, Atlas tossed her a sceptical yet charming look. "Prove it."

"Not falling for that one," she replied coyly. "Besides, I've had enough boob talk for one night. I want to talk about you."

"Pfft, no you don't," Atlas told her.

"Yeah I do!" she insisted. "Like about the fact that you threw a beer bottle over the edge all grumpy. What, was it expired?"

Atlas looked gloomily down at the palms of his hands, callused and hardened after years of opening bottles. "No, nothing like that. It's just…I've had a bad experience with alcohol recently."

Quinn slid in closer so that only the armrests were between them. "What happened?"

"It would be like a six-chapter flashback and that is not something I wanna get into," he informed. "Besides, it…it doesn't matter anymore. Just seeing Levi like that earlier made me do some thinking."

"Thinking?" she repeated.

"Like, existential thinking! Things like who I am as a person and all that shit. I was wondering if his outburst was partially my fault."

She was about to ask another question and Atlas decided it would just be more efficient to answer before she got the chance. "Though it may be hard to believe, I haven't been all peaches and cream towards him. He can just be difficult to deal with and I'd lash out at him whenever something irked me, which, happened frequently."

Quinn nodded. "No, I understand. Veronica is the same in the sense that she can be a total dictator sometimes, emphasis on the *dick*. And after what happened before we met you three, it doesn't even seem like she's the same person I shared a bunk bed with for over a decade."

"What happened?" It was Atlas's turn to ask.

"Just like you said: too long to explain. Another time," she promised.

"It's a date," Atlas said jokingly.

"Sounds good," Quinn said sincerely.

Silence fuelled by sexual tension ensued. Atlas looked over to her and noticed her not so subtly press her boobs together with her elbows. He fought desperately to ignore them, afraid that another screw up on his part would result in the deaths of his fellow survivors.

"I don't know… I guess I miss my friends. Sure, they were stupid assholes, but they were *my* stupid assholes. Now that they're gone, I've got no one to talk to."

Quinn's plan worked. She gave him a passionate, drawn-out stare and bit her lip. She then stood up, undid the single string tied around her neck, and let gravity take her dress to the floor, revealing her lack of underwear.

"Uh…" Atlas drooled confusingly.

She slowly stepped toward the steps declining into the pool, her butt producing a perfect jiggle with each movement. Quinn looked back at him so that only the side of her face and the edge of her left breast could tease him. "What? Do you really want me to swim alone?"

Atlas felt an increasing bulge against the interior of his navy shorts. He stood up and cautiously stripped, taking off each garment carefully in case she suddenly changed her mind. Fortunately for Atlas, her mind was made up and when he dropped his boxer briefs, his erect penis stared her down…No. Fuck this shit. Staring her down? Really? No penis I've seen has a goddamn eyeball! This really took a turn to the *Fifty Shades* territory, huh? How about this, I'll substitute penis for…uh…Cellphone? Sound fair? He walked into the pool with his *cellphone* leading the way until his torso was submerged with the illuminating water. His heart rate accelerated, as it now had to worry about pumping…power…to his *cellphone*.

Quinn gasped as her teenage hormones trembled. "Judging by your *cellphone*, you must have really wanted this."

He laughed nervously. "Are you sure this a good idea?"

She frowned. "What, you've never made a *call* before?"

Atlas backed away and started to speak faster in hopes of shrouding his bout with embarrassment. "Of course I've made a *call* before! I've *called* so many girls! I've been *calling* girls since I was in junior high!"

She smiled as if she was looking at a newborn puppy. "Aww, this is your first *call*! Don't worry; I'll go easy on you. Sometimes it can be hard to get *reception* the first time."

Atlas shut her up by pressing his lips firmly against hers. He licked the back of her teeth and just as she was about to make another jab, he licked her ear and nibbled on her pierced lobe.

"Don't treat me like a child," he ordered.

He pulled back her hair and kissed her jawline.

"Holy shit you're good at this," she gasped.

Atlas sucked on her perky *speakers* (Jesus…) all while feeling inside of her, causing the water above to swish. She gave him one final kiss—a thank you—and took a breath of air before she went underwater to… what's another way of saying blowjob?

She came up for air and she bent over, resting the top half of her body on the edge of the pool. Quinn pressed her *bass* against his *cellphone*, playfully teasing him. Then…well, I don't know what else to say. They had sex.

At the peak of dusk when everyone was either sleeping or struggling to get reception, I slung my backpack over my shoulder and headed for the door. Before I could force myself through the doorway however, I turned my head and glanced over at the desk in the far right corner where an unused notepad resided. I knew it would only make things harder but…she deserved that much. I had to say goodbye. Goodbye to the one living person that I even remotely cared about, despite knowing her for the duration of two days.

I drew the blue inked pen to the notepad and began scribbling. "Dear Annabelle…"

When I finished my awkward and pointless letter, I creased it down the middle and carried it to the hall. There, I was met only with the hollow, *Shining*-esque darkness that slithered up and down the corridor. Scared that someone would run into me—a person that shouldn't exist anymore, perhaps—I tiptoed with absolute frailty down the hall and paused in front of her door. My eyes fell down to my chicken scratch and with a hesitant back and forth hand, I dropped it at the base of her door. I closed my eyes and released a pressurized breath. Then a door two to the right of me slowly creaked open and my breath stopped as my lungs refused to function.

"Levi?" the familiar shadow asked.

I thought of not answering. Making a clean getaway might've been the only shot I had at escaping. But, the thought of someone chasing after me was nauseating.

"Josh?" I whispered back.

He stumbled out of his room, wearing a gray university hoodie and gym shorts. "What're you doing?"

I took an uncomfortable moment of silence to process through my library of lies, unable to find a suitable checkout.

"Why aren't *you* sleeping?" I asked instead of answering.

"I'm an insomniac," he said, as if I were to know that. "Usually can't get to sleep until I see the sun rising. What's your excuse?"

"Hungry," I responded, it being the first word that popped into my head. "I was hungry. Never got to eat much at dinner cause, well, you know…"

"Yeah…" he said, unsure of accepting my answer. "But why're you bringing your backpack?"

My teeth clenched. Why don't you take your goddamn nose out of my goddamn business, I thought. "Heh, you never know how hungry you can get."

Josh took a step into the hallway, a look of sympathy decorating his stereotypical athletic face. "I may be stupid, but I'm not an idiot," he explained. "I can see that you're trying to ditch."

I opened my mouth about to protest, but closed it and shook my head. "…You don't know what I'm doing."

He stepped closer and raised his voice to a volume that I worried would wake the others. "C'mon buddy! Yeah, this evening was kinda messed up, there's no denying that, but you can't just leave! We need you here!"

I released a soundless laugh. "Need me here? For what? An example of what not to be? Please don't attempt to patronize me, all right? I don't need your sympathy. What I need is for you to get back into your room and forget about this."

Josh was determined. "No," he insisted, taking large steps so that he blocked my path. "What about the two months of us three by ourselves? We survived together! We became friends!"

"I have no friends," I replied coldly.

The affliction that I caused Josh was noticeable in his facial expression, yet he shook it away and stood his ground. "Be that as it may, I can't let you leave."

I blinked slowly, full of annoyance. "Josh, get out of my way."

"No."

I took a step toward him and as he grabbed my forearm, I swung it around and locked it around his neck in a chokehold. My desire to leave overpowered his brute nature, as he was left helpless besides a few slaps and claws to my neck. I pinched his nose and squeezed my bicep harder and harder until I could feel his body loosen. I let go and his limp body flopped to the floor, snoring with unconsciousness.

"Well, shit…" I muttered as I scratched my head.

Knowing that his body being left here would cause even more distress, I knew that he had to be moved back into his bed and stage it so that it was nothing more than a vivid dream. But as I knelt down to drag him away, I could hear shuffling feet from inside an indistinguishable room, leaving me no choice but to make a run for it.

The following morning, Annabelle emerged from her room to find Josh sprawled out at her feet lying in a puddle of warm drool. Confused and slightly weirded out, she bent down and poked his chest the way a child would test the liveliness of a dead rodent at the park. His eyes fluttered open and immediately his face condensed as the delayed headache was finally taking full effect.

"Was th…" Josh mumbled, still groggy and lacking an appropriate level of oxygen to his brain.

"What are you doing?" Annabelle questioned. "Were you…spying on me?"

Josh sat up with his eyes bulging out and his face glossy with the residue of secreted drool. "Levi? Where's Levi?"

Annabelle became increasingly befuddled. "What the hell are you talking about?"

"He left! Knocked me out!"

Before she could respond, she noticed the folded letter that I had left her resting between her bare feet. She picked it up, flipped it open and read it.

> *Dear Annabelle,*
>
> *For most people, they look to friends or family for salvation. They try and find that sense of belonging and purpose. Unfortunately, I am not one of those people. After last night, I realized that I couldn't stay here anymore. The reason being that I can't trust myself to be around you guys. I'd never want to hurt you. So, I gotta go and be with the only person that I trust: myself.*
>
> *Goodbye and thanks for the talk. You gave me a reason to stay longer than I should have.*
>
> *-Levi*
> *P.S. You should talk more. You have a beautiful voice.*

She read the note twice and felt a tinge in her chest. At the moment she wasn't certain whether that pain was anger or drowned feelings. Perhaps both.

The door four down to the right on the opposite side opened up and out came Atlas and Quinn. His hair was unruly and she was wearing his shirt that was translucent enough to show her black lace bra beneath. It took less than a moment for Annabelle to realize what they had done. It took Josh several.

"Well this is a weird pairing," Josh pointed out. "You two friends or something?"

Annabelle raised the note eye level. "Levi left," she explained, though she was careful not to show the insides of the letter.

Atlas retracted his arm from around Quinn's waist and approached Annabelle with his forehead dented. "What do you mean he left? For like a supply run?"

"No. He's gone."

Silence burrowed in Atlas's throat as he wiped his mouth in contemplation. Though the true perpetrator that caused my disappearance was seemingly still nestled in her bed, he couldn't help but feel somewhat responsible.

"...I see," he managed to say. "Have you told her yet?"

"No, I just woke up," Annabelle replied as she walked over to Veronica's room.

Josh stood up. "I caught him leaving," he said responsibly. "He wouldn't listen to me and before I knew it, bastard had me in a choke hold. He must've really wanted to leave without us knowing."

Atlas shook his head. "He's a dumbass for leaving but this is Veronica's fault. Shouldn't push a guy like Levi."

Quinn squeezed Atlas's arm innocently. "I'll talk to her. She should hear it from her sister."

Atlas nodded and as he beckoned her to the door, Annabelle had grown impatient of knocking and barged in through the unlocked door. After a brief moment of waiting and shuffling feet, Annabelle returned with a worried look on her face.

"Uhm...where's Veronica?"

# 19. "L-Levi? Is that you?"

I awoke to the sound of a decomposing hand slamming against the passenger window. It took a few frantic side to side glances before realizing where I was. After my encounter with Josh, I knew it best to flee before things worsened. I found a rusty plumbing van on the side of the hotel with the keys still in the ignition and after a long night of painstakingly slow driving, I found myself parked on the outskirts of a neighbourhood. Specifically Aspen Gardens, where I had been woken up by one of its remaining residents.

The pale man clawing on the opposite side of the glass was charred and seared. His eyes were a coagulated cream colour that resembled hard-boiled eggs. The clothes on his back were only shredded tatters of fabric that failed to shield his flesh-exposed body from the scorching sun. We made eye contact and he made it very clear that he longed for my taste as he literally licked what was left of his lips. Annoyed that he had disrupted a semi-satisfactory sleep, I stumbled out of the van and grabbed him by his wispy gray strands of hair, jerking his head back. I escorted him three steps ahead of the van's headlights where a lone yellow and black fire hydrant resided. There, I heaved his head down onto the peak of the hydrant's lid, the sound resembling a smashing pumpkin. I pushed down, lifted him up and pushed him down again and again until my hands were gloved with gore and the peak was visible through the gaping hole in the back of his head. That'll teach him not to interrupt my sleep.

Clearly a failed attempt at ridding the infected, my neighbourhood was nothing more than a fire pit. Trees reduced to stumps, parks turned into graveyards, and little to no infected mobile. Perhaps the only thing in the entire neighbourhood with an untainted pulse was myself. As I strolled the streets, my morning shadow felt heavy, almost as if it was housing two hosts: a follower and myself. I spun around on the soot-littered street and saw nothing. There was the possibility I saw the top of a person's head ducked behind a dumpster, but my mind was too focused on the mission at hand to really care.

After a long walk through the ashy air, I finally reached the all too familiar cul-de-sac. Most of the houses in the semicircle were simply charred frames in empty lots, but three of them had survived the bombings. I decided to raid the one closest to the right, a white panelled bungalow with a baby blue trim around the garage doors. The screen door creaked with a shrill tune that inverted my neck. I rushed inside to cease the achy hinges but I couldn't make it three feet into the heavy restricted interior, as boxes and trash were stacked to the ceiling. My nostrils flared from the rich aroma of mothballs secreting from stowed-away clothes bursting out from water-stained cardboard. The kitchen was merely a four foot box traced around the sink and oven that housed cans of soup and boxes of half-eaten macaroni. The microwave was shoved into the side of a mound of books and as I peeked into the dusty window, something moved inside.

"The one house I decide to raid and it was owned by a hoarder," I complained to myself.

After collecting the bare minimum that was even worth a contemplation of consumption, I slowly shimmied through two columns of stacked furniture that seemed to be holding up the sagging ceiling. But before I could reach the escape, a hand emerged from the foyer and grabbed a hold of my ankle.

"Shit!" I shrieked, more feminine than I would care to admit.

I lost my balance and collapsed into a pile of dresses triple my age. Now in a clearing, I was able to see who or what had latched onto me.

"No way...Ms. Simmons?" I acknowledged in disbelief.

Ms. Simmons was an eighty-three-year-old spawn of Satan who lived as long as she did for the sole purpose of traumatizing kids like me. Her nose was crooked and witch-like, her breasts drooped down to her belly button, and her eyes were as dead as her soul. She had a single braid of antique hair that I would frequently imagine choking her with. This disgusting hag of a woman was so messed up that she once mistook me for her lover in the forties, leading me to find naked pictures of her in my mailbox the following morning. When I went over to confront her, she 'conveniently' lost that misconception and pepper sprayed me when I rang the doorbell. One more thing: She's been confined to a wheelchair for more than three decades.

"Wait a minute…" I said as she weakly nibbled on my shoe. "You can't get up, can you?"

I stood up and loomed over her, noticing that her legs refused to move.

"So…disabilities carry over?" I asked myself. "Are you still in there? Can you hear me?"

Her toothless gums extended out to me, snapping at my face. I stared intensively into her red and purple eyes, trying to unveil any signs of life. Sadly, all that I could find was a mindless paraplegic.

"Well, I'd say goodbye but you were an unstable bitch. So, yeah…"

I turned around to the door but as I did, her shrieks and gurgling cries loudened. I peeked over my shoulder and saw her arm reaching out for me desperately. Through her beckoning fingers I could tell that she didn't want me to leave her. Well, leave her like this.

"You…you want me to kill you?" I asked Ms. Simmons.

She opened her mouth and closed it, freakishly resembling a nod.

"Jesus," I exhaled. "Well, alright."

I stepped toward her and she crinkled her neck up with what little drops of energy remained. Reaching into my back belt loop, I pulled out my crowbar and raised it to her wrinkled forehead.

"Hope this is what you want, you wackjob."

A simple jab was all it took to press through her gelatine-like skull. Once I pulled it out, her dead corpse released a choked breath that was more like a sigh of relief. Now she could rest in peace, whatever the hell that meant.

Breaching out into the hot summer atmosphere made muggy by clouds of smoke, I crossed over her lawn, passed a scorched lot, and stopped in front of the next house that was left perfectly untouched. Of course it was. What kind of story would it be if fate hadn't led the protagonist back to his birthplace?

"Home sweet home," I said with a heavy voice.

The first thing I noticed was the grass. The colour of cheap beer, my father didn't so much as acknowledge it in over a decade. I was the one that got my hands dirty when it came to mowing the grass or taking out the trash or bring his empty bottles to the bottle depot; every visit was guaranteed a cash return in the triple digits.

The house itself was a decaying shell of a once prosperous life. The wooden panels below the overhanging rooftop had become rotten and the originally crisp army green paint had chipped away to a speckled wreck. The cement pathway that led up to the door cracked and splintered, providing hundreds of weeds a bountiful life. The keyhole next to the broken doorbell had countless scratch marks etched across it thanks to the many drunken nights of fumbling keys. I reached into my back pocket instinctively to grab my pair, only to realize I wasn't living my sad, day-by-day life anymore. I gave the doorknob a turn and as expected, it was unlocked.

When I walked in, it was as if I passed through a veil of vulnerability that instantly eradicated the emotionless shell that I had spent so much time building up. The moment I walked through the door, I became the little boy that found out his mom had been sent to the loony bin. Step by step, I moved with my arms at my side and my eyes glued to my feet, terrified at what may potentially be ahead of me. Then I came at the crossroads of my hallway; one way leading to the kitchen and the other leading to the living room. I was unable to decide until I heard a slumbering groan emerge from the living room, making the decision for me.

My chest filled with unprocessed breaths, functioning like a machine with a missing gear. An imaginary clunk rattled over and over until I was face to face with a glass door, which was when everything stopped. Absolute, irrevocable silence that made me dizzy.

"Hey Dad," I whispered, my voice fogging the glass panel opposite my lips.

There he was. Peppered stubble sheltered his wrinkled and sunken cheeks. His thick, brooding eyebrows flickered with life as he awoke from some sort of sleeping hibernation. The eyes of the father found the eyes of the son, hazel rings looking at one another with misplaced familial love. His wedding ring clinked on the wooden floor as he heaved himself up to a crawl. Bringing himself out into the light, the sickly, maggot-infested bite mark carved into his shoulder could be seen through his beer-stained sweatshirt. Unfortunately, this wasn't the worst state I've seen him in.

"So, how have you been?" I said, then pausing. "…Well that was stupid of me."

I looked up from my feet and knelt down, now level with his gnawing body.

"I, uh, I don't know what to say. I spent the whole car ride here trying to come up with something to say, but now that I'm here…"

My gaze fell onto his lips licking ravenously at the sight of me.

"I don't know how I'm supposed to do this. It's not like they sell books or provide twelve-step programs on how to cope with your infected, cannibalistic father," I said with a depressed chuckle. "I guess I came here to say goodbye. Well, that and tell you how much of a piece of shit you are. Sorry. *Were,*" I corrected.

He clicked his teeth in acknowledgement.

"I need to start off with saying that what happened with…with… Sienna…it wasn't your fault. No one could've ever expected something like that to happen…but it did. Life is shitty but it moves on so you don't need to always make it shitty. You blamed yourself but you took it out on me. Mom only saw the bare minimum of your torment and that was enough for her to try and end her life. She didn't slit her wrists because of what happened to Sienna or hell, even me. She slit her wrists because of what happened to you. You were what ruined this family."

I exhaled, allowing more than a decade of pressure to be released.

"I've wanted to say that for so long. I…I don't know why I never did before. I guess…I just always felt sorry for you."

While I glanced up at the indifferent ceiling, unable to look at his rotting face, there was a shift of branches behind the far left living room window. All that I could see was a silhouette darting into invisibility, but nevertheless it was indeed there. The possibility of someone spying on me did occur momentarily but I had been in such a raw state that I didn't give it much thought.

"I'm on my own," I admitted. "Well, not entirely. I was with a group of people, two guys, and we came across three girls. One of them… she's messed up…like me. But of course that wasn't enough for me to stay. I remember what you said when I was eight, that "I was too ruined to have friends." As terrible as that sounds, you were never wrong. I left because I can't be around anyone. That, and I was forced to come here to get my medication. If it were up to me, I would've let you rot away to nothing. But no matter how unbelievably horrendous of a father you were, all the beatings, all the neglecting, all the drinking, there's no denying that you made sure I always had my meds. Maybe that was your way of showing that the smallest possible shred of compassion had remained."

With gentle fragility, I raised my hand and rested my fingertips on the glass. "I'm not going to cry for you. I can't. That was taken away from me the day of the carnival. But even if I could, you don't deserve my sadness. You deserve what has happened to you."

I pulled my hand away and stood up. Turning away, my mind was set on leaving him trapped in that shitty little room for the rest of his shitty little life. That's what the old Levi would do. That's what I wanted to do. But then I thought of Britney all the way back to the first day and how she was so kind and pure. And when she was infected, through all of the animalistic rage and contorted spasms, she was still in there. I looked at my father and I could see that the man who held me in his arms for the very first moments of my existence was still there. Through both his sickly infection and his abusive, broken nature, there still remained the soul that had shown me the meaning of life at such a young age. That was enough for me to reach into my backpack and pull out the snubnosed pistol that Felix used to end his life.

I aimed it at the only man who knew me for what I truly was. "… You're still my dad. And if I can't end my misery, at least I can end yours."

The gun fired its final bullet and shattering through the glass like paper, it lodged itself into my father's brain. A dizzying splatter shot out from the base of his skull and when his cold body hit the floor, a faint smile of contentment formed on his dead face.

The events following were a bleak disarray of nothingness. The moment I fired the gun and made myself an orphan, I suddenly found myself sitting in the driver's seat of my van. Time and space were irrelevant. All that mattered and all that seemed to exist was the three-month supply of red and blue pills held in my grasp. A kneejerk-like gust of wind collided with the van's windshield, acting as a stern warning for what was soon to come. Like a teaser trailer for a feature presentation that was premiering shortly, my goosebump-ridden flesh felt a storm looming.

"Alright," I said aloud. "Let's get started."

Before I could turn the keys, a terrifying scream filled the air. My head snapped to the source of the sound like a whip, only to witness a family of four being swarmed by pale ones across a shrub-covered meridian. A mother and her two children, a boy and a girl, were trapped inside of their minivan as the father tried dreadfully to fend off the snapping humans. By the way his body moved and that fresh look of hesitation scratched into his face, it was clear to me that he had little to no experience with taking on this undead threat. Perhaps they had the luxury and security of their unscathed home or they had somehow managed to make it this long without facing the anomaly that now dominated the earth. They have never had their nostrils filled with that decomposing scent of death that had a tinge of unforgivable sweetness to it; a cheap perfume purchased in the afterlife. They were weak and didn't deserve my help. I was not going to help them. I was not going to help them. I was not…crap.

I started to sprint as fast as I could to the house across from me. The crowbar dangled and swung at my waist with each step then suddenly rose in the air as it craved the taste of infected blood and brain tissue.

"St-stay back!" the man yelled at the zombies, expecting a response.

It was kind of pathetic to see him prodding their lunging bodies away with the end of a hockey stick. It reminded me of the first time I took the reanimated life away from a beast, stealing a portion of lingering innocence along with it. Now the killing seemed like second nature.

"Get down!" I ordered the man.

As he slumped to the pavement in a panic, I took the curved end of my weapon and slammed the zombie's head against the back of their vehicle. A miraculous splatter of red, purple and gray had been plastered on the back window as the flattened head slid to the ground. I looked to see three pairs of petrified eyes locked on to me, something I found incredibly unsettling. Before I continued on, I grabbed the attention of the mother.

"Cover their eyes! They don't need to see this."

The mother slapped her hands over their eyes and shielded their bodies with her own. The two children could feel their mother trembling.

Another one approached. I gave the dad a look, expecting him to assist me in some way, but he had been unable to comprehend the idea of taking a life, and that made me mad. Simply relying on my foot as a viable weapon, I jammed my heel repeatedly into the temple of the squirming zombie, moving less and less with each stomp. With one last step, I managed to pierce the skull and squirt thick clumps of brain matter onto my anchored sneaker. Overkill.

"Holy Christ," the man breathed.

"Grow a pair!" I angrily yelled back.

The remaining three converged onto our location and I proceeded with my varying attacks. First: a lunge to the eye. The crowbar pierced its way through. One down. I spun around and roundhouse kicked another body in their chest, sending it tumbling to the ground. That would have been a lot cooler if I didn't realize midway through that I had a crippled stomach and nearly buckled to the pavement. Regaining my balance, I knelt down and stuck the metal through the base of its chin six inches deep. Another one bit the dust. Now only one left. This one was fast. She latched her murky fingers onto my arms and snapped at my neck. I put a resounding effort in keeping her back but she kept on pushing to the point that we were rolling on pavement as the man watched, not knowing what else to do. Thanks, asshole.

The crowbar fell from my grasp and the gun was conveniently out of ammo. I wasn't willing to beat her to a pulp with my fists and she would take a bite out of my leg before I could have the chance to use my foot again. I needed to find something fast since her dead weight began to strain the muscles in my arm, showing that I couldn't hold her off for much longer.

Then I saw a manhole cover a few feet away. Perfect.

With all my strength, I heaved her body off of mine and as she landed on her back, I scrambled to my feet. I darted to the circular entrance in the ground and bent down to lift the heavy metal cover off. A thick, electrical surge of agony shot through my spliced organs that nearly caused me to release it. Her body rose from the cement and without any time to recuperate, I heaved the disc into the air and squashed her head beneath it.

The man looked behind me with widened eyes. "B-behind you!!"

I turned around to see a zombie mere feet away from my exhausted body. His jaw was open and I was completely helpless. Then out of nowhere, a thin sheet of metal came from behind and sliced into his neck, wiping it clean off from his toppling body. As he collapsed disgracefully, my saviour appeared holding a stop sign. I couldn't believe it.

"Veronica?"

She stood in front of me, panting heavily. Black specks of blood were spat onto her shirt. "Huh…Hi…"

I was right all along. Someone was following me and it just so happened to be the one person that I was willing to rip apart.

"You…you were following me?" I asked, rage spurting over the brim.

"…I had to see where you were going. After what you did to Josh!"

My surroundings were muted. Unable to contain myself, I lunged at her throat and started to choke her.

"YOU…SHOULD NOT…BE HERE…" I said through teeth clenched so tightly that they would soon shatter.

"L-let her go!" the man pleaded.

My eyes shot over to the man and then to his family in the rear window behind him. Each had varying degrees of terror depicted though all demonstrated a consensual message: I looked like a monster.

My grasp loosened and with a built-up sigh, I released her. She collapsed in a stutter of coughs and I turned to the family. Catching a glimpse of myself in the side view mirror, seeing my blood-splattered apparel and gory crowbar held in my hand, I didn't blame them for their concerning expressions. I dropped the curved metal and lifted my hands in the air defenselessly.

"I apologize," I said, averting their gaze. "We…have complications that we need to work out."

With my head pointed downwards, I could hear an unbearable gasp.

"L-Levi? Is that you?"

I sadly smiled at Mr. Rodney, secretly livid that he had recognized me. I babysat his kids a few times and they even let me sleep over when my dad had gone on a bender. This was not something I needed at the moment.

"Yeah…Hey, Mr. Rodney. Sorry to meet again on these terms."

He shook his head in disappointment. "My boy, what happened to you?"

"The end of the world," I replied. "Have you been holding up in your house all this time?"

"Yeah. But they kept coming, ya know? We had to leave." He looked down at the zombie with its head caved in. "How can you…"

"If you don't kill then you die. It's the sad truth."

Mr. Rodney rubbed his forehead with his sleeve and scratched at his patchy scruff. The look on his face suggested that he had been talking to a complete stranger.

"I'm sorry…I'm just having a hard time seeing you like this."

His wife called from the now open car door multiple times but Mr. Rodney just couldn't rid his stare from me.

"John! We need to leave. The kids shouldn't be seeing this."

I was fairly certain she was referring to me.

He paused. "Well… I guess I'm off."

"Keep them safe," I said in an ordering tone.

He nodded and backed away to his awaiting family. Just before he hopped into the driver's seat, he stopped and gave me one final look. "You saved my family as well as myself. Know that I'll never forget that."

Then, with utmost haste, they drove off. Their daughter was still sitting in the back, facing the rear windshield. She gave me a solemn, unguarded wave and I returned it with a broken smile. Once the car passed the exit onto 127$^{th}$ street, the smile dropped and I faced Veronica.

"Calm down!" she snapped. "If I wasn't here, you'd be dead. I saved your life."

"Jesus, you're just like Atlas. I had it under control!"

"Yeah, sure looked like it!"

I could not even comprehend my hatred for this girl. "Did you stalk me all the way here looking for a fight? I have nothing to say to you. You pushed me and pushed me and I don't ever want to see your face again. I'm doing *you* a favour!"

It was clear that the hatred was mutual, yet a sprinkle of guilt resided in her eyes.

"Don't feel sorry for yourself! It seems like you're trying to go out of your way to be the 'damaged' guy and beg for an audience. I'm not buying any of it."

I shook my head. "I'm leaving."

She leaned in and jabbed her sharp finger in my chest. "You're retarded if you think you'll leave me here."

"I'm taking you back to the hotel," I said coldly.

"But we are not even close to finishing this!"

I walked away. "Yes, but if I hear you say one more word, I might actually kill you."

# 20. "Whose car is that?"

We drove for nearly thirty minutes in silence. The tension made the vehicle reek with distrust and lividness. Clearly I was not interested in talking but that didn't stop her.

"I saw what you did to your dad," she muttered.

I could tell she noticed my jaw clench. My eyes had now been fixated on the hilly landscape ahead of me, avoiding her sight at all costs.

"How could you just kill him like that? Your own father?"

I cleared my constricted throat. "I was putting him out of his misery. As terrible as he was, family is family." I looked at her through my peripherals and tightened my gaze. "You wouldn't understand. What have you had to sacrifice?"

I could hear her rage fuming. "You have no idea what I've had to sacrifice. No idea!"

"You're right! I don't! See, these past few days you've always been on my case for being mysterious and having unclear motives. But *you're* the one that no one knows jack shit about! At least my problems are out there for the world to see!"

She laughed in a way that made me want to claw out her voice box. "I don't have anything to prove. I'm not trying to make a name for myself. But here you go again with that mental instability bullshit. Have you ever heard of *Catch-22*?"

"Yup," I replied, flashbacks of English class on the fateful day playing in my head like PTSD night terrors.

"One of the main points of that story is that if you think that you're crazy, you're not actually crazy. Truly insane people would never dare classify themselves as 'damaged'. You're not crazy, you're only hoping to get the attention that you never received as a kid."

Even in my state of hormonal fury, I couldn't deny her valid points. Perhaps I had spent most of my time and effort saying that I didn't care about what anyone thought of me by caring what everyone thought of me. Still, that didn't negate the fact that she was a bitch.

"…Maybe you are right. Is that what you want to hear? Feed your never-ending desire for female righteousness?"

Veronica shook her head and looked at me with those glossy, forever angry eyes. "God you're an idiot. What I'm trying to say is that I know you're not a lunatic. I pushed you and though you reacted hastily, I know you didn't mean it. It's the closest thing to an apology you'll ever get from me."

"That's an apology? Wow, thanks."

"You're welcome."

Another bout of silence commenced until I saw the cylinder style of the hotel approaching.

"One more thing," she said, this time her voice resembling a guarded friend.

I grunted in acknowledgement, eyes looking down the speeding road.

"You need to stay away from Annabelle."

The car shifted to the left as I momentarily lost control. I looked at her as disorder fluttered through my mind like a drunken bee.

"What are you talking about? What did I do?"

She let out another laugh, this time taking form as the universal chuckle of judgmental annoyance that was encoded in female DNA. "You're such a fricken boy."

"Last time I checked," I stated. "Do you think I'd hurt her or something? We're barely acquaintances."

"I'm not worried about *you* hurting *her*," she said, implying the opposite. "She's more of a wild card than you could ever dream of being. She's the kind of insane that doesn't think she's insane. Besides, she has the hots for you."

The first two sentences were gibberish to me. My ears reddened at the sound of the third. "…Bullshit."

"Don't go begging for reassurance," warned Veronica. "I may not know anything about her but I do know that she's a girl and that's enough. In her weird, silently freaky way, she's interested."

A smile pushed on the inside of my lips but I was quick to swallow it back down.

"It doesn't matter. It's not like I'm staying."

"Well whatever the case—"

As we entered the parameters of the hotel, she was interrupted by an unusual sight.

"Whose car is that?" she asked.

There appeared a black Cadillac parked in front of the revolving doors. Neither friendly nor an immediate threat, it was shrouded in an unbreakable veil of mystery. The only clue of its origins came from a white cross cleanly painted on the rear windshield. The vehicle was empty, but I feared that its owners were not simply looking for a one-night stay.

"Whose car is that?" Veronica repeated, more anxious.

Putting the van in park, I slid off the driver's seat and examined the vehicle as a heavy downpour of varying situations arose. "Maybe it belongs to someone who's looking for a place to stay?" I suggested unsurely. "A hotel like this, it's not that far-fetched to think we weren't the only ones interested."

"You best hope that you're right," she snarled, insinuating that I was at fault for whatever would unfold.

We rushed inside and climbed the steep, cement stairs as Veronica loudly listed everyone's name in hopes of a response. Reaching the sixth floor, she forced her way into Quinn's open room without knocking and as expected, no one was there.

"No…this can't be happening," she tried to convince herself. "It can't be!"

I inspected Atlas's room, which appeared to be more like a crime scene than anything else. Open drawers, overturned chairs, a shattered television, muddy footprints from multiple pairs of shoes tracked across the carpet, all signs that made it clear things weren't looking good.

"Anything?" Veronica called out, already knowing my answer.

"Nope. But wherever they went, they left in a hurry. All their belongings are still here."

Pacing and angrily searching in circles, Veronica was at a loss. "You don't think…" she couldn't finish, referring to death by biter.

"We would have found some by now," I assured with a smidgen of compassion. "The infected weren't the reason for their departure."

"Then where the hell are they!" she spat at me from the hallway.

I stood up from inspecting the wide, masculine footprints in Atlas's room and met her desperate eyes. "Freaking out will do nothing for them. Right now, all we can do is look for clues."

"Clues?" Veronica repeated with disregard. "Levi, this isn't a board game. We can't just pack this up and leave it for another day. Our friends are missing!" She paused. "Apologies, *my* friends. Jesus, my sister!"

Before I chose to lob another remark in our pointless match of back and forth, something in the corner of my eye caught my attention. Next to Veronica, there was a substantially large stain found where Josh and I had our little engagement the previous night. Unfortunately, I did nothing that would've made him bled.

"First clue," I said, pointing at the stain next to her.

She spun to the side like a wind-up toy and immediately took a weary step back. "Is that blood?"

I joined her in the hall. "Well, I don't think they had a Merlot for breakfast."

Her sadistic eyes pierced me at full throttle. "Christ, how can you be some calm? Don't you see? All of this is your fault!"

To put it bluntly, I was ready to smack a bitch. "My fault? What are you talking about?"

"Wasn't it you who said we always had to stick together? You leaving made them vulnerable!"

I laughed angrily. "You really want to play the blame game? You left too! Do you need to see a replay or do you remember smuggling yourself in the van?"

She didn't respond. The expression on her face made it seem like she had gotten the wind knocked out of her.

"What's up with you?" I finally said.

"Replay…" she repeated to herself. "…Does this hotel have surveillance?"

I understood where she was going with this. "When you guys boosted up those generators, power came back to everything." I looked up to the top right-hand corner of the hallway and stared at the electronic eye. "If we're lucky, that means that those were turned on."

"There's a room in the basement that might help us. Let's go."

She didn't wait for a response before she bolted for the stairway. I looked up at the camera once more. To think of using them was something I would've easily overlooked. Huh, I might have doubted this one. *Maybe.*

With the help of a keychain flashlight found on a dead security guard's waistband, we slowly crept down into the nightmarish hollows of the hotel basement. Veronica was more determined than frightened but since this had been my first time down there, I was undoubtedly the latter. Being in such a lifeless and faded atmosphere brought me back to my unenviable childhood. Oh, how I wish I could have played hide and seek without hyperventilating.

"In here," directed Veronica.

We entered and just like every film with a surveillance room, screens stacked upon screens covered the wall where a single swivel chair sat in front like an audience member too close to the movie. The middle screen resting on the desk booted up and had shown a login screen.

"Uhm...what do you think?" I asked as she sat down in front of the collage of monitors.

"Password?" she said aloud as she typed the word. Try again.

"Well at least we can be comforted that the security here wasn't primitive," I said.

We looked around for a post-it note or a random collection of numbers, but to no avail.

"Qwerty?" she suggested as she plucked the first six letters in the top row. Try again.

I wasn't keen on spending hours on end conjuring up common passwords and partake in a numbing session of trial and error. There was bound to be a clue somewhere and that clue just so happened to be a pin-up of a familiar, lingerie-wearing star in a rather unthinkable pose behind the door.

"Try...Sasha Grey?" I mumbled.

She frowned curiously and typed it in. Access granted.

"Who is that?" she asked as she navigated the mouse to the daily footage files.

"Don't play stupid," I said simply. "Everyone masturbates, even you."

The reddening of her cheeks was visible in the screen's reflection. I couldn't help but smirk.

"Whatever. Just shut up and watch the footage."

She clicked the play button and the fifteen screens simultaneously booted up. Each screen included seven different shots from seven different cameras. We had the pleasure of sifting through over a hundred perspectives throughout the course of last night and this morning.

"Go to the sixth screen," I asked. "Maybe each screen belongs to its corresponding floor."

Bingo. There I was in the green filter of the night vision, choking out Josh.

"How did you learn how to do that?" wondered Veronica.

I shrugged. "I used to watch a lot of *Cops*."

She scrolled across the horizontal bar on the main computer and time sped up. There I saw Veronica inspect Josh's body shortly after I sped away, her chasing after me, six hours passing by with Josh drooling on the floor, then finally the money shot. We sat back and let the room around us disintegrate into millions upon millions of pixels, absorbing us into the footage of the past.

# 21. "The Tom Cruise or Will Smith of the apocalypse."

"Awe balls. Nosebleed!" Josh said as he pinched his nose.

A heavy flow of nasal redness dripped down his wrist and onto the floor where he had forcibly slept.

"Josh, get in here!" Atlas called out as the girls were gathering in his room.

"Just a second!" he yelled back. "Man, it's a real gusher."

With his head tilted up to the ceiling, he carefully directed himself into the room where everyone had met for their debrief. Each of the perplexed teenagers had changed their apparel for the final time in this story. Atlas found a charcoal gray tee and a scuffed-up leather jacket. His jeans remained the same. Josh wore a tank top with a black and white American flag on the front. A baggy pair of cargo shorts only added to his already dripping douchebaggery. Quinn wore a pair of white jean shorts that were so high up, her butt cheeks made a lengthy appearance. A light blue crop top barely held on her accentuated breasts by a string around her neck. For Annabelle, it appeared that her wardrobe was incredibly limited. She had to resort to the summer dress she wore the day we met, something I couldn't complain with.

"All right," Atlas began, "now at approximately 2:30 AM, Levi got out of his room and ran into Josh." He drew two stick figures in a poorly sketched hallway on a standalone whiteboard.

"How did you get that board from the conference room all the way up here?" asked Josh, head still tilted.

"Don't worry about it," he swiftly replied. "Anyways, they have their little chit-chat, Josh approaches him, Levi goes all Rambo on him, thus dropping him like a sack of potatoes for the rest of the night."

"That drawing looks like he's humping me."

Atlas faced the board once more. "Morning arrives, Annabelle finds Josh at what…7 AM?

Annabelle nodded.

"Sooo, that gives us a four and a half hour gap where both Levi and Veronica vanished, presumably together," finalized Atlas as he popped the lid onto the marker. "Where could they have gone?"

"Even with this 'lovely' play by play, we have learned absolutely nothing," Annabelle spoke in a high-strung tone. "He made it pretty clear in the note that he was leaving for good. But why did Veronica go with him?"

"Hold on," Quinn interrupted. "Why did he leave a note only to you? Were you two lovebirds?" She made kissy lips that were accompanied with sounds and resembling body movements. Josh cleared his throat anxiously.

"Shut up, latex," Annabelle said dryly. "If you weren't too busy munching on Atlas, you would have been with Veronica before she snuck off."

Before the cats had their fight, Atlas intervened. "As much as I love girls talk about munching on me, pointing fingers won't do us any good. We need to come up with reasons why she left."

"Maybe she didn't leave on her own," Josh suggested, now with a wad of tissue in each nostril.

"What're you on about?"

Josh sat back on one of the beds and sighed. "Let's think about this realistically. She pissed Levi off. He storms off to do God knows what. And then we can't find Veronica? Doesn't that seem a little too *Dexter-y* than normal?"

Quinn scoffed with 50% absurdity, 50% concern. "What, you think Levi kidnapped Veronica? He's a wacko but he's not a murderous wacko."

"How do you know?" Josh questioned back. "You've only known him for a couple days. Hell, I've been by his side for more than two months and I ain't even know the guy's last name. It could be Lector or Bundy for all we know."

"It's Finch," confirmed Annabelle, "and he wouldn't do that. I know him."

Quinn repeated her kissy lips, this time with more sexuality. "Annie and Leviii sitting in a treeee, F-U-C-K-I-…"

"I'd slap you but I don't want to get chlamydia," snapped Annabelle, her voice frozen with ice.

"Enough!" Atlas interjected, this time with complete seriousness. He looked to Annabelle with a wondering smolder. "What do you mean you know him?"

All eyes were on her. "…He's not a bad guy. You guys disregard him because either you don't trust him or you think he's weird. He feels like he can't trust anyone because he can't! Why would he trust a bunch of strangers? Even you," pointing at Atlas, "he said that you two were together since the very start and you guys still hardly speak to each other. Aren't guys supposed to become friends in like an hour and best friends in two? By the sounds of it, he at least tried to make the effort. Did you?"

Atlas's stubborn wit was nowhere to be found. He stuttered, a rare occurrence for him. "I…"

"—treated him like shit. I know. 'cause you thought he was too odd to be worthy of your respect. But you know what? Some of the things I've been through make him look like a saint. So instead of trying to find the source of his and Veronica's disappearance, maybe you need to look in a mirror."

She stormed out and let the mouth-opening silence course through the veins of the three remaining occupants.

While Annabelle was busy being engulfed by untainted silence in her room, Atlas and Josh took it upon themselves to continue the search for anything that could link to Veronica's disappearance. Their first venture: the seventh floor.

"You sure it's a good idea that we're doing this?" Josh hesitantly asked as they scaled the palely lit stairwell.

"I've told you a dozen times: They are not zombies," reiterated Atlas. "They're *living* people that have been infected to make them *living* maniacs. If we find any dead bodies up there, that's how they'll stay. Dead."

Josh nodded unsurely. "Yeah…but still, why are we even doing this? Are you expecting to find her safe and sound?"

Atlas scratched his unshaven face. "No, but I guess I'm just hoping that we don't find the opposite."

He pushed the lever of the door and their two beams of light sprouting from their flashlights pierced the musky darkness. They then waited.

"Hear anything?" Josh whispered.

Atlas extended his baseball bat out and made a loud tang on the closest wall. Once the sound finished reverberating throughout the uncirculated air and was met with an embrace with nothingness, he nodded. "All good. Like I said, we only have the dead to keep us company."

"How upbeat of you."

They then searched each room with a collection of keys dangling on a ring the width of a bowling ball. Atlas had picked it off of a guard down in the generator room the day before.

By the third room, Josh was getting restless. "Soo…do you think I've got a shot with Annabelle?"

Atlas perked his ears up, though continued to rummage through desks and bedside drawers. "Annabelle? Like, *our* Annabelle?"

"Yeah!"

"I've never seen you two exchange so much as a glance," admitted Atlas.

Josh chuckled at Atlas's seemingly naïve attitude. "You should've seen it! We shared this incredible moment this morning when she found me unconscious. There I was, lying there like a man-damsel in distress, and there she was, swooping in to save me." Josh beamed but through his closed eyes he could feel Atlas's corrosive judgment. "I don't gender stereotype," assured Josh. "I'm a feminist. She could wear the pants in the relationship, I don't mind."

In the bathroom of the fourth room, Atlas gave himself a look in the mirror and shook his head as if he were in a comedy mockumentary.

"Uhm…" Atlas spoke up, though not sure where his words would take him. "…I don't really know much about her. She seems all right but it looks as though Levi and her have…*had* a thing."

Josh rolled his eyes and exhaled routinely. "Ahh yes, of course. Why am I not surprised?"

Atlas looked at him for the first time since their conversation started with a concerned, almost offended gaze. "What do you mean?"

Josh slumped down on the queen-size bed in room 725, the fifth room of their search. A thin cloud of dust burst out beneath him and levitated to his torso.

"You can't honestly just be seeing this now, can you? If this whole story of ours were a movie, Levi would be the star. The Tom Cruise or Will Smith of the apocalypse. Us? We're part of the goddamn ensemble, supporting cast on a good day. No one pays to find out about our story. We simply exist because we fuel Levi's story! *The Expendables* should be about us because that's exactly what we are: Expendable."

Atlas leaned on the mounted TV opposite of Josh and shined his flashlight in his eyes. "Stop feeling sorry for yourself. Why'd you even say that? Is your ego bigger than I thought?"

"Just as big as yours," Josh swiftly replied. "C'mon, tell me you don't feel a teensy bit jealous of all the attention he gets. Do you not care about making a name for yourself?"

"I don't care about what anyone says about me," Atlas made clear. "Ain't nobody messing with me except me, yeah? Anyone that thinks attention is a good thing is a big 'ol juicy sack of shit."

Josh sat up, the highlighted shade of blue in his eyes glimmering in the streaks of window light while Atlas's sombre hue faded into the dark. "Granted, but you must at least care about some things that you'd like everyone to know. Like, none of you or the girls have ever asked about my interests or hobbies or what I wanted to do after high school!"

Atlas rubbed the sandy specks of crud from his eyes that were as dry as his interest. Still, he saw no harm in playing along. It wasn't like they had somewhere to be.

"...Fine. Josh, what are your interests? What are your hobbies? What did you want to do after high school?"

He lit up like an overly ecstatic Christmas tree. "Funny you should ask! I was our school's best basketball player so that took up most of my time, but I also love working out, The Beatles, and girls. Most people would think I wanted to go into basketball—judging by all the scholarships I was offered—but my real passion is...well, you're going to laugh..."

"No, tell me..." Atlas attempted to produce a shred of care.

"A magician! Man, magic is tight!"

Atlas closed his eyes, exhausted by how long of a time he had spent with a boy trapped in a full-grown body.

"What did/do you want to do?" Josh asked as if they were on a first date. It was clear who was having more fun.

"This is stupid," Atlas finally released. "There's no point in talking about this."

"Yes there is. What do you want to be?"

His frustration was clawing away at his insides, burning at the slightest touch. If only he had the liquid that could flush it all away.

"Uhm…a drummer."

"Really??" Josh asked with surprise.

"Yeah? What's it to you?"

"Nothing, I just thought of you as a plumber or construction sort of guy."

"Yeah well screw you too," Atlas tossed back. "I don't know, I picked it up when I was eight and it was the best way I could get my anger out without pissing off the folks. I then started to play because I actually liked it and pretty soon, I got good." Atlas smiled to himself. "Man, banging at the kit in perfect tempo? There's not a feeling like it. You ever see *Whiplash*? Great movie. The whole chair-throwing and car-crashing is a slight exaggeration but the passion is dead-on. To have something that you can care about…to call your own…that should be what drives you. It's what drives me at least."

They sat in a pocket of silence that gave Atlas enough time to hide his smile.

Josh chuckled. "Just a magician and a drummer at the end of the world. Unlikely duo, huh?"

"Yeah, especially after all the shit we did to each other as kids," reminisced Atlas.

"Yeah…" Josh joined in.

Before things could become any more personal, Atlas stood up. "C'mon, we should head back."

He left the room and made for the staircase, neutral on whether or not Josh would follow him. But when he reached the door, that's when it happened. That's when it all fell apart.

"Jesus, it's Levi!" Atlas called out, approaching the window overlooking the parking lot.

Josh joined him. "It's him? Really?"

The slender black Cadillac parked in front of the entrance. Josh thought to himself for a moment. "Where would Levi have gotten a black Cadillac?"

They both waited in anticipation for the owner of the car to reveal him or herself. Then he did. Vacating the driver's seat was a twenty-something-year-old man with a Jesus beard and long brown hair pulled up in a man-bun. He wore a loose, white cardigan that drooped down to his knees and wore a pair of slim jeans that made sure to show off his worn-in loafers.

Josh frowned. "That's not Levi."

Then a second occupant arose from the car. It was a black woman with buzzed hair wearing a sparkling white crop top and white jean shorts to match. Her dazzling eyes were visible all the way from the seventh floor as they were decorated with a curvaceous swirl of fiery red and deviant blue.

"That's definitely not Levi," Atlas muttered.

Then the third person came out. When his boots collided with the pavement, the earth shook. He ascended up nearly seven feet into the air, producing a behemoth presence that made Atlas and Josh gasp in disbelief. The beast was as muscular as a roided-up bull and wore a white wife-beater that was struggling to contain his impossibly large pecks. He was as bald as a cue ball and he had a defined handlebar moustache that twisted up at the corners.

"I don't know what the fuck *that* is!" exclaimed Josh, backing away from the window. "What do we do? What do we do??"

Atlas would be a hypocrite if he told Josh to calm down as his heart was vibrating like a hummingbird on cocaine. "We don't know what they want! They could just be looking for a place to crash!"

Josh jabbed his index finger through the air in front the window and vigorously shook his head. "Do you see Mr. Stone Cold Handlebars there? He ain't looking for a little nappie time!!"

Fat beads of sweat trickled down Atlas's face and soaked into his T-shirt. He felt this compromising sense of fear that he had never experienced before, maybe because he now had something to lose.

"Uh…uhm…they don't know we're here! It's not like they're going to check out every floor in this goddamn building, right?" he asked rhetorically. Josh chose to answer anyways.

"If they're looking for something or-or someone then maybe!"

In the far distance seven floors below them, the posh voice of the dark-skinned female carried back to the two scared boys.

"Hey, I think I saw something move on the sixth or seventh floor."

"Oh shit…" Josh said breathlessly.

"Let's check it out," Man-bun said.

"Oh SHIT!" he cried out loud enough to make Atlas slap his hand over his mouth.

"You need to shut up and breathe," Atlas said as his covering hand trembled. "We'll hide in one of these rooms. They won't be able to get in without a key."

"With that slab of beef, he'll just have to sneeze and the door will open. We're straight dicked."

Atlas's eyes widened even larger than they already were. "…The girls. They don't know!"

"Well then let them know!" Josh whisper-yelled back. "I'll stay here and shit my pants in privacy."

"The hell you will," Atlas denied. "You're coming with me!"

He grabbed Josh's shirt collar and dragged him back onto the sixth floor, accidentally leaving the ring of keys behind. Already Atlas could hear the echoes of the stranger's voices ricochet up the stairwell. They had less than a minute.

"Annabelle! Quinn!" Atlas called out mid-stride, still retaining the panicked whisper.

Quinn didn't respond but Annabelle did and the moment she did a convoy of terrified statements bombarded her. With the fast-pace speaking of the two boys, she could only catch fragments of what each of them was saying.

"…black Cadillac…"

"…strangers coming…"

"…guy with a man-bun…"

"…moustached monster…"

Annabelle breached the comforts of her room and stepped toward them with a look of complete disorientation. "…What? What're you even saying?"

Atlas brushed his floppy hair back and it stayed, as it was now slick with sweat. "No time to explain. Go to Quinn's room and hide. Shut the door behind you. Don't answer unless you hear our voices, okay?"

He pushed her away before she could respond and with a leap to the opposite side, she closed the door, leaving the boys to desperately find a hiding spot. Judging by the loudness of their now comprehendible voices, they had to be on the floor below them.

"Your room's still unlocked!" noticed Atlas. "Go! We shouldn't both hide in the same spot!"

"Where'll you go?" asked Josh as he was already through the doorframe.

"I'll improvise."

Josh gave him a worried nod and shut the door. Using his room as a hiding spot would make the most logical sense, but Atlas didn't have time for logical sense, or any sense for that matter. With counting down seconds, he forced himself to hide in a trashcan. Just as the lid settled on his skull, the stairwell door swung open and they had arrived.

Once Annabelle had entered Quinn's room while Atlas had become one with the trash, she could hear a buzzing sound fade in and out coming from the bathroom. Too adrenalized to have the courtesy of knocking, Annabelle barged in on Quinn who had been masturbating.

"Annabelle!" she yelped. "Get out!'

Quinn closed her legs and sat upright on the toilet, pulling a bulky blue object out from inside her.

"Is that an electric tooth...forget it! We need to hide!" Annabelle ordered a pantless Quinn as she pulled her into the bathtub with her. She extended the shower curtain and Quinn dropped the toothbrush in the tub with her. Annabelle then shut her mouth and filled her in with the uncertain situation unfolding in the hall.

A pair of eyes peered side to side through the thin garbage slate. The black woman approached the garbage can, sending an intoxicating aroma of cherries and vanilla into the slit. She paused, as if she was about to open it, but then turned around and rested on the trash bin. Her butt was pressed up against the hole and though oxygen was unable to flow inside and out, Atlas's heart finally started to beat again.

"Ehh, must've been a sinner," she muttered while licking a glossy, blue ring pop. "It's not worth it to look through every room."

"Be patient, darling," Man-bun spoke, his voice as soft as silk. "We've always brought prospects back with us. Every time. I know someone's here. I can smell their cheap perfume."

First off, it's cologne, Atlas argued internally. And secondly, it was very expensive. The price tag was still on it when I swiped it from that boutique. Dick. Atlas already hated him.

"Gonzo? You find anything?" he asked the behemoth.

Surprisingly, Handlebars said nothing. He simply shook his head and sighed a noiseless sigh.

"Oh well. They're probably on a different floor," Man-bun assumed. "The sign out front said there's a rooftop pool. We ought to check that out."

Then, as proven on multiple occasions, fate continued the streak of stirring our shit up. Just as the beast named Gonzo had turned around, a sudden vibrating sound caught his silent attention. Quinn had accidentally sat on the toothbrush.

"No shit stop!" she swore as she fumbled with the off switch. When she finally did, it was too late.

Gonzo pointed his sausage-size finger at the door and the dazzled-eye woman waved her ring pop in the air for him to commence. He took one step back, raised his army boot to knee height, and then proceeded to kick the door clean off its hinges.

"Oh no," Atlas whispered at the slightest decibel.

He took one surveying glance at the empty room and turned his body to the bathroom. With just his iron grasp, he grabbed the handle and pulled it open with ease, despite it being locked. He saw the silhouettes of two crouching girls on the shower curtain, pushed it aside, and he flashed his set of yellow teeth in the form of a psychotic smile. Screams flooded the hotel and Atlas knew it was over.

# 22. "So we've got a silent giant, a candy-loving ninja, and a hipster."

As the other two made their way into Quinn's bedroom, Atlas was faced with a moral conundrum: Should he stay or should he go? He had approximately thirty seconds before they would return to the hall in search of others, giving him enough time to make a run for it and follow my footsteps. The thought made him sick to his stomach—granted it may have been the wretched stench of the garbage—but he didn't immediately rid the thought from his mind. Though there isn't a set time where an individual should feel responsible for the well-being of their peers, Atlas thought that three days didn't meet the criteria. Annabelle was basically a stranger to him, Josh said it himself that he was expendable, and Quinn? Well, as shitty as it sounded in his head, sex was sex. Doing someone didn't make them your problem. So as he seemingly convinced himself that he was justified to leave, the three suddenly returned from the room with Annabelle and Quinn, looking terrified and confused. They were inches away from Gonzo, making any resistance pointless. Now, Atlas had to see if the girls would rat him out.

Man-bun cleared his throat. "If anyone can hear me, I want to assure you that we mean you no harm. We have no intention of hurting or robbing these girls in any way. I only ask for anyone to come out, if they're hiding, so we can just talk. We're here to help, not hurt."

Atlas could taste the bullshit in his mouth. Unfortunately, Josh lacked the common sense taste buds and emerged from his room.

"W-what do you want?" he hesitantly asked.

Man-bun smiled. "Hello, my friend. Are you the only one?"

All three of the teenagers refused to speak, giving away Atlas's existence nonetheless.

"I'd be more comfortable if *everyone* was here to speak with me. I don't want to worry about an ambush."

Then Quinn surprised them all and decided to speak up. "Atlas? It's okay to come out. I-I don't think they're here to hurt us."

"Well shit," Atlas exhaled.

Now faced with the degrading image of emerging from a garbage can, he attempted to do so with utmost fluidity. Unfortunately for him, the lid remained on his head and his foot got caught on the rim of the bin, causing him to trip blindly. With both the contents of the garbage can and his dignity spilt on the floor, he slowly removed the bin as if it were a knight's helmet and shook his hair out from his closed eyes.

"Nice of you to join us," Man-bun spoke. Atlas was unclear whether he was making a joke out of him.

Now with no chance to escape, Atlas thought it would be best to endow a rigid and impenetrable persona to make him feared. Though he would never admit it, I think he did it to show that he cared about these survivors, even if it was only slightly.

"What do you want?" Atlas said sharply, refusing to blink.

Man-bun flashed his closed-lip smile and approached him with an extended hand. "My name is Jeb. You must be Atlas, I presume?"

Atlas decided to answer his question by avoiding it with his own question. "Jeb? As in…Jebediah? Really?"

His smile didn't lessen. "God-given name. I don't know, I think it makes me sound like a cowboy. Don't you think?"

Atlas nodded slowly. "Think what you want, it doesn't make it any less stupid."

Jeb placed his hands together and returned Atlas's nod. "You're on edge. I get it. Meeting new people these days can be difficult to say the least. I remember meeting Zara for the first time," he told, gesturing to the third member of his party. "She nearly swiped my head clean off my body with that staff of hers."

Atlas looked at Zara and just noticed that she had a slender, four-foot tall bō slung over her shoulder. She blinked her dazzling, cursive eyes and gave him a slight head tilt, lowering her ring pop from her lips.

"If you keep staring me down then he won't be the only one," she threatened, causing Atlas to alter his gaze at Gonzo instead. As expected, he said nothing, only clenching his jaw. His burly moustache made it seem like he lacked a mouth.

"What's your deal?" Atlas asked.

"Gonzo here doesn't say much," Jeb explained on his behalf. "He may look intimidating but he's got a heart of gold." Then he paused, as if remembering something. "Well, as long as you're on his good side."

Atlas scoffed at the sight before him. "So we've got a silent giant, a candy-loving ninja, and a hipster. As interesting as that sounds, can you please get to the point where I should give a shit? Why are you here?"

"Of course," Jeb agreed. "Could we sit down?"

"No."

"…Alright," Jeb said, desperately trying to lighten the situation. "I usually recite this piece that I have memorized, but you seem to be quite…uh…"

"Stubborn? A hard ass? Lacking of any shits to give?" Atlas suggested. "Take your pick."

"What I'm trying to say is that you seem to have your mind set before the question is even asked. What I'm here to do is to provide the question and convince you to say yes."

"Yes to what?" Atlas sceptically questioned.

"We have a place where everyone is welcome and everyone is safe. No ifs, ands, or buts. There are walls, an abundance of food, and a nearly unlimited supply of water. If you choose to come with us, you'd help us break one hundred."

Atlas waited for a continuation but Jeb appeared to be done. Annabelle decided to join the conversation. "So you came here just to recruit us? Why?"

"Because God has been deemed murderous and we strive to prove his innocence. We want you to join us without anything in return because God is loving and accepting."

Atlas burst with an uncomfortable fit of laughter. Everyone looked at him either offensively or perplexingly.

"Sorry…" he mumbled in-between giggles. "It's just now I understand your game here. You're a cult."

Gonzo tightened his fist, imagining Atlas's throat in his iron grasp. Jeb raised his hands defensively.

"Not in the slightest. We only want what's best for our people and to praise God with good deeds. We could only be considered a cult if you think Christianity is a cult."

Atlas shrugged, "Well, God does seem like quite the narcissist…"

"Please don't speak of God in such a derogatory manner," Jeb said, his voice becoming thick.

Atlas was infamous for his stubbornness. However, when it came to religion, he went to a whole new level.

"You honestly believe that God is good? So let's just say for one moment that I believe in God—disregarding the fact that the idea of him is complete dickshit—and play along here. How can killing billions of people be considered justified? And if that's not enough, causing a virus to infect the people that managed to survive? How retarded can you possibly be?"

"God didn't cause the virus!" Jeb exclaimed, his rising temper now noticeable. "He wiped those sinners off the planet to restore balance! Doing so created the perfect amount of humans. But mankind has burdened him with so many of our wrongdoings that he was forced to infect us. We strong-armed him into plaguing us because we have let him down one too many times. It wasn't his fault! It was ours!"

"Sinners?" Atlas repeated, hearing only that one word come from his lips. "My friends died that day. Good, honest people! Christ, I even saw babies that were killed by your so-called god! Are they sinners too?!"

Jeb chuckled, this time in a spine-chilling manner. "God works in mysterious ways."

That was the tipping point for Atlas. He didn't remember sprinting towards Jeb and he didn't remember throwing a right hook into his cheek. Atlas only found himself aware of his surroundings when Gonzo approached him and forced his fist into his stomach, literally sending him flying back. The moment Atlas's back met the floor, Zara drew her bō from her back and aimed it an inch away from his face.

The girls were in shock. Josh was the only one who could speak. "Atlas!" he cried out.

"Not now, Josh!" Atlas spluttered back.

Everyone was silent. It was as if a realization blanketed the hotel and embraced the three perpetrators with incredible disbelief. Zara's bō retreated from Atlas's face and with a wind-breaking spin, she now aimed it at Josh.

"Whoa, hey, what did I do??" he asked feverishly.

She pierced her eyes at him with unbreakable seriousness. "What did you say your name was?"

He looked side to side at his helpless friends. "I…I didn't…"

With a flick of the wrist, she snapped the rounded end against his cheek, creating an immediate tear.

"Ow! That hurt!"

"Then don't be stupid," she warned. "I'm going to ask one more time. What is your name?"

"Josh…" he muttered childishly as he rubbed his cheek.

"Last name?"

"Valentine…why?"

She took a step back with her mouth fallen ajar. Looking back at Jeb, he shared this look of divine disbelief.

"I can't believe it…we found him…we actually found him!"

Saying that everyone was confused would be an understatement.

"Found who?" Annabelle asked as her forehead frowned.

Avoiding the question, the three huddled up and spoke with newfound excitement. As Atlas slowly staggered up to his feet, he didn't take his eyes off of Josh who was just as befuddled as the others. When they finally stopped their whispering, Jeb turned to us and grinned as maniacally as Gonzo had done.

"God has given us a gift today," he announced. "A gift that we'll be claiming. Josh, you're coming with us."

Before he could protest, Zara was already behind him and had his arms in a painful bind. Quinn was the first to go to his aid. If only she knew what she was doing.

"Wait! You can't just take him! What did he do?"

Jeb rubbed his freakishly smooth hands together, nearly exploding with joy.

"Oh no, no, no, my dear, you don't think we're just taking him, do you? We'll need you as well. All of you are coming with us."

"FUCK that!" Atlas yelled, grabbing his bat from the overturned garbage can that he had been hiding in. He couldn't even raise it for battle before Jeb pulled a revolver from the back of his waistband and fired it out of his hands. The bullet cut a hole in the top end and threw it back, sending a painful vibration through Atlas's hands.

"It's cute when they fight back," Jeb remarked, his smooth, outgoing voice nowhere to be found. "If you try anything like that again…" He placed the end of the pistol against Quinn's temple. "…We'll kill your lovely ladies."

A stream of tears flew down her face, smudging her mascara.

"Now move."

Now that they had arrived at the mysterious Cadillac, their group increased from three to five. The first of the two sat cross-legged on the hood of the vehicle, playing with a metallic yo-yo that burned the eyes of the living with each flick. He wore a jean vest and sand-coloured kakis as well as a pearly white undershirt, indicating that there seemed to be a not-so-subtle trend within the group. His hair was cut and shaped into a towering Mohawk the colour of a setting sun. Opposite of him was a stubby male with greasy muttonchops that looked to be poorly glued on each of his cheeks. His balding head formed a cul-de-sac hairline and he wore an untucked white dress shirt littered with food stains. Seeing the prisoners drew a smile to his face, though he appeared to find more enjoyment in the fresh female meat.

"Yo Boss, who're the kiddies?" Mohawk asked, barely glancing away from his ascending and descending toy.

"God has awarded us, Brother Bucky," Jeb said joyously. "We have found the boy."

Bucky caught his yo-yo as his focus became prioritized. He jumped off of the car and slowly turned to Jeb with the look of confusion and dismay mixed into one. "You mean…*his*…"

"That's the one," Zara confirmed, now with an elastic piece of bubble gum bouncing between her teeth.

"What are we going to do with them? Why have you brought others?" the fifth man asked eagerly.

"They'll be of great use to us when the time comes, Cricket," Jeb replied as if he were reading scripture.

"Boss, aren't they too young? Ya know, for the event?" Bucky asked.

Jeb turned to him and pulled a cigarette from his cardigan pocket. "We'll leave that for *him* to decide."

Things were not looking good. Being within arm's reach of Gonzo and lacking any weapons besides his fists, Atlas was guaranteed a definite defeat if he resisted. They made sure to pat him down twice for any weapons but they made the mistake of leaving Annabelle untouched. With her closely in front of him, she carefully pulled a sheathed knife from her waistband and handed it to Atlas. Careful not to whisper anything audible, he simply took it and shoved it in the front of his jeans. Now it was time for him to decide how he was going to use it.

"I have to piss," he said, not thinking of a better plan.

Jeb exhaled a cloud of nicotine and squinted at his random immaturity. "We haven't even left yet! Can't you hold it?"

"Do you want to learn the hard way?"

Understanding that he didn't want the seat cushions soaked with urine, he waved him off. "Fine. But if you try anything stupid, we won't hesitate to open fire. We don't need all of you."

Atlas gave the leader a sarcastic smile and wandered over to the far side of the Cadillac overlooking the rest of the parking lot. While he relieved himself, an uncomfortable silence drowned both the captors and the teenagers, while the teenagers shared confusing glances with one another as they found Atlas's behaviour odder than usual. Once he finished, he seemed to have dropped something and before he stood up, a loud release of air drew immediate attention.

"What was that?" Jeb asked.

Bucky faced the car and noticed something unordinary. "Uh…why is the car on a slant?"

Jeb and the others realized in less than a moment and their eyes clouded with rage. Gonzo appeared to unleash that rage on their behalf as he charged Atlas and lifted him from the gravel, causing something to slip from his grasp and hide beneath the car. He raised his tattooed arm into the air and sent his fist crashing down into Atlas's face. Bruising blood immediately encompassed his eye socket as he rolled on the ground in dizziness. Gonzo raised his fist again for the final blow when Jeb intervened.

"That's enough, Gonzo."

The silent brute released his first audible sound in the form of a reluctant groan and he dropped him down effortlessly.

"Did he just…that son of a bitch," Zara snarled.

Jeb spun on his heels and struck Zara across her face with such force her gum launched into the air.

"Swearing is for the weak. You are not weak. I made sure of that."

She bowed her head and rubbed her cheek silently as Josh did a moment ago.

Jeb faced his audience. "He's a clever one, that Atlas. He must've thought that little gag of his would do what, exactly? Somehow convince us that he's got too big of balls for us to handle? That we'd just leave you teens be and ride off in the sunset with our tails between our legs? Nope. Nuh-uh. You see, God has given us these wonderful things called legs, so I think it's time we use 'em for once! We'll walk."

The bandits groaned in disinclination. Cricket stuck out his bottom lip and frowned.

"Boss, That'd be a three day walk at least!" informed Bucky. "Us being out in the open might not be a good idea."

"We've made it this far with no problems and the big man upstairs will see to that continuation. Besides, once we return with these brats, we'll be rewarded beyond comprehension."

Now on his barely functioning feet, Atlas cleared his throat loudly and spat out a glob of blood. He looked up at Jeb.

"This isn't going to end well for you," he explained. "Ya think we're going to let a couple of psychos order us around?"

"That's exactly what's going to happen," Jeb informed.

"I can promise you one thing. I don't know when, I don't know where, but I can guarantee that I will be the one that kills you."

Jeb released another cloud alongside a chuckle. "Man, that's a morbid thought. Positive vibes are what makes the world go around. Don't be all down in the dumps." He looked back at his fellow captors. "Let's get going!"

The four men and Zara threw their packs over their backs and forced the teenagers to move ahead. Josh skin was fainter than the shade of pale and seemed as though he was a gentle tap away from collapsing. He couldn't fathom what these people wanted with the likes of him and couldn't understand whether to feel special or damned. The two girls were in that state of uncertain denial as the true gravity of their situation had yet to sink in. All that Annabelle knew was that she wanted a certain someone by her side. And Atlas? Well, he may have faced another in a long line of injuries but at least he was able to produce something out of it. Anticipating my return, he chose to leave a message that he was certain I was capable of deciphering. He knew deep down that I would ultimately fight to rescue them and I'm not ashamed to admit that he was right.

# 23. "...You wear lip gloss?"

Once their bodies escaped the frame for good, I sat back and rubbed the grainy images away from my eyes. Though their predicament may have seemed black and white, the lack of audio made things frustratingly gray. The entirety of the surveillance felt like a silent film with dialogue provided by the only two audience members watching. We didn't know who those people were, what they wanted, where they went, and most importantly, how we would track them down. Knowing Atlas, it was certain that there would be a clue of some sort. Sadly, knowing that did nothing for us.

"So what, they got kidnapped?" Veronica asked unpleasantly.

"Guess so," I muttered back.

"Why? What could those religious hippies need them for?"

My eyes continued analyzing the screens, watching the silent hotel remain painstakingly still. "The important part is that they were taken *alive*. If they wanted to kill them then we would've found them by now. The fact that they were kidnapped is at the very least a good sign."

The resentment she gave me felt like a scalding shower.

"How is that a good sign???" Her spit speckled the back of my hair.

"Because that gives us the chance to find them! We've got everything we need to know right in front of us, now we just need to fit the pieces back together."

Veronica closed her eyes, trying to rid her temper that would have me crucified. "...Okay. Try and find out why they took them in the first place."

I scrolled the bar backward and watched the previous hours rewind until it stopped at their first encounter.

*"Not now, Josh!" Atlas spluttered back.*

*Everyone was silent. It was as if a realization blanketed the hotel and embraced the three perpetrators with incredible disbelief. Zara's bō retreated from Atlas's face and with a wind-breaking spin, she now aimed it at Josh.*

*"Whoa, hey, what did I do??" he asked feverishly.*

*She pierced her eyes at him with unbreakable seriousness. "What did you say your name was?"*

*He looked side to side at his helpless friends. "I…I didn't…"*

*With a flick of the wrist, she snapped the rounded end against his cheek, creating an immediate tear.*

*"Ow! That hurt!"*

*"Then don't be stupid," she warned. "I'm going to ask one more time. What is your name?"*

*"Josh…" he muttered childishly as he rubbed his cheek.*

Pause.

"She points her staff-thingy at Josh. Why? He piss her off?"

I squinted at the sixth monitor and highlighted his frozen face with my finger. "It looks like he says…his name? I'm not the best lip-reader but that's what it looks like. So unless she REALLY doesn't like the name Josh, she must know him. Maybe a family friend?"

"You kidnap your family friends often?" she asked me acerbically.

"Well clearly they're not on good terms. Maybe none of them are. To some, that's enough of an excuse."

Veronica nodded and nibbled at the lid of a pen she found on the desk. "Okay, so they or at least she has it out for him. But where are they going?"

I fast forwarded up until their descent to the main floor and found nothing. We searched and searched and searched some more and reached the same ending of their departure every time. Tensions were high and the cramped surveillance room reeked with dissatisfaction.

"Damn! There's nothing!" Veronica released, her head tilted to the ceiling.

My forehead kissed the keyboard, typing V, B, and N over and over again in the search tab. "There's gotta be something. There always is."

She ruffled her hair with such violence I feared she would pull out a clump.

"Just…hell, I don't know…go back to the part where that mountain-looking guy clocks Atlas. That part still confuses me."

"There must be a reason they don't take the car," I said mostly to myself as I enhanced the main screen and brought up the parking lot.

*Atlas gave the leader a sarcastic smile and wandered over to the far side of the Cadillac overlooking the rest of the parking lot. While he relieved himself, an uncomfortable silence drowned both the captors and the teenagers, while the teenagers shared confusing glances with one another as they found Atlas's behaviour odder than usual. Once he finished, he seemed to have dropped something and before he stood up, a loud release of air drew immediate attention.*

*"What was that?" Jeb asked.*

*Bucky faced the car and noticed something unordinary.*

Pause.

"Right there!" I pointed out. "He looks at the car and says something that makes the other guy punch Atlas."

"Did he slash their tires?" Veronica said, providing another example of her practical thinking that I was envious of.

"That's…that's actually a very good guess. Only one way to find out!" I said with a tinge of excitement. "If you weren't such a bitch I'd kiss you right now."

I slipped out of the room before she could hit me.

As we reached outside, the day went from bad to worse. Like I pointed out earlier, the weather was the fan and shit was brewing. Said shit was about to hit.

Veronica took a step back. "Yup, he slashed 'em. Look at how it's on a tilt."

We tracked the front tire on the driver's side to be the victim and both knelt down like wannabe detectives.

"Well…that's definitely a sliced tire. Glad we cracked that!" Veronica said with her natural mockery.

"No, no, no…" I stopped her, running my fingers over the split rubber. "It's not just a regular cut. He made it into a shape."

Veronica peered closely and frowned. "An eight? Why would he carve a goddamn eight into a tire?"

"I…I haven't thought that part through," I admitted. "Jus' give me a second."

She stood up and paced angrily and unknowingly. "Well that's just great! My sister is probably in the midst of getting raped by that hippie Jesus and you're busy playing CSI!"

"Veronica, your mouth is open. I suggest you shut it," I said impatiently.

While she pouted, I continued to stare at the eight as if it was an optical illusion, focusing and un-focusing my eyes until it finally hit me.

"It's not an eight!" I declared.

"What?"

"It's not an eight! Look at it sideways."

Tilting her head, she understood what I was saying but didn't understand where I was going. "Okay, it's an infinity symbol. Your point?"

I couldn't help but smile at Atlas's unexpected genius. "Where did we say that we were all going?"

"Uhm...that place...Safehaven?"

"—Which you can only get to when you take the bridge out of town. Know what the name of that bridge is called?"

"No Levi, I don't know what it's called. I don't have a book nearby on fucking bridge names."

"It's called Infinity Bridge," I finished.

Realization hit her but it hadn't been to the same extent as I had hoped. "You understand how much of a stretch that is? So you think that's where they're taking him or where he's going to end up?"

"Whatever it is, that's where they'll be. Now you can either wait here and sulk or come with me to bring them back. Your choice."

She approached me with a passionate anger. "Whoa, just wait a second. *You* were the one that left in the first place! Now you've suddenly had a change of heart? I don't think so. What's in it for you?"

I looked down at my hand where Atlas's baseball bat was held. When we first discovered they were missing, I felt obliged to take it.

"Look, even I can feel guilt. I don't want their blood on my conscience so I'm going to make sure that none of it gets spilt. You okay with that?"

Veronica shrugged her shoulder so that her backpack rested properly. "Fine. But I'm coming with you. No way you are getting all the credit."

I flashed my teeth mockingly. "It's a date."

I walked over to the van with Veronica trailing behind, not realizing she had picked up something from beneath the Cadillac.

The air felt different. There was an embodied heaviness as though gravity decided to double. The trailer of food and supplies—which we had retrieved off of our originally abandoned truck and attached it to the van—rattled behind us like a dragging muffler. As always, bodies of death or infected were placed alongside the highway, fallen from their vehicles, limping or crawling in a seemingly state of abandon, yet the body count felt uncomfortably minimal. The drive toward the city felt like heading into a spoiled surprise party, longing for the inevitable to just happen already.

Heavy rainclouds rolled down the sky and swallowed each other into a vast, murky ceiling above us. Wind blew at incredible speeds, pulling victimized trees from their buried roots like it was nothing. The thunder and lightning being relinquished through the sky was as lethal as it was dazzling. Even with the headlights turned to the highest notch, we struggled to see more than a few feet in front of us through the dense rain falling from the sky. Then, as if things hadn't reached the appropriate level of creepiness and oddity, Veronica spotted something as we crossed a hurrying river.

"STOP!" she demanded.

I stomped on the brakes and our van came to a painfully screeching halt.

"What?" I asked, picking my torso up from the steering wheel.

She pulled her sleeve up so it covered her palm and wiped a circle into the fogged-up window. Her eyes locked onto something that was resting on the bank of the river.

"Do you see that?"

I leaned in to her window and struggled to make it out. "Is it a person? I can't tell."

Whatever the thing was, it had knelt down in prayer position and frenetically scooped the rushing water into its mouth. The fast-pouring rainwater mixed in with the river, raising the water level to a reaching height.

"Look at how it's moving," she pointed out. "The way its limbs are contorting and twitching? It seems like it's…an infected?"

The way it moved was reminiscent of a prehistoric Neanderthal whose survival instincts were full-fledged. The scene was so raw and barbaric that it took me a moment to realize how much of a game-changer this really was.

"They…they drink!" I exclaimed.

"Nothing gets past you," she replied.

"These aren't zombies, Veronica. I had a feeling before but this… this proves it. Something dead wouldn't need the primary resource for life, right? They're more intelligent than we thought."

She rested back in her seat. "So what does this mean?"

I gripped the steering wheel. "It means they're living. And we're killing them."

Finishing the conversation on a morbid note, I shifted from park to drive and was met with a vicious rumbling. Beneath the hood of our vehicle, the engine started to splutter and release the sounds of grinding metal. Eventually, a thin layer of smoke seeped out and fused with the murky atmosphere. I was getting so sick of our infamously horrid luck.

"ARE YOU FU…" I stopped. Took a breath. Held it in for four seconds and released it with another four. Just like how they taught me.

I felt Veronica's worrisome glare through her peripherals as if she was frightened to look at me head-on. You're taught to never look at a wild animal directly in its eyes.

"…You good?"

I inhaled and chewed on the swallowed air. "I'm good."

She eased up. "The battery's probably drained. Either that or the engine's shot."

The base of my skull embraced the headrest forcefully. "What do you know about cars?"

Unintentionally, my question may have come across as both sexist and inferior because the look of unlawful anger embedded in her eyes stabbed me.

"What's your problem?" I asked.

"Nothing," she said, too quickly to mean it. "You handle it then. Go on. Check the fucking thing."

I blew out and raised my eyebrows, as that was the universal expression for males alike when we didn't understand women's anger. As I would later find out, I had been in the wrong.

Stepping into the storm, I clung to the edge of the van's hood and pulled myself to the front bumper. Smoke rose through the outline of the hood and I lifted it up to see an array of tubing and metal contraptions. I mindlessly looked down at it whilst stroking my chin.

"Alright…well that's the engine…Uhm…Maybe…Christ, what am I even doing?" I asked myself hopelessly.

Examining countless parts that had no meaning to me, I managed to spot a red tube that wiggled more than it probably should have.

"Okay that doesn't look right. When in doubt, pull it out."

I pulled it out, only to have steam billowing from the opening and into my face.

"*Cough* Ahh, the steam is working," I spluttered sarcastically. "Check that off the list, Veronica."

Through the foggy windshield, I slowly saw her finger spell out something.

"Suck…my…rude."

I plugged the hole where steam poured out of and focused my eyes on the engine, expecting something to magically fix itself. Giving up on me—which was a completely valid thing to do—Veronica rolled down her window. "Hurry up! This is not the ideal place to be right now!"

She couldn't have been more right. A stream of lightning electrocuted the sky with ear-popping thunder following a half-beat too late. Once the sky dimmed back to its blackness, an army of shadows appeared on either side of this bridge ten feet above water. As if the lightning assembled them miraculously, there was no plausible explanation for them to suddenly be there at such a magnitude.

"What the…there's no way…" I uttered, breathless.

Their silence was incomparable. They appeared with such fluidity and prowess that it couldn't have been do so randomly. Like a wolf stalking a rabbit, they were patient and they were calm. They were there because they planned it. And on came the feast.

"Veronica, stay in the car," I said with my raised hand extended to her. "That's an order!"

Even when I was trying to be the good guy I was the bad guy.

"Go fuck yourself, Levi. Get in the car. Now."

I ran for the door of the van but instead of the driver's door I opened the back passengers, where a crowbar and a baseball bat rested side by side. I grabbed the bat and slid the door shut.

"Van won't hold for long," I told her, though it felt like screaming. "If I can take some out, then you'll have a shot!"

She stared at me like I was an alien. I could see that she had an internal feud on whether to join me or not. But before the decision could be formed, they had arrived.

Men and women, children and past friends, all sizes and varying stages of decomposition, all with only the desire to feel my susceptible flesh rip between their teeth. They could instantly smell the vulnerability on my skin through their collapsed noses and started to swarm in a circle. I swung at one's head, knocking it into another, and another, and another like a curve of dominos. Backhand and forehand, left and right, I kicked and I shouted, I killed and I missed, but no matter what I did, they kept coming for me. A woman latched her grimy fingers on me and dug her wedding ring into my shoulder. She found my groan of pain enjoyable and smiled.

"You're all sick..." I grunted.

Stronger than her skeletal appearance had implied, she pressed me against the concrete barricades that separated the bridge from open air. Then, with a shot of adrenaline mixing with a reckless teenage mind, I tipped back and took the both of us down into the rapid waters.

"Levi!!" Veronica screamed, hands pressed against the glass.

She snapped at my face as we were free falling. Her gastric breath was enough to make me vomit but we impacted the rushing floor before I had the chance. The moment water filled my lungs, I realized that I might have overlooked a slightly important fact: I didn't know how to swim.

While the bubbling water licked my eyeballs, I couldn't help but think back to the single swimming lesson I took when I was six. It lasted eight minutes, my dad figured it would be a good idea to bring a six-pack while watching from the bleachers, we both got kicked out, and that was the extent of my learning. Funny how you think about the things that never seemed important at the exact moment you need them. But that might have been an afterthought since I was too preoccupied with drowning. My insides felt like dumbbells and my brain felt painfully constricted until...it softened. With the woman gone—dying upon impact—I was in a solitary bliss and I started to fade away.

1...2...3...1...2...3...listen...1...2...3...1...2...3...listen... nothing...breath...kiss...

Water expelled from my mouth and returned down to lather my face. I looked up to see rain and a familiar face. Then I was out again.

The drizzle of a fading storm pattered on the seasoned windows of the fifties-style diner. The Ink Spots were etched on a vinyl that echoed statically. Shiny, red plastic seat cushions pressed up against my unconscious back. I heard sizzling, cooking perhaps. I felt warmth against my eyelids, artificial light that hummed and hissed. Wait a minute…lights don't hiss…

Groggily, I heaved my eyelids open and blinded myself with the hanging lights. Sitting up dizzily, I wiped them clear and opened them to see nothing but confusion. Firstly, there was an antique woman who stared blankly into space. Her skin tone was that of a faded brown and she wore a hijab over her head, both indicating that she was of Middle Eastern descent. Though her eyes were pale and blind, she had a facial expression that resembled eternal contentment. Secondly, Veronica was standing behind the counter in front of a stove. She was cooking. And last but not least, I felt a heavy weight piled on my legs. Looking down, I saw that it was a snake. A motherfucking Samuel L. Jackson *Snakes on a Plane* kind of snake.

"What the hell!" I shrieked.

The surprised python jerked its head back and slithered away to its master. Veronica rushed over to me with a steaming frying pan.

"You're up," she pointed out. "…Good to have you back."

There were questions of questions that I needed to ask but whether it was my weary state or my male immaturity, I decided to say the one stupid thing I could've said.

"…You wear lip gloss?" I muttered, rubbing my grinning lips.

She slapped me so hard I blacked out for the third time.

## 24. "Poppycock. You're not giving us fuck all except for a problem."

Past the sea of forestry that pierced into the skyline, a wide, dream-inducing meadow rested on the earth as if it was a blanket knitted by the hands of gods. The storm had passed and the land remained untouched as if an invisible orb encapsulated it preciously. Birds chirped, frogs croaked, bugs buzzed, and leaves rustled, adding dashes of serenity to the natural masterpiece. Not a single sign of man's presence could be identified, aside from the parted trail in the tall grass made by the moving legs of four teenagers and five captors.

Though the storm had passed, their considerably moist clothes still clung to their respective bodies. Makeup smeared and the girls were now on bare display for all the starving men. Annabelle's black bra was like a magnet and the blatant staring made her wish she was locked in her room. That, however, could not be possible. Seven hours away from the hotel that they briefly called home, Atlas, Josh, Annabelle, Quinn, and the group of marauders stumbled forward at a steady pace. Atlas's head drooped and his face frowned in a quizzical fashion as he pondered a plan of escape. With the landscape at his disposal, he had been able to conjure up four ways of fleeing, none of which would successfully bring his fellow survivors along with him. Selfish decisions that came to him instinctively were forced to be forgotten. The moment he emerged from that garbage can he was reluctantly responsible for them. More than he would care to admit, he felt somewhat at fault for their predicament that only stoked the embers of guilt faintly burning in his chest, acting as a constant reminder of a potential fire. So until he could find a way to rescue himself as well as the people that trusted him, all that was left was to keep on walking.

Cricket scratched at his overly protruding stomach and pinched the collar of his shirt to fan himself. It wouldn't be hard to believe if this was the most he had ever walked.

"*Hff*...can't we...can't we find a car?"

Jeb withdrew another cigarette and popped it between his smooth lips. "Any car out here is either shot or stuck in traffic. If you want to clear a path for us on the highway, be our guest."

Cricket lifted his lethargic gaze and dropped it on me. "If only this motherless, scar-faced greaser didn't slash our tires." He stumbled slightly faster to reach up to Atlas in their line of prisoners. He leaned in so that his grubby snout grazed the hairs above Atlas's ear. "You're gonna love what's in store for you, kiddy. You're gonna wish your mom had gotten that abortion."

His anger was flickering but Atlas was smart enough to keep it in check. His mouth, however, not so much. "Abortion? Really? At least *pretend* that you're religious."

He pushed his frameless glasses back into his piggish face. "I worship God with every ounce of my being."

"What's your god supposed to be? A cheesecake?"

Cricket raised the back of his sausage fingers in the form of a slap but was silenced by Jeb's abrupt shushing.

"Over there," he pointed at a moving shape that broke through the tree line.

Everyone looked up to see a brown doe with white speckles galloping through the grass, only to slow its speed and recede to a calming state. Daisies and lilies kissed at its hooves while it quietly tromped through the field. Suddenly, the head of the doe rose precipitously at the sound of twigs snapping beneath their feet.

"Would you look at that," muttered Bucky.

"It's beautiful," Quinn said with a glimmer of hope.

For a moment, no one spoke. Even the brutal nature that was found in the five captors had been suppressed at the sight of the elegant creature. The chirping of birds faded away into the background, as did the buzzing of the insects, issuing complete silence in the field. This didn't last long as a firing bullet that shot from the bushes shattered the silence. The doe couldn't even turn its head before the lug of metal pierced through its skull and splattered blood onto the fresh flowers. Quinn released a small gasp and even Atlas couldn't help but widen his eyes.

"What the hell was that??" asked Atlas in a raised tone. "Was that one of you?"

Jeb looked at his group of fellow worshippers to see not a gun raised. It wasn't until the cries of happiness and cheers were heard in the distance did the true killer reveal himself.

"It appears we are not alone," Jeb said happily. Zara pulled out her bō and took on a battle-ready pose.

A plaid-wearing man with a beer-stuffed gut (substantially smaller than Cricket's) emerged from the forest with a rifle in his clutch. His salty goatee lifted with his smile, eager to feed the hunger rumbling in his belly. The smile on his face was quick to drop however, when he caught sight of the nine individuals that were watching him. He stopped walking and looked over to them.

"H-hello," he called out shakily. "Sorry, folks. Wadn't expecting anyone out 'ere."

Jeb gave him an acknowledging wave and grinned in a friendly fashion that reminded Annabelle of their first encounter. Atlas saw this hunter as the key to their escape and decided to jump at the opportunity.

"Help us!! These men are holding us hostage!! Please He--"

Gonzo's right hook routinely slammed into his stomach, shutting him up.

"Guhh…" Atlas wheezed with a sense of déjà vu.

The hunter stirred in place and watched the commotion with confusion and fear swirling in his head. He gripped at the handle of his rifle but immediately dropped the weapon to the ground at the sight of Jeb's aiming pistol.

The hunter raised his hands and surrendered. "Puh-please, I d-don't want any trouble, sir."

Jeb approached the man until they were in speaking distance from one another with his gun still raised. He sighed and pulled at his beard curiously.

"Hmm, we're in quite the conundrum, aren't we? You see, I was about to invite you to come with us, but something tells me you're not interested in that."

The hunter momentarily glanced at the teens and proceeded to back away. "I ain't seen nothing, man. Do whatever ya want with those kids, I ain't judging. Just let me take my buck and I'll leave you be. No questions asked."

Atlas grimaced at the man's cowardice.

Jeb's smile dropped. "You come across people who have kidnapped children and believe they are deserving of "whatever we want" to do to them? Your ignorance is sinful and downright disgusting."

He didn't wait for a response and pulled the trigger, shooting the man in the heart. The bullet lodged itself into a valve, causing the organ to explode from the inside.

"Jesus!" yelped Atlas. "You killed him! You actually killed him!"

Jeb calmly stepped forward to the dead hunter and knelt down beside him. Dipping his finger in the gushing blood, he brought it to his forehead and swiped a streak of blood downwards.

Zara popped a gum bubble emotionlessly. "We only consider it killing if they are one of us; a person of god. Not a sinner like him."

Jeb stood up and faced them. "She's right. God made it so that we would cross paths with this beast. I'm able to determine how sinful one is with a single glance." He beckoned Atlas over and though he was hesitant that stepping out of line would result in another beating, he eventually made his way over to the fresh corpse.

"Overweight, tracks on his both of his arms, cheap dentures, and…" Jeb flipped over his body, "just as I thought."

Tucked in his back pocket was a half-filled mickey of vodka.

"People like him don't deserve to live. Soon, you'll understand why."

Jeb walked back to the group and pointed back at the deer. "Gonzo, get the deer."

He responded with a grunt that dripped with annoyance. Atlas took a moment and when he joined everyone else, the vodka was no longer with the hunter.

The day came and went, leaving them in the company of the homicidal darkness. Being forced to vacate any roadways and streets for the infected to claim, the captors came across an abandoned campground.

"This'll do for the night," Jeb decided. "Gonzo, look for any inferiors lurking about."

Like a battered donkey, he trotted away disgracefully. While the rest waited for his all-clear, Annabelle spotted the name of the campground, Blackberry Grounds, and her brain activity flatlined. She backed away with a look of sheer corruption and agony carved into her pale face.

"Ann?" Quinn asked. "You okay?"

Annabelle looked at her for a moment before returning her gaze to the out-of-focus surroundings that clawed at her. A painful lump lodged into her throat, pressurizing her panicked breath. Nothing about the way she acted was normal. Granted, the world was far from whatever could be considered normal, but whatever had taken hold of her was on an entirely different level.

Gonzo returned and announced the safety of the campsite by giving them a thumbs up.

"Perfect. Gonzo, Find a barbeque for us to cook up the deer while we find a site to set up camp. Hopefully God is gracious and provides us with spare tents and trailers."

"What about them?" Bucky asked about the teenagers as he spun his yo-yo.

While they walked to a spotted plot, Jeb peered behind the group and noticed Annabelle had refused to move.

"Hey…what're you doing?"

Bucky approached her and when he grabbed his arm to pull her forward, she resisted. Like a dog that knew something the others hadn't, she fought desperately to avoid entering the campsite.

"Don't make this harder than it needs to be," Bucky told her with an audible strain in his voice.

"No! NO!" she pleaded.

Annabelle bent her head to his forearm and bit down, puncturing pockets of blood.

"Dammit! Bitch bit me!" he angrily complained.

Now lacking patience, Bucky gave her a single resounding tug on her arm with enough force to tear joints. She fell into the camp's boundaries and yelped.

"Don't you dare touch her again," Atlas threatened. Josh stood behind him, trying to back him up whilst burying his fear.

"What're you? A buck ten soaking wet? Shit, I dare you to try and threaten me again without your voice cracking," Bucky snarled back.

"This is not necessary," Jeb ended. He turned to Atlas. "I was going to let you all snuggle up in a tent together. Clearly, none of you brainless toddlers can be trusted with that. So, I'm forced to do what I feared might happen. Zara, reach in your pack and grab the stuff."

Zara looked at him quizzically. "You sure? We don't have much left. You said it yourself that this is specifically for—"

"Just do it!" he cut her off.

She shrugged and unzipped her backpack. After rummaging through cans of fruit and lukewarm bottled water, she pulled out a bundle of thick rope.

"Here," she passed to him. "That's all I got. Bucky probably has some more."

Bucky pulled out the rope that he had. "You want me to?"

Jeb nodded. Bucky tucked his yo-yo in his pocket and proceeded to tie one around Annabelle's neck.

"You bastards are going to hang her?!" Atlas asked frightfully.

"Calm down, boy," Bucky said. "It's just a leash."

While Annabelle looked to be too dazed and traumatized to protest, Quinn spoke up on her behalf. "We're not dogs! You shouldn't be doing this to us!"

Jeb shook his head irritatingly. "We also have duct tape. Should we use that as well?"

Quinn shut up.

"Good choice."

One by one, Bucky tied a complex knot at the back of their necks and formed a suffocating leash for the three of them. When he came to Atlas, no rope was left.

"Damn, ain't that a bummer!" Atlas said cheeringly, hoping for the off-chance they would leave him be.

Jeb waved his index finger left and right like a metronome. "Ah, ah, ah, I just so happen to have the perfect thing."

Reaching into his personal collection of goodies, he pulled out a bike chain and a padlock.

"You have got to be kidding me."

With a smile that couldn't seem to disappear, Jeb dropped his pack and sat on a slanted stump. The smell of cooking deer wafted around the campgrounds and formed a potent, carnivorous cloud above them. The teenagers' stomachs screamed for hunger, but when Josh looked over to Gonzo who used a barbeque that was as sterilized as a toilet seat, he advised against it.

They were fed scraps. When Atlas was parched, he asked for water that Jeb annoyingly handed to him. Explaining his disappointment that it didn't turn into wine made Atlas without water for the rest of the night and Jeb self-conscious about his Christ-like beard. This was about the extent of their 'dinner' and when it came to bedtime, the teens were separated and tied to trees, one on each opposing side; Atlas with Josh and Quinn with Annabelle. While the captors took turns throughout the night for both guard-duty and perimeter watch, Jeb was the primary candidate for the boys, Zara for the girls.

Unable to sleep sitting upright against a tree and with a noose around her neck, Quinn tried to make conversation.

"Your eyes are very pretty," she said with a weary smile to Zara.

Now that she had a moment to actually examine them, she could see the intricate detail around each eye. Her left one was a midnight blue that swirled and curved at the edges. Precise spacing could be found between each wave and that patience was passed on to her right eye that contrasted with a cherry red. The design was more static and fiery, yet balanced and contained appropriately. It was truly a masterpiece sketched on her face.

Zara blew and popped a bubble. "Thanks, I made them myself."

A painfully awkward laugh wheezed out of Quinn. "No haha, I meant the designs."

"So did I. Tattooed them on when I was around your age."

"Tattoos? Jesus, that must've hurt!"

Zara shrugged, suggesting that pain was not a problem for her. "Nah. A bee sting's worse. As long as you're okay with biting down on leather then you're golden."

Leather was a trigger word for Quinn as she suddenly flashed back to three years prior where she found herself in a dingy basement. Her arms and legs were strung up like a calf at a rodeo and a thick wad of leather was slipped between her teeth. A lone lamp dangled from the sweating ceiling, flashing glimpses of a gimp suited man on top of her.

"I…I wouldn't know," Quinn said, a reminding pain trickling below her waist.

The rest of their conversation was minimal and usually resulted with Quinn asking to be let free. On the opposite side of the tree,

Annabelle had dissolved into the darkness. Using this to her benefit, she bit and chewed at the rope like a rabid beast. Her gums were becoming torn and her teeth ached but it was a small price to pay in order to flee this hell she found herself in. It was like an animal chewing off its limb for survival, except Annabelle needed all of her limbs for what she was planning on doing to her captors. I was unaware of the reason for her paranoia at the time and when I eventually found out, it made my childhood look like a spin-off of *Happy Days*.

Moving over to the men's tree, Atlas glued his eyes on Jeb, whom had been reading a passage from his personal Bible. Seeing Jeb's calm nature made the stumps of where his ring and little finger once were itch incredibly. He had no idea why.

"Can I ask you something?" Atlas spoke up.

Jeb remained silent while he finished his page. When he was done, he slammed it closed and beckoned Atlas with his hands. "Lay it on me."

"What do you gain from this? Kidnapping all of us, I mean. It's clear you need Josh for whatever kinky, religiously fetish thing you've got planned—I don't really give a damn—but what about us? What's our purpose here?"

"I can still hear you guys…" Josh feebly called from behind the tree.

Ignoring him, Jeb nodded with a smile. "Right there! Exactly what you said! That's why we've taken you kids. We are giving you a *purpose*."

Atlas snorted. "Poppycock. You're not giving us fuck all except for a problem. We were perfectly fine before your hippy ass came barging into our home."

"You lie to yourself," Jeb was quick to reply. "Perfectly fine? Remember what I said about being able to read people? Well, when I look at you kids, I see flawed individuals. Each and every one of you, there's something that's broken."

"Oh yeah?" Atlas said in a challenging tone.

Jeb cleared his throat but spoke at a volume only they shared. "The blonde one, Quinn? She's addicted to sex and pleasure. With the help of the shadows, she is touching herself as I speak."

Atlas nonchalantly peered to the side and sure enough, he could see her arm moving up and down while Zara walked the perimeter.

"Josh," he continued, "he is weak. And his blood is tainted."

This confused Atlas. "Wait…he's infected?"

"Yes…but not in the way that you think. A much worse kind of infection that will be dealt with soon enough."

The foreshadowing was too strong for Atlas to deal with. He raised both of his eyebrows and exhaled heavily.

"The quiet one, I believe her name is Annabelle, she is broken. You may think this as well, but you have no idea how bad it really is."

"And me? What's wrong with me? Please, I'd love to know."

Jeb paused for a moment, studying Atlas's piercing eyes. "You… you are lonely."

Atlas frowned. "And that's a sin? Well fuck me sideways."

As he said it, he remembered the very first day when Tibbs was the first to go; the day his mother died.

"I wasn't finished," he clarified. "Due to your loneliness, you drink. A lot. Some may even consider it alcoholism."

Atlas laughed, but said nothing.

"Don't think I didn't notice you take the vodka from the hunter's body. I can smell it off your breath."

"I don't have a problem. I can stop anytime I want to."

"Then why don't you?"

Atlas smiled. "Because I don't have a problem."

Jeb let out a genuine laugh. "Heh, that's good. You're pretty funny. It's a shame what will happen to you."

His smile faded instantly. "What will happen to me?"

Jeb opened his Bible up once more and gave him one last glance over the top of the page.

"Now that would just be ruining the surprise, wouldn't it?"

The next day, clouds of a dusty gray parted ways and revealed a morning blue sky. Down on the drying land, the living had woken alongside the sun and used this morning solidarity to cover some untouched land. Whether or not the halfies slept or could even comprehend the idea of sleep, they were always nowhere to be seen at the break of day.

"How much farther?" Josh asked, pulling at his leash. "I'm getting neck burn."

"I've got a solution for that," Zara said, now tossing back candy coke bottles. "First, you need to think really hard. Then, with enough effort, you'll be able to grow some balls and suck the fuck up."

Jeb was about to confront her and her swearing, but her raised bō was faster and at the ready, making him decide against it. Atlas couldn't help but form a weak smile.

Another hour of silence passed and Josh could feel holes forming in the heels of his shoes. His fear and uncertainty had come and gone and now he was just exhausted. He didn't care what was happening, he just wanted it to be over.

"Hey…I gotta ask," he spoke up. "Are you guys cannibals? Like, that'd be the shits and all that but at least we'd know. It's pretty early on to resort to humans though. Like, if you went a year of Spam and stale Cheetos, then at least I'd understand."

Jeb lit another cigarette from his seemingly unlimited supply. "We would never resort to such a disgrace. Why would we ever taint our bodies by ingesting people below us?"

Josh shrugged. "Well, you ate the deer…"

Jeb puffed a smoke cloud. "That's because deer are worth eating."

That seemed to shut everyone up. Well, until Josh ran his mouth off again.

"Just in case you guys are cannibals, you should eat Atlas first. He's got way more muscle than me."

Atlas shook his head. "That's the weirdest compliment I've ever received."

"Quiet!" Bucky said just below a yell. He pointed to the left of them where they looked to find a church.

"Have we claimed this one yet?" Jeb asked hurryingly.

They looked back to Cricket who had pulled out a small notebook and a golf pencil. After flipping a few pages, he looked up from his frameless glasses and shook his head.

"Perfect," Jeb said happily. "Zara, Gonzo, you know what to do. I'll join you."

Zara shook a finger at him. "Nuh-uh. You're not going. Whenever you come along you just watch and don't do any of the work. At least if you're out here, you can help fight off any biters. Besides, we don't have any more rope. I told you we didn't have much left, didn't I?"

"Yes you bloody told me that!" Jeb cried crankily. "…Fine. I'll stay here. Just make sure that you two don't mess it up. Boss will use you next if you do."

Zara looked up at Gonzo and then back to him. "What're we supposed to use?"

"Just figure it out! At least one of you has a brain so use it!"

Biting the air in her closed mouth, Zara turned around and stormed off to the church with Gonzo lazily following behind. Now, all that was left was the confusion.

"Uh…did I miss something?" Atlas asked his fellow teenagers. "What's going on in the church?"

In an outburst of rage, Jeb rushed in so that he was mere inches from his face. "You're not worthy of witnessing it, you boozer cretin." He turned around and faced the two remaining captors, Bucky and Cricket. "How dare that nigger talk to me like that! I'm next in charge! I was there for the very first time *he* did it!"

Bucky pulled out his yo-yo and rested on a park bench. Downtown was in the nearby distance.

"I don't know what to tell you, Boss, other than to shut up. The infected are worse than ever. We don't need an army of them on our asses right now."

Feeling the power and authority slipping from his grasp, Jeb slumped down against a fire hydrant whilst whispering hypocritical swears. Josh, Atlas and Quinn stood there, unsure what to do. Annabelle was still in an upright comatose state.

"So…we wait?" Quinn wondered.

"Yes!" Jeb said impatiently. "We wait!"

And so they waited. But what they were unaware of, however, was what had been occurring inside of Cricket. You see, ever since he laid eyes on Annabelle and Quinn—two girls thirty years younger than him—he had wanted to do sinful, barbaric, unspeakable things to them. Ranging from imagining them swapping urine to wearing each other's skin, his psychotic sex drive was unable to be contained much longer. Seeing Quinn with a leash on was too much to bear and he wanted to take advantage of his superiority.

He removed his glasses and dropped them. "Oops."

Looking at Quinn, she looked back at him puzzlingly. "Uhm…you dropped your glasses."

He inhaled, hoping to catch her scent. "Pick them up for me."

She hesitated. "What? Why can't you—"

"Now," he repeated sternly.

Not wanting to worsen their situation, she confusingly bent over to pick up his glasses, exposing her round, bubble-shaped rear that was covered by her white, see-through jean shorts. He faced her raised bottom and immediately got hard.

"Stay there," he ordered with a maniacal smile. The other teenagers started to worry.

She stopped mid-bent and looked back at him. "What? Is there a bug on me?"

His smile widened. "Get on all fours."

That's when Atlas intervened. "Alright, you pervert…"

"You keep your mouth shut, you spineless shit of a child!" he screamed.

Somewhat frightened, Atlas looked down at Jeb, who appeared to be interested in what was unfolding. He did nothing.

"Get on all fours."

"But…" Quinn began to protest.

"Do it. Now."

She looked down innocently and slowly proceeded to drop to her hands and knees. Once there, He leaned in so she could smell his gnarly breath. He sniffed her hair and suddenly yanked it back, making her yelp.

"I want you to bark. Bark like a dog."

This was too much. Atlas stomped forward with a fury plaguing his mind, but he was tugged back. Jeb got up from the ground and grabbed hold of his dragging chain. He pulled back sharply and Atlas dropped to the ground as his throat momentarily collapsed.

"Bark like the bitch you are."

Quinn felt true fear. As she struggled internally, Josh stood up but hesitated fearfully. Annabelle did nothing visible but behind her back she was frantically scratching at her frayed rope.

"*BARK*!"

She barked. Cricket moaned with excitement.

"Beautiful! Now…lick me."

Tears trickling down, she shook her head. "N-no…"

He knelt down and faced her, his massive gut almost touching her face. "What did you say?"

"I…I won't…"

Cricket struck her, again and again. "Don't *SMACK* you ever *SMACK* say no *SMACK* to me!!"

While Quinn's face became swollen and tender, she thought back to another basement, this time designed like an elementary classroom. She wore a skimpy, tissue-thick schoolgirl outfit that was torn away to nothing. A neon pink gag ball was shoved in her mouth, strapped on with shiny leather. Two guys were behind her. One was a fifty-year-old man in a toddler outfit and wore a propeller hat on his head, the other a slimy looking 'teacher'. Together, they had their way with her. A third man was by her face, watching and pleasuring himself. This... this was not forceful, nor was it degrading. It was a sexual discovery and a mutual tool for enjoyment that was being given and received. The thought was troubling and one that not many would enjoy experiencing. Quinn was one of the few and was barely fifteen years old at the time.

Atlas fought as best as he could but Jeb had his chain in his grasp and his shoe on his skull. Bucky took no part in it, only throwing his yo-yo up and down with a solemn look. Josh started to cry. Annabelle finally scratched through the rope but just as she was ready to claw that overweight pedophile, a loud train-like whistle grabbed all of their attention. They collectively looked up and Atlas could not believe his eyes.

Josh's mouth dropped. "Is...is that...a cowboy?"

## 25. "We're dogs, remember? I'm marking my territory."

My brain felt like liquid. Every little movement made it swish and my vision trailed along like a fat boy suffering an 800m race. With a slow, wavering shuffle, I managed to reach the front counter and slumped down in a high-top swivel chair. My head fell to the checker-tiled counter as if both were magnetized.

"Don't slap a recently concussed person," I grumbled through my folded arms. "I'm all…fuzzy."

Veronica turned around wearing a new and clean outfit—an undone red and black gingham button-up overtop a white, Joan Jett T-shirt and bleached jeans below—and slid a plate of lukewarm pancakes next to me. Her look of eternal discontentment and judgment was ever so present.

"Awe, thanks for jumping in a river to rescue me," she spoke in a baritone impersonation of myself. "Thanks for resuscitating me back to life and dragging my dead weight back to safety. Thanks for the goddamn Aunt Jemima pancakes."

I raised my head and heaved a drone through my diaphragm that felt both bruised and exhausted. "…Thanks Veronica. For everything. You saved my life and…I'm not going to forget that."

She scoffed, assuming I was being facetious. I pulled the plate toward me and jabbed a chunk of pancake into my mouth with a permanently stained fork.

"Except for the pancakes," I added. "Taste like cardboard dipped in lard."

"I wasn't going to make them from scratch just for your sorry ass. I'm amazed this place still has power. It was either here or a strip club called *The Dusty Flamingo*. An easy choice considering how I wasn't keen on facing pale ones with their pastied-tits flopping out."

I chuckled. "Smart." Lifting my fork, I directed attention to the blind woman and her pet snake. "Just a small question: What's up with the gypsy and python? Does that not weird you out…like, at all?"

She curved her mouth to one side and shrugged. "She let me in before they could get me *or* you. Doesn't speak English though. And I'm not entirely sure she knows we're here, but she's nice all the same. The more important question though is what the hell were you thinking? Jumping in a river? I hope you know we lost all of our food and supplies."

I scratched my unshaven puberty beard and breathed out guiltily. "I wasn't thinking. That's on me. I…uh, I don't know how to swim."

She snorted. "Clearly."

"Like I said, I'm sorry." I paused, looking at the stopped clock between a picture of Elvis and Gene Kelly. "…How long have I been out? I mean, before you slapped me."

Veronica leaned over the counter and peered through the door window. "Around ten hours or so. If we leave now, we'll be able to make it to the bridge in a day, two at most."

I stood up, my joints and muscles screaming for mercy, and gave her a reassuring smile. "Then let's get a move on."

She nodded. "Lemme just grab some snacks and water for the road. I'm…not sure, but I think she said anything in the back is fair game."

"Please try and find me some new clothes," I asked. "I feel like a goddamn cartoon character."

She gave me a thumbs up above her head and vanished through the swinging doors, leaving me with a gypsy and her reptile.

"I…uhm…" I muttered confusingly.

The hijab-clad woman continued her stare in an unspecified direction. Her snake flickered its tongue at me sneakily.

"Well this is just weird."

Waiting for Veronica, I returned to the booth I awoke from and found Atlas's bat perched up against the opposite bench. It's literally taken a bullet and my crowbar was nowhere to be found. Seeing as I loathed guns, I would have to find another weapon; a trademark to who I am. In an apocalypse, your weapon was like your I.D. It became a better representation of who you were than your own face. Flipping through a mental catalogue of weapons, I dog-eared a couple pages. Hmm…perhaps a bō…

"You there…" a faint voice of broken English spoke.

I snapped my head back and found nothing to have changed. Veronica hadn't emerged, the snake continued licking the air, and the woman stared. Then, her wrinkled lips opened.

"I…I know…you…"

My forehead creased. "Uhm, are you talking to me?"

For the first time, she turned her head and stared me down with her pale green eyes. I wasn't certain where of me she was 'looking' at but it felt as though she was reading me like a book.

"Over here…come…" she beckoned with a near-skeletal hand.

I'm not going to lie. She gave me the heebie-jeebies.

"Okay…"

I stepped carefully until I could've touched her with a hesitant hand. She pressed her flattened palms down into the air, gesturing for me to lower to her level. I did so and the snake swayed its head side to side ponderously.

"You…hurt…" her bottom lip trembled.

I nodded sympathetically, careful not to disrupt her clearly fading mentality. Then I realized she wouldn't see that.

"Yeah, yeah. I…do hurt. The world is getting pretty rough out there."

She shook her head as if I had insulted her. "No. No…No." She lifted a finger and tapped my forehead. "You hurt here."

My confusion started to morph into paranoia. I wasn't just weird out by her anymore. She started to frighten me.

"What do you mean?" I asked, tempted to play along.

She released a sigh, burdened by a near-century of age. "Pain… terrible, terrible pain. I see you…I see little boy. Little boy and…no mother. Little boy…trapped…in man's body. Frightened…scared… orphan."

Something kicked the inside of my skull. It felt as though someone put a gas nozzle in my ear and pumped my skull full of poisonous fluid.

"You don't know…" I hesitated. "…Who are you?"

She continued, gently stroking her snake's jade-scaled head. "You want love…scared of love…broken and damaged. I see you…"

Her hands lifted and simultaneously grasped both sides of my face. Shivers trickled down my neck and spine. "You're here…but…she's not. She haunts you…greatest failure…Sienna…"

The record player scratched and a new song played: I've Told Every Little Star. That was it.

"VERONICA!" I blared, shooting up to my legs. "Get out here! We're leaving."

After a crash of stacked pans, she emerged from the kitchen doors with a duffle bag slung over her shoulder.

"What? Are they here?" she frantically asked.

"No…just, we're leaving…"

She stopped moving and studied my tightened face. "What happened?"

I shook my head and bit my lip like a cranky thirteen-year-old. "Nothing. She just…she talked."

Sceptical, Veronica dropped her bag and approached the suddenly silent woman. Leaning in, the python hissed and jerked its head, causing her to kick back. Veronica realized something wasn't right about the woman's stare, for it wasn't blind but more so…lifeless. Slowly to avoid a snakebite, Veronica gently checked her neck and then her wrist for a pulse but felt nothing. In fact, she was uncomfortably cold at the touch. Veronica receded.

"Levi…she's dead," she pronounced. "I think she's been dead for hours."

I scoffed frustratingly. "Bullshit. She…she spoke to me! In English!"

Veronica looked at me and back at her. "I don't know what to say. She's dead, Levi."

The song plucked and poked at me and I just couldn't take it anymore. "Will you turn that fucking song off!"

Veronica didn't remove her gaze. "What song?"

"Are you stupid?" I asked, pointing at the record player. "That song!"

When I followed my finger to the player, I suddenly realized that no sound was being produced.

"Levi…there's no music. It's not even plugged in…"

She reached behind the counter and pulled out the cord that hadn't been plugged in.

I opened my mouth and let it catch the wafting air of disarray. Unable to look at Veronica and her judgmental stare, I walked over to the bag, slung it over my shoulder and made my way to the door.

"Let's go. We don't want to lose them."

I tossed the bat to her and she caught it with shock. "But…what about her?"

The door opened, activating the welcoming jingle.

"The snake will take care of that."

If I were to go with one word to describe Atlas's current state, I would go with flabbergasted.

Down the road, a burly man with a pipe pinched between his teeth rode towards them on a black stallion. The man's coal-coloured beard was wide and fiercely thick, resembling an untamed forest of masculinity. If he were to be placed next to Jeb, he would make him look like a prepubescent boy. On top of his shoulder-length hair rested a gentleman's top hat that had a single white lily tucked in the lined bow tie. He wore a collared shirt of tartan fabric beneath his open vest and his cowboy boots clacked against the saddle with each stride the horse took.

"Jesus Christ," choked Jeb.

Immediately, Jeb frantically gathered the four teenagers into a tight circle so that their leashes were minimally visible. Quinn was unable to stand up before he trotted over to speaking distance. With a slight tug of the reigns, the horse came to a halt and he simply stared down from the clearly superior position he formed.

Jeb nervously brushed loose strands of his hair behind his ear and puffed his chest out in an intimidating yet friendly demeanour.

"H-hello, brother," he stuttered, pulling the fakest of smiles between his stuttering cheeks. "How are you doing this fine afternoon?"

As expected, the cowboy said nothing. He squinted his mahogany brown eyes at Jeb, to the teenagers, then back to him.

Jeb also peered back at the leashed teenagers and thought it best to justify their state.

"You must be wondering about their leashes. W-when the virus hit, I…uh…was working my shift at a day care for disabled children! Their parents didn't come for them and since…since I care for them so much I knew it was up to me to keep them safe. They can sometimes get a little challenging…so we have leashes to make sure they don't run off. Ya know?" Jeb pointed to Quinn and let out a chuckle. "That girl even thinks she's a dog! What a bunch of goofballs, huh? We just play along to keep them happy."

With utmost stillness, the cowboy pulled his pipe away and exhaled a smooth cloud of unfiltered tobacco. His mouth was hardly visible through his tangled block of facial hair but it was safe to assume that it wasn't smiling.

"…Do you speak?" Jeb nervously asked.

Finally, a thin line creaked open from his beard. "Those aren't your kids."

His voice was husky and bruised by overconsumption of hard alcohol and smoke. Potentially two octaves below the rest of their voices, the man sounded like he chewed on gravel for sport.

Jeb looked back at both Cricket and Bucky but received nothing in return. Bucky's eyes were glued to his yo-yo and Cricket was as pink as an embarrassed pig.

"Heh…what makes you think that? Why'd you say such a thing?"

The cowboy shrugged. "Because I'm not a goddamn idiot. I've got eyes, and they saw what that bald thumb was doing to the girl."

Cricket noticeably squealed and shot uptight like he had been impaled. Jeb realized that any shot of tricking the mounted man was futile and decided to pull his gun out.

"Alright, Sundance, you had your fun. I don't want any trouble and I'm sure you don't either. So how about we go our separate ways and forget this ever happened. Deal?"

The cowboy glanced down at his horse and chuckled, resembling the sound of an old car struggling to start. "And if I don't…you're going to shoot me? Is that a threat?"

Jeb swallowed his nervousness, causing it to lodge halfway down his throat. "Mmhm… that's right. So why don't you ride off in the sunset and let us do God's work, okay?"

Sincerely disappointed, the cowboy rubbed the corners of his eyes the way an adult would do so in the presence of misbehaving children. He looked up at his opponents and pointed to each with a finger gun.

"Head…Head…Throat…"

It all happened with such precision and immediacy that Atlas didn't even see it occur. At first glance he saw Jeb in front of a cowering Cricket and a silently scared Bucky. Then he blinked. In that fraction of time, the cowboy drew a silenced pistol from his jacket and fired three perfect shots. The first victim was Bucky, having a silver slug pierce in the direct center of his forehead. The second shot spiralled towards Jeb and also hit him in the head, but this one went right between his eyes. The third and final shot rocketed towards Cricket and blew apart his throat, elongating his doomed life, which had been exactly what the cowboy had intended. An array of brain juice and murky blood splattered in the air like an exploding bottle of wine, shrouding the teenagers in their deceased captors.

The three bodies slumped to the road almost synchronized.

Annabelle gasped, Quinn shrieked, Josh threw up in his mouth, and Atlas turned to look at their saviour. The cowboy blew away the trailing smoke from his gun barrel and locked his gaze with Atlas.

"What're you looking at me for?" he asked, disgruntled. "You should be running by now."

Atlas shuffled through his disoriented brain for an appropriate response. "You killed them...I...thank you."

The cowboy tipped his top hat so that it casted a shadow over his eyes. With a click of his boots against the horse's thighs, they both were on their way.

"Wait! Wait!" Atlas called out. "That's it? You're just going to leave us here?"

The cowboy stopped. "Excuse me?"

Atlas immediately shut his mouth and took a step back. The cowboy swivelled his horse around and faced them once more.

"I saved your ass. Asses. By my count, I don't owe you a thing. My conscience is clean."

Atlas looked down at the bodies and studied the two deaths and a suffering. When he looked up, the cowboy turned around and it was clear he wasn't doing it again.

"You're free," he called back without stopping. "This world...you get a second chance. Hell, look at me, I'm a goddamn cowboy."

Atlas's mouth flung open with shock and envy. "What's your name?"

"I haven't decided yet!" he called out.

And with that, he was off. Atlas couldn't lift his jaw closed.

"Atlas!" Annabelle broke his daze. "There's still Zara and the bodyguard! They'll be here any second!"

Atlas looked back at them and shook his head in disbelief. "Did you SEE that? He had more hair on his face than my head! Fuuuck, I'm so insecure with my body right now…"

"Focus!" spat Annabelle. "We need to leave. Now."

With a nod, Atlas agreed. "Okay…but just give me a second!"

Dragging his chain behind him, Atlas stood over Jeb and unzipped his pants.

"What're you doing?" Annabelle asked.

"We're dogs, remember? I'm marking my territory."

While Atlas proceeded to urinate on Jeb's bullet-ridden face, Josh peered in the opposite direction and watched the cowboy become a silhouette. Beside him, however, was an unusual sight. Josh started to panic.

"Guys? There are two people over there. Are they with these guys?"

Atlas zipped up his pants and turned away. "Whoever they are, we clearly don't do well with strangers. So let's make like a tree and bust off."

Josh pointed down to Cricket, who was still writhing and spluttering. "What about him?"

Quinn stood up and spat on his barely living body. "Let him suffer."

Then they were off. They ran and ran until they couldn't and then they ran some more. Even through all of the tension of what had just occurred, they liked to believe that they could put all of it behind them. The problem, however, is that the 'it' was a 'they' and they were chasing after them with a bloody vengeance.

## 26. "Here's to you, kid."

I could not believe how many dead bodies there were. And I don't mean the upright, contorted meat. No, I mean the men and women that were luckily enough to stay on the ground. Even though we had been a couple miles out from the downtown area, it was virtually impossible to look in any given direction without being welcomed by cold flesh. Veronica and I made an unspoken game out of it, seeing who could go the longest without stepping or tripping on a dead body. She won after six minutes.

It's interesting how there was an abundance of meat—albeit not the freshest—laying around and yet the halfies didn't even acknowledge their existence. Maybe they thought they were too good for the truly dead, arrogant that they had claimed a comfortable place in-between. To be fair, my first instinct when I see a rotting cow isn't to cook up some hamburgers.

"We should stop and eat some lunch," suggested Veronica, gripping her vocal stomach. "Besides, I don't like how little of biters are out here. It makes me think they're...conspiring."

I nodded, still trying to find my footing. "Yeah. Good idea."

She took a double step to catch up with me. The last thing I needed right now was to talk to someone.

"I think you should talk to someone," she said. "You seem far from being alright, even by this world's standards. We may not be friends but I'm all you got right now. You may find it hard to believe but you can actually talk to me."

I nodded once more and gave her a weak, lying smile. "I'm fine, thank you. Let's go find somewhere to eat."

After a couple minutes of passing burnt-out convenience stores and boarded-up strip malls, we spotted a church nestled up in a bundle of trees. The wooden shutters had been spray-painted with multiple phrases and warnings, varying from *God help us all* to *why am I here?* One thing that stuck out in particular, however, was a phrase that was repeated over and over: *The Sins of the Father.*

"I mean, I'm not entirely sure if it's Sunday but...wanna check it out?" I asked.

"This looks like a place where someone gets exorcised..." remarked Veronica.

"We don't have to buy the place. Just to have a roof over our heads for an hour or two."

She sighed and beckoned to the place with confirmation. I stepped forward and felt a trio of bodies under my foot. This wasn't out of the ordinary seeing as there were usually more corpses than there was pavement, but I looked down nonetheless. The man-bun and red Mohawk gave me a realization.

"Uhm...Veronica? Are these guys who I think they are?"

She looked down and released a gasp. "These are the guys that took them! They've been uh...shot. Should that worry us?"

I knelt down and examined Jeb's body. There was a faint gloss on his Jesus-esque face that when smelt reminded me of that cat piss beer from oh so long ago.

"At least we know Atlas was here," I determined, the corners of my mouth slightly curving.

"What makes you think that?"

I pointed to Jeb's urine-soaked face. "He's been peed on. Who else would do something like that?"

Veronica smiled. "That *is* an Atlas thing to do. But wait a minute... what about that black chick and the..."

"Mountain?" I finished. "Doesn't look like they're here. They still might be out there. Good news though is that we have less of a problem to deal with. They've got them outnumbered four to two. Six to two when we catch up with them." I gave Veronica a reassuring smile.

She took a deep breath and felt somewhat better. "At least we know we're going the right way. Should we check the church for any clues? It's the only accessible building around here."

"Sure."

We walked down the road and turned onto a gravel path that led to a small set of classic church stairs. Handing the bat to Veronica, I opened both of the large oak doors and the empty church was exposed. Well, empty might not be the best word to use.

"What the hell is that supposed to be?" Veronica asked, pointing the tip of the baseball bat to the altar.

I entered the church and as I walked down the aisle, I saw what she was talking about.

On a hastily built cross erected on a pedestal, an infected had been mounted on with nails lodged into its wrists. Below it was a circle of candles that surrounded engravings and satanic symbols etched into the floor with a knife. Above the cross was a blood-written message reading, "Please don't forget us". In the middle of the ritual site had been a pile of ash, presumably from a fire beneath it as the beast's legs had been entirely charred. It lifted its weak head and pathetically snapped its jaw at us.

"Jesus, I told you!" exclaimed Veronica. I told you we'd find an exorcism here!"

"That's not what this is," I stated curiously. "It's more like a remembrance or…a plea."

Veronica gagged. "Either way, I've suddenly lost my appetite."

The air felt vulnerable. Instantly I had a connection with the pale one and approached it.

"Do you have a knife?"

Veronica hesitated but ultimately handed one to me; the same one Atlas used to slash the tires. I stepped in the marked circle on the floor and looked up to its bulging eyes. As I raised the knife to its temple, it suddenly ceased its attack and looked deep into my eyes like a frightened child. I saw something awful in the beast. I saw myself. Then in the blink of an eye, the reflection was gone as I buried the blade into it. Standing in silence with the newly bloodied knife clutched in my fist, I turned to Veronica, overdosing on the vulnerability in the air.

"I…I think it's time to tell you what happened to me."

I tucked myself in the back right-hand corner of the church, basking in a thin beam of sunlight pulsing through a fractured glass mural. Veronica collected a heap of black and white choir robes from a backroom and spread them out beneath us like the floor to a pillow fort. Facing me, she sat cross-legged with a can of corn in one hand and in the other a steak knife she took from the diner. While she carved the lid off the can, I stared down at my fidgeting fingers with intensive purpose. I was scared and rightfully so as I hadn't once shared this with someone before her. My parents only knew because they were victims of the event. So why did I want to tell her? Because the bottled-up burden was near-expulsion and I decided that I should at least be in control of opening it.

"So," she began, unwrapping a plastic spoon and knife, "you want to tell me why you're an introverted, uncaring sociopath? Colour me intrigued! I've wanted to know the deets ever since I saw you. You've got that look to you."

I glanced up, smiled briefly, and then looked back down at my hands. This was the only way I could open up without becoming a dangerous mess.

"This isn't gossip," I clarified. "Hell, I don't even know why I'm telling you. I just...look, it's messed up okay? For five minutes can you not be you? Just...be there. That's all I ask."

Veronica swallowed a mouthful of corn and surprisingly complied with ease. She sat back with full attentiveness and I took one final deep breath. Then I was falling.

*Falling...*

*Falling...*

*Falling...*

Falling until I was no longer the seventeen-year-old me. When I hit the pavement, I was three years old. When my feet hit the pavement, I was happy.

Cotton candy. Burnt popcorn. Overpriced stuffies. Rigged games. Vomit-inducing rides. The carnival was in town and I was mesmerized. In my right hand was a wound of blue raspberry cotton candy that resembled a wispy beehive. In my other hand was the hand of my father. Back then his hair was a wavy, midnight black that drew the attention of any audience. He was dressed casually yet classy and the happiest smile you could even imagine found a comfortable spot on his stubbled face. With a job like his—a graphic novel artist highly regarded throughout the States—he was literally a superhero to me. Back then I used to think that his superpower was 'girl-getter' since it didn't make sense how he could've possibly landed my mom. She walked ahead of us, more beautiful than comprehension. At the time she was thirty-one but with her glimmering face and near-perfect physique, you wouldn't guess a day over twenty-five. A talented photographer, her skills behind the camera landed her a job in front of it and skyrocketed her fame in the model industry. Every detail about her was so precise and hypnotic that my father couldn't prevent the constant double takes from people passing by, both men and women. For some reason, the one vivid memory I have of her is her brown to blonde ombre hair that barely grazed her shoulders. It reminded my of a paintbrush that could be found in my dad's office; a perfect fit. Even at such a young age I understood how lucky my father was to be married to her. Even at such a young age I understood how lucky my sister and I were to have her as a mother.

Yes, that's right. I had a sister. Her name was Sienna and she was my best friend. Her being seven, I was more of a personal assistant rather than her brother. She'd give me makeovers, blamed me for anything and everything, yet I liked spending time with her too much to care. Her hair colour was identical to mine but her personality was everything but. While I was scared of my own shadow and shy beyond belief, she was so outgoing and vocal that I would frequently forget what silence sounded like. One time, this red-haired little shit kicked sand in my eyes and a minute later Sienna had him pinned down near the swings shoving sand in his mouth. A boy in her class once grabbed her butt because "he saw it in a movie" and a minute later he was getting sand shoved in his mouth. I never understood Sienna's obsession with sand but unless I wanted the same fate as the sand-kicker and butt-grabber, I opted against asking.

The trip to the carnival was a split birthday present for both Sienna and I as we were born a day between each other save the four year gap. Everything about it was rigged and overpriced but it was a hell of a lot of fun. While my dad and Sienna took off for the adrenaline rides like the Big Dipper and the Zipper, my mom and I ventured off for rides more on my level: the Ferris Wheel and the Merry-Go-Round. After an hour and a half of my mother and I making silly faces at random people, we finally met up with my dad and sister. That was when it happened.

Some famous pop singer at the time—I have no idea who—had decided to make an appearance at the carnival. No concert or anything like that, simply to eat mini donuts and get mauled by fans. We came across the initial burst of fans and as they came faster and more vigorously, it became difficult for the four of us to stick together. Fans spliced Sienna and I away from our parents and after being engulfed by bodies—legs, in my case—we both felt tugging on our arms. Assuming it was Mom or Pops, we followed the tugging without hesitation and once out of the crowd, Sienna and I were holding hands with a complete stranger.

"Who are you?" Sienna asked, trying to yank her hand away.

He knelt down to her level and gave her a welcoming smile. "My name's David. I'm a security guard here. I'm here to make sure neither of you get lost!"

The man was the definition of normal. He had thinning blonde hair and a goatee, no-framed glasses that stuck closely to his face, and wore a fleece jacket over top a collared shirt. Nothing was special about him in any way. He was just there.

I smiled up at him, my toddler teeth barely visible. "Mommy and Daddy are over dere!" I pointed. "We get separated. They're just over dere!"

He shook his head politely. "To avoid searching all day, we get all the parents who have lost track of their kids to meet at a place. That way, I can take you straight to them!"

I hooked my finger in my mouth curiously. "Oh…well…oh-tay."

I grabbed his hand and we both followed the man, though Sienna was more sceptical than I. She bit the inside of her cheek and walked with caution. Even for a seven-year-old, she could tell when something was off. But why was she going to question it? After all, he *was* a security guard.

We walked with him for what felt like hours until we reached the outskirts of the carnival. There, we found a collection of buildings and rides that appeared to be shut down/out of order. The one that he led us to was a House of Mirrors that had a flickering light above it.

Sienna frowned. "Where are our parents?"

"Inside!" David assured. "Just follow me."

While he led the way, I tugged on the bottom rim of her shirt.

"Se-Se? When we get back c-can you win me that tiger? The ring toss is stupid hard."

She rolled her eyes and smirked. "Fine, you twerp."

He beckoned us in and when we passed the door, we were met by nobody. Then the door locked behind us. Darkness was there when I squeezed my eyes shut and it was there when I opened them. It was the only constant in the event. Darkness was all that I could rely on.

"Se-Se! SE-SE!" I yelped at nearly a dog whistle pitch.

She screamed for me but I drowned her out. My throat was raw and my insides ached as I had screamed in utter despair. She sounded like a dying car horn that was sucked into the darkness further and further. I felt a heavy set of hands pull at my shoulders and drag me away blindly. I assumed that it was David but one could never know as not a sound was made. No shoes, no grunts, not even his goddamn breathing, just a soundless mass. I kicked and yelled and begged for my parents, to no avail. He forced me down on a chair that might as well have been suspended in space and bound my wrists to the armrests with zip-ties. Fading into nothing, I was left alone in the dark with piss in my pants and puffy slits left for eyes. This would be horrifying for anyone so imagine experiencing it as a three-year-old. It was surreal. It was what nightmares feared. Hell, I wasn't even certain that I was alive. Time didn't exist where I was, only darkness.

After a few minutes, each one equipped with an eternity, my damaged eyes continued to suffer due to a sudden power up of the lights. Once I blinked back my vision, I saw my reflection dozens and dozens of times, each at a tilted angle. Not knowing where to look or if I myself was a reflection, I was forced to look upon the set of reflections that did not belong to me: the ones that belonged to a strung-up Sienna.

"Se-Se…" I cried voicelessly.

Her clothes were gone. She only had the darkness to hide her young body but now that it had evaporated, nothing was hidden. Now, we would take baths together and I had seen her prepubescent body before, but this was different. I felt sick to look at her, almost as though I was to blame. She obviously could see me as a fresh batch of tears poured down her splotchy cheeks. All she could do was shake her head.

"Don't look, Lee! It'll be okay!" she lied.

My body was paralyzed, as was my hearing, negating any choice to avert my stare. Then without any sounds of warning, David was there behind her, unshaven and bare.

"Your skin smells intoxicating," he licked into her ear. "I've been doing this for a long, long time but when I saw you, I knew this would be my grand finale. Tell me, my sweet child, have you bled?"

Sienna's eyes were wider than what was physically possible. "B-buh-bled? I don't…"

"Gotten your period," he rephrased, adjusting his glasses.

She shook her head. "What is that…?"

David moaned and grabbed his crotch. "Y-you know exactly what to say!"

At his feet was a radio that he knelt down to and pressed play.

PLAYING: I've Told Every Little Star by Linda Scott.

The upbeat tune bounced off the mirrors and into my ears forever. He decided that would be the moment in time to acknowledge me. Looking at me, unsure if it was a reflection or myself, he smiled widely and extended his hands out. "I hope you enjoy the show."

Then…well he…there was so much blood…pooling on the floor… the image of him doing that … it was devastating but…hearing her screams…that's what did me in. Once he was done and my sister dangled there with her humanity and virginity dripping on the floor, he moved onto his final act and pulled out a pistol. As he loaded it, his eyes never left mine.

"My dream is to create something more damaged than myself. Here's to you, kid."

He positioned the gun down at her…you know…and aimed it upwards…and fired. Her head went from dangled and drooped to stiff in a flash and a spurt of blood popped out from the top. He clapped and lights faded to black. Only seconds passed before sobbing could be heard and he was now sprawled across the floor in fetal position. The gun was next to him.

"Dear god…I'm innocent! She was not mine!"

He heaved up to his knees, trembling from head to toe, and lifted up the gun to his head.

"Don't forget," he whispered to me.

A second gunshot rang out and this time it was his body that fell. Lights fell once more and I had yet to speak. There was nothing to say. It was over for me.

*** 

Veronica was fighting angrily to prevent herself from crying. Even now, after all those years, my eyes continued to remain dry.

"That's not possible...Christ, you have to be lying!" She shook her head, looking to the floor of the church. "You're lying to me...that sounds like a story on freaking *Dateline*..."

I released an ironic chuckle. "It was."

Her eyes shot up at me, brow furrowed. "Shut up."

"Did you ever hear about something called the Reeves Raping?"

She nodded. "Yeah...they talked about it in psych class last year."

"That was Sienna."

Veronica gasped painfully. The first droplet of tears stained her clenched cheeks. "No...what? But...the name..."

"Levi Reeves," I answered. My mouth felt odd, as though I had bitten down on something I had never tasted before. That name hadn't reached my lips in more than a decade and it tasted as such. Veronica wasn't able to create an answer so I took over and finished the story.

"I was there for around thirty hours. The song was on repeat. Clocking in at two minutes and twenty seconds, I listened to it eight hundred and eighteen times. And every second of that was merged with a faint yet audible sound of just...dripping...and dripping. I'd try so hard to keep my eyes closed but either it would hurt too much or I'd fall asleep since I would always end up looking at my sister's strung-up body. My eyes adjusted to the dark, making her perfectly visible. They found me—my parents and an army of police officers—and I was reborn as damaged goods. My family was all our town could talk about and we were forced to relocate with new identities and new lives. Levi Reeves became Levi Finch, but here's the punchline: Remember when my sister and I first got captured and we were both pulled away? She wouldn't have moved in the dark by herself. Now since David's hands were on my shoulders, who had grabbed Sienna?"

"You mean...there were two of them?" she asked rhetorically.

"Twins, most likely. One was swapped with the other when the lights went off and the 'innocent' one was who shot himself. Well... that's at least what I came up with. A coping mechanism, ya know? It made me feel less guilty for some reason. I pieced this all together myself but who'd believe me? I was a delirious kid that had experienced terrible trauma. My dad wouldn't believe me...he couldn't. How could he live knowing that there was someone alive out there who took everything away from him? Even if he did believe me, going to the cops and the press would only expose our real identities and that would only make things worse. My dad *chose* not to believe me. My mom did believe me and that's what drove her to slitting her wrists."

Veronica covered her mouth. "Are you kidding me…your mom is dead too??"

I stopped and looked in realization. "Right…I never told you that part, huh? She's not dead…at least, not to my knowledge. Either way, she's long gone."

Once I finished, my lungs inhaled a breath of air that had been waiting for thirteen some years. Veronica was now bawling and putting herself down.

"That song…that goddamn song, I tormented you with it! I'm such a bitch!"

I shrugged. "You couldn't have known. That's not on you."

She looked at me with teary eyes and averted them. Shamefully, she reached over and grabbed my unexpected hand.

"I'm sorry, Levi. I'm so, so sorry."

Trembling static tickled my hand up into my arm. No one had ever apologized to me in the way she had and it was uncomfortably…nice.

"Don't be sorry," I cleared my throat of sadness. "The past is the past and I don't intend to be digging too much into it. Frankly, I don't have the time to. But for what it's worth, I forgive you for everything. I forgive you for the song and for Tasering me…everything except for those pancakes. Those were inexcusable."

Veronica sniffled a chuckle and wiped her fading tears away. She looked up to me and smiled. "Yeah well screw you."

I replied with laughter and looked down at my hands, which had ceased to fidget. "You're not half bad, Bangs. Hell, I guess in this world we would be considered friends."

"Not if you call me Bangs," she warned, swiping her even hair to the side. "Atlas calls me that and I hate it. It makes me sound like a pornstar."

"Not unlike your sister," I said under my breath yet loud enough for her to stand up.

"How do you—"

"I may be messed up but I'm still a guy. I know what porn is."

She shook her head, her eyes rolling inside. Then, with a glance to the burnt corpse, a process of contemplation occurred within. As I stood up from the corner, the sheet of sunlight now illuminating my torso, she spoke up.

"Listen…you opened up to me. Maybe I should do the same and tell you something about me."

Before I could encourage her to proceed, a loud thump boomed on the outside of the church doors.

"We'll have to put that on hold for now," I told her. "Gather your things. Grab the bat."

As she shoved the spilt insides of her backpack back in, I slung mine over my shoulder and stepped down the aisle, knife in hand. I don't know what I was expecting or if I wanted some sort of response but for some reason I called out.

"Hello?"

Apparently not learning from any horror movie ever, the word was a death sentence that triggered an overblown temper tantrum created by the infected. They bulldozed the doors and all halted as one unit to stare us down.

"Not good. Not good!!" I yelled doing a 180 to the rear. "Head into the back room!"

"What good is that going to do us?" complained Veronica, though joining me nonetheless.

"Old church! Bell tower!" I said in-between breaths.

A squadron of them moved with such synchronicity that it would make a marching band envious. It was as if there were two types: the silent but deadlies and the full-on freaks. Half of them filed down the aisle slowly but purposefully while the rest climbed and hurdled over the prayer benches like it was track and field. Their eyes burned with hasty hunger, implying they were the ones that had gone longer without eating. Just as they could latch their spider-like fingers onto our backpacks, we dove into the back office and slammed the door shut. As I had expected, there was a ladder attached to the right-hand wall.

"How could you have known?" she asked, her back pressed against the door alongside mine.

"Complete guess."

"Ah good," sighed Veronica. "Okay, hold the door, I'll climb up first."

"Why do you get to—ah forget it."

She gave me a reassuring nod and left the door, burdening me with double the weight. Veronica climbed the rungs until she reached the hatch and flung it open.

"Okay…Now!"

Using their pushing as momentum, I thrust forward and jumped onto the ladder. They busted through the door with terrifying smiles, resembling a dozen Jack Nicholsons from *The Shining*. They grabbed onto my ankles and begged for a bite, but even I knew my story wasn't over just yet. I kicked and shimmied them off until I climbed through the hatch and slammed it shut. If they had known how to climb ladders, I wouldn't have even bothered going forward.

"Great…now we're on a roof…on a building…surrounded by infected. Stellar plan," Veronica remarked.

It turned out that it was in the worst way possible. Not a second later we heard rapid barking approaching fast. In the corner of my eye, I saw a scruffy mutt that had curly, chocolate brown hair and cinnamon eyes to match sprinting as fast as its little legs could move. A trio of biters had been chasing the poor thing and either done so purposely or coincidentally, they lead it right to the clump. Seeing a new target, most of the infected surrounding the church converged towards it, rendering the dog helpless.

"No, no, no…not the dog…"

"I'd rather watch humans die all day than to let a dog die…but we have no choice."

Veronica shook her head and let out a saddened groan. "Levi we can't!"

"Don't go soft on me now!" I ordered. "Move."

She swore tremendously and began to scale down an unwatched pipe. Once she was out of view, I looked back at the dog and bit my thumb until blood was drawn.

"I…I'm so sorry…"

As we escaped, all we could hear were the shiver-inducing yelps from the dog that was being feasted upon.

## 27. "Suicide is the weakest thing a person could do."

Less than a decade prior, the sign welcoming cars to the city was accompanied only by farmland and forest. If we fast-forward nine or ten years, shopping malls and apartment complexes carved their concrete skeletons into massacred soil. With the downtown area only a mile away, this outer section of man-made structures was like an appetizer to prepare oneself for the main course. Construction sites were as common as the parking lots that surrounded them, each with a varying degree of potential consumer potency. One in particular found a place in the city skyline as it rested just before the hill ascending to the main metropolis. Two exoskeletons of future business skyscrapers stood tall and naked, as production had come to an indefinite halt. A walkway was built to connect the two, creating an oversized letter H. It was in this construction site that Atlas and company came to a collapsing halt.

"*huff* Do you *huff* do you think we're *huff* safe?" Josh asked, his hands pressing deep into his bent thighs.

"We ran a goddamn marathon…" Atlas remarked, "I sure hope so…"

The contents of the construction site were fairly standard. Piles of gravel left and right, massive cement cylinders resting horizontally, stacks upon stacks of wood planks, heavy machinery that was getting a prolonged sunburn, you name it. Quinn slumped against one of the cylinders and hid in the shade it produced. She was in rough shape.

"Water…anybody have water?" she asked in a near beg.

They all shook their heads.

"There's probably a vending machine in that portable office over there. We can check it out but…give me a second." Atlas felt like he was strapped a little too tightly to a Tilt-a-Whirl.

"I found a jagged piece of metal," Annabelle stated quietly, her dry tongue struggling to rest back in her mouth.

Quinn let out a laugh that turned into a painful cough. "Great... we can use it to slit our throats."

"Don't joke about that," Annabelle said sharply. "I meant we could use it to cut these leashes off and keep what little dignity we have left."

"Unless I find a blowtorch, I'm gonna be excluded from that group," Atlas muttered, swinging his chain sadly.

She knelt down to Quinn's level and grabbed her rope. While she sliced roughly, Quinn looked down at the blood speckled on her baby blue crop top. She didn't even know whose blood it belonged to.

"I wasn't joking..." she murmured at a hush tone. Annabelle was able to hear her.

"Excuse me? What did you say?" she asked, now standing up to cut off her own.

Quinn's eyes welled with tears. "You know what I said! We have no food, no water, psychos chasing after us and for what? To go a week longer of suffering before the inevitable comes to fuck us? No, I think we should end this before they do it for us."

Josh pulled off his sliced noose and allowed his forehead to crease with concern. "You're not suggesting what I think you're suggesting, are you? Not after everything we've been through! Hell, I've got religious nuts gunning for me and I have no idea why but I'm not just going to give up 'cause of it."

Quinn stood up shakily and crossed her arms in hopes of making herself look more stable. "Why should we force this upon ourselves? Yes, I'm suggesting it! Without any weapons, we're basically bait for those monsters and I'd rather take my own life than get eaten alive or raped by those sickos!" Quinn looked to Annabelle with doleful eyes and placed her trembling hand on her tense shoulder. "What's the point? Besides, Levi and Veronica are most likely long gone by now. We can join them!"

Atlas pulled Quinn away from Annabelle and slapped her hard enough to send her crashing down to the ground. She clutched her cheek in horror as the tears started to unravel. Atlas glared down at her with unshakeable disdain.

"Shut your mouth right now," he spat.

"...You...you slapped me!" she said shockingly.

Atlas shrugged. "What are you going to do about it? Kill yourself?"

"You can't speak to me like that! You're n-nothing without me! I'm the only one who would ever fuck you!"

"You'd fuck a dog," replied Atlas. "That's why you enjoyed the collars, right? I know you, Quinn. I know how you are a nymphomaniac in every sense of the word. How dare you say that you worry about rape when the very idea of rape gets you off. When that fat pig was hitting you, I know you enjoyed it. I also know that you only had sex with me so that I'd watch out for you. Why? Because you are hilariously weak."

She bit her lip to cease the tears but they were automated. No matter what she did, nothing could cover up her pitiful stench.

"Don't…don't talk to me like that! *You're* the weak link!"

Atlas was at a point of no return.

"Your existence is meaningless. The only thing that you are to me is a sex object, and an expendable one at that. All that you do, all that you've ever done, is complain. You have never contributed to anything beneficial for this group, and you know what? I was fine with it. You're weak. If you were to have killed yourself it wouldn't have made much of a difference." He knelt down to her level and leaned in until they were face to face. "But the moment you try and take advantage of someone else and bring them down to your level, that is when I intervene. If you ever attempt to convince Annabelle, or anyone for that matter, to kill themselves, I will personally make sure that you are completely and utterly alone in this world. Do you understand?"

Quinn opened her mouth to respond, but nothing came out. Her eyes fell to the gravel and sobbed uncontrollably.

"I-I cuh-can't d-do this alone!"

Atlas scoffed and belittled her. "Didn't you just say that you were going to kill yourself? Well, what're you waiting for? No one is stopping you! Or did you say that to gain our sympathy?"

Quinn felt worthless. "I'm suh-sorry…Please…I don't want to kill myself!"

Atlas gave her a single nod and began to back away. "Good. Then get your ass off the ground and pull yourself together. We're leaving in five."

He spat to the floor and strolled over to a panel of the surrounding fence. Josh crept up behind him nervously.

"That was cold, man," he whispered.

"No, it was necessary," Atlas clarified. "Suicide is the weakest thing a person could do. Hearing anybody even say the word sets my teeth on edge."

Josh tucked his hands in his James Dean jacket and breathed out. "Remind me never to piss you off."

They both looked at the way they came through the metal hexagons of the fence. Watching in silence, they almost achieved a moment of peace before a black woman carrying a bō ruined that from happening.

"Is that…" began Josh.

Atlas bowed his head into the fence and groaned. "Perfect."

Like a crack of a bullwhip, Atlas pushed away from the chain-linked wall and darted to Annabelle and Quinn. There was a weird look to his face, for it wasn't the common expression of annoyed exhaustion created from the sight of infected. He looked both peeved and confusingly distraught, leaving the girls with similar looks only amplified.

"What is it?" Annabelle questioned, one arm on Quinn's shoulder as a result of lifting her up.

Atlas opened his mouth to speak and with perfect timing, Zara entered the vast construction site and announced her presence.

"Think you can run, you brainless, hormonal voice cracks?" she taunted. "You killed three of us. That doesn't go without consequence. Try and hide if you want…here I come."

She dragged one end of her bō in the gravel, acting as a guide to how close she was to them. The four teens clumped and frantically looked for a way out as if they were experiencing their first day as freshmen. With the multiple forklifts, bulldozers and piles of varying elements, an unintentional maze laid before them and they had to find their way to safety. Since the only exit was in current sightlines of their attacker, there was only one way left to go: Up.

"We'll lose her in the skyscraper. Doesn't look like there's any electricity so make sure everybody sticks close."

They collectively nodded and Atlas was quick to create a diversion. Approaching fast, he had to think even faster and that meant resorting to one of the most primitive techniques of Distraction 101. In a forklift, a rotting driver was in the process of being dead. Using his unfortunate fate to his advantage, Atlas scurried to the base of the machine and quietly creaked the door open. In case the carcass suddenly rejuvenated with life, Atlas cautiously untied the driver's shoelaces and slipped off a cold boot. With that in hand, he lobbed it in the air over to the shipping container-style office. Making a subtle yet noticeable *thump*, her dragging staff came to a halt, paused, and drifted away from them.

"Okay…now's our chance!"

As if the sky was four feet high, they all scuttled to the right-hand building half-ducked. Once out of sight, they stopped all things cautious and ran full speed ahead. Their feet clattered like heavy raindrops on the cement floor, only accompanied with wheezy and staggered breaths. Scaling level by level via a single grated staircase, the light of the dinnertime sun was becoming increasingly difficult to access. Soon, they stumbled upon pitch darkness that was created by draped tarps on the walls. This was something they were forced to endure, as backtracking was not an option. That's when they realized they weren't alone.

"You here that?" Annabelle asked.

There was a collection of moans and wordless whispers. Atlas found a battery-powered spotlight and waved it around the room they found themselves in. A corridor to their left, they slowly sifted by. Trying to find a suitable hiding spot, Atlas opened a door to a finished office, only to flash the spotlight on nine pale ones. The infected were jubilant at what they saw.

"Run! Run!" Atlas cried as he backed away.

The light shook and bounced messily as they ran in no particular direction. Both parties were screaming and sweating, each for different reasons. Running with his head down, Josh was at the back of the group and felt the tug of death pulling at his wife-beater.

"Get off!!"

Atlas dodged a pillar and frantically looked for an escape. "We need to get them off of us!"

Thinking fast, Annabelle darted into the lead and dove to the side in a men's bathroom. This was the last room until the draped tarps, thus giving an undesirable momentum to the infected. Atlas sprinted until his nose grazed the fabric wall, and then jumped to the side, leaving the chasers a surprise. As expected, they didn't stop and one by one collapsed through the wall. A ten-story drop awaited each and every one of them.

"*huff*…good…thinking…" praised Atlas.

Everyone looked at each other, realizing that there was only three out of four.

"Uhm…where's Josh?"

Atlas peeked through the closed door with his spotlight in hand, but instead of finding any pools of blood or a broken body, there was only silence.

Down a narrow, emotionless road, Veronica and I walked in deafening silence. I aimlessly kicked evaporating puddles of past rain, my brain flooding with nothingness. Half a day had passed since the recollection of my childhood trauma and an unbreakable cloud of awkwardness followed us ever since. Neither one of us wanted to tackle small talk or address the elephant trailing behind, so we continued on in silence, thus putting my focus elsewhere. My target was on the infected or in this case, lack thereof. Their behaviour was impossible to decode. Hours ago I saw them rush with ravenous haste in the burning sun and now they were nowhere to be found. Besides a lethargic halfie here and there, the land was as empty as my knowledge of the infected anomalies. As of this moment in time, I knew four facts about them, one more of an educated guess.

1. They were not zombies. Not once had I witnessed a completely deceased body reanimate.

2. They required the same basic resources as us humans. This was proved to me when I saw the Neanderthal-like biter slurping from the river a day prior. Seeing this also explained the bite marks I saw on various closed containers such as pop cans and that gas canister.

3. They were smart. Unlike their stereotypical movie depictions, these beasts understood the pros and cons of attacking alone and had a terrifying sense of patience. They needed our meat for nourishment but they weren't above waiting for it.

4. Who they once were had still survived. Though unable to prove this, subtle personality traits seem to still latch on, making each pale one as unique as their peeling fingerprints. The last fact was not something I liked to think about, however, as it made killing them much, much worse.

"Well this is awkward," Veronica finally spoke up.

I sighed. "Now it is."

She let out an impatient groan. "Listen, you can't just drop that on me and expect everything to be roses and lollipops. It's… going to take some getting used to. Besides, I cried in front of you. That shit is as rare as a unicorn snorting cocaine."

"Should I not have told you?" I questioned, tricking her into thinking this was her fault.

"No! I mean, yes. Yes you should have. Christ Levi, I'm not good at this kind of stuff."

"That makes two of us," I said, scratching the scruff on my face in confusion.

"What I'm trying to say is that I'm glad you told me. I can be a bitch, I'm fully aware of that, but that doesn't mean I can't have friends. The fact that I've given you every opportunity to knock me out and you still decided to open up, that…it means a lot. It means that you're willing to trust me, and I think I can do the same."

I felt a painful burn in my cheeks that I wanted to slap away. I was blushing.

"Well…thank you," I said awkwardly. "I guess our little adventure hasn't been that terrible. We've probably had a laugh or two."

"*Probably*," she repeated with a chuckle. "We can't try and pretend nothing happened and we shouldn't. Let's just move on and keep our minds occupied."

"How so?"

She bit her lip and ruffled a side of her black liquorice hair to try and force out a suggestion.

"Uhm…cities? Where would you like to visit?"

I raised my eyebrow. "Our options are kind of limited these days, don't you think?"

"Disregarding our current…predicament. If you could go anywhere, where would it be?"

This was a thought that scarcely flickered through my mind. With my father in the state that he was, vacations were fairy tales. I adopted a routine of worrying about bills and bills and more bills on a daily basis that if I were actually given a break, I would've been more stressed than relieved.

"I don't know," I said, somewhat surprised. "The only time I've been on a plane was when we moved here."

"Seriously? C'mon, everyone has a place. This world…there's a lot of them. Just say the first one that comes to your mind."

My brain wasn't allowed to think as my mouth did all the work.

"Japan," I said unconsciously.

"Why?" she asked.

Now my brain had to pull its weight. "I don't know…just seems… peaceful? I remember in the second grade we learned about Japan. I was in a group and we all sat around this, uh, tape player. I remember wearing these giant, rubbery headphones and just letting hours go by listening to the thing. The kids went out for recess, to lunch…but I just sat there. There were only a couple photos shown in class but the narrator was so descriptive that I didn't need any. Still, I've always wanted to see what she was talking about."

I stopped walking and smiled to myself. I thought I forgot that memory. It was rare that something *good* was retained in my mind.

"That's awesome, Levi," Veronica said with a smile. "See? Everyone has a place! For me, it'll always be Jasper. I know it's biased because of my cabin, but it'll always be home for me. Hopefully, Dad is…"

Before she could finish, a blaring gunshot shut us up.

"Where'd that come from?" Veronica asked, pulling out her knife.

My head snapped to the right and examined a rusty school bus depot. Once my focus settled primarily on the wide, brick-covered garage, screaming and shouting could be heard coming from inside.

"In there," I answered. "Do we check it out?"

"I don't know…there's obviously someone in there, but should we make them our problem?"

My neck ached at the thought of someone else's life in my hands.

"There's a chance it's *them*…besides, this is a bus depot. The worst deal we could get out of this is a potential ride into the city."

"No, the worst deal we could get is dying," she corrected. "Brutally."

"Lovin' that optimism."

Ultimately we decided to check it out. Worryingly unlocked, we treaded through the grossly lit lobby straight out of a B-list horror film. Child-drawn pictures of busses and their respective drivers decorated the walls, only adding to the creep factor. As we moved closer, the yelling grew louder. After two failed attempts at doors, we came to door #3 with our prize indeed behind it. All that was left was if we wanted to claim it.

"So...do we go in?" I asked in a whisper.

"Try and figure out what they're saying," she asked.

Now that we were inside the depot, it was nearly impossible to hear anything. Perhaps the yeller had cooled down or perhaps he was currently being eaten. The only thing I could do was try and make out what it was.

"Okay...I can here a man talking...he's crying...begging...okay shifting gears, now he's threatening..."

Veronica was growing impatient. "Let me hear!" she asked childishly.

"Stop pushing!" I told her.

Her leaning body pushed me past stability and turning the doorknob just the right way, we crashed through the door and made ourselves known. Everyone inside—five men, three women, and a baby—turned to us in shock and silence took over. The gunman, a homeless-looking black man with electrocuted hair and missing teeth, frantically aimed his gun at us.

"Perfect," I muttered.


Darkness was broken by the sudden exposure of fiery sunlight reflecting through the walkway windows. Atlas, Annabelle and Quinn pushed through the doors and immediately felt the metal beams beneath them rattle unnervingly. Nothing was certain and everything was fucked.

"What is going on?" Quinn yelled, trying to find someone to take responsibility. "Where did he go??"

Atlas ran his fingers through his grease-induced locks alongside an exhausted exhale. He was perspiring in more places than he could imagine and he knew it wasn't about to lessen anytime soon.

"Bastard must've got lost!" Atlas suggested, unsure. "I don't know, okay? Candy chick might've gotten a hold of him."

The tension between them had reached an all-time high. The sound of each other's voices was enough to create a burning frustration fuelled by empty stomachs and dry throats.

"We might have a bigger problem," Annabelle said, pressing her finger on the grimy glass.

The three watched in horrifying curiosity as an army of troops fought ruthlessly for the downtown sector. Continuous gunfire played like a broken record, only the barely audible death screams mixing in with the soundtrack. Explosions were heard for hours but this was the first glimpse they had at the gravity of the warzone. The main siege was not visible but the sprouting battles were painfully so. Thousands upon thousands of infected worked together to create an opposing threat worthy of tremendous fear. Attacking soldiers and machinery alike, they were able to latch their infection on the resistance and in bursts of agony, were even able to momentarily turn the soldiers against each other. One bite to an arm sent a fury of spasms that unintentionally fired bullets in every direction. The infected weren't capable of using guns, but they didn't need to be. With their near-hypnotic bites and spasm-inducing saliva, they got their victims to shoot on their behalf. The battle was far from over but the frequent splotches of blood had told the three teenagers that the body count was to be exponential.

The door slammed open and in came Josh, panting like a frightened dog.

"Holy shit!" Atlas exclaimed as his heart momentarily forgot its purpose. "Where the hell have you been?"

Even if he was painted red, Josh's paleness would've been worryingly vibrant. He looked as though he'd seen a ghost, and that ghost had seen a ghost.

"I…I…" he struggled to think, "I'm sorry…I heard a voice… Thought I should check it out."

Quinn frowned. "But…you just vanished! They were chasing us!"

Annabelle looked disgruntled. "Let me get this straight. We're currently running from a crazy person, you hear a voice, so you decide to go *towards* it?"

Josh grabbed the railing for support. "No, no…it wasn't like that! I thought I heard…a kid's voice? I'm sorry, guys…I don't know what came over me."

Atlas squinted with scepticism. "So…you didn't come across her at all? She didn't say anything to you?"

Josh shook his head with a glazed look to him. None of the three noticed him stuffing a Walkie-talkie further down his back pocket. Clearly there was more to this but the interrogation came to a halt when Quinn shrieked.

"Guys! GUYS!" She drew attention back outside, several blocks away on the perch of the hill. A tank was parked and its barrelled spout had randomly fired at a classy jewellery store. "What's it doing?"

There was a slight pause where anticipation was dripping. Then it turned upwards and aimed directly at the teenagers.

"No…it wouldn't…" Atlas muttered in disbelief.

But it did. For no justifiable reason, except perhaps another case of a biter hypnotizing a soldier with its spit, a cloud of smoke erupted and piercing through it was a hurdling rocket straight for them.

"MOVE!" Atlas ordered.

Everything was stuck in slow motion. Annabelle was in the lead and she sprinted for the opposing door. Quinn was behind her and a fresh batch of tears streamed from her shut eyes, slowly and meticulously floating down to the rumbling ground. Atlas was next and his immediate instinct was to endow his tunnel vision and easily overtake his allies. However, he was not known to follow his instincts. Instead, Atlas grabbed a hold of a paralyzed Josh behind him and heaved him forward. The moment his grasp let go of Josh's arm, the rocket met its target and eradicated a series of beams on the first tower. Their entire surroundings shook and with the structural integrity demolished, the building started to collapse. Rubble and shattered glass sprinkled violently through the walkway as it started to split down the middle. The sound of ripping steel and breaking floors filled their ears, disorientating their mind and their status of current existence. None of them realized what Atlas had done until it was too late. Annabelle peered back and saw Atlas standing completely helpless. He had a look of childish fear on his face that was sinking lower and lower. Without warning or any preparation, the collapsing tower swallowed Atlas's body. No famous last words. No parting words of wisdom. Simply nothing. He was gone.

# 28. "I don't know, maybe it's a dad thing."

It was a Mexican standoff and by Mexican standoff I mean not at all. As awesome as that would be, the only gun in the mix was in the hands of an off-the-rails black man while we were left holding nothing but our dicks. Well, metaphorically speaking.

"Who are you?" he said with incredible instability.

"Uh…" I said, biting my tongue. "No one…we'll get out of your way…excuse us."

It's a good thing I didn't place any bets on the success of that.

"S-Stay right there!" he ordered with a trembling gun. "You're w-with them!"

"This day just keeps getting better and better, huh?" I muttered to Veronica as we stood up. Our hands reached for the air above our heads, allowing the bat and knife to clatter on the floor. The others looked to us with a quivering amount of fear since they at least knew the motives of the gunmen. Thankfully, Veronica took charge to clear any confusion.

"We're not going to hurt you, mister. We don't even know what the Sam-dick is going on here. We heard screaming…we came running. That and we wanted a bus."

Well at least she's honest, I thought. The man's dilated eyes flickered back and forth between the two of us like he was playing a sped-up game of *Pong*. He wore a stained, unbuttoned Hawaiian shirt that was overtop an even further stained wife-beater. Cargo shorts rested loosely on his lanky waist and just below his knee a fresh bite that already turned rancid could be found. He reeked of sweat and desperation and was clearly out of his mind.

"He's bit," a moustached man in a trucker hat informed us. "H-he wants his kid."

"'Cause it's my blood!" he interjected. "I ain't infected worth shit! Five minutes it's been and nothing! It takes seconds, a minute at most! I'm still living!"

The high-pitched shrill of an infant came from one of the three school buses. He pointed his pistol at the location of the sound and shouted wordless noise.

"My child! You can't do this! I'll kill every one of you!"

His aim drew back and forth at the frightened hostages, each provoking some kind of plea or wince. It appeared that Veronica and I were the only one that didn't share the passing fear. We looked at each other and with a single glance we shared the same plan.

"Sir?" I said to him calmly. "I don't know you. Hell, I don't give a shit about you or what happened to you. That's your story and I'm not going to mix myself in with that. But I *can* offer you something. Words of wisdom, perhaps?"

He flashed his teeth like a rabid dog. "What can you give me? *They* got my little boy!"

"And maybe that's for the best. You're mad…you're desperate…I get it. I knew someone that shared the anger that you're feeling right now. Someone was taken from him and his anger clouded his judgment. He hurt the people close to him, the ones that were innocent and victimized by his anger. Now there's no fixing your fate but you can come away from this a redeemed man. You are going to die…that's a fact, but if you convince yourself it's not then your son will die. Don't let the sins of the father determine the fate of the son. You love him, yes?"

He nodded through burdening anger and fractured tears.

"Then you can let him go. You give him the chance to survive then you can die a hero. Isn't that what you want?"

He had now been completely overthrown by sadness as he dropped to his knees in a sob. "He's my boy…I can't leave him…I love him, man…I can't…"

"Yes you can," I encouraged, kneeling down. "Just give me the gun, okay?"

The second he dropped his guard, Veronica took the base of the bat's handle and knocked him out. While I had taken his focus and softened his rage, Veronica had snuck behind him with Atlas's bat entirely unnoticed.

"Good work, V," I said, standing back up. My sympathy was gone.

When we looked at the huddled group, they stared at us with alien eyes. To them, we might have been more dangerous than the gunman.

"W-w-what are you going to do with him?" a pregnant lady asked. The sight of her reminded me of Cecilia and that was not a memory I needed to process at the moment.

"What am *I* going to do?" I asked with slight frustration. "No, no, no…we subdued him. Whatever happens next, that's on you. It's not our job to determine his fate. We just made it easier for you people to do it."

The judges, jury and potential executors looked at one another. The five men—varying from twenties to late sixties—collected together and discussed what they were willing to do. While a freckled, ginger-haired girl cradled the squirming baby boy, an elderly woman was in the process of consoling a grief-stricken woman. Judging by how she acknowledged the unconscious gunman, it was safe to assume she was either his wife or sister. Her stomach stuck out like an un-popped bubble that was nearing five-six months pregnant. Whether it was the gunman's son or nephew, I never found out.

"So…do we leave?" I asked Veronica with an awkward neck tilt. The two of us stood isolated from the others like it was a junior high dance and we were the punch bowl.

"Not yet. They have vehicles. I'm so sick of walking."

I shook my head. "They're weak. Looks like they've been held up in here since day one."

Crossing her shockingly muscular arms over her chest, Veronica shrugged. "We were like them."

"But we're not anymore. That's the important thing."

The council of men seemed to have reached a verdict but wanted to speak with the women before finalizing their decision. Judging by the sister's/wife's response, it was clear that it wasn't merciful.

"Take him out back," the trucker hat man told the others reluctantly.

A man in overalls halfway zipped and the eldest of the men (who had the face and body of a war machine) each took an arm and dragged his downwards facing body out into the back. Thankfully, Veronica had hit him with enough force that he would never realize his fate.

"Thank you for that, son," the leader said somehow both warmly and coldly. He extended a hand that was permanently stained with engine grease.

"I'm not your son," I replied without shaking his hand. "And you're welcome."

The pregnant woman approached me, her nose still sniffling with grievance. "What you did…it was the right choice. Whatever you need…it's yours…"

"Are you people using any of those buses?" Veronica asked with a hinting tone.

"Yes, actually. We were just about to head into town and cross the bridge. We've heard of this sanctuary off the coast of Vancouver. Why?"

Veronica and I looked at each other and smiled at the convenience.

Fast-forward an hour and twelve minutes, we were resting against the front of the second bus. A soothing evening breeze whistled through the open doors, the city taunting us in the distance. In the far left corner outside of the garage was a pair of boots horizontally lying behind a dumpster. I was almost certain they were the same footwear that the infected gunner had worn but I didn't care enough to quench my curiosity. The group of people—who we learned were the drivers and employees of the depot—were busy piling their substantial supplies into the bus. What were we doing? Well, as our infamous luck would have it, the owner of said boots behind the dumpster was the sole mechanic and their only shot of using the buses. They had a surplus of gasoline but the engine itself was messed far beyond my inadequate vehicular knowledge. We all remember the last time I tinkered with an engine and both Veronica and I agreed that I would be the 'nurse' in this setup. By that I mean that I handed her whatever tools she needed. And by her I mean Veronica, something that was equally as shocking to me as it is to you.

"So let me get this straight…you know how to fix cars?" I asked with an amazed tone.

"My dad taught me for years," she reminisced. "While most girls were busy playing with Barbies and getting their periods, I spent my time mending chassis and keeping rear ends lubed."

I scrunched my face up. "Dude, phrasing…so wait, you didn't get your period?"

She flicked my forehead and rolled her eyes. "The point is that I know what I'm doing. Hand me that belt tension gauge."

I failed to process the foreign language and handed her the closest thing to my right, proving to be the proper tool.

"Wait a minute...on the bridge..."

Veronica smiled deviously. "Oh yeah...I could've got it running in less than a minute. You were just too busy being a discriminative douche that I thought you could have a crack at embarrassing yourself. You passed."

Listen, I didn't doubt you because you're a woman, I doubted you because fixing cars is not usually something a seventeen-year-old knows how to do! But I've seen now that you're more than capable of taking care of yourself. So I'm sorry...but screw you I almost drowned!"

"*Almost*!" she repeated, attempting to lessen the stakes. "I jumped in after you, remember?"

"I remember something alright," I muttered, rubbing my lips jokingly. I was soon rubbing my bruised arm seriously.

Resting against the overturned hood, I examined the city and saw none of the bloodshed. With heavenly clouds the colour of orange and violet gliding above, everything almost looked normal. It put me in a sentimental mood and Veronica was victim to that.

"What's going to happen when we reunite with the others?" I asked somewhat solemnly.

"We smile and be happy. That's what people do when they see their friends, Levi."

"Obviously. But I meant...what happens next? It feels like a lifetime ago but I do remember you saying this was a temporary co-existence. We scratch your backs and all that jazz, yeah?"

She set down a tool I had never seen before and joined me in city-gazing.

"We're going to have that talk now? Alrighty. Levi, you knew we have two separate end goals. Us girls have my father's cabin and you boys have that underwater city thingy. I'll admit you three have been substantially better than I gave you credit for but that doesn't change the facts. As corny as it sounds, we want different things."

I chuckled and nodded, the sun reflecting perfectly to create a shadow glare over my downward gaze. "Yeah I know...but we've got each others backs, you and I. I'm sure they're doing the same just as we speak. I'm not going to get all sappy, but why throw away something that works? We don't need to have two separate end goals."

Veronica shook her head and put on mocking eyes. "You just have the hots for Annabelle, you slut."

Her sense of humour still struggled to translate properly. "Forget it. Forget I said anything."

I turned to board the bus but she grabbed my shirtsleeve to pull me back.

"God you're so dramatic. Yes, all right? I think we should stick together. Whether or not Safehaven is legit, Papa Rhodes always loves having guests."

My grimace turned into a smile but then froze agonizingly. It slowly drooped at the exact speed as my realization. Soon, my face was a cracked rock.

"Sorry…who?"

"Papa Rhodes?" she replied, nonchalantly. "His name is Jim but he always refers to himself in third-person. I don't know, maybe it's a dad thing."

I was unsure if my heart was vibrating at blinding speed or came to a despairing halt. Cold sweat seeped from my forehead and armpits as I was trying to convince myself that it was only a coincidence.

"And he, uh…he taught you how to fix cars?"

"Yup. My elementary was only a couple blocks from his shop so every day I'd run down 26th Ave and work with him!"

I bit my teeth together so painfully that I was certain one row was going to snap against the other. Jim Rhodes…Mechanic…26th Ave… Jesus Christ. Maybe there was another. Please for the love of God let there be another. I only had one shot left.

"Veronica…what's your last name?"

My questionnaire was clearly frustrating her. "Uhm…Rhodes? Are you retarded?"

I had to grip the edge of the bus so that I wouldn't collapse. Now finished with the engine, she slammed the hood shut and took a step closer to my averted eyes.

"Lee? What's the matter with you?"

I would've rather placed a bullet in my mouth and bite down than be in the position that I was in. My past took its sweet time to creep up behind me and it finally caught up. After spending all my time trying to avoid my childhood trauma, I completely overlooked my recent trauma.

"Christ…Uh…Okay. Okay. You may want to sit down."

Her anger was brewing. "Just spit it out!"

I blinked, never wanting the fraction of darkness to end. The darkness was always my constant but it wouldn't help me now. Nothing would.

"…I met your dad. The very first day it hit, I met him. We…Atlas, me and…some cops…we came across his garage. There he was."

I could tell her entire body was clenched. The most desperate fight took place inside of her as she fought valiantly and hopelessly to prevent tears.

"Was he…was…he…"

"No. No, he was alive."

The sigh of relief nearly broke me. I wanted to cry. I wanted nothing more than to break down and relinquish my sadness. I couldn't, however, as the man at the carnival took that away from me.

"Yeah…he was alive but there…there was a bandage on his arm."

A relapse of fighting occurred. "Was he bit?"

I shook my head. "No. Well…I don't know. Veronica, you need to understand that everything that day was so…fucked. It was like there was something in the air that made sane people…lose it. One of the police officers took his injury as a potential threat and she…well she… shot…him…"

Her eyes widened and closed. Every ounce of breath inside of her expelled from her body, leaving her lifeless. She didn't know where to look or how to feel. All that she could do was form a single question.

"Who was the officer?"

I groaned. "Veronica, it doesn't…"

"WHO?"

My eyes blinked away my shattered emotions. "Atlas's mom."

I will admit that the rest of the conversation has faded from my memory. It's as though I can picture fragments of the argument with it on mute, allowing the sound of silence to accompany us. I remember lots of shouting and tears and pain, but most of all I remember the resounding look of betrayal stitched into her drooped face. I knew that I wasn't at fault but she still blamed me and for some reason, I accepted it. Perhaps it was an overdose of empathy that made me absorb the blame, understanding the pain of taking it on single-handedly. I pitied her and if it meant hating myself, so be it. Unfortunately, that wasn't enough for her.

"I can't be with you right now. I need to go."

"Go where?" I asked with annoyance. "It's not like you can go to a bar and be by yourself! Veronica, I'm so incredibly sorry for what happened. I'd do anything to prevent it from ever happening. Unfortunately, I can't and we can only move on. Just get on the bus and we can take it one step at a time."

I reached out for her shoulder but she slapped my arm away like it was a bug.

"Don't you dare touch me! I decide what I want to do and right now, I want to be as far away from you as possible."

I shook my head at her haste. "C'mon, don't be ridiculous. What about Annabelle? Or your sister! They're waiting for you!"

"Then you can tell them why I left."

Her stone posture and lack of appropriate thinking had shown me that she was being serious. The driver slammed his palm on the horn twice, initiating an ultimatum.

"Let's go! It's gonna be dark soon."

I waved him off and took a step back, hoping she would join me. She didn't.

"Goodbye, Levi."

"No. No! You don't get to do this! You can't just check out when something pisses you off! Get on the bus or so help me God I will make you."

Her jaw extended outward slightly with passionate rage. "Don't make me turn this against you. I have a long list of things I could say that'd break you. If you have any shred of compassion left for me, leave. Right now."

In the few days we shared together, she slowly became my second sister. Now, by her choice, she was leaving me too.

"…Please," I pleaded.

"Go," she muttered coldly. Her feet turned as did her body and she walked away from me.

With a rich taste of shame tainting my mouth, I boarded the bus and immediately walked to the tail end as it roared to life. I stood like the orphan child I was and watched her through the emergency door window. I silently begged her to turn around with a sudden change of heart but as I've said, she was the second most stubborn person I knew. Even if she regretted her choice, she stuck to it. The bus drove toward the city and away from her. Just like that, without any sarcastic quips or even a single nod of life-altering acknowledgement, she was gone.

## 29. "This world is filled with unmotivated pussies, that's a fact, but you gotta be the one that'll break the mold."

The city's sign of welcome came and went but I for one missed it entirely as my face burrowed in my callused hands. There was a multitude of raw emotions expelling from one side of my neurons to the next. A feeling of heartbreak, though she wasn't my girlfriend. A feeling of betrayal, though she wasn't my enemy. A feeling of trashed familial love, though she wasn't my sister. I didn't know how to feel but the fact that I was faced with the uncertainty had demonstrated progress.

"She your girlfriend?" an older man asked gravelly, sitting in the opposite aisle.

I pulled my eyes from the window and back at him. "I'm sorry?"

"The girl we left back there. One with the bangs. She your girlfriend?"

"No," I answered firmly. "A friend...I think. She found out something and thought it best to go our separate ways."

He exhaled judgmentally and threw a handful of sunflower seeds into his cigarette-stained mouth.

"And what now? You're coming with us?"

His tone aggravated me. It was as if it belonged to a grandfather who shared a trait with his smokes: lacking a filter.

"Yes...I mean, no. I'm meeting up with some other people at the bridge. Hopefully, they're still alive."

"And that's where you meet your girlfriend?"

I thought of Annabelle but refused to mention her. "I don't have a girlfriend, gramps."

He crunched down on the shells and spat them out the window. "Oh…you one of those gays?"

My nostrils flared and my teeth clenched. "No, you arthritic fart. I'm not "one of those gays"."

He smiled through his tense cheeks, implying this was a rare occurrence. "Can I give you a piece of advice, boy?"

"No."

"Well I'm gonna give you some anyways. Ya see, when I was your age, my folks were constantly busting my balls on when and who I was gonna marry. There was one, a cashier at the station where I bought most of my smokes, but I never had it in me to ask her out. In the sixties I was enlisted to fight in 'Nam and I flew as fast as I could pack my bags. I did this, hoping it'd help me become a man. What's manlier than fighting kooks in the pouring rain? After two years of service and a couple dozen deaths under my belt, I went back with my head held high and the balls to ask her out. But when I went to the station and asked the owner for her number, know what he told me? He said she went off and got married…to an architect, no less. To this day I've never married. A few fucks here and there but I've been alone ever since."

My mouth opened and then closed, not really understanding the point.

"I'm sorry to hear that…but where's the advice?"

He spat a seed in my direction and frowned. "Calm your impatient little ass and listen. My point here, boy, is that you've got a finite time. That was a fact before this undead shit. Now, it's even more so. Love is a bitch of a drug but I can see that you're already addicted. I see me when I see you. Whether you gonna go after bangs back there or go after one of your 'friends', it doesn't matter. I don't give a shit. But you better do *something* instead of waiting for nothing. You could be like me and wait until you're ready, or you can grow a pair and just do it. No one's ready for love. This world is filled with unmotivated pussies, that's a fact, but you gotta be the one that'll break the mold."

I never thanked him for his advice. He turned away from me and enjoyed his stale sunflower seeds as if I had never existed. I hated getting advice because it made me feel like a helpless child. You never really want advice until you need it. Unfortunately, his advice made me think about both girls. However, this wasn't a Betty and Veronica conundrum. I had my mind made up almost a week ago.

The city was smaller than I imagined. Now in the heart of the storm, I realized that there was more rubble than there were buildings. It was smaller, yes, but so much louder. We turned down Jasper Ave and like a stealthy wave, the sound of gunfire and death hit us hard. Suddenly, we were driving through a no man's land.

"Everybody keep your heads down," the driver ordered. "We gotta move slowly here."

Everyone tried so desperately not to scream, fearing they would single-handedly cause our demise. Eventually, after slowly treading over dead soldiers and through bustling hordes, no one proved to be at fault. Our downfall was an overlooked claymore hidden beneath a quartet of fallen cops. Without warning, there was a massive explosion that decimated the front of the bus.

"Shit!" a man bellowed as the seared body of the driver covered him.

Most of the bus had remained intact but this didn't matter. With most of the front controls down, the collapsible door folded open, allowing the infected to board. Screams of passing infection and termination bounced around the curved walls, forming a domino effect. With me at the back of the bus, I knew this wasn't a proper finale. I unhinged the escape door with bat in hand and left the rest to suffer. It was wrong and sick but I had no other choice and I guarantee none of you would have done differently. I had a mission and it wasn't going to come to an end at the back of a goddamn bus.

My feet landed on the ripped asphalt and immediately I was in battle. The overwhelming sound of gunfire overpowered the halfies nature of stealth and patience, forcing them into unhinged survivalists. I swung at biters with Atlas's bat, performing a sort of dance in the middle of raining bullets. A doctor's jaw broke off entirely upon impact and ricocheted off of a pale female soldier. Once a backhand swing took care of the doctor, I waited eagerly for her to approach me. Within biting distance her mouth gaped and I swiftly shoved the end of the bat into the hole. Prodding the bat backwards, I guided her back into the parked bus and proceeded to jab forcefully, pushing the bat through her skull. She dropped and I momentarily thought I had time to make a getaway but a behemoth stopped me from doing so. My jaw literally dropped.

Across the street where soldiers and infected alike fought to the death, a pale beefcake watched me like a tempted bull. He had tree trunks for legs and from head to toe was clad in a bomb-disposal suit, creating a hellish juggernaut. The tinted helmet hid his face from me, thus making it all the more frightening. Knives and guns and explosives coated his reinforced body but none of it mattered for he chose to take me on with nothing but the terrifying, impossible muscle beneath the suit. He charged at me with limp arms and I tried to swing the bat but that turned out to be as effective as hitting him with a Fruit Loop. With freakish speed he tackled me before I could dive out of the way, driving me straight into the closest point of impact. Sadly, this was in fact a rather large mirror. At least, I thought it was a mirror. He tackled me through but when I expected the solid wall behind it to stop me, we just kept going. It turned out that it was actually a one-way mirror and on the other side was a high-class nightclub. With glass shards tucked in every crevasse on my body, we hit the bar floor with him on top of me.

"You're…crushing…everything!!"

I smacked and slapped him like it was an elementary fight as I felt both the air and life draining from me. While his helmet proved advantageous for me in the aspect that he couldn't bite, I had no kill point. Desperate for anything, I grabbed around his waist and felt the ridged handle of a Bowie knife. With my other free hand I tilted his helmet down so it was pressed against my own skull and preceded to stab the nape of his neck. Again and again, the squishing sounds became increasingly juicy and thick. Once the beast's life was ended, I used what strength I could conjure up to save my own. Heaving myself out from under the dead weight, I gasped for air and could finally catch my breath. Then the cocking of a shotgun behind me stopped that immediately.

"Move and you die," a whispering voice threatened.

Wheezy and collapsed, my voice resembled a fire billow more than anything.

"Okay…take it easy…I'm just going to turn around slowly…"

With my trembling hands raised, I turned and gently rose to my feet. Once eye level, the gunman was in fact no stranger. She was the same brown-haired girl wearing the summer dress that threatened my life nearly a week ago.

"A-Annabelle?"

Emerging from the shadows, her entire body trembled with hesitation. She wanted nothing more than to believe that I was who I said I was, but previous experiences prevented certainty.

"You're not him…you're wearing his face…YOU'RE WEARING HIS FACE!"

With the shotgun fully pumped, she fired a burst into my stomach. Well, she would've if the gun hadn't been empty. She pulled the trigger again and again, expecting a bullet to magically appear in the barrel. I took a series of deep breaths that got caught midway down my throat. My eyes locked on her and hers on mine. Both of us operated on hesitancy. I longed for it to be how it was before my departure but it was clear that she had gone through something horrific during these past two days. Her delusional behaviour was warmly familiar and I knew not to question it, only to assure her.

"Annabelle, it's me. I'm here. I'm Levi."

Two tears trickled down her face, one following the other with a slight delay. She yelled wordless screams through biting teeth, showing that she was fearful in believing me. I knew that I had to prove myself.

"Uhm…I, I saved your life! Remember? The day after we met…in the field? I-I told you about Cecilia and the farm! Annie, remember? You asked me to make you care. I made you care about me!"

Like a code word awaking a sleeper agent, Annabelle's eyes flickered and she was finally there.

"Levi…" she muttered in disbelief.

"I'm tougher than I look, right?" I reminded with a weak smile.

She dropped the gun and stumbled forward with exhausted strength. The chemistry through our stare was erupting and I took it as a sign for me to plant a kiss. However, she interpreted it in a much different sense and I suddenly had the outline of her hand embedded in my cheek.

"What…why?" I asked feebly, rubbing the swollen redness.

"You left! You think a note is good enough? Damn you, Levi. Damn you!"

The spotlight was burning my skin with embarrassment. Lest we forget that a woman's nature remains intact even if an apocalypse is thrown at her.

"I'm sorry?" I said, weary of sudden slaps.

She shook her head. "You should be…"

At her height she reached just below my collarbone. With a sigh of relief, she looked up at me with those extravagant eyes of hers and I melted. She was now in charge and her delicate hands landed on each of my cheeks. Annabelle pulled my face towards hers, our lips meeting with a warm embrace. I kissed her as if my life depended on it, holding nothing back. When we pulled away, she gave me a smile that made me feel reborn.

"…because then we couldn't have done that," she finished.

I exhaled gentle laughter and hugged her as tightly as my rattled body would allow. Once my nose was buried in her hair—which somehow still smelt amazing—a scream behind her made me look up to see Quinn and Josh.

"Levi?! Is that you??"

I nodded with a grin, initiating a heavy sob from Quinn as she ran for me. Prying Annabelle away from me, she now latched on but instead of an embrace of passion, it was of hopeless desperation. Annabelle may have looked roughed-up but Quinn was a complete mess. Her day-old mascara smeared violently, resembling the love child of a dumped prom queen and a raccoon. She smelt of fearful sweat and her neck was wrapped with rope burns. I wanted to ask but something told me I didn't want to know. Josh, on the other hand, stood distant like a guilty child that had yet to have their crime discovered. I gave him a nod and he returned it with averted eyes. His skin was sickly white and his eyes were incredibly bloodshot. Judging from his appearance, he looked infected. The sad thing was that he wasn't.

"It's awful…it's just awful…" Quinn said in-between stuttered gasps. I looked at Annabelle with question eyes but she didn't return with an answer. She was keeping something from me. I could tell she knew that I was catching on so Annabelle was quick to change the subject. Of course, she had to bring up the one thing I wanted to avoid.

"So? Where's Veronica?" Annabelle asked.

Quinn's head popped up from my chest at the sound of her name. The question formed a crossroads where once a path was taken it could not be retracted. Should I have lied and said that we got separated in the chaotic streets? Should I have told the truth and face the inevitable backlash of not chasing after her? In the end, I did neither and perhaps both.

"Don't worry…she's alive. We got separated…out there…but she's fine. I'm sure she'll find her way to us sooner or later."

Before the two girls could question me further, it was then my turn to ask the inevitable question.

"So? Where is he? I've got something of his that needs to be returned," I said, picking up the bat.

Quinn suddenly choked up. "W-wait...you didn't tell him??"

"Tell me what?" I asked.

Annabelle seized up and bit her lip with doleful eyes. "Well- I, h-how am I supposed to?"

"Tell me what?"

Both the girls looked back at Josh for help. Looking at them and then me, he was utterly perplexed.

"I-I...he...oh Jesus Christ!"

Josh burst into a messy sob. "Wuh-we c-couldn't do anything! The tank just shot at us! H-he fell and-and..."

Before he could even fall to the floor, my hand grasped onto his collar and lifted him back onto his limp feet. I smacked him on the back of his skull and jabbed my finger only centimetres from his nose.

"Tell me. Now," I ordered.

Through blubbering words, each of them took turns in unraveling everything that they had endured. From the initial kidnapping to the mysterious cowboy to Atlas's demise, the day and a half had been laid out in front of me as the city slowly crumbled around us.

"The rubble and ash was too thick to see anything," Josh concluded. "But we were so scared of a second attack from the tank that we left the grounds as fast as we could. There's nothing that we could've done."

The nightclub held a considerable quantity of darkness, making it difficult to be spotted by biters roaming the raging streets. This allowed me to process everything, as well as refuse to accept it. The final sentence that Josh said struck me to my core. When I heard that, I knew that I couldn't forgive myself if I was part of the we in "nothing that we could've done". Sure, people perished ever second of every day and even more so now, but I was not willing to let Atlas perish in such a sudden and rushed act. Surveying these three living teenagers, I realized that it was Atlas's doing for me to have located them. I left, but he knew that I wasn't stupid enough to leave for good. After everything that we've been through, all the fights and daily hardships, the contradicting philosophies and opposing personalities, through all of it, I couldn't deny the familial bond that we shared. He may have been the brother that I always fought with, but a brother nonetheless. If he was capable of surviving a plane crash, a car crash, sixty-five days on the road, and a kidnapping, no way in hell was a building going to be the death of him. That was something I owed to him, and was the sole reason for me to remove the demolition suit from the halfie.

"W-what are you doing?" Annabelle asked.

This entire conversation was spent with me armouring up. It was not an instance on television where a single cut between cameras was all it took for me to suit up. Believe me, it was sixty pounds of life-saving apparel.

"Where did he fall?"

Josh flipped through his memory for an address. "Uhm…42$^{nd}$ street I think…seven or eight blocks from here."

"Did you see his body?" I asked the three of them, buckling up the boots.

An exchange of uncertain looks was as good of an answer for me.

"Exactly. So, I'm going find him and bring him back."

The fury erupting from Annabelle's eyes pulsated down into her body and limbs, making me wonder if I should've started with the helmet…or a cup.

"Do you have any idea how idiotic you sound right now? Yes, I get it. The deaths of people close to you can be agonizing. I understand that you feel the need for closure but that's not a luxury that we're given these days. This city is a warzone and the fact that you made it back to us once is a miracle in itself. We've finally been granted good luck and you want to go and shit on it?"

With my kneepads and bulletproof pants tightened on, I reached for the self-contained arsenal and attached it piece by piece. While I was preoccupied with this, I explained my reasoning to her.

"The very first day, Atlas and I were in school. Josh was there too… but he was quick to leave. I accidentally got locked in a classroom, moments before the plane hit. Atlas was still in the school and before he left, he caught a glimpse of me through the window. Now, he could've easily kept on moving. Hell, I would've! But he chose to open the door. In the end, that didn't do much since we were *both* in the classroom when it hit. The point of this is that it doesn't matter what the outcome of the rescue attempt was. The only thing that matters is that he opened the door for me, both figuratively and literally. A menial gesture, but him showing that shred of care was more than I had received in a long time. He saved my life in multiple ways and he deserves for me to do the same. Even if he is dead, at least I can die knowing that I tried. That's good enough for me."

I slipped the arm gauntlets on and rotated the shoulder pads into position, leaving only the helmet. Annabelle stood in front of me and she was holding it.

"You don't always have to be the good guy," she assured with trembling sadness.

I took the helmet from her and allowed a simple, genuine smile to approach my face.

"No…but sometimes I do."

She blinked and tipped her head, ashamed of showing the vulnerability in her sadness.

"If I die, at least I got to kiss you twice," I stated joyfully.

"What do you mean twi—"

I interlocked my gloved fingers around her slender waist and kissed her for a second time. This one was more passionate, more savouring. My heart was petrified but my mind was euphoric. There was a very good chance I would never see her again so I needed to make it count. And, well, I think I did a pretty good job.

Once I pulled away from her lustful enticement, I caught a look of pure distraught on Josh's pale face. It was as if I had offended him in some way. Honestly, it was the least of my worries because now I was a self-promoted soldier in a dying world. I didn't have the time or care for teenage jealousy.

"If I'm not back in one hour, find a way to the bridge. *Carefully.*"

I walked to the shattered window with the bat in my hand and a dozen other weapons on my waist. It felt as though my feet were in blocks of ice. The important thing, however, was that they were *bulletproof* blocks of ice. With one final look back, I gave them a cheesy thumbs up.

"I hope to see you soon…" I paused. Bit my tongue from exposing any foreign compassion. They deserved more but I could only give them some. "…Thanks for giving me a shot."

Like the wind, I faded away. As cool as that would be, it felt like I was covered with cement from head to toe. I awkwardly stepped over the window ledge, dropped the visor on my helmet, and embarked on what I could've only hoped to be my final life-risking mission. Let's be honest here: We all know that's bullshit.

# 30. "Because we're animals, plain and simple."

Retold by Annabelle.

I sat behind the bar with my knees drawn to my chest, bathing in stale liquor. The floor vibrated at a randomly precise tempo and infinite gunfire coaxed my ears with shivering music. Quinn was next to me but that only included her physical presence, for her mentality was in a different world. Neither of us spoke, yet that uncomfortable lump at the back of our throats could be felt from excessive talking. In her mind, she was ranting about her psycho-erotic tendencies that allowed her pain to be disgustingly desirable. In my mind, I thought about Levi and the devolved gender he was a part of.

I wish I could come up with some deep-seated metaphor for them, but they themselves were an idiosyncratic species that differed from women like a lizard to a sparrow. If you were to ask any woman, regardless of their sexuality, they're likely to agree that man was the best and worst thing that happened to them. Men were their own paradox in every sense of the word, which evoked impulses in us girls that formed this desire to both tear their clothes off and wring their necks. Yes we kissed and yes it was nice, but I hated it. I hated it because it made me emotionally viable and that itself was the worst death sentence out there. There was a strong chance he was going to die and if we hadn't kissed, my feelings would've left with him. Now, there's that 'what if?' that would be cemented in my brain until the day I die and that was not something I was wired to deal with. If it hadn't been abundantly clear already, I was a virgin. The idea of a penis made me immediately compare it to a naked mole rat. However, this didn't mean that I was a lesbian. Believe me, I could go on and on about my hatred for our lady parts. I had crushes and I went on dates but that never amounted to anything because commitment issues could be found highlighted in the index for my personality. It's not that I didn't want to date and have sex, it's just I couldn't trust someone to do it with. That was the main catalyst for my anxiety before all of this and after the events shortly following Day Zero, it only got worse. So why could I trust Levi? Well, for the longest time I didn't. I could only relate to him because he was the only one I knew to truly understand what it means to be ruined. Our semi-friendship that dipped the toes in flirtatious waters was more than enough for me. But then he had to go and mess it up by kissing me. I mean, I kissed him first…but that's not the point! That brown-haired douche ass went on his suicide mission, leaving me with what I could only assume to be some form of worried-widow syndrome. Like I said, the best and worst thing to happen.

Quinn stirred, reminding me that she was in fact right next to me. "I liked it…"

I turned to her, flinching from an explosion a block over. "What?"

She inhaled a series of spliced breaths. "…I'm an addict. When I look at myself in the mirror, that is the only thing I see. When guys stare at me…I like it. It shows me that they see me for who I am. When we wore the leashes…t-that, uhm…that is hardly the most degrading thing that has been around my neck."

I nodded slowly, blinking the most sympathetic eyes I could fake. "So you're into some kinky stuff…so what?"

Quinn chuckled at my understatement. "You have no idea. Being dominated…it puts me in my place. It shows me that we're the same as the animals we pay to see at zoos. Because we're animals, plain and simple. That is the one constant for me. And, well…when that fat pig of a man made me go on all fours and bark…I liked it! It makes me sick to think about it but it was the best rush I've had in years."

It was impossible to shield the look of uncomfortable disgust on my face. I had nothing that I could tell her or was willing to tell her that would make her feel normal, so I changed the subject.

"Whoever you are doesn't matter to me. As long as you're willing to work together, that's what counts. That's what Atlas would've wanted…"

A sudden rush of frustrated steam shot out of her like a cartoon bull. "Bastard."

"How can you say that?"

Quinn reached across from her and pulled out a 1969 spirit that had a crusty, arenaceous coating around the bottle. Yanking the cork out with her teeth, she threw back a murky swig and wiped the residue from her lips with her forearm.

"He humiliated me. No one had ever spoken to me like that. Lies too…I'm not weak! I was the leader when it was just us three. Me! I led most of the ambushes and made sure all of us were stocked up on tampons and deodorant. But once he showed up, I faded into the background without a choice." She took another gulp. "And he couldn't have been more wrong when he said that I was his sex toy. Two nights ago on that roof, *I* was using *him*! The two most important things in this world, Annabelle, are sex and security. If I promised him one I would get the other. Plus, I got to have sex, so that's a win-win."

My facial expression demonstrated that I disagreed completely. "How can you possibly think that's the right way to live? Whoring yourself out for *protection*? A little ironic, don't ya think?"

Quinn scoffed, trails of blood-coloured liquid dribbling down her chin. "If you asked me two months ago what's the single most important thing in life, what would be my answer? Money! I don't care how sentimental your viewpoint is, even love is a struggle when you can't buy the roof over your head or the clothes on your back. Bills may be obsolete but the idea of currency will never end. Maybe it'll be weapons or medicine or water, but whatever it is, lust is chained to our DNA and will not be pleased with any of the above. Sex, Annabelle, is what rules this world. Sooner or later you'll understand that and see that men will kill for it. If I have to bang somebody to make sure that I live then so be it."

An interesting philosophy, yes, but kind of misplaced in our conversation.

"I think you went on a little tangent there…" I pointed out.

The alcohol was beginning to activate. "My point is, Atlas was a piece of shit for saying that…he didn't understand it and he took that out on me…and then he had to go and be a heroic dick and sacrifice his life so that we three would make it! What an asshole…"

Being patient was getting me nowhere. "Ok I'm lost. How the hell does that make him an asshole?"

"Because he died a good guy!" she explained, expecting me to understand. "He said all that shit to me and then died saving us. That makes me look like the bitch if I talk shit about him! He died making me care about him and that's why he's an asshole. Heroic, yes, but an asshole nonetheless."

I stood up from the sticky floor and rubbed the corners of my eyes.

"Alrighty…well, you think on that and I'm going to go check on Josh. He's been oddly quiet."

While she entertained herself with the wine bottle (perhaps in more ways than one) I ducked my way to the slender hallway across a blank dance floor. A few minutes after Levi left, Josh told the both of us he was going to the bathroom and hadn't come back since. With blind arms waving in front of me to guide through the darkness, I came across the men's washroom door. Before I knocked, a thin green illumination from the door outline stopped me. Then voices began to whisper. Not just his own. *Voices.*

Retold by Josh.

Sitting on the porcelain toilet being blanketed by blackness, I finally came to the realization that I was too oblivious to see before: I had no friends. Atlas never trusted me from the get-go and then he died. Veronica said maybe two words to me that included "fuck" and "you". Quinn was the definition of a hot mess but thought all guys were perverts unless they looked like Zac Efron. Levi was the closest thing I had to a friend, which was tremendously sad as he had both choked me out and kissed the girl I was in love with. That left Annabelle and we might not have been friends but I would've done anything to become more. She was the only thing that held me back from going through with it…but I convinced myself that she would understand.

I was pathetic. My only chance at success died on the basketball court when the infection spread. Everyone else in my group had the qualities of becoming truly memorable and there I was, plagued with a curse of being forgotten. I had nothing or no one to prove myself. That is, until a couple hours ago when a radio was slipped into my back pocket by a bō-wielding woman. Informing me with knowledge that I couldn't believe, she presented me with a choice and in that spray-painted, cum-stained bathroom, I had to make up my mind. I wanted to do it, I really did. I had settled on an option but lacked the balls to actually go through with it.

Resting my hand on what felt like a skinny dildo, I soon realized that it was in fact a glow stick. Cracking it like it was the spine of a worthless animal, I shook it to full illumination and examined myself in the water-splotched mirror. I was disgusted at who I was looking at, but was I capable of becoming something that I could be proud of? That *he* would be proud of? I begged for it to be so. I just needed that little push, which just so happened to be resting on the lid of the toilet's water tank in the form of a thin, powdery white line. An expired hotel key card rested beside it, as did a fifty-dollar bill, bent at the corners as if it had once been rolled into a tube.

"Cocaine. Perfect," I muttered, desperate for anything at that point.

Before my common sense could wake up, I rushed over to the toilet, rolled the bill into an expensive straw, and snorted the dry, contaminated blow.

My head kicked back and my nose burned with a foreign sensation. I opened my eyes expecting a life-altering state of being, but nothing. I felt a tingle and…that was it.

My hands gripped the porcelain as I began to panic. "No, no this isn't good…I need this! I need it!"

There were three remaining lines of mistakes waiting impatiently to be absorbed. So, as anyone that would want any and all stress to be relieved, I snorted three strips without a breath in-between. A new threshold was reached.

"J-Jesus…" I moaned as it immediately took effect.

It was euphoria mixed with grandiosity and I was indestructible, invincible, and ready to take on the world. I could feel every muscle in my body and they wanted to move. I knew what I was doing was right because it felt oh so good. Once I pulled the radio out, the rest was easy.

Retold by Annabelle.

Everyone talks to themselves. Anyone that says otherwise is either a liar or a new brand of schizophrenic. Josh, well, he was always weird. But talking to himself in different voices? That was reason enough to eavesdrop. The other voice was robotic and carried interference, yet almost definitely female. I pressed my ear against the wood to try and make out the mysterious conversation.

"I already told you! C'mon, get a move on! You're taking forever!" Josh said frantically.

**Just calm down,** a familiar voice replied. **The roads are backed up with corpses but we'll be there in a few minutes. Repeat the location so the others know.**

"Jesus, how many people are you sending?"

**Enough. Ya know, so nothing happens like last time. That guy with you, Globe or something, he really stirred some shit. Boss ain't happy with him.**

"Atlas! Like the god! And he's dead. Deader than dead."

**Awe, send me the details of the funeral when you have a chance. In the mean time, tell us your location. Now.**

"Orbit Nightclub off Jasper Ave. Just...you're not going to hurt them, right?"

**No. Not yet anyway.**

Confusion and paranoia made for a terrible concoction, overpowering me without warning or discretion. I opened without knocking to see Josh hunched over in a corner with a Walkie-talkie in his hand. His head snapped to me and a look of guilt shrouded his face.

**Stay put. We'll be there in two min-**

Josh turned the dial off and hid the radio behind his back as if that would ease the situation. He shot upwards, wiped his runny nose and smiled.

"A-Annabelle! Just the girl I wanna see. You're so, so beautiful, ya know that?"

"Who were you talking to?" I asked, a sense of panic rising in my body.

"What? No one! I-I was just listening to the radio! Honest!"

"Who were you talking to??" I repeated. "Who's coming?"

The effects of the drug were slipping away with haste, swiftly allowing Josh to comprehend his impending damage. He looked in the mirror and saw not only disgust but also self-betrayal.

"Annabelle...oh shit," he whispered, clasping his hands at the back of his neck. "I never wanted to hurt you. You can stay with me and we'll be okay! I promise you!"

Seeing him in such a disgraceful manner made the gravity of the situation sink in instantaneously. The world was ending but there was a much worse threat I had to face. If only Levi hadn't left.

"You…how could you…" I mumbled in disbelief.

Josh lifted his head and directed this pain-stricken look to me that felt like a vial of poison being injected into my bloodstream, causing my insides to corrode slowly and agonizingly.

"Puh-please! I-I luh-love you, Annabelle! S-stay with me!"

Using love as a ploy to keep me from leaving? Big mistake. I was done with being the silent one. I was done letting people make decisions on my behalf. Most of all, I was done with this piece of shit. I threw an uppercut to his stomach, my fist clenched with boiling vexation. He tumbled back and clutched the sink fearfully.

"Fuck you, traitor. I'm taken."

I slipped through the door before he could pull me back into his slimy grasp. Though I wouldn't know for many days to come, the way I treated him may have been the biggest mistake of my entire life. But I'll get to that later. Because once I turned the corner and faced the shattered window, I had no time to think about repercussions. My mind was solely focused on the gun jabbing into Quinn's temple. We were finished.

Back to me.

Foggy glass. Heavy breathing. A shooting jab cascaded through my warped ribs, as if my soul had been rattling them like flimsy jail bars. Biters of every age and of every clique saw me as a challenge but were only able to achieve shattered teeth and empty stomachs. I barely raised a weapon and instead pushed through the bustling mob. I was safe but in return I was completely trapped. I was impenetrable in my suit of armour yet I had never felt more vulnerable.

There was a chrome knob on the side of my bubbled head that allowed for sound to pass through. I turned it off and allowed only my breathing rate and speckled rubble pattering on my helmet to break the silence. It soothed me. Screams of the infected were bad enough but the screams of the living were much, much worse. Their suffering was present and through my ears I shared their agony. Turning my ears off, I let my eyes do all the heavy lifting and boy, did they not disappoint. Looking up, I paused and examined our future. Fire and blood painted on a canvas of colossal smoke clouds scaling skyscrapers. On the ground level where us mortals laid to die, a climactic battle was unfolding less than a dozen blocks away. From the napalm-coated streets to the abundance of mobile freaks wandering aimlessly, I knew moving forward would achieve nothing other than an abrupt, throwaway termination. I knew that, yet my legs kept moving forward. It was as if my brain had sent a message to my legs, copied and pasted the shit out of it, only for the overload of impulses to remain stuck in my waning mental realm like a congested highway. Just to make things clear, I was not heading over to the battlefield. The thought never even crossed my mind. Atlas's rescue was my first and only priority, which just so happened to reside on the very brim of the fight. What I didn't take into consideration, however, was my apparel. Sure, taking on the pale ones was exponentially easier, but side effects to my choice of attire included: abundance of sweat, restricted movement, and the fact that I looked like a goddamn soldier. This didn't bode well for me.

I was probably fifty meters away from the street where Atlas had fallen. Not even a minute away. Now, you know how fate to me was like the bitchy ex-girlfriend who strived to shit down one's throat? Well, fate had a bipolar sister that went by the name of luck. She wasn't sadistic but more so bored and felt the need to mess with me whenever she felt like it would spice things up. Because of course, what would my life be without seemingly impossible coincidences to occur that took me on exhausting detours? One step was all it took to trigger some sort of imaginary tripwire, causing freaks to pour out from doorways, alleyways, cars, the sky, I didn't even understand. Once I was literally surrounded at every corner in the open street, the cavalry was quick to follow. Two hundred men and women in camouflage risking their lives and there I was looking like the fucking Michelin Man.

"Flank the left!" a bald beefcake called out. "Watch for the alleys!"

Suddenly my two hundred and fifty pound body was vibrating from the action movie gunfire. Flashes of burning light zoomed past me and I was hit with two bullets, one in my thigh and the other in my lower back. The padding was enough to stop damage but did nothing to soothe the tremendous stinging. The wounds burned and pulsated, bruises already forming before I fell to my knees. I took a moment to let my heart beat again, giving the opportunity for chunks of brain and bone fragments to circle around me like some psychotic ritual. As the ground was covered with only death, I shot up like a compressed spring and joined the layer of the living. I reached around awkwardly at the comfortably holstered assault rifle on my back, making it seem like a failed attempt at pulling a *Die Hard*. I finally got a hold of it and fired, but this wasn't like the movies where it took five minutes to master a weapon. When I fired a shot, the kickback jammed into my shoulder blade so fiercely that the bullet soared high above their heads. After an entire round of pathetic shooting, I managed to take down a total of five, making a highly unnoticeable dent in the sea of freaks. Unsurprisingly, the soldiers were a different story. They fought with passion and their kills were comically graphic. There had actually been a moment where I ceased fire and watched them slowly get overrun. They formed a circle around an overturned limousine that also acted as my hiding spot, but it was getting smaller and tighter. Once I turned the hearing knob on, one woman called for cover to refill her ammo and when she did so, she noticed me. I waved like the pathetic shit I was.

"A seeker?? What are you still doing here?! Why aren't your claymores going off??"

I looked at my selection of weapons and found nothing. Slowly I was starting to understand what my job description had been.

"Claymores…what claymores?"

She continued to look at me as if she was expecting a response. I repeated myself but the same look was given. Turned out I had a knob on the other side that allowed my voice to be heard.

"WHAT CLAYMORES?" I said, my voice robotic and tinny. Finally she heard me but she wished she hadn't.

"Ramirez!!" a soldier nearby yelled. "Get back up! We need you here!"

She waved him off. "Just a second!" She turned to me, her life-despairing eyes widening. "You planted claymores around the perimeter right? That's your job! Without them we have no chance!"

I felt obligated to apologize even though I was not the person she thought I was. I felt obligated, yes, but was never given the chance to go through with it. As if it were a coin toss, the infected won and immediately doubled their rage. In that moment, I was not the hero that I ventured off to become. I was weak and my knees ached to prove that. In the end, I fell back down with the limo as my shield and watched a massacre that made the farm look like a romantic comedy.

What I had watched was a scene of such devolved brutality that made me believe it to be a tragic painting with blood as the primary colour. Blind freaks, smilies, biters with mutated limbs, they all seemed bullet proof. They had planned and they were precise. One biter ripped a trachea out of a soldier and another converged on a nearby brother of arms. They looked out for each other. When one had a kill, he or she backed away for safety and proceeded to attack from a different location. Guns didn't matter for they had fear on their side.

"Grenade! PLEASE!" Ramirez begged to my quivering body as she fired an empty gun.

I patted my body down and lobbed the avocado-shaped bomb to her. She caught it, pullet the pin with her teeth, and held onto it. I watched her entire body cease to exist as her sacrifice took the lives of six biters. Six new ones eagerly took their place and it was as if her death meant nothing.

"Christ…" I breathed.

With what shred of dignity and courage I could gather, I eventually joined the fight to do my part. The bat became so slimy with juices that I was losing my grip. All but one of my knives got lost in their throats and skulls. My gun was empty and my gloved fingers were too fat to reload it. I had no grenades but the bald leader did. We were in arms reach of one another when a blindly thrown grenade landed at his feet.

"LOOK OU--"

Explosion. We were both sent flying through the air and my face landed on a rough slab of concrete, creating a ripple of cracks down my mask. Climbing up, I released concussed noises that sounded like static and grinding metal. Blinking myself back to proper vision, I looked for him through a cracked view.

"You okay?"

I ducked beneath the firing bullets over to the leader and found him in a dugout with his face in his hands.

"We're alive, sir. We…"

He lifted his head from his hands to reveal that his entire face had been blown off. Two gaping holes remained where both his nose and left eye previously resided, his shattered cheekbones rattled each time his mouth opened, and all that was left intact were the exposed muscles stretched across his face.

"Hyhh…mmm…ghuu…."

When he slumped over, death graciously infected his body.

I stood up silently, unaffected by the hurdling slugs of death. My mind felt like a river of swirling sentiment, colliding with the inside of my skull after each step I took. The bullets became fewer and fewer as did the soldiers. What gunfire that was left grazed by my helmet like deadly whispers. I saw a man with no face. He had no face. Then…right then, I knew. I wasn't a soldier. A friend, yes, but I was not a soldier. The glass container of my sanity was oozing onto my mental floor. I had to leave before I voluntarily dived in front of the bullets without my fiberglass mask.

"I'm…s-s…sorry…"

The dead soldiers didn't care for my apology. They died with malice lining their taste buds and formed tainted memories of my betrayal. Not even with the claymores but with my cowardice. The infected smelt my vulnerability through the vents of my suit and seemingly made an effort to avoid me, prolonging my suffering. Occasional bullets hit me but instead of relating the harsh impact to pain I made it synonymous with sensation. It made me feel something and I would sometimes crave a bullet so I wasn't walking numb. Turning left and then two rights, the pale ones were scarce, soldiers were corpses, and I walked aimlessly. Did I care anymore? Nothing seemed to convince me until a charred sign of 42$^{nd}$ street passed by and the collapsed tower rested on its brother. What amazed me was that rather it being a complete pile of rubble, most of it had simply tilted onto the support of the other. I looked at the concrete mammoth and its broken partner as if it were a mirror. It was unbelievable. Atlas's chance of survival skyrocketed because he had something to fall on. He had something there to catch his fall. It taught me that even when one is broken, it doesn't necessarily make it destroyed. I was gone, but was I too far gone? Also, did the fallen tower symbolize Atlas or myself? Through all of this, the searching for medicine and the search for Atlas, was that all that I was searching for? I knew what my true motive was. The thought of Atlas, Josh, Quinn, Veronica, Annabelle and I all around a makeshift dinner table eating canned tuna and jarred beets, it was the idea of family. That is what forced me onwards to locate my friend who had given me every reason to believe he was dead. Family.

Now I was running. The gates of the construction site provided a silent welcome and soon I was hurdling over bent metal and fallen concrete blocks. The damage was bad, but was there hope? I faced the two towers, took a deep breath, and surveyed for movement. The surviving building was a concrete and metal jungle that had scaffolding scaling it like vines. An orange crane loomed over it with a single steel beam that had still swung with gentle force since the unexpected demolition. The fallen brother resembled a toppled tower of *Jenga* that had a wall to prevent it from hitting the floor. It ached and creaked like an arthritic back and its stability matched a house of cards; a misplaced touch was all it needed for a flimsy downfall. For hour-long minutes I stared blankly at the abiotic structures until I spotted a limp hand nearly three stories up. Deep in the tilted rubble was a cave-like burrow that looked like a bird's nest. There was no movement, but a hand was all I needed.

"Atlas! I'm here!" my voice cried out, dried and beaten.

Unless I wanted to cause further damage, I had to scale it from the outside. Like a jagged rock climbing course, the steel bars cut through my gloves and caressed the blood out from my palms. I didn't care. I climbed as my muscles pleaded for me to stop. Loose chunks of building constantly came loose and usually softened its fall on my helmet, further cracking the glass. When I heaved myself up to the third level platform and saw him, the floor shook with nauseating uncertainty. He was there and his eyes were open. They saw death and the interstellar quandary that it embodied. They did not blink and they did not flicker. His head drooped over like a dying lily. His once gray tee was now red and his leather jacket had become pathetic tatters. I was unsure how much blood he had lost but the fact that he seemed to have been bathing in it was not a good sign. Thinking that the chain leash around his neck was a source of complication, I took out a pair of bolt cutters from my right thigh pocket and snipped it off. Still nothing.

"Atlas…Hey Atlas…wake up…"

I slumped to my knees and my fallen weight rattled our surroundings. My sliced glove reached out to him and my tinted helmet tilted slightly.

"Come back…" I begged, my robotic voice cracking with remorse. He blinked.

# 31. "Happy thoughts, happy thoughts,"

"...S-so...God's...a giant...robot?" Atlas asked with a voice filled with blood and dust.

His crackled words paddled my chest, sending pulses of shock and awe through my contained body. He was alive. He was actually alive.

"Not exactly..." I finally said, reaching back for the helmet latch. Pulling it off, it made an unsealing sound as if an airtight jar of pickles was opened. My oily strands of limp hair shrouded my eyes but nonetheless he knew who was standing over him.

"Great...you're God...that's disappointing..."

I chuckled dryly. "Nice to see you too..."

Hobbling on my knees slowly and cautiously, I approached Atlas and examined the damage. Though his insides probably resembled a bone-potent smoothie, his outer damage was minimal as only a single piece of shrapnel was dug into his calf.

"Heh...déjà vu, huh?" he said, his lips peeling back to show his bloodstained teeth.

I removed it without warning and released a thick spurt of deoxygenized blood a shade too black. He wanted to scream but it was too much work. Atlas simply released a half-assed fury of profanities I'd rather not repeat.

"The girls...Josh...they alright?"

I nodded, craving Annabelle's lips at the thought. "They're alive. We all made it...because of you."

His head fell back against the fractured stone headboard and he groaned. "Let's not get all sappy, okay?"

I smiled thinly but retained a sincere look. "I know… it's just, everyone thought that you were dead. But I know you and everything we've been through. You don't die easily."

"After all this, I'm almost guaranteed a shitty and non-spectacular death…AIDS, maybe."

"Regardless," I continued, "you're alive now. I know we haven't seen eye-to-eye much and I left you, but I never stopped respecting you. You're the only one that got me and you knew to leave that clue since I was going to come back one way or another."

"Levi…" he tried to stop me.

"No, I need to say this. I can only imagine what you've been through these last couple of days and yet you took care of them. You may not think it, but you're a goddamn leader. You care about people and…and I never thanked you for caring about me in that classroom."

"Levi! My leg!" he yelled without a voice.

Looking down I realized that the faucet in his open leg produced the red pool he bathed in. Blood poured steadily and with each ounce gone, another step to death was taken.

"Crap…uh, bandages…I've gotta have bandages on me somewhere…" I muttered, swivelling my torso left and right to search my endless pockets and pouches.

He shook his head. "No…I think it…sliced an artery. Bandages won't stop the bleeding."

My mind was working overtime as I thought relentlessly to try and conjure up a solution. The main one that I kept coming back to was removing his leg entirely but that would only lead to further blood loss. I needed something to seal the wound, not cover it up. Then it hit me.

"You're not going to like this one bit," I warned.

"Like what?" he asked, unsure if he wanted an answer. "Like what?"

I reached into a slender pouch on my utility belt third from the center and pulled out a flare.

"Awe fuck man," he complained with a whiny rasp.

I popped the cap off, struck the scratch surface over the ignite button and created a static flame with thin smoke.

"Sorry about this," I said in advance.

Screaming was not too much work this time. I held the flame right up against his squirming leg and even had to sit on his stomach to hold him down. After twenty seconds of cooking his flesh, the vacating blood decreased and his throat became raw from screaming.

"Not over yet. You're more likely to die from the infection than the wound itself."

Atlas laid his exhausted eyes on me and blinked painfully. "...So?"

Half-expecting to make a Molotov cocktail during my rescue mission, I made sure to grab a small glass bottle of whiskey from the bar. That, and I figured if I was going to die I should go out with a buzz.

"Happy thoughts, happy thoughts," I reminded him as I unscrewed the bottle. I poured it over the burn and the flesh was still hot enough to make it sizzle. This time, screaming was no work at all.

"All done!" I pulled out a wad of gauze and dressed his leg.

Atlas sighed through his clenched teeth and looked out at the nighttime horizon. From this view, it was almost impossible to find any specs of life.

"This...this is fucking war, dude."

"Which is why we need to get out of here," I told him. "Here, take my hand."

I carefully lifted Atlas to his feet but no blood rushed through his body as a hefty chunk of it was covering both the stone and myself. He was intoxicated with disorientation.

"I can't...walk..." he said, the world spinning three times over.

We were three stories above ground. The most logical solution for us to safely reach the floor would have been for me to lend him my containment suit. Unfortunately, logical thinking wasn't a specialty of ours. I picked him up in a bridal carry, shuffled over to the fractured cliff and jumped.

"W-wait!! Shit!!" Atlas yelled.

For a brief moment the rushing wind muffled everything else, letting me breathe. I was free falling and it was peaceful. It was frighteningly familiar and the thought of a beach came to mind but I couldn't place it.

Steel upon rock. As I put the boots on back in the bar, I noticed a spring-like contraption in the heel, reminiscent of a certain cake-lying video game. I took a gamble by landing on my feet and the second I hit the ground, the cards were revealed. Luck finally threw me a bone and neither of us were harmed. I let Atlas down and he instantly fell to his knees to vomit a bloody pile of his insides.

"Why'd...you...do that?" he mumbled through a filled mouth.

"The faster we get back to the others and get out of the city, the faster we can *properly* patch you up. So stop complaining and let's move."

Atlas crinkled his neck back to me and frowned. "Have you…seen me? Dude, I'm dead weight. Just go and make sure—"

"Shut your mouth," I interrupted. "No way did I go through all of that for you to give up on me. I watched someone lose their face! Either you take *your* bat right now and grow a pair or I'll Negan the shit out of you. Understood?"

He stood up, his stance having a noticeable curve. "…You take the bat. It won't do me much good now." He looked at my remaining stock of weapons. "Those pistols…give 'em to me."

With an accepting grin, I handed him both pistols that were holstered on each of my thighs. A fresh batch of explosions had been produced on 42$^{nd}$ street, sending a heavy wave of rubble and smoke through the hexagonal holes on the fence. Every remaining soldier had retreated onto this wide street in hopes for a final takeover. The war had caught up with us.

"Get ready," I said, raising the bullet-holed bat.

"*\*tt\**Whatever you say, *Hurt Locker*," he replied as he loaded a bullet into the barrel.

Simply put, the magnitude of this battle scene made the other one—where I personally witnessed a woman explode and a man receive a botched facelift—look like child's play. A monumental downpour of bullets scorched through the smoky air and desecrated anything that stood in their way. A constant detonation of triggered mines and newly thrown grenades created an array of bloody fireworks that erupted in the streets. The violent humming of nearby fighter jets and explosive reinforcements caused a vibrating sensation that carried through the dense air. The military had thrown everything that they possibly could at the doomed threat ahead of them, seemingly securing a victory. That is, until the dead flooded the streets in every. Single. Direction.

I spotted a deep, mortar-induced crater where a posh cafe once resided, causing me to sprint for the cover as Atlas painfully dragged behind me. Putting our lives ahead of his agony was a worthy sacrifice and with my mind solely focused on moving forward, I let Atlas keep his mind occupied with something other than the pain.

"I run! You shoot!"

I immediately heard the gunfire, knowing that Atlas was happy to comply. Left, right, corner, right, left, Atlas had buried his suffering and adapted an adrenaline-powered state of machine-like vigour. Not a bullet was wasted as he paved a path for me to follow, but the density of the smoke had made the surroundings nearly opaque, forcing us to move ahead utterly blind. Once we passed the corner of an overturned delivery truck, a trio of drooling mutants emerged through the smoke and came at us in a frenzy. Atlas had been busy with the endless amount of freaks pooling behind us and now it was my turn to demonstrate why I was a worthy survivor. A businessman with a goiter bulging from his throat, a taxi driver with a smile forever carved into his face, and a waitress without a jaw was what stood ahead of me. I belted a tennis player's grunt and I brutally murdered the new species. Three fully ruptured skulls later, I continued on until we dove into the crater. I hit the jagged rock and was followed by a stumbling teenager with a limp.

"They just…keep…coming!" Atlas yelled.

"We…we're almost there! Two more blocks! TWO MORE BLOCKS!" I reassured.

Peeking over the edge to spot any further cover, time slowed exponentially as a new wave of death crashed down into war-ridden streets. Everywhere I looked, men and women that had promised their lives for their nation had their promise cashed in. For every biter shot down, the rotting corpses swarmed two soldiers, delivering a slow and agonizing demise. There were tens of thousands of the infected and a fraction of the living. Now, they had only one weapon left at their disposal. On top of a charred fire truck was a silver canister that was dropped from a supply plane only an hour earlier. Soldiers approached it, turned a knob, and dove for cover. Suddenly, thick, yellowish clouds of gas mixed in with levitating dust and swallowed $42^{nd}$ street. Any surviving soldiers placed gas masks over their faces, leaving us victimized by this mysterious gas.

"Mask…I need a mask!" Atlas frantically stated.

I was safe with my bubble-like helmet. At least, that's what I thought. As the clouds of a yellow storm crept closer and closer, Atlas rummaged through the bodies of every dead soldier. Two seconds more would have been all it took if he hadn't found a gas mask in time. He drooped to his knees in exhaustion and I was about to join him when it hit us. He was fine, but me? Thin strands of gas seeped through the cracks of my helmet and tickled my nostrils. Though it wasn't the full dosage, I still felt every single side effect. Gaseous poison seeped down into my suit and through every pore in my body, constricting and burning like my torso had been placed inside of a clamp. I clawed at the splintered glass hovering over my face, the pain too foreign to explain. My eyes seared as if they had been dosed with a mixture of salt water and bleach. When I closed them, my tainted mindset produced jagged, erratic flashes of blue and red lightning that lit up beneath my eyelids. The bright, pulsating flickers had frightened me more than my outer surroundings, causing my throbbing eyes to see that the soldiers' plan had both succeeded and failed. Freaks became all jittery, as if their infected hearts had been hooked up to a revved-up engine. Some collapsed lifelessly, some fell in a convulsing rhythm, and some become more frantic and psychotic than ever before. Regardless of the varying results, it was clear that the components of this gas had a serious effect on their brains.

I felt Atlas's trembling fingers clasp on my shoulder pad. He hoisted himself up and reversed the role of hero and damsel in distress as he was now leading me away from the smoky massacre.

"We...need to *cough* get y-you out of here..." he spoke less than a foot away from my ear, but all I heard was muffled, broken sounds like words put in a blender.

"Hyhh…Wu...a..."

My vocal cords felt like rusty nails penetrating my throat. I could not speak, I could barely walk, barely hear, yet death did not approach me. However, the truly terrifying effect of this gaseous compound was about to take hold.

While dying soldiers soaked in the gas and the infected were nonsensically affected by it, Atlas led me to the next street through a tight alleyway. Once there, I found myself in a new world. Atlas was no longer beside me. The sky was filled with fiery despair and below me was an infinite sea of blood-drained corpses. Gravity evaporated in the air that it held down and I became inverted with all as my dreary body was carried into the hellish sky. I began to gain speed and floating bodies of the ones I knew, loved, and cherished slipped past me in the burning atmosphere like a handful of sand falling through my fingers. Before I could reach the roof of this surreal hallucination, walls of metal and concrete floated through nothingness and encapsulated me in a corroded factory. This was it: the factory in my nightmares. Broken gears cranked against one another, alarms and sirens blared a familiar tune and faulty pipes rattled as a thick fluid pumped through, acting as the veins of this behemoth. I took exactly seven steps on the grated floor, each panel slightly decompressing beneath my weight. When I looked up, I knew to expect someone close to my heart in the fatal position ahead of me. Veronica, Atlas, Annabelle… but it wasn't any of them. It was myself. I approached the other me cautiously and gazed at my mirrored image, which appeared equally puzzled. The other Levi started to whisper things; words of the future that were renounced as gibberish through my unworkable mindset. Blood dribbled from his wide eyes, painting over them with a lively red hue. He continued to speaking as the red liquid filled his mouth and I was only able to recognize one word that he/I uttered: Safehaven. With that, he was gone. The pipes burst and down came a tsunami of blood onto my body. It wasn't until the tip of my head was submerged in the gore was I brought back to reality.

"LEVI!!"

My eyes flickered open and there stood Atlas, whose eyes were glossy with tears. Not tears of sadness but of those that belong to someone who had witnessed a truly demented scene.

"…You collapsed," he sugar-coated. "Took me ten minutes to haul your body down the street. Jesus, man, I didn't know if you'd come back."

"Where are we…?" I asked, rubbing my bruised scalp.

"That bar or whatever you said the girls and Josh were held up in? It's just across from us. I just…I didn't want to bring you in the way you were."

I didn't know what to feel. Shame? Embarrassment? Gratefulness? I had no idea. My mind felt inverted and shaken sadistically. That gas was straight out of a comic book and I was the lab rat in the super villain's experiments. The only cure was a one-way ticket out of the city alongside my reunited friends. At the end of the alleyway and onto 49th street was the bar and things would have finally worked out, right?

"C'mon…they'll be worried," I said, selecting embarrassment from the three.

A silent nod was received and we reached the end of the alley. The Orbit Bar and Nightclub was exactly where it should've been and the mirror window had stayed smashed. However, things were not how I had left them. Though the majority of the gas cloud had remained in the past streets, the air tasted poisonous. Something was tampered with. *Someone* was tampered with.

"What the...?" Atlas murmured.

Two black hearses were parked up on the sidewalk in front of the club. They appeared unmanned until the drivers and their passengers began to emerge. Eight men in total vacated the bar and while most appeared average and unimportant, two men stood out. One was a black, six-foot-five monster of a man who wore a white tank top so tight it could have been painted on. The other was a sharply dressed man with trimmed stubble and two different coloured eyes, one an ivory green and the other a coffee brown. The last member of the group stood out the most, however, as she was a female who carried a bō and had tattoos around her eyes.

"No, no...is that...?" I wondered, flashing back to the security footage.

Then their victims filed out of the bar. Two girls with leather bags over their heads and their wrists bound were directed to the funeral vehicles. Beneath the bag on the shorter girl was sprouting hair that was like silk at first glance. There was only one girl I knew with hair like that.

"ANNABELLE!" I screamed, my mind clouded with fear and fury.

She spun to the sound and yelled through a gagged mouth. They stuffed Annabelle and Quinn into the first vehicle that drove off the second the doors slammed.

The car drove off toward the bridge and new bullets drove toward us. Atlas ducked behind a dumpster and fired his gun blindly but only created sounds of empty barrels. Six assailants with a gun to each of their names versus the two of us: wounded and without ammo. Our only shot of making it out alive was to retreat and that's exactly what we did. The final battle was surely not going to take place across from an STI-ridden nightclub. It was going to take place at the opera. This, ladies and gentlemen, would be a proper finale.

# 32. "Sayonara, kid."

Down the street was a square of crumbling architecture; the remnants of a bustling society. Here we found abandoned shopping malls, five star restaurants, platinum hotels, and most importantly, the opera house. Cue the overture.

As we raced for our lives past the box office and towards the auditorium, I couldn't help but realize that I had never been to a concert before. Since I had been too busy dealing with my father drowning himself in beer to consider making friends, common social gatherings were lost along the way. I had never experienced the dazzling lights and melodic harmonies and overpriced tickets of live music. In the world that we currently inhabited, first experiences were limited. An abundance of time wasn't given to us to be wasted on swimming lessons or skydiving. The firsts that this world granted us were things like a first kill or feeling flesh being ripped from your bone for the first and (presumably) last time. Was life worth living in a world where sheer brutality was a necessity? I couldn't answer that. One thing was certain: Regardless how I left the theatre, whether dragged out lifelessly or covered in my victim's blood, there was no denying I would be different. Dodging bullets and swerving through obsessive hands of the infected, it was a moment that we collectively knew to be a turning point in our lives. You know when you experience something that is influential and life-changing but you don't know it until later in life? We knew from the moment we entered the revolving doors. I wouldn't have hallucinated monolithic orchestral music for nothing.

The expansive and grand hall that stood between the auditorium and us was once a hidden gem buried in our city. People would pay hundreds, even thousands of dollars for a sub-par seat in the theatre and a single glance at the magnificent entrance would already be worth the price. A waterfall was placed between two marble staircases that lead to the first of three balconies, where an endless flow of diamond-like droplets rained down to form a shimmering cloak. Obsidian pillars towered over the wealthy, holding up the elegant masterpiece. I've always been intrigued by the impossible standards of this opera house, and unfortunately it took a worldwide apocalypse for me to see what a run-down slum that it had become. Graffiti-styled names of the living and dead covered the wall and flames of fire-filled garbage cans licked the dank air as black smoke added to the already poisonous atmosphere. The waterfall that once gleamed had been bone dry, with only a large bloodstain that dripped down halfway. We could hear hushed whispers wafting from the auditorium and hoped that they belonged to survivors that were willing to help. With around twelve seconds of space between our pursuers and us, we were just able to painfully climb up a flight of stairs and open the first balcony doors when they trickled in. We slipped inside and while Atlas slowly closed the door to avoid detection, my weary eyes were fixated on the contents of the theatre. Instead of a handful of people like I previously assumed, I was slightly off by a little more than a hundred. The prestigious opera house that often hosted world leaders and A-list celebrities had now housed sickly drug addicts and their starving children. The first balcony doors flung open and a wave of excrement and infection lined our nostrils with a putrescent coating.

"This is just depressing," Atlas groaned with achy bones.

Each of them had been so strung out that we were mere flies on the wall. They didn't acknowledge us and continued injecting rusty needles into any flesh that hadn't already rotted. Most of the children were toddlers and all were dehydrated and addicted. In nearly every row I would spot bloody bundles of blanket that I refused to further investigate. Now, it was only about *our* survival.

"If any of you can hear us, forget that we were here!" I asked pleadingly.

We simultaneously rose our fingers to our lips to signal discretion and slid down a rickety, wood panelled bridge that connected the second floor to the first. Since our chances of survival would double if we separated, we chose to split up. Atlas hid in a tight compartment in the pit of musical instruments at the front of the stage while I crossed over the stage and found a man cover that led directly beneath it. Sure, our chances would double, but two times zero still equals zero. The cover was barely on top of my head when I started to hear gunfire.

"NOBODY MOVE!" a heavy voice screamed.

The sound of fireworks erupted above us. The druggies and their children were finally directing their hazy focus to something other than the open air. Some screamed in fear of realistic hallucinations, others simply watched the religious gunmen with quant, wondrous curiosity. I crawled on top of a pile of sandbags and found a peephole that surveyed the entire audience. Now it was time to see whether or not an audience of junkies would sell us out.

The sharply dressed man with heterochromia spoke with a calm resonance. "Eh-hmm. Ladies and Gentlemen. My name is Cain and we are not here to hurt you. Each and everyone one of you in this room are absolutely safe...except for two. One of them is wearing a bomb disposal suit and the other looks like he's got bones made of sawdust. They just so happened to be in the wrong place at the wrong time, and, well, here we are. These two lives are most certainly not worth the lives of your own, so this should be rather simple: Tell us where the two boys are hiding and we'll leave quietly. If you do so, God will reward you."

The moment I laid my eyes on him in the street I knew he was Jeb's replacement. He had the attitude and persona of an egotistical cult leader, yet something told me that even he had someone to answer to besides God. Whoever he answered to was not important in that moment in time. Right then, he was the superior man. So how would the addicts treat him? There was complete silence. I watched helplessly as meth heads and smack enthusiasts tried to comprehend the idea of allowing the execution of two teenagers. To my utmost disbelief, not a single word was spoken from the hundred and some survivors. This would only make things worse.

An impatient laugh was released from Cain as he gently tucked back a single loose strand of blonde hair.

"Well, that didn't work as well as I hoped. Time for plan B."

Cain reached into the audience and pulled out a boy no older than four. While the boy was aware enough to wet his pants, his mother tiredly waved him off. Foam was bubbling from the mother's mouth.

"Shh-shh. Don't you cry little boy." Cain ruffled the boy's hair and pressed the barrel of the gun to his tear-soaked cheek. The six other men had their guns pointed to a separate chunk of the population, making any resistance futile. Zara watched with annoyance.

Cain looked around and smiled. "For every minute that passes without telling me where they are, I kill a kid. Starting with this one."

The malnourished, fine-haired mother shifted in her seat and finally showed a smidgen of compassion for her bloodline. "Don't...do that..." Her trembling finger jabbed towards the stage. "They're under the stage... In the pit..."

Once he tossed the boy back to her like worthless trash, Cain flashed his shining smile that had gold fillings on his top canine teeth.

"Pleasure doing business with you," he sang out.

The men marched towards us and though I should've been angry at the mom, I knew that I would've done the exact same thing without a moment's hesitation. Now I just had to prepare for my upcoming departure.

Four men, led by Cain, raced to the stage like kids at recess, while one man was remained at each door exiting the theatre. I knew I would eventually be found and likely killed, but I had been handed a decision of whether or not I should attempt to save Atlas. They were cornering the instrument pit like a pack of wild dogs and it would be only a matter of moments before one of them sniffed him out. I stared out through the peephole as they crept closer...closer...closer...

"Stop!" I yelled, emerging from a panel with my hands raised.

The men snapped their guns at me, the clicking noises of their cocked weapons added as a near echo. Cain popped his head out from the pit and frowned, almost as if I had taken away the pleasure of personally finding me.

"You know, you must be truly terrible at hide and go seek," he muttered. "But you don't match the description Zara gave me. We only just saw you running away with that shit stain. Were you there when your friend gunned down my men of faith?"

My armour creaked as I shifted confusingly. "Gunned down? What are you talking about?"

Zara slid down a railing onto the main floor and popped a gum bubble. "He wasn't with them, Cain. I don't know who the fuck that is."

He rolled his tongue of over his golden teeth, making a suckling noise. "Well then. You mind doing me a favour and telling me where he is?"

I said nothing.

"…You wouldn't give yourself up for nothing, whoever you are. I'm assuming we've gotten pretty damn warm to finding shit-disturber #1?

It didn't make any sense. Atlas should've been in plain view from where they were standing. I cautiously approached the corner as they held their guns on me, only to discover that Atlas had somehow vanished from his hiding spot. Cain noticed the confusion in my eyes and read it as a victim of betrayal.

"…he abandoned you, didn't he? Man, that just tugs on the heart-strings, don't it?"

I couldn't believe it. Did Atlas leave me behind? He would never do that. After all I went through to save his ass? No, he couldn't…

My head slowly rose to my oppressors and I began to back away onto center stage. The men formed a circle around me, giggling to themselves sadistically, as if they wanted to feel the warm spray of my exploded brain on their giddy faces. I looked at these men with disgust, morbidly laughing at how they thought they did this for God and God alone. At the head of the surrounding circle, Cain raised his pistol.

"It's a shame. A whirlwind of shit started because some of our own just wanted to share our mission for redemption. I wish it didn't have to go down this way. I mean, I love God. Killing kids ain't a gold star in his books, but at the end of the day, all you gotta do is ask for forgiveness. Sayonara, kid."

My eyes closed in defeat as I braced myself for the final sensation of pain. But instead of hearing a gunshot, I heard a faint click. Then wind, almost as if something was free falling. I peeked through one eye just to see the final second of a massive stage light falling before it came crashing down on the neck and spine of the henchman next to Cain.

"Christ!" he blurted out.

The man beneath the shattered light released a punctured scream as the blood began to flow.

"Muh…My back! My fucking b-back is broken!!"

Everyone looked up at the darkness overhead, fear seeping into their bodies. Another light came crashing down. Then another. Then another. The men fearfully scattered as lights rained down upon them, making them fire blindly at the ceiling. While Cain and his men picked themselves off the floor, Atlas slid down a rope and planted his feet on the glass-ridden floor.

"You bastards messed with the wrong people," he said as he raised his bat once again.

Without looking, Cain shot the man with the shattered spine and snarled in pure hatred.

"You wanna try and kill us? Be my guest. But let's see how tough you really are. No guns," Atlas demanded.

I tossed my nearly opaque mask to the stage floor and raised my steel-knuckled fists.

"Let's do it," I said.

With an entire audience too captivated and too high to leave, Cain almost had an obligation to give the people what they wanted: a fair fight. He tossed his gun to the floor and the others followed, but no guns didn't mean no knives. He pulled out a deadly blade from his waistband and smiled.

"I've waited a long time for this."

The drumroll commenced. The stage held the corpses of half the orchestra as they must've suffered from the outbreak in the midst of a rehearsal. As imagination took hold, they rejuvenated with life, propped up their instruments at the ready and turned their sheet music to the opening note. The strings took the lead. Then the brass fluttered in. The battle had started and the opera singer prepared to belt.

Cain and Atlas charged at each other until their weapons clashed. Another man joined their fight while the remaining two converged on me. One of them had tattoos inked across every inch of his body while the other one was the black beefcake that looked as though he could pile drive a tank. So, you know, a fair fight. I swung my fist at the tattooed one and hit his rib, temporarily knocking him down. The tank sprinted at my like a charging rhino, tackling me to the floor whilst winding me in the process. Now on top of me, he threw a punch at my face, which I barely dodged, causing his fist to break through the wood. With my free arm, I desperately grabbed for anything lying around and found a violin that I proceeded to smash against the back of his thick skull. He groaned and I managed to slide beneath him while he pulled his fist out from the stage. The tattooed one was now back on his feet and sucker punched me in the eye. He threw a flurry of punches, some that I was able to block with my padded wrists, and others that I wasn't. With the taste of blood now in my mouth, I improvised and spat the liquid into his eyes, blinding him for a precious second. Now that I had a free shot, I elbowed him in the chin and kicked my steel foot into his knee, causing it to snap and the jagged bones of his leg pierced through the skin.

"Aiiyyeeeehh!" he yelped. One down.

I took one second to glance out into the audience and noticed Zara was nowhere to be found. I couldn't spend any more time focusing on her whereabouts.

Even in his heavily weakened state, Atlas proved to be a worthy opponent as he had been able to dodge every knife jab that Cain threw. With the trusty bat in his hand, he smacked the other man—a scrawny, weasel-looking fellow—across the face with enough impact to send a few of his teeth flying from his mouth. Atlas kicked his un-cauterized leg back at Cain's chest, which he caught and twisted it downwards.

"Shiiittt..." he groaned as he fell to the floor.

The two men double-teamed him and brutally kicked his squirming body until Atlas was able to slip his bat between Cain's legs and flick it up, making him fall on his back. Atlas pulled himself up and after grabbing the scrawny man's arm under his armpit, he jabbed the base of his palm into his throat, rupturing his trachea.

"Hhguyhh...Acgg...Gygh..." he spluttered as he dropped to his knees. Atlas paused, unsure if he had just killed a man.

While this was happening, the tank had gotten the jump on me. With his fist now free, he yanked my leg out from below, causing me to face plant on the wood. He bent down, pulled my head up by my hair, and smashed my face back down. I felt my brain slosh back and forth against my skull. Colours blurred and the world vibrated. I tried to crawl away only to have him slam my head again and again. The cracks began to spread across my skull. But while I was crawling away, Cain was in the midst of climbing to his feet. Atlas had just shattered the throat of the scrawny man and Cain used his vulnerability to his advantage. He came up from behind Atlas and grabbed him in a chokehold.

"You're done, little boy."

The tank may have been stronger than me but I was faster. He threw a devastating punch while I was halfway up but I saw it coming a mile away. With a single knife left on my suit, I unsheathed it and jabbed it into his armpit once he extended his full fist. I knew I wasn't capable of killing but I was more than okay with hurting. He didn't appear to be in too much pain until he lowered his arm, catching the blade on a nerve bundle. The tank shrieked and cowered down in agony. This gave me just enough time to grab Cain's pistol and aim it at him. His remaining men aimed their pieces at me and I at them. Finally: A true Mexican standoff.

"You let him go, Cain. I don't want to kill you."

"That's cute," he grimaced. "You should know something: I was never going to kill either of you. But him…I should do it." Cain directed attention to a physically drained Atlas. One of his men went beside Atlas and yanked at his arm until it protruded straight out. "Except, even though I'd love nothing more to blow this kid's brains out, his existence is not mine to decide. Boss man said that we need ALL of you kids, and that means this sack of shit included."

"This doesn't need to end this way!" I pleaded. "People shouldn't have to fight other people when there's already a threat out there! Why are you doing this to us? Why'd you come for us??"

The main level doors swung open and Zara appeared once again. By her side was a boy our age that averted his shameful eyes.

"J-Josh?" I asked in shock.

"This is why. Initially, he was our only mission. But with you kids all together, we just couldn't pass up the opportunity! He was the one that contacted us. He sold you guys out."

My anger surpassed any form of words. I looked into his beady, little eyes and made sure he looked back. I made sure he knew what he was doing. Atlas was too exhausted to even fully comprehend the situation.

"Guys…they were going to kill me…" Josh tried to explain.

"And now you get to see first-hand what Boss wants to do to you kids. He's honoured me with performing the first act so…I hope you enjoy the show."

The man holding Atlas's squirming arm straight reached behind him and pulled out a machete. A machete from my suit. I looked down and realized he must've taken it away from me. For that, I'll always feel guilty.

"Wait…" Atlas mumbled through blood and exhaustion, "what're you…"

Then it happened. The man handed the long blade to Cain and he exhaled laughter. A psychotic tinge struck his eyes and instantly he drove the blade down on Atlas's upper arm. The music stopped. The only sound that existed in this world was of chopping meat. It occurred in three layers. The first was the skin, fissuring easily as if it was made of butter. Then the muscles and tendons were exposed, sawed down like a rare steak. Last was the bone and that didn't slice evenly but rather splintered off into two jagged ends. Once three cuts were made, his detached limb fell to the opera floor and Atlas immediately passed out. The potency of his shock negated any screams to arise.

"NO!!" I yelped horrifically, pulling the trigger on my gun. Of course, the clip was empty.

His arm was on the ground. His limp body in the arms of Cain was draining of lively colour. If the blood loss from his leg wasn't enough, now he was faced with a gushing stump. I was convinced that he wouldn't leave the theatre alive.

"How could you…" I said, broken and beaten.

Cain shrugged and gave a nod to someone behind me. A slender, blunt object collided with my skull as Zara had struck me down and knocked the consciousness out of my body.

From then on, haze shrouded me. I was intoxicated off of trauma and my mind was incapable of latching onto the solidity of my surroundings. There were multiple skips in my vision where I would find myself being dragged through the opera lobby and then suddenly in the back of a car with my hands zip-tied together. The car stuck with me however, as it was a hearse. Yes, to twist the blade even further, they put Atlas's fading body into a coffin. There was a single breathing hole at the head of it but something told me he wouldn't need it for very long. I was in the back seat with Zara driving, Cain in the passenger seat and the man with the damaged throat next to me. Their existence meant nothing to me. I chose to drown them out by falling into a trance. My head leaned against the mobile prison window and watched countless pale ones pass by. I wanted to know more about them. They were monsters, yes, but they were superior to us. They would never face the barbaric cruelty that us teenagers endured. They hunted for meat but they did so only because it was necessary to survive. Enjoyment was not found in their killing and suffering was not their intent. The people that captured us? I wish I could say the same thing.

His arm was in the backseat next to me. Palm up, it dribbled with blood as the fingers were permanently extended out. I didn't even attempt to think what they planned on using it for. Instead, I took the time to think about Annabelle and Quinn and their unknown whereabouts. I thought about Josh and how he had forsaken us. I also wanted to think about Veronica—a person I might have eventually considered as sister—but she was not someone I had to wonder about. The reason for that was because I saw her. I fucking saw her. Only for a fragment of a second, Veronica was behind the wheel of a school bus that she must've fixed up. She was there and when the hearse reached the bridge and sped by her bus, we made a fraction of heartbreaking eye contact. Why did she have to come back? Seeing her, I knew this was her story now. My fate was in her hands, whether she liked it or not.

They didn't put a bag over my head so I saw when we crossed the bridge. I saw them place these theatrical white masks on, where there was no mouth and only slight indents for eyes. Each of their masks had various sins written over them. I...I was truly frightened. When we pulled up to the gate of an abandoned university, with Atlas's dying body in the coffin and another masked man beckoning us in, I had one final thought: Our story didn't deserve to end like this.

*To Be Continued...*

# Epilogue

The seventeen years had caught up and I was back in the interrogation room. My muscles ached and my throat was wrinkled with dryness. Tom and Godmother each sat across from me, both adopting looks of a child who begged for one more story before bedtime. But I was tired, and sleep was now the only place where the nightmares didn't follow.

"…And? What happened next?" Tom asked, his index finger tucked in his gnawing teeth that never ceased to move.

"…I'm done for the day," I sighed. "My friend…I want to see my friend."

Godmother was compliant but Tom was not. He was now invested in the story and was immortally unsatisfied.

"Levi, I appreciate that you're working with us…but this is not reserved only for when you're feeling up to it. We have a finite period of time and the closer we cut to the date, the less of a shot we'll have at taking him down."

I tilted my head and licked my bottom lip curiously, caressing the hairs of my beard with a wandering tongue. My hands came up from the underneath the table, the rope that once bound my wrists now dangling from my left palm.

"What…how…?"

I stood up, ignoring the searing strike of pain that arose from my forgotten leg. "Like I said, I'm not a prisoner…not anymore. I need… time. Even a crazy man has a limit. We'll pick up tomorrow."

Tom gave a look to Godmother, who had a glazed look of artificial happiness. I knew something was bothering her. Perhaps she wanted to know more. Perhaps she knew too much. Regardless, she gave him a gentle shake of the head and looked at me.

"...That's fine, Levi. You're free to go. My men will escort you to a safe room."

I each gave them a glance, looked at the dark corner where my imaginary companions waited, and nodded.

"No one's free...not anymore. We're all still here."

Heaving my casted leg one step at a time, I vacated the room and gave them the opportunity to speak. The closed door hadn't even clicked before Godmother collapsed with remorseful sadness.

"Godmother!" Tom exclaimed. "What's wrong? Are you okay?"

She sat cross-legged on the floor, tears dribbling through the creases of her wrinkles. Her wrists stung.

"I had a feeling...But I didn't want to...I couldn't..."

Her sobs overpowered her words. Tom embraced her confusingly.

"Godmother, please...what are you talking about?"

She looked into the corner where my imagination found a home and she delicately ran a trembling hand through her bob.

"...A mother should never have to see her son like that."

It took a few moments for it to sink in, but it finally hit Tom. He got it. It all made sense now. This wasn't only for the salvation of the nation. No, this was more than that. This was a family reunion.

# Thank you

Well…Shit. Now I have to thank some folks. Here goes something:

As cliché as it sounds, I have to start this off by thanking my parents for the inexhaustible love and support that they have given me. My mother has not only spent every waking moment of her life caring for the well-being of others but also done a hell of a job at doing so. She has encouraged me more than anyone to pursue my passion because she is aware that forcing me on an undesirable career or life path would only lead to resentment. Also, I made a promise to her that if I ever become a successful actor or writer, she'll be my date for the award ceremonies. My father is just as loving as my mother, but he goes about it a different way. He is the personification of a *Dad-Joke* and having his humour around the household brings warmth that anyone and everyone can be embraced by. He is loving and accepting, but has also made sure to bestow the knowledge and morals I need to not be an irresponsible, immature asshat. He has taught me what it means to be a gentleman.

Next up is my brother, Connor. For most of our lives, we were in separate worlds isolated from each other even though we grew up under the same roof. I'm not going to sugar coat it: We didn't like each other. But as time passed and we matured, a fondness emerged that morphed into a resounding sense of respect. From his dive-bomb handshake to his businessman's persuasion that could convert a pair of Jehovah's Witnesses, he is shaped by his well-tailored suits and ability to demonstrate what it means to be a brother. My father may have taught me what it means to be a gentleman, but Connor has *shown* me what it means.

I'd also like to thank Xlibris for having the patience and confidence in both the novel as well as myself. They were more supportive than I could've possibly imagined and I don't know what else to say without it sounding like they paid me to give them a shameless plug…so I'll give them a shameless plug: Check this company out. Seriously.

The photo of the two flowers was one of my initial inspirations for this story and I would never forgive myself if I didn't credit the phenomenal photographer. His name is Baptiste Esteban and what he is able to capture is truly mesmerizing. I thank him for letting me use one of his many works of art.

I'd be a pretty awful friend if I didn't mention my buds. From Bob and Piper, two amazing guys with a sense of humour that I attempted to pay homage to with as many jokes as I could fit in, to Sam and Nick, who actually took the time to read it and tell me it wasn't crap, I don't have enough things to say about my friends. There are countless individuals that I am incredibly grateful to and I apologize for not being able to list them all. However, there is one that deserves a spotlight, as he is the one that this book is dedicated to: Connor McCormack.

I have two brothers. One is by blood and the other by bond. Coincidentally, both are named Connor. The Connor that this book is dedicated to is also the inspiration for Atlas, arguably my favourite character. I've known him since I was three and it was solely because of him that this book came to be. In a hilariously boring English class in grade 10, he was doodling and drew a picture of us as zombie fighters. Because of that drawing, I knew that I had to create a story. Initially, this was supposed to be a graphic novel with him as the artist, but the timing didn't really work out. He has promised that when he gets to the level of talent that he strives to be, we'll reunite for a graphic novel version. I'm holding him to that.

Thank you. Each and every one of you have helped me in some shape or form and I know that words on a page aren't able to capture how appreciative I am but they'll have to suffice (for now). To the readers, I thank you for taking the leap of faith and giving this book a shot. If you liked it, don't worry, there is much more to come. This is the first book in a series of five and I sincerely hope that you will join me as we continue this journey with Levi, Atlas, and the gang as they go through even more shit.

# List of Songs

If This Were a Movie…

Sh-Boom – The Chords
*Played at: The morning routine*
Turn Around, Look at Me – Bee Gees
*Played at: The daydream in class*
Wonderful! Wonderful! – Johnny Mathis
*Played at: The plane crash*
Memories of You – The Ink Spots
*Played at: The TV broadcast*
Twentieth Century Blues – Noel Coward
*Played at: The drive downtown*
The Wonder of You – Ray Peterson
*Played at: The trek for the deer*
Put Your Head on My Shoulder – Paul Anka
*Played at: The hotel room with Annabelle*
Tears on My Pillow – Little Anthony & The Imperials
*Played at: The garage daydream*
Born Too Late – The Poni-Tails
*Played at: The car crash*
Sweeter Than You – Ricky Nelson
*Played at: The comatose dive*
It's All in the Game – Tommy Edwards
*Played at: The farm massacre*
I've Told Every Little Star – Linda Scott
*Played at: The conversation, the diner, and the church*
Sincerely – The Moonglows

*Played at: The nighttime escape*
Unforgettable – Nat King Cole
*Played at: The return to home*
It's Raining- Irma Thomas
*Played at: The rainy breakdown*
The Gypsy – The Ink Spots
*Played at: The diner (beginning)*
I'll Never Get out of This World Alive – Hank Williams
*Played at: The cowboy confrontation*
Crying in the Chapel – The Orioles
*Played at: The church (after the reveal)*
La Vie En Rose – Edith Piaf
*Played at: The unexpected tower collapse*
Daddy's Little Girl – The Mills Brothers
*Played at: The reluctant revelation*
You Always Hurt the One You Love – The Mills Brothers
*Played at: The rescue for the fallen (post-kiss)*
Nessun Dorma – Pavarotti
*Played at: The final battle*
At The End – Earl Grant
*Played at: The end*